The Foursome

ALSO BY TROON McALLISTER

THE GREEN

The Foursome

Troon McAllister

DOUBLEDAY

New York   London   Toronto   Sydney   Auckland

PUBLISHED BY DOUBLEDAY
a division of Random House, Inc.
1540 Broadway, New York, New York 10036

DOUBLEDAY and the portrayal of an anchor with a dolphin are
trademarks of Doubleday, a division of Random House, Inc.

The Foursome is a work of fiction. The characters and events exist only in the
author's imagination and any resemblances to real life figures are purely coinci-
dental and unintentional. In those cases where real life figures make cameo
appearances in the novel, they do so in a purely fictional context and no repre-
sentations of factual accuracy are implied by the author or should be assumed by
the reader.

LIBRARY OF CONGRESS CATALOGING-IN-PUBLICATION DATA

McAllister, Troon.
The foursome: a novel / Troon McAllister.
p. cm.
1. Golf—Fiction.   2. Golf resorts—Fiction.   I. Title.
PS3557.R8 F68 2000
813'.54—dc21

Book design by Richard Oriolo

ISBN 0-385-49910-8

Printed in the United States of America
May 2000
First Edition
1   3   5   7   9   10   8   6   4   2

For Shawn Coyne

The Players

The Course at Swithen Bairn

HOLE	PAR	YARDS*
1	4	410
2	5	530
3	3	170
4	4	385
5	4	429
6	4	405
7	4	350
8	3	205
9	5	522
Out	**36**	**3,406**
10	3	140
11	5	520
12	3	195
13	3	175
14	5	540
15	4	444
16	4	429
17	4	392
18	5	580
In	**36**	**3,415**
Total	**72**	**6,821**

* Measured from halfway between front and back of tee boxes. Total yardage from front tees: 6,252. From back tees: 7,295. The course has not been rated.

Why do you think they call the devil "Scratch"?

—EDDIE CAMINETTI

Chapter 1

⊞

Several years ago I had a truly life-changing epiphany. Unfortunately, I can't remember what it was.

But I can tell you about something that happened to a couple of other guys . . .

JOE ARONICA, AT AGE FIFTY-TWO, had arrived.

He owned the patent on a miracle metal, owned 51 percent of the Aeronica (get it?) Aircraft Corporation, had an on-paper net worth of some $5 million, at least if you didn't factor in the surely temporary illiquidity of AAC stock, a gorgeous wife, three gorgeous kids, membership at the most exclusive country club in Danuba, Connecticut, a 7-handicap and a source at Dunhill in London who sent him two boxes of Havanas each month buried deep within crates of metal tissue dispensers for use in rehabbing aging Boeing 737s. Best of all, he was known as the inventor of Arondium (get it?), and his reputation as a businessman-scientist was secure.

Aronica stared morosely around his professionally decorated office and wondered why he was so damned miserable.

Five foot eleven, stocky to the point of beefy and with features more like those of a meat-packer than an engineer—Aronica's whole physiognomy seemed designed to telegraph a pugnacious disposition. Although the upper part of his face was somewhat flattened, his jaw jutted mildly, giving the impression that here was a man used to defending his character, albeit usually in the form of defiant belligerence rather than by actually demonstrating whatever qualities he wanted you to believe he had. Yet despite that perpetually contentious look, his physical movements often betrayed an underlying uncertainty: He was given to being easily startled, at which times his normal coordination devolved into an almost childish awkwardness, as if he were constantly preparing to flee from something as yet unseen.

To anybody casually observing him, though, few reasons for such incipient unease would be in evidence.

Arondium was an honest-to-God marvel, and Aronica was its honest-to-God creator. Often sharing the lecture podium at business conventions with scientists who'd invented such things as superglue and Naugahyde, he presided over AAC, a corporation he'd set up to license the production of the miracle metal, he not being of the temperament or inclination to bother with creating and running an actual manufacturing company. The corporation practically ran itself: He made the deals, then sat back and waited for the royalties to roll in. Whatever true effort he expended was largely relegated to badgering the dim-witted knuckleheads who ran the really big companies into seeing the true potential of arondium and dreaming up more and more applications for it. Despite his patent on an alloy that had the strength of titanium yet was ten times more flexible and resilient under repeated stress, the only deals that had thus far been negotiated were for bicycle frames, tennis rackets and rudder assemblies for refurbished 737 cargo planes, all of which he made by using outside contractors rather than doing the work himself. The rudder deal was his largest contract, and had spawned the name of the company, which sounded a lot better in the annual country-club registry than Aronica Sporting Goods.

The country club. That reminded him of at least one chore he could turn his mind to other than reading movie reviews in *The Wall Street Journal*, which was much like getting opera information from the 4-H newsletter. This year it was his turn to plan the annual golf trip that had become a tradition among his regular foursome.

Having mentioned golf, let me digress for just a moment and introduce myself: I'm Alan Bellamy, a professional golfer. Okay, that's overly modest. I'm actually one of a handful of professional golfers who can be said to inhabit the elite stratum in the firmament of professional golfers. I've won a boatload of big tournaments, including two majors, and was the PGA Golfer of the Year three times. I captained the last U.S. Ryder Cup team, too, which is how I came to be involved with one Eddie Caminetti, but that's a whole other smoke, and I'm getting ahead of myself anyway.

I'm telling you this story because I'm about the only one who can. Or, more correctly, the only one who will. I pieced it together from a variety of sources, including a guy named Carlos who worked for Eddie, a Haitian golf-course maintenance supervisor, a drop-dead gorgeous former cardiothoracic scrub nurse and amateur athlete who once helped Eddie fake his own death, and even some of the guys in Aronica's foursome, who sometimes informed more by what they elected to withhold from me than what they chose to disclose.

The only person who wasn't all that helpful was Eddie himself, who insisted that he had no idea what the hell I was talking about. A bunch of guys came down, they played some golf, a little friendly betting money changed hands . . . why did I keep asking him dopey questions as though it were more important than that?

I've taken a few liberties where gaps needed to get filled in and made some assumptions about what was going on in people's heads, but my guess is I got it pretty close to 99 percent right. For one thing, I know golfers, maybe better than anyone except Eddie himself. And a golfer is a golfer, whether he or she is from Toledo or Uzbekistan. Certain traits characterize them all, although the events in this particular story surprised even me.

Anyway, here was Joe Aronica, mooning unhappily over his great good fortune and getting ready to turn his mind to the task of planning a golf vacation. Reaching for the stack of brochures his secretary had gathered for him, his hand slipped, and as he reached to stabilize the bunch of paper, he saw a white envelope flutter to the floor. He put the stack in the middle of his desk and bent down to retrieve it.

His name and business address appeared on the front in calligraphy made elegant by its very understatement. There was no return address. He tore it open and took out a single four-by-six card. The front read, "The most memorable golf vacation you've ever had." Sighing in disappointment, he turned toward the wastepaper basket when the rest of the sentence caught his eye: ". . . or you don't pay. No money up front."

He read the smaller type below. "Our twelve-room hotel is located right on our own private championship course, open only to our visitors. One of the finest layouts in the world, Swithen Bairn sees barely twenty rounds a day and is in pristine condition all year round. Qualified individuals only."

The card itself was of fine linen, the printing rotogravured engraving. There was an 800 number listed. . . .

Aronica picked up the phone and dialed it himself. It was answered before he even heard it ring on the other end. "Swithen Bairn, good day?" Female voice. Like a bell, and already totally focused on the call, not distracted like a front-desk clerk might be.

"Ah, uh, my name is Joe Aronica—"

"Yes, of course, Mr. Aronica. Delighted to hear from you."

How many of these invitations did they send out, or was it simply a trigger response from a well-trained customer service rep? "I'm, um, I'm calling to verify the details in this card you sent me. I'm planning a golf vacation for me and some friends, and—"

"Certainly, sir. There not being many details supplied, you want to know if the guarantee is valid."

"Now you mention it . . ."

"I understand. It's quite literally true." She pronounced it "littrally," British style. "There are no catches."

"Seems a little far-fetched. How do I know—"

"It's simple, Mr. Aronica: Since we take no money from you up front, there's really no risk involved, is there?"

"Just the risk that I'd have a lousy time."

"How does that differ from any vacation that requires all your money in advance, with no recourse if you're unhappy?"

"Well, I might have been to those places before and known what to expect."

"But that wasn't so the first time you'd been there."

True enough. "Any chance of checking with some of your past guests?"

"None whatsoever. Strict confidentiality is one of our primary concerns. I think you can appreciate that, Mr. Aronica."

"Sure, sure. Well, then, what do you have to do to be a 'qualified individual'?"

"If the invitation was addressed to you, you're most likely qualified. As a formality, we do require a detailed financial statement signed by your accountant and notarized. A mere precaution, I'm sure you understand. In this fickle financial atmosphere, today's sultan is tomorrow's—"

"I got it. No problem. But, like I said, there's these other guys, too, and—"

"Oughtn't to be a problem, sir. If you submit the financials, we'll have a determination within twenty-four hours."

"Yeah, but, uh, a couple of these guys, they're a little skittish about—"

"As I said, complete confidentiality is assured. You needn't worry."

Aronica tried to think about what he should do next. In the silence that ensued, he sensed no impatience at the other end, and felt comfortable taking his time. "Okay, look: What I'm gonna do, I'm gonna talk to the other guys, see what they—"

"By all means, Mr. Aronica. Confer with your colleagues and call back whenever it's convenient."

"All right. Thanks, then."

"Good day, sir."

"Hey, wait a minute! Hello?"

"I'm right here."

"Say, where is this place anyway?"

"A little difficult to describe. Just turn over the card . . ."

Aronica did so, and read, "Your stay includes a private room, three gourmet meals per day with drinks and cigars, all the golf you can handle, lessons from our professional staff, and transportation to and from by private jet."

A private jet. "Doesn't much matter where you are."

"Not in the slightest. We'll look forward to hearing from you, then?"

It was an assumption, not a question. Only after she'd hung up did Aronica realize that not only had he not gotten her name, he'd also forgotten to ask how much it would cost if it *did* turn out to be their most memorable vacation ever.

Chapter 2

■

AS HE DEPRESSED THE SWITCHHOOK and dialed another number, Aronica wondered if the handwritten invitation had been sent to every other member of the Royal Connaught Golf & Country Club as well, or if he'd been singled out somehow.

"Advanced Wellness Systems, how may I direct your call?"

Now there's a nice, cozy name for a medical practice, Aronica thought. *Positively reeks of nurturing bedside manner.* "Dr. Perrault, please."

Half a dozen clicks and pops later, he heard, "Administration, may I help you?"

"I'd like to speak to Dr. Perrault."

"May I ask what this is—"

"Just tell him Joe Aronica's on the line."

"And may I tell him what this is—"

"Yeah, tell him I'm two seconds away from towing his Bentley and if he doesn't pick up the phone I'm gonna haul it over a gravel road all the way to the next—"

"Who the hell is this?"

"Goddamnit, Pete, what're you, the freakin' Pope?"

"Love of Christ, Joe, you damned near gave me a heart attack!"

"So what . . . you're a doctor, ain'tcha?"

Aronica heard some mumbling along the lines of Perrault telling his receptionist it's okay and yeah yeah she did the right thing putting the guy through. "So what's the rumpus? Thought up a place for us to go golfing yet?"

"Matter of fact . . ."

Peter Perrault, a 5-handicap, was the sole owner of a ninety-physician group medical practice, which, contrary to the universal trend, was actually making money in a progressively strangulating managed-health-care environment that was squeezing everybody else out of the business. Not only that, he was doing it while taking on the more difficult cases that his peers shied away from because they cost too much to treat and returned too little by way of insurance reimbursement. A popular speaker on the lecture circuit, Perrault gleefully castigated his whining competitors for their inability to control costs and their failure to appreciate things from the insurers' point of view.

It was their own fault, he told them: If they hadn't spent so many years overcharging, to the point where a bandage that cost ten cents at Wal-Mart came in at $6.75 on the hospital statement, they wouldn't have gotten caught so flat-footed when the insurance companies said enough was enough and refused to keep knuckling under. Now, instead of doctors deciding what was best for their patients, they had to get permission from some medical-school dropout at Blue Cross whose job it was to make sure the patient had one foot in the grave before so much as an aspirin was prescribed. "Decapitators, all of you!" he'd thunder, referring to the *capitation* method by which many of his competitors were paid: They got so much per patient from the insurance company, regardless of what the ailment involved. So the only way they could make money was by providing as little service as possible; the fewer patients they saw, the more profitable the practice. The less time they spent with each patient who did manage to get an appointment, the more money they made.

"Why would anybody in his right mind sign up for your plan under those conditions if he had an alternative?" Perrault would ask rhetorically, and hold himself up as just that alternative. He knew how to hold costs down and still provide quality care, which was why he was willing to take on the difficult injuries, the chronic diseases, and why people were practically breaking down the door to see the doctors at Advanced Wellness Systems. Perrault might have started a counterrevolution in health care but was perfectly content just to run his own group and take good care of his own patients, and he wasn't a bit ashamed to be making a decent buck while doing it.

Perrault listened, intrigued, as Aronica spoke. Enthusiastic risk-taker that he was, his excitement was predictable until Aronica got down to the administrivia. "You gotta be a qualified individual, is all."

"Which means . . . ?"

"Not much. Just a detailed financial statement, notarized and so forth."

He could feel Perrault tense up at the other end. "I don't know, Joe. I've a pretty damned complicated financial situation here, you know that. My own people can hardly sort it out."

Aronica knew he kept it that way purposely. If the insurance companies found out anybody was actually making money in medicine, they'd conjure up a way to put a stop to it. "What of it?" he asked, trying to ignore Perrault's upper-class, pseudo-British speech affectation. "You think these guys, they run a golf club, you think they're like Merrill Lynch or something? Throw some numbers together and print 'em fancy, what the hell are they gonna know?"

"You've a point there."

"Sure. Besides, that little snot who does your books, pay him enough and he'll certify you're homeless or the Sultan of Brunei, either way. Just gin up something looks normal, is all."

"Normal, right. Have you informed them that you're bringing two sets of clubs, Mr. Normal?"

Aronica caught the sarcasm in Perrault's voice but could never understand why the other guys were always embarrassed when he showed up at some resort valet stand lugging two bags. "No, I didn't tell 'em. Why should I?"

"They're going to be providing transport on their own jet, that's why. Even a touring pro doesn't carry two bags."

"That's 'cuz they got half a dozen freakin' trailers full of clubs following them all over the country, vendors drooling all over themselves trying to give the damned things away. Besides, the second set's my lucky ones."

"Some scientist you are. If they're so lucky, why don't you use them all the time?"

"They're not lucky if you use them all the time, and if you got a problem with that, you can sit your ass home and I'll ask Sam Coolidge along instead, okay?"

Aronica was instantly sorry that he'd mentioned Coolidge, but it was too late. In any event, it settled Perrault down. "Okay, okay, don't throw a hissy fit. Have you phoned the other fellows?"

"Getting ready to. Lemme give you a fax number so you can send your financial statement."

"Fax. I don't know, Joe. You don't have a secure line, and what with all the—"

"Not to me. Straight to them."

"Ah, okay. Let's have the number."

Chapter 3

■

"HWWUFF?"

Aronica closed his eyes as panting sounds rustled their way through the phone. "Chelovek, why do you even pick up the phone if you're in the middle'a doing your secretary and—"

"Admini—" *Hwwuff* "—strative—" *Hwwuff* "—assistant." *Hwwuff Hwuff.* Then some prolonged sighing followed by a few muffled smacking sounds. "That's what she is, that's what she likes to be called, my little lamb chop. Mmmhmm-mmhmm . . ."

"Give it a goddamned rest, Jerry. Can't somebody there just take a message for you?"

"I'm running a business, Joe. Can't expect me to let things slide just on account of— Yeah, run along, pumpkin, that's a good girl. Type something, whatever. Look busy! What I was saying—"

"I like how you run a business. You need a partner?"

"There's no explaining the creative mind to a cretin. Whaddaya want?"

Jerrold Chelovek, a genius in the advertising world as attested to by the Clio Award proudly displayed in his company's reception area, was a senior partner in the firm of Cardosi, Perlis and Bell and a 7-handicap. Six years ago he'd been a copywriter sharing a desk with a college sophomore, churning out slogans for such stylish products as swimming-pool chemicals, coyote traps, pop-rivet kits and aftermarket replacement ribbons for Bolivian-made shelf-labelers.

What had lit the fuse on his career was his realization that a major, developing market was being all but ignored by manufacturers and retailers, that of newly landed immigrants fresh from their teeming shores and yearning to spend freely. He convinced his clients to come up with services and products aimed at helping these people assimilate themselves into the bewildering maelstrom that was American culture, with fierce brand loyalty as a side benefit; not only would the customers appreciate the attention, "They'd be profoundly *grateful* and become your best salesmen when all the grandparents, aunts and uncles eventually come over," as he liked to tell his prospects. It may have been obvious in retrospect, but it hadn't been when Jerry Chelovek began pushing it, and by that time his clients had pretty much cornered what was turning out to be a surprisingly lucrative market.

"You can't be serious with this, Joe," Chelovek said before Aronica had gotten three sentences into it. "Don't you know a scam when it smacks you upside the head?"

"But what's there to lose? I spoke to these guys on the phone and they're serious: no money up front."

"Yeah. But when we get there, maybe they stick us in some roach-infested tent and it turns out the gourmet food is nothing but warmed-over Shit McMeals and then they offer us the 'deluxe upgrade option,' which we have to take just to make sure we don't get malaria or the squirts—"

"Christ, you're a cynical bastard, Jerry."

"I'm in advertising; what do you expect?"

"But here's the thing: Let's say we get there and it's just what you say. So we go find a better place, and the plane ride was free."

"True. So where is it?"

"I don't know." Aronica heard a long exhale at the other end and said quickly, "What's the big deal here, Jerry? Let's take a chance for once! It isn't like we can't afford to buy our way out of it if it goes south."

Chelovek had to admit that was true enough. In the last several years their fortunes had risen dramatically, through hard work, creativity, and more than a little serendipity, and what was the point of having a fat bank account if you couldn't step out on a limb once in a while? Besides, it wasn't like throwing half a million at a chancy stock. Spread a few bucks around and they could always find a good place to bivouac and play golf no matter where they were.

"Damnit, Joe, you're right. Life's too short to play it safe all the time. Sign me up and let's see what happens. You gonna call Deke, or you think maybe we ought to let Sam in on this one, it being free and all?"

"I didn't say it was *free*."

Sam Coolidge again. Was Chelovek serious or just getting himself on the record as worrying about their old friend? "Who'd we leave out if we asked him, Jerry?"

"I was just thinking, with Deke's bad ticker and all, if we get stuck and have to scramble, maybe the stress won't be such a good thing for him."

Aronica saw the opening for a graceful way out. "Maybe you're right, but that should be Deke's call, not ours. Besides, we gotta send them financials, and I don't think Sam's would get him a subway token at this point."

Aronica wondered if he oughtn't to cluck some reflex sympathy, even though Chelovek didn't need to be reminded that Coolidge just hadn't kept up in terms of socioeconomic status and therefore couldn't afford the kinds of places the rest of them liked to play. A cardiologist and former medical partner of Pete Perrault, Coolidge had gone off on his own to found a series of charitably subsidized clinics in poor neighborhoods. "Nice guy, sure, but you want to go back to being a member of the Pile o' Shit Golf Club in Bumfuck, Missouri?"

"Yeah, you're right," Chelovek said, and Aronica bit his tongue: Leave it to old Jerry to shift the burden elsewhere. "So put it to Deke first and let's see what happens. And do me one other favor—make a backup set of reservations somewhere else in case this craters before we ever even see a plane."

Chapter 4

::

"**A**RE YOU KIDDING ME? *ANYTHING'S* better than this rat hole I work in every day!"

The "rat hole" was Deke Savitch's basement. He was ostensibly general manager of the retail division for a boutique Wall Street brokerage firm, but if he actually got into the office once a month, it was a lot.

Savitch, a 3-handicap and the best golfer in the group, had been the star of the Fayez Maranjian, Morris, Short and Hopper trading room before a lurking heart condition had been diagnosed during a routine company physical. Partially because of his outstanding record, but mostly because of his frequent appearances on financial television shows that were good for the firm's image, senior management had cut him a great deal of slack in order to keep his name associated with theirs. The "general manager" title sounded magisterial when he was interviewed, and most financial-talk-show hosts rarely asked exactly who, or what, he actually managed, which was pretty much nobody and nothing.

These days Savitch was primarily a program trader. He had a bank of computers in his basement hooked into all of the world's major exchanges, as well as direct lines to Fayez Maranjian's floor traders. He analyzed the volatility indexes of thousands of stocks, as well as the trends in timing differences, looking for high-probability opportunities for trades that would exploit the combination of variability and timing.

If Acme Plungers was bouncing between 8 and 8½ in London, and if that activity was being mimicked in Chicago but with a few minutes' delay, Savitch would wait at his terminal until the next time it was 8½ in London and 8 in Chicago, then immediately put in a buy in Chicago along with a limit order to sell automatically at 8½. Based on the previous hour's activity, there was a good chance that the stock would be somewhere above 8 in Chicago shortly after his having bought in.

While a quarter or half a point doesn't sound like much, it adds up if you buy a lot of shares and do it very often. A thousand of Acme Plungers and Savitch could be in and out of the stock with a five-hundred-dollar profit in less time, as he liked to put it, "than a short crap." Which was about as profane as he ever got.

It didn't work perfectly, of course, but all you really needed was to be right more than half the time. Savitch's hit rate of 62 percent, even with Fayez Maranjian's modest trading commissions, made him very rich and was very easy on the heart.

Aronica was surprised at Savitch's easy acquiescence to his proposal. Usually he got the standard every-time-I-even-get-up-to-pee-it-costs-me-money line. "What got into you . . . the computers go on strike?"

"Joe," Savitch said thoughtfully, "way I figure it, what's the point of sitting around making money all day if you don't get to enjoy spending it, you know what I mean? Get out and smell the flowers?"

"Damn, what's this? The new you?"

"Your health starts to go, it makes you think. Count me in. You bringing that idiotic second set of clubs again?"

Chapter 5

∷

AT THE ROYAL CONNAUGHT GOLF & Country Golf, you couldn't put on your golf shoes in the parking lot; the members thought it would make the place look like a muni trunk-slammer instead of the sporting field of the local hoi polloi. You couldn't even wear shorts. Couldn't pull a hand cart either, or ride in a golf car or carry your own bag. Everybody had to take a caddie and walk the course, unless you had a medical waiver, in which case you could ride. The degree of unhealthiness among the club's 380 members was truly alarming, judging by the number of waivers issued, as was the peculiarity of crippling infirmities that enabled one to endure multiple sets of tennis while rendering one unable to walk the golf course.

The aversion to walking was less a function of laziness than embarrassment, owing to the fact that while the average handicap of the members was about 11, that of the caddies was more like 5, resulting in acute discomfort whenever a member shanked one into the azaleas and his caddie remained perfectly still and said not one word, which the member usually read (correctly) as a clear expression of extreme derision. Thus, via no particular design, it became a badge of honor to risk taking a caddie, and the pecking order of the Royal Connaught was established as those who walked versus those who rode. While the members would vehemently deny that such a situation actually existed, of the nine board members and four officers, only two ever rode in carts.

Joe Aronica, Pete Perrault and Jerry Chelovek, being 7-, 5- and 7-handicaps respectively, always walked. Deke Savitch, because of his heart condition, rode. Since Savitch had to ride anyway, he took a "four bagger" cart that could carry all their clubs, and thus were they saved the necessity of tipping a caddie.

"Could prove amusing," Perrault said, picking up his ball after holing out for a par on the seventh. He always knelt to retrieve a ball, never bent over from the waist, unwilling as he was to assume any posture that could be remotely construed as undignified. His favorite description of himself was "patrician," and the case could be made that his angular, almost feminine features, trim and slightly underweight physique, and the helmet of carefully coifed, salt-and-pepper hair he affected with the aid of chemicals easily obtained by a physician, did give him an air of having descended from some ancient, noble bloodline, but even a cursory examination would disclose that it was the kind of aristocratic veneer more apt to have been purchased than inherited.

"Has an air of mystery about it, don't you think?" he asked as he adjusted the tennis sweater draped casually about his shoulders and smoothed out a thin mustache consisting of bristles so stiff a force-five gale couldn't have mussed them up in the first place.

Aronica carefully lined up his three-footer, which he needed to sink to neutralize Perrault's par and save a skin. "Hope you guys don't hold it against me, it turns out bad."

The rest stayed quiet as he struck the ball and sank it. As it rattled around the bottom of the cup, Chelovek said, "Still sounds like a crock to me."

In contrast to his physician friend, Chelovek seemed not only untroubled by his own generally disheveled appearance but prideful in its connotation that, unlike his borderline-snobbish compatriots, he was a man of the people who, regardless of the amount of monetary wealth he might accrue, would never dream of abandoning his blue-collar roots. Six foot three and saddled with a doughy frame that had made him wretchedly self-conscious in high school, he'd learned how to exploit his size as a tool once he realized that prospective clients were subconsciously impressed by a strong physical presence, as though the simple fact of his solid and unmistakable *there*-ness somehow signaled that he would be an enduring asset, as opposed to the effete and ephemeral waifs who traditionally populated the advertising world and who would just as soon jump to your competitors if the price were right, or if they could find more artistic fulfillment in, say, hawking Teletubbies rather than Beanie Babies.

Everything about Chelovek, though, from his thatch of unruly hair to his pronounced lips, from his large, workingman's hands to the habit he'd picked up long ago of speaking like a Brooklyn cabbie working the swing shift, gave the impression that he couldn't give a rat's ass *what* you sold, so long as you let him help you move the product: Pay him to be on your side, and Jerry Chelovek was your man.

Aronica was leaning down to pick up his ball but stopped. "Listen, Jerry, don't fuck around. You want to back out, fine, but don't come back later and give me any of this I-told-you-so crap. You know the deal, I didn't talk you into a goddamned—"

"Jesus, take it easy, will ya? What're you gettin' so touchy—"

"You know damned well why! If you're gonna stand there and start giving me shit—"

"Hey, both you boys calm down, okay?" Savitch waved them off the green, and as they walked back to the cart, he said, "Nobody's gonna blame you, Joe. We all know we're taking a chance. That was part of the deal. Jerry, all he's saying, it sounds fishy."

"Of *course* it's fishy," Aronica said. "That's not new news, so why keep bringing it up?"

Chelovek threw his arm around Aronica's shoulders and squeezed, then knocked him sideways off balance. Grinning, he said, "I wasn't jerking your chain, asshole. What I was gonna say before you jumped down my throat, why don't we make some backup reservations somewhere, 'steada figuring we can get something once we're there? You don't even know where the hell it is, so who wants to be traipsing all over East Jesus lookin' for a cot 'steada playing golf?"

Stumbling and recovering, Aronica said, "Could run into a lotta dough, we don't show up for the backup res."

"So we buy trip-cancellation insurance," Chelovek said.

"Don't you need a medical reason or something?" Savitch asked. "And a letter from a doctor?"

"Oh, dear!" Peter Perrault, M.D., exclaimed, stopping dead in his tracks and slapping his forehead loudly. Looking at Savitch in feigned anxiety, he said, "Now, how do you suppose we're *ever* going to convince a doctor to write us a letter!"

When they finally stopped laughing, Chelovek dropped his putter back in his bag and said, "Ah, what the hell. How safe can you play life anyway, right?"

"I quite concur," Perrault responded. "What kind of a name is Swithen Bairn, anyway . . . Scottish?"

"Beats me," Aronica admitted. "Then again, what the hell kind of a name is Connaught?"

"Darn," Savitch said. "Sure would be nice to let Sam Coolidge in on this." Plastering a sad expression on his face, Savitch had the hangdog look of Humpty Dumpty following the fall, looking over parts of his body that were strewn about beneath his feet. "Rotund" was the kindest word that could be applied to him, but not the sort that could be further delimited as brawny or burly or strapping or any other adjective connoting serious musculature beneath a deceptively flaccid exterior. Savitch was *fat*, was what he was, and his pasty skin, diminutive stature, small ears flat against his head and almost complete absence of a neck did nothing to distract from that basic diagnosis.

Into the sudden gloom the corpulent stockbroker had just brought down around them, Aronica said, "You know, Deke . . . you got a real knack for pissing on everybody's parade."

Chapter 6

■■

JOE ARONICA HAD SURPRISED THE rest of them on this one. Usually the very picture of reticence and a plodding trekker of the safe route, he was the one who'd come up with this dice-throwing venture and seen it through. He'd even struck back when Chelovek, with his typically vaunting suspicion of everything human, had turned his keenly honed bullshit antenna in the direction of this harebrained vacation idea.

Aronica had gone through three cups of black coffee at Savitch's house, trying not to bite his fingernails as they waited for the promised limo to arrive. Savitch's wife, Binky (née Florence), with the good humor naturally characteristic of one who no longer needs to get upset about problems involving only money, good-naturedly chided the foursome about their naïveté and, when she wasn't pointedly avoiding getting anywhere near Chelovek or even making eye contact with him, pretended to scratch out Swithen Bairn's phone number from the pad on the refrigerator while circling that of Hilton Head, where they'd made their backup reservations.

When her grin devolved into shock, the others turned to where she was looking and beheld through the window (and past the wrought-iron, remotely controlled electric gate with a gold-plated S in swirling script) a stretch limo in muted gray turning into the graveled drive. As Aronica broke into a triumphal smirk and the others continued to stare, Binky jumped to answer the chime and pressed a button that caused the gates to swing open majestically.

The four scrambled to hitch themselves up and head out, Savitch taking the time to clap Aronica on the back. "Damn, Joe!"

Perrault nodded, and even Chelovek managed a grudging "Well, it's a start," not willing to grant Aronica complete exoneration just yet but also not wishing to somehow jinx the whole deal by being unduly skeptical.

By the time they got outside, a uniformed chauffeur already had the trunk open and several suitcases stowed but suspended his efforts as he leaped to the doors and got them opened with a cheery "Good day, gentlemen! I trust I'm not late?"

"Not a bit," Aronica assured him. "Right on the button."

"Splendid. Step right inside. Won't be but a jif."

Perrault thought he detected a slight hesitation as the chauffeur mentally added up five golf bags instead of four, but the man bent to the task without mentioning it. "Least he knows to put the clubs on top," Chelovek said, but Binky nailed him with an icy glare and told him to behave.

She kissed Savitch, the last to get into the car, and said to the chauffeur, "Like a cup of coffee?"

"Ah, thanks very much, but it's quite unnecessary. Car's fully stocked, you see?" He waved once, and they were off.

And fully stocked it was. Cleverly concealed panels held brewed coffee, hot water for tea and a variety of bags, freshly squeezed orange and grapefruit juice, croissants, brioche, sourdough toast and four kinds of jam. Fine china, silver cutlery and linen napkins all bore the letters SB in hair-thin script, which led Perrault to remark, "Their own limo? How can they have their own limo?"

"Why not?" Aronica answered, his confidence level rising by the second.

"Well, they'd have to have one in every city in the country, would they not?" Perrault explained.

"Beats me," Savitch said. "Pass the butter, wouldja?"

"Easy on the cholesterol, Deke," Chelovek cautioned.

Savitch ignored the advice. "Once in a while, what the heck, right, Doc?"

Perrault reached for the carafe of orange juice. "Depends on your specifics, Deke. I'm not your physician, and I'm not here to baby-sit you."

IT BEING A SATURDAY MORNING, the ride to the Westchester County Airport was smooth and traffic-free. The driver carefully slowed down for potholes and speed bumps lest his charges slosh coffee but otherwise remained quiet on the other side of a smoked-glass barrier.

"Just a few minutes remaining, gentlemen," he announced softly over an intercom.

They pulled into the airport and turned off the central road before reaching the main terminal, heading for the ramp area where private aircraft were hangared. Chelovek and Perrault looked enviously at the gleaming Falcon, Cessna and Westwind jets bearing the corporate logos of such blue-chip giants as IBM, General Electric, Time-Warner and Exxon. There were any number of unmarked planes as well, including several Bell Ranger turbojet helicopters and a garishly liveried 737 bearing a crown logo and the name TRUMP emblazoned in letters four feet high.

The limo passed by them all and, as puzzlement began to cross the faces of the passengers, turned left at the last hangar. As it swung around behind the building and away from the morning sun, there before them gleamed a Gulfstream IV painted in the deepest green and polished so exquisitely it might have been coated with crushed diamonds. Light danced off the silvered cowlings of the engines, the vertical fin shimmered, and even the tires seemed to have been Armor-coated within the previous ten minutes.

The forward airstep was down, and two uniformed attendants stood patiently, a man at the top and a woman with shoulder-length hair at the bottom. As a fuel truck began pulling away, its driver stopped, got out and wiped at a stray trickle of gas beneath the left wing, something he'd probably not done to a plane since his four-week probationary period when he'd first gotten the job fifteen years ago. As he got back in and resumed backing up, the rear section of the fuselage was revealed. It bore the same thin-lined logo as the china and linens in the limo, SB in muted gold, the letters barely twenty inches high.

"Are we ready, then?"

The chauffeur's voice startled the staring passengers, who'd not yet realized that the limo had come to a halt at the bottom of the airstairs. By the time they got out, the chauffeur had the trunk open and the golf bags on their way to the rear baggage compartment.

"Good morning, gentlemen," the attendant at the bottom of the stairs called easily. "Pleasant ride in?" Up close they could see that she was a beauty of the strong, corn-fed, Midwestern type.

They all started responding simultaneously, Savitch and Perrault stammering a bit, Chelovek and Aronica more in control of themselves. The attendant seemed to take no notice of their momentary disorientation. "Great day for flying. Right this way, please."

Chelovek led the way as the attendant at the top called down, "Welcome aboard! My name's Carlos. Take your time coming up." Carlos had a mildly swarthy look to go with his Latino name, but his barely discernible accent had more of the lilt of the Caribbean. About six feet tall and slender, his was an immediate but not imposing presence. Like the chauffeur and the other attendant, Carlos seemed appropriately deferential but not even remotely subservient, giving the definite impression that his service function in no way implied a subordinate station in life.

Chelovek paused at the bottom of the stairs, leaned against the railing and began speaking in low tones to the female attendant. He didn't notice as the pilot, visible in the cockpit window to the left, smiled and waved pleasantly. Perrault saw him and waved back, saying sideways to Aronica, "We've been here but two minutes, and Jerrold's on pussy patrol already."

Savitch didn't see the pilot because he was looking at the fuselage to his right. "Hey! There's no windows!"

Carlos nodded enthusiastically. "The reason for that is simple, Mr. Savitch. It's for—"

"God*damn*, Carlos!" Aronica exclaimed, banging his hand on the rail opposite the side Chelovek was leaning on. "I been telling those knuckleheads at the FAA to yank the windows for years!"

Perrault turned around as Chelovek, annoyed at the interruption, said, "What the hell're you talking about, Joe?"

"It's a safety thing, pure and simple! A window's a piece of weak plastic, and you take away structural metal to put one in. Time you get done slapping a hundred of 'em into an airplane, you might as well be flyin' around in a toothpaste tube, all the integrity the structure's got left."

"Quite right, sir," Carlos agreed.

"I'm in the business, you know."

"Aeronica Aircraft, of course, sir."

"So why do they put windows in planes at all?" Savitch asked.

"I'll tell you why," Aronica shot back. "Because the paying public is too stupid to protect their own asses. They wanna look outside and watch the ground go by, then sue the hell out of everybody for building shitty planes when one of 'em bellies in and crumples like a paper cup!"

"Gee, tell us how you really feel about it, Joe," Perrault said. Then he thought about it for a second while the others savored his jibe at Aronica. "It seems, whenever I fly, passengers become incensed if you even put a shade up, complaining that they're utterly unable to watch some insipid movie. Makes one feel the callous clod merely for wishing to look outside."

"I hate flying commercial, too, Dr. Perrault," Carlos said. "Personally, I ride along on Swithen Bairn's cargo plane instead of a commercial flight when I'm off duty: no windows and no movie, just a cooler full of lagers. Speaking of which . . ." He motioned them inside the plane.

Chelovek turned back toward the stairway just in time to see the female attendant walking away. "Hey, where you going?" he called out.

"I'm not your type," she said without turning back.

"What d'you mean?"

As Savitch walked in front of Chelovek to get to the stairs, the attendant called back over her shoulder, "I'm not inflatable."

Red-faced, Chelovek tried to ignore the snickers from his supposed friends. "Fuck you and your safety campaign," he grumbled to Aronica as he turned to follow Savitch and Perrault up the stairs.

"What'd you say to her?" Savitch asked from inside the plane.

"Just asked her what her favorite position was."

"Whud she answer?"

"CEO." He took one last look at the woman, just in time to see her hoist both of Aronica's heavy golf bags, one in each hand, as though he'd forgotten to put any clubs in them.

"You wouldn't last two minutes with that vixen anyway, Jerrold," Perrault said as Chelovek gulped, then grabbed him by the arm and pulled him inside.

Aronica was rubbing his hands together and practically ran up the stairs now. "Well, Carlos, I like the cut of this operation's jib, yessiree. When are we wheels-up?"

"You gentlemen are the only passengers, so it's your call."

Aronica was last aboard, and as he entered the cabin, he looked around and clucked his tongue disapprovingly, an interesting reaction considering that the others were already sinking into the calfskin seats and drinking in the rich appointments. "Ah-ah-ah, Carlos. You disappoint me!"

"And why is that, sir?"

"Seats facing forward." Aronica waved his hand toward his friends. "Bad thinking there! Much safer to have them facing backward."

"Whyzzat?" Chelovek asked, still irritated.

"Crash happens, you get thrown toward the nose, not the tail. So which is better, full-length of padding down your back or a tray table between the eyes?"

"So that's why the flight attendants are always sitting backward?" Savitch asked.

"She coming along?" Chelovek whispered to Carlos.

" 'Fraid not, sir."

"For heaven's sake, Joe!" Perrault said to Aronica, throwing a theatrical glare toward Savitch at the same time. "Will you sit down so we can close the door and open the cooler?"

As Aronica did so, Carlos stood and idly scratched the side of his face as he looked around. "Good point, that," he said to Aronica. "They face backward in the cargo plane. I'll bring it up to the owners."

"There you go," Aronica said, satisfied.

Chapter 7

❖

INITIALLY NONPLUSSED BY THE LACK of windows, the four of them quickly forgot about it altogether as Carlos, even before the growl of the closing wheel-well doors fell away, opened several wall panels near his seat to reveal a liquor stock that made up in quality what it lacked in volume. There was Hennessey XO and Grand Marnier Cent-Cinquantenaire, three bottles of Lafitte lying on their sides in a separate minicellar, several Taittingers and Dom Pérignons chilling in the refrigerator next to a small aluminum keg sporting a protruding tap and a Tuborg label, Zubrowka vodka with a reed visible in the bottle, Terre Firma tequila . . .

"Bit early, don't you think?" Chelovek said.

"It's five o'clock somewhere," Perrault countered, pointing to a bottle of Bombay Sapphire and a Schweppes.

"Soon as we level out, I can open the galley," Carlos said as he began to fix a gin and tonic for Perrault.

"Say, how long's the flight anyway?" Aronica asked, feeling around under his chair, which he'd discovered could swivel 360 degrees and move some two feet fore and aft or sideways.

Carlos pursed his lips and rocked his head. "Hard to say. Three, four hours, depending on the winds."

Aronica's hand stopped moving. "This a flotation cushion down here? Didn't know we were going over water."

"Not certain we are," Carlos replied, squeezing a fresh-cut lime into a glass. "But we're ready to pick up anywhere, so it's a precaution."

"Any chance of visiting the front office?" Aronica jerked a thumb in the direction of the cockpit. "I'm a licensed—"

"Sorry, sir," Carlos said, pausing over the drink and looking genuinely distressed at having to deny the request. "Safety above all else, I'm afraid."

As Aronica threw up both hands in mock surrender to show he understood, Perrault held a finger in front of Carlos and twirled it. The attendant quickly resumed mixing the drink.

Several minutes later they could feel the engines being throttled back gently, then a muted chime sounded and a voice came over the intercom. "We're in level flight, gentlemen, so you're free to walk about the cabin. Appreciate it if you kept the belts on when you're sitting down, though. If you haven't driven a car since 1962 and need a lecture on how to fasten them, Carlos can show you how for three strokes a side."

The captain's wisecracking blew apart any last vestige of polite decorum as the passengers threw off their belts and stood up, stretching a bit and shooing Carlos toward the galley. Perrault reached into a panel and gingerly withdrew one of the Lafittes. "Okay to crack this beauty later?" he called, holding up the bottle.

"Certainly," Carlos answered automatically, without looking back.

Chelovek came up behind Perrault and peered at the label over his shoulder. "Holy shit . . . that's a '61!"

"You're telling me?"

"What's it cost?" Savitch whispered.

Perrault looked around for some kind of posted price list, then rummaged through the magazine holder in the side of Aronica's seat but didn't find anything. "Feels a tad chintzy to ask," he said.

"What's it usually go for, roughly?" Savitch asked tentatively.

"Approximately what your clubs go for," Perrault answered.

"Fuck me!" Chelovek cried loudly. "Yo, Carlos!" he yelled as Perrault turned away in embarrassment. "What's the tab on the Lafitte?"

"Don't worry about it," Carlos called back. "Like the invitation said, everything's included."

The four friends stared at each other, but only for a second. Carlos came back nto the cabin wearing an apron and wheeling a four-tiered serving cart. On the top shelf was a platter of smoked salmon, a dish of quail eggs, an open tin of caviar, and small china cups holding diced hard-boiled egg, onions and parsley. "Here, let me get that for you," he said, reaching for the wine.

As Perrault let go of the bottle, Savitch bent down to look at the second tier. There he saw paper-thin prosciutto and wedges of cantaloupe alongside a shallow bowl containing a pile of stone crabs and freshly shucked oysters. There were also several boxes of ordinary breakfast cereal.

"Hey!" he heard from behind him, turning to see Chelovek reach for one of the cereal boxes.

Chelovek looked at the box and held it up. "Trader Jim's cereal: I designed this box!"

"Really?" Carlos said. "You mean the picture?

"Hell, no, all of it, right down to the last letter!"

Carlos turned to the others, exclaiming, "Well, how about that!" but they didn't seem equally impressed, likely having heard it one or two thousand times before.

Carlos turned his attention back to Chelovek. "Maybe you can explain something to me. Right here." He set the wine bottle down and took the box, pointing to an ingredient listed on the side panel. "What the heck is 'crystallized evaporated cane juice'?"

Chelovek folded his arms across his chest, smiled and closed his eyes. "That, my man, is sugar."

"Sugar!"

"Yes indeed." Chelovek opened his eyes and reached for the box, rubbing the surface lovingly. "Came up with that little beauty myself. Had to, on account of people just aren't buying into that 'fructose' bullshit anymore, knowing anything ends in O-S-E is sugar no matter how you spell it, so we hadda come up with something else."

"Well, I'll be go to hell. Sugar!" Carlos handed back the box and picked up the wine bottle. He cut the foil off the top and pulled a corkscrew out of his apron pocket. "Anyway, I can whip you up some omelets, pancakes, a dozen kinds of crepes—pretty much whatever you'd like, but don't go crazy: I'll be serving lunch in about an hour."

As he put the bottle between his knees and yanked the cork with a satisfying pop, Savitch whispered to Aronica, "Tell me we're not dead."

"Who gives a shit if we are?" Aronica replied, never taking his eyes off the stone crabs.

Carlos poured a small amount of wine into a glass, held it up to the overhead light, swirled it around a few times and then, to their surprise, took a sip himself. He swished it around in his mouth and then swallowed, half closing his eyes as he did so. Smacking his lips in satisfaction, he said, "Damn, this is a good job! Who wants some?"

·

"I CAN'T FIGURE THIS FELLOW out," Perrault said quietly to Chelovek between sips of the Lafitte.

"Like, should he be sweeping floors or running an airline?"

"Right. Or even where he's from. Half the time he sounds like a Jamaican cabdriver, the other half like Neville Chamberlain. I say . . . Carlos!"

"C'mon, Pete," Chelovek whispered sternly, a stone crab poised above a jigger of cocktail sauce Carlos had made from scratch. "Don't embarrass the guy!"

"Relax, Jerrold. The man lives only to serve."

"More wine, Doctor?"

"No thanks, Carlos. Take a sit and have a breather."

"Thanks." Carlos removed his apron and took a seat opposite the two of them, then reached for a wineglass without asking permission. "But this job's not exactly digging ditches."

"I can see that," Perrault said as he took up the wine bottle and gave Carlos a generous pour. "May I ask you something?"

"By all means." Carlos twirled the stem of the glass between his fingers and took his time appreciating the bouquet before taking a small sip.

Perrault leaned forward and put on his most comradely *entre nous* expression. "What's the scoop on this place, this Swithen Barn?"

"It's pronounced *Bairn*, actually. Rhymes with harem, except one syllable. And what scoop would that be, Doctor?"

Perrault shook his head and dropped back against his seat. "I'm curious. How can the proprietors risk not getting paid after providing"—he waved his hand around the plane—"all of this?"

Carlos nodded knowingly; this was obviously not the first time he'd heard the question. "The owners pick their visitors carefully, and most people do pay. But you want to know what I think?"

By this time Aronica and Savitch had swiveled their seats around to face the others. "What's that?" Chelovek asked, taking up the cue.

Carlos looked around, as though entertaining for a half second the notion that there could be someone else on board who might overhear. "I don't think the owners really need the money. I think the whole place is just one giant tax deduction."

He ignored their wide-eyed looks and set down his glass, then put his elbows on his knees and leaned forward, gesturing with his hands as he spoke. "I'm not saying I really understand this kind of stuff, but these guys, the owners, they have other businesses, see? Some of them pretty big. And those companies have some . . . uh, I don't remember the term, but it's chunks of the business that don't make money but they can't get rid of them. Damn, what's the—"

"Nonperforming assets," Perrault suggested.

Carlos snapped his fingers and sat up straight. "That's it, Doc! And what happens is, the nonperforming assets, all they do is make the profit smaller and not much else. So what the owners did, they said, 'Let's build this resort, make it a completely separate corporation, and we'll sell some of those non-performing assets to that corporation.'"

"So Swithen Bairn now owns pieces of these other companies?" Savitch asked.

"Exactly. A little steel mill outside of Pittsburgh, a chain of dumpy motels in Nebraska, even an HMO in Iowa. Swithen Bairn claims gigantic losses every year and never pays a dime in taxes but recoups most of its operating costs by charging just enough to the original companies that owned those assets for their use." With a satisfied grin, Carlos took another sip of wine and waited for the reaction to his speculative tale.

"I'll be damned," Aronica breathed in admiration.

"Hang on a second here," Chelovek said. "You telling me the IRS doesn't smell a scam here, this corporation nothing more than a black hole sucking funny money into its books?"

Carlos hurriedly swallowed and shook his head. "But it *is* more than that, Mr. Chelovek. They have enough customers to make it a legitimate operation, and each of the owners plays some kind of an active role in management, and that's on-site management, not some kind of, uh . . ."

"Absentee?" Savitch ventured.

"That's it. Not some kind of absentee thing."

"Which justifies their being at a posh resort in the first place," Perrault said.

"Because it's business-related," Carlos concurred.

"You've got to admire the creativity," Perrault admitted.

"What I still don't get," Chelovek said skeptically, "is why they went through all the trouble. Bottom line here, no matter how you spread it around, the same amount of money gets lost. All you really did was move around whose books the losses appear on."

"Thought he said most of their guests pay, though," Savitch argued. "So that's new income you didn't have before, right?"

"No, Jerry's right," Aronica countered. "You may have new income, but you also have new expenses, running a resort with a golf course on it. I mean, look at all of this . . ."

Perrault rested his chin on his hand and thought about it. "Has to have been something else, some other reason . . ."

Carlos laughed. "Well, of course there's another reason. Isn't it obvious?"

"Isn't what obvious?" Savitch asked, wondering if he should feel insulted.

Carlos turned up his hands and let them drop onto his lap. "You're right, of course, Mr. Chelovek. Net net, there's basically no more money going in or out across all the companies. But instead of just obsolete steel mills and crappy motels, now they've got obsolete steel mills, crappy motels, and one of the most beautiful golf courses in the world they can use whenever they want to, and that their friends can use, and as long as enough outside people pay enough money to legitimize the place as a real business, they can go on doing what they really love the most."

"And what's that?" Perrault asked.

"Why, play golf for money, Doctor. That's kind of the whole point."

Chapter 8

THE SOFT DRONING OF THE engines was the only sound inside the cabin following Carlos's candid speculations about the *raison d'être* of Swithen Bairn.

As the others gaped at the attendant, Chelovek asked warily, "Play for money? Is that what we're expected to do?"

"Expected to—" Carlos jerked his head up sharply, shock and concern registering on his heretofore tranquil features. "No, no, Mr. Chelovek! My God, I hope—"

Sweat broke out on his upper lip. He gulped, then looked down at the wineglass on the arm of his chair, grabbed it and stood up. Before any of the others could stop him, he quickly dumped what remained in the trash receptacle and put the glass aside, then reached for his apron and put it back on.

Perrault smiled and held up a calming hand. "Relax, my good man. No need for fretfulness."

"The owners . . . What did I . . . If they thought I was giving you the impression you were expected to gamble there . . . !"

Aronica stood up and clapped a hand on the attendant's shoulder. "F'Chrissakes, Carlos, what do we look like, government informers?" He turned toward Savitch, who nodded his concurrence that Carlos's fears were unfounded, then pointed toward the discarded wineglass. "I know it's included, but you pour any more of that down the shitter at twenty bucks a sip and we *will* turn you in!"

Carlos managed a weak smile as the others laughed and urged him to sit back down. "Sorry," he said as he resumed his seat but left the apron on. "Sometimes, nice bunch of guys like you, I forget who I'm working for, or even that I'm working."

"So we're *not* expected to play for money?" Chelovek asked, the only one keeping his mind on the business at hand.

Carlos shook his head. "Of course not. That's *their* thing, the owners. Got nothing to do with you. You're on vacation, is all. The real money players who visit, they know what's up in advance."

Chelovek took some mild umbrage at that. "Who's to say *we're* not real money players?"

"Yeah," Savitch piped up. "We've been known to put a penny or two on a round."

"Not saying you don't, gentlemen," Carlos replied. "No offense intended."

"How did they select us?" Perrault asked, trying to ward off any unpleasantness. "To send the invitation to?"

"They didn't pick *us*," Aronica corrected him. "They picked *me*, and *I* picked the rest of you."

"I don't really know," Carlos said. "Thing is, these guys are absolutely dead damned nuts about golf. And nuts about people who're nuts about golf. What I'm guessing, all they care about is you all love to play, and you can afford Swithen Bairn."

Perrault took a toast point and scooped up the last bit of caviar. "And their level of play?" he asked as casually as he could as he popped it into his mouth.

"Real good. Not hustlers either. I'm not saying they can't get a little clever once in a while, but it's just part of the fun, and they keep it clean."

"They win a lot?" Aronica chimed in.

"More often than not. Especially against guys who know how to play golf but don't know how to make a bet. It's a real art, believe me, what with some of the crazy games they come up with."

"What kind of handicaps do they carry?" Aronica asked.

"Pretty close to scratch, some of them, and they— Hey, wait a minute! You guys aren't thinking about—"

"Heavens no," Perrault assured him. "Merely making inquiries, getting the lay of the land. As Deke said, we've been known on rare occasion to entertain modest wagers ourselves."

"Yeah," Aronica added with enthusiasm. "But it's getting boring, same old assholes week after week."

Chelovek scratched the side of his nose. "Glad you said it first, Joe."

"Thing is, Carlos," Perrault said, "what with all the time we've been play-ing together, everything pretty much evens out over the long haul. At least if you don't count Deke."

Savitch took a deep breath and let it out slowly. "Here we go again. You guys get so torqued about losing, why the hell do you bet in the first place?"

Aronica pointed to Savitch and said to Carlos, "This sonofabitch, you lay a couple coins on the line, he'll play under his handicap every damned time."

"Quite eerie," Perrault agreed.

"I keep telling you guys," Savitch said defensively, "it isn't the money, it's the competition. Makes me focus. Isn't that the whole point of putting some-thing on the game? Besides," he added, pointing toward Aronica, "Joltin' Joe over here, every once in a while he hauls out those 'lucky' clubs he lugs around with him—*he* wins darned near every time!"

"That's why they're lucky," Aronica said in mild embarrassment.

"Then how the hell come you don't use them all the time?" Chelovek chal-lenged.

"Because," Aronica said with exaggerated patience, "they're not lucky if you use them all the time. Defeats the whole purpose."

Perrault waved the debate, clearly an ancient one, into silence. "So, Carlos, whom do we see about perhaps arranging a contest with your employers?"

The attendant shook his head forcefully. "I told you. Forget about it."

A chorus of "whys" assaulted him, and he said, "Four guys get off a plane, all strangers, and they march up and say, 'Let's put a little something on it'? Forget it. They'll smell something fishy right away. Wouldn't you?"

"And if we don't say anything," Aronica argued back, "we're stuck playing with each other for a whole week. So what've we got to lose?"

Carlos considered it. "Only thing I can tell you, if it's not too busy, maybe they'll chat you up and see if you're interested in something. But believe me, you approach one of them, it'll never happen. Wait until you're invited."

Aronica, Perrault and Savitch sat back, thinking it over, totally intrigued.

Chelovek looked around and sneered. "You ask me, I think we're being scammed."

CHELOVEK'S SNEER TURNED TO AN all-knowing smile, and he beamed it on the attendant. "Gimme a break, Carlos. You gonna sit there and tell me you're not setting me and my buddies up?"

Carlos frowned. "What are you talking about?"

Chelovek laughed and shook his head. "Took you all of fifteen minutes to get these schmucks so lathered up they're probably going to wire their banks for betting cash before the plane comes to a stop!"

"Hey, who do you think you are, Jerry!" Savitch spat at Chelovek. "What makes you so gosh-darned smart?"

"Indeed," Perrault chimed in. Addressing Carlos, he said, "This man, if someone sells him a newspaper on the street, he checks inside to see if he was swindled out of the classifieds."

"Captain Bringdown, here," Aronica volunteered he inclined his chin toward Chelovek. "Thinks anybody smart enough to tie his own shoelaces is trying to rip him off."

Chelovek wasn't about to get sidetracked by insults he'd been hearing from them for years. "Maybe, but this one's so transparent even you assholes can't tell me you don't see right through it. Hell, way he's got it set up, you're all gonna spend the whole week practically begging these owners to take your dough! No offense, Carlos."

"No offense?" Carlos responded incredulously, but good-naturedly as well. "You just accused me of being the front man for a sting, but no offense?"

"Don't pay any attention to the cynical bastard, Carlos," Aronica advised.

"What can I tell you?" Chelovek pleaded with a smile. "I'm in—"

"Yes, yes, you're in advertising," Perrault finished for him. "How tiresome. Carlos, you seem to know a good deal about the goings on. Now, why would that be?"

"I sometimes caddie for them, make a couple extra bucks. Nothing brings out a guy's true personality like a round of golf, and you can learn an awful lot just by hanging around and paying attention."

He leaned forward and dropped his voice slightly. The others, without realizing it, leaned in to catch his words. "One time I'm carrying a bag, and Ted Turner's in the foursome?"

"*The* Ted Turner?" asked Chelovek, impressed despite himself.

"Himself. Anyway, I heard him talk about how he was going to merge his company, and I didn't give it any thought. Sure enough, a couple months later he joins up with Time-Warner."

The intercom chimed softly, but Carlos ignored it and sat back, shaking his head ruefully. "I'da picked up some of that stock, I'd own this jet instead of serving drinks on it." Remembering once again who and where he was, he held up his hands and said quickly, "Not that I mind, don't get me wrong. But believe me, I'm saving every penny I can scrounge for the next time a tip like that comes along. You don't get—"

"Gentlemen," the intercom intruded, "we're going to begin our descent in a couple of minutes, so we'd like Carlos to get everything put away while you all get strapped in. Should be on the ground in about thirty minutes."

"Shit!" Carlos exclaimed as he jumped up, then apologized for his language. He set about re-stowing everything in the galley and side panels and then began checking that all their seat belts were fastened.

AS THE SOUND OF THE engines dropped half an octave, Aronica looked at his watch and said, "Damn, that seemed fast. Been up over three hours, though."

"You're kidding," Savitch said, looking at his own watch.

"Carlos, tell me something . . ." Perrault reached into his jacket pocket, took out his wallet and opened it. Withdrawing a hundred-dollar bill, he held it out to the attendant. "How good are these gentlemen, truthfully?"

Carlos looked at the hundred but made no move to take it. Perrault shook it back and forth. "Couple extra shares when you get that great stock tip . . . ?"

The others nudged their hands in Perrault's direction, urging Carlos to go ahead and take the bill. Eventually he did, and tucked it into his back pocket.

"The main guy, Eddie, he'll tell you he's a two. Argue back that he knows the course better than anybody, so that's gotta be worth something. Keep a sense of humor, don't get nasty, and eventually he'll probably let you talk him down to scratch."

Aronica, not to be outdone, took a hundred out of his own wallet. "Hey, Carlos . . ."

"Fellas, c'mon!" Carlos threw up his hands and backed away. "I told you, they're not going to play you, so you don't need to—"

Aronica shook his head. "Forget it. You did a hell of a job on the flight. Just showing you a little appreciation. Come on, take it. I can afford it."

Sighing, Carlos stepped forward and gingerly accepted the bill. "When people first get there, the tees are usually set up front, so you play real well. But when you play for money, they'll knock 'em back as far as they'll go."

"How much of a difference could that make?" The words were out of Chelovek's mouth before he could haul them back in. He prayed that nobody would call him on his 180-degree change of heart, and nobody did.

Including Carlos. "Huge. That's the way the course was designed, so they could set it up for all kinds of golfers. Play it from the forwards and it's a very pretty cream puff. From the tips and it's like falling off your local muni and landing at Pine Valley." Which, in case you didn't know, is generally considered the toughest course in this corner of the galaxy, although for my money that distinction should go to Ko'olau on Oahu, where the rule of thumb is to bring as many balls as your handicap.

It was Savitch's turn, but as he reached for his rear pants pocket, Carlos stepped away and said, "Hey, whoa! No more!" They could tell he meant it, and Savitch sat back again.

"Fellas," Carlos said, "why waste your time trying to play against people who know the course that well? There'll be other people there; you want to bet so bad, set up a game with some guys who're as new to the place as you are."

"But them you don't know," Aronica counters. "How do we know they'll be honest about their handicaps?"

Carlos explained that the resort took golf and betting very seriously. The pro will call another player's home club and verify his handicap for you immediately. In fact, it's a house rule. That way nobody gets offended at their honesty being questioned.

"So basically," Chelovek said, "this whole place centers around betting on golf, and you're telling us we don't have to if we don't want to?"

"Mr. Chelovek, lounge around the pool or play fifty-four holes a day by yourselves for your entire stay and nobody will care one way or the other, believe me."

Carlos dropped out of the crew seat and began pulling the shoulder strap out of its retainer. "Course if you do that, and have a good time, you really ought to pay for your stay."

"And how much would that be?" Savitch asked, realizing as they all did that nobody had paid any attention to that minor detail.

Carlos snapped the strap into place and leaned over to locate the lap belt. "Eighteen grand each for the six days, plus ten for the jet, which you can all split. Mind locking those seat swivels into place, gentlemen?"

Not hearing the sounds of the seats being correctly positioned, he looked up, just in time to see several variations of barely repressed alarm on the passengers' faces.

Tilting his head dismissively, he said, "But like the invitation said, you don't think it was worth it, don't pay."

THE GUYS HAD MANAGED TO pretty much talk themselves out of their shock by the time the Gulfstream slowed on the ramp and came to a gentle stop with nary a squeal or rumble from the undercarriage. As soon as he heard the engines spooling down, Carlos unsnapped his belts, stood up and walked toward the cabin door. Upon hearing two knocks from the outside, he fished out a pair of sunglasses, swung the release arm over, pulled the door inward to break the pressure seal and then shoved it outward.

The four passengers had their eyes trained on the door but winced and drew back or covered their faces with their arms when it opened. The light that lanced through their dim-adapted eyes was naked and fierce, and all they could perceive in those first few instants was a riot of indigo and emerald swirling kaleidoscopically through the doorway.

"Take your time, gentlemen," Carlos said. "Yo, Jake!"

"Hey, Carlos!" a cheery voice answered from outside above the sound of the airstairs being lowered. "Anybody coming out? Or they like the plane too much?"

Aronica, blinking painfully, was the first to near the door. As his pupils contracted, the chaotic splash of brilliant colors began to resolve itself into sea, grass and trees. Set on fire by the sun, the scene before him shimmered silently behind the heat waves rising from the black tarmac beneath the plane.

Savitch came up behind him and looked past his shoulder. "Damn . . ." he said as Perrault and Chelovek followed suit.

"Gentlemen," the man Carlos had addressed as Jake said, "welcome to Swithen Bairn."

Chapter 9

✱

Day One

TWO SIX-PASSENGER GOLF CARTS stood a few steps away. Their luggage was already being loaded into one of them, and Jake, a young man with seen-it-all eyes, held out his hand toward the other one. Unable to tear their gazes away from the achingly beautiful panorama that stretched in all directions, the newly landed guests shuffled slowly into the cart and somehow got themselves seated.

Jake got into the driver's seat and slowly pulled away from the plane. As it left the lingering jet fumes behind, they took deep breaths and got their first whiff of the complex and intoxicating mix of viburnum, jasmine and stephanotis that perfumed the air of the resort.

"The main house—that's what we call the hotel—it's only a couple of minutes. Want a little tour on the way?"

Jake grinned as an assenting chorus arose from his charges, then turned onto a path of crushed pastel coral overhung with broadleaf palms and delicate ferns so lush that sapphire crystals of sky peeked through only occasionally. Sunlight filtering through the translucent leaves created the illusion that the tunnel-like path was illuminated by soft light emanating from within the plants themselves. Impossibly bright and multihued birds, excited by the cart that brushed aside branches as it proceeded, flitted back and forth and expressed their outrage in a continuous stream of whistles, hoots and boisterous screeches.

The path had turnouts about every twenty-five yards. Each had a wooden bench and a cooler filled with ice and several bottles of water. Jake pointed to one as they passed, and the guests looked to see a vervet monkey perched atop a bench and eyeing them expectantly. As the cart slowed, the monkey leaped onto the front of it, grabbed a cookie that had appeared in Jake's hand, then jumped off the side opposite the one he'd arrived on and swung from a branch by one arm, all of it in a single continuous, fluid motion.

"You got any food on you, you go walking around here," Jake said in a soft Southern drawl, "best keep it away from Mambo, that little smart-ass."

"Anything in there liable to be dangerous?" Aronica asked.

Jake shook his head. "Nothin' poisonous on the entire island, although the insects can be annoying, you don't have some repellent on. Best lay off the aftershave and cologne, by the way. Drives 'em nuts. Hang on . . ."

He swung the cart hard right onto a side path. In less than a minute the dense thicket ended abruptly, and they emerged on a small hill. Jake aimed the cart at its crest and, topping it, stopped and applied the toe brake. Spread out before them was a small beach of pinkish sand, stretching less than a hundred yards end to end and bounded by stands of palm trees. Dotting the curving beach were umbrellas, rattan mats and chaise lounges. An attendant manned a booth in the middle, well back from the water, on which they could see piles of towels. There were boxes of fins and masks alongside, flotation mats stacked behind, and a miniature bar close at hand. The attendant, who was the only person on the beach, turned and waved, and the men in the cart waved back.

"Doesn't get a lot of business this time'a day," Jake said. "Mostly early morning and late afternoon."

"How come?" Aronica asked. "Sun too strong?"

"Nope," Jake answered. "I'll show you."

He put the cart in reverse and got it turned around, then plunged back into the mini-jungle and found the main path. Several minutes later they came upon a clearing that was about fifty feet across but looked from where they were positioned as if it might stretch a good deal farther than that to the left and right.

Jake stopped the cart and set the brake again but said nothing. Perrault looked around and said, "What's this?"

Jake inclined his chin toward the clearing ahead. "First tee."

It took a moment for that to sink in. Then Chelovek stepped gingerly out of the cart and walked forward into the clearing. The first thing he saw as the trees on his left fell away was two planters full of violet orchids set about twenty feet apart. To his right and about thirty yards away he saw a second set of planters, this time of yellow flowers, and still farther back a single one of blue, backed by a wall of bamboo plants. He noticed that the setback wasn't straight but curved away, so that only one blue planter was visible, and he guessed that its twin was somewhere off to the side.

As he looked at the planters, puzzled as to their meaning, he heard Savitch behind him cry, "Tee markers! They're tee markers!"

Suddenly understanding, and quickly realizing that the blue plants were the farthest set, Chelovek turned around at the same time as Savitch and saw Aronica and Perrault, apparently having caught on a little faster, staring in the other direction.

"Jumpin' Jesus . . ." Chelovek breathed.

There was another set of markers up ahead, this time of white flowers, and beyond them a near-phosphorescent fairway boldly slashed its way down a gentle slope, turned right at the bottom around a stand of stately palm trees, and ended at a perfectly round green surrounded on three sides by the ocean. The cobalt blue of the sea was separated from the deep emerald of the green by the same kind of coral they had seen on the beach, giving the whole target area the look of a giant eye. The white flag fluttering off center looked like a gleam, completing the illusion perfectly.

Jake, still sitting in the cart, watched with satisfaction as the four guests stood there looking for all the world like awestruck tourists gazing stupidly at the Sphinx or the skyscrapers of Manhattan. He pulled a cigarette from a pack in his shirt pocket and stuck it in his mouth. "Go on, now," he called out. "Have a good look!"

Shaken out of their reverie, they nodded absently and started forward. Crossing the rough in front of the teeing area, they emerged onto the fairway, and Aronica knelt down to run his hands along the grass. "Lord, would you take a look at this!"

Savitch peered at it for a few seconds and said, "I've seen *greens* didn't look this good. Like it was spray-painted on."

Perrault bent over and nodded his agreement, but Chelovek remained standing, taking in the entirety of the number-one hole. "Most beautiful damned thing I've ever seen," he said softly, to no one in particular.

Perrault stood up and looked past the fairway, where portions of other holes were visible in the distance. "Not a soul on it either."

"So what do you think?" Jake asked as he appeared behind them, taking in a lungful of smoke.

"Jake!" Perrault said before anyone could answer, grabbing the staffer's arm. "What's the local time here?"

Jake took a moment to exhale a blue-gray cloud that drifted off lazily toward the fairway. "Hell's the difference, Doc? You wanna play, go for it. Dinner's whenever you want it, and I can bring a couple sandwiches out to the course, tide y'all over."

"What about checking in?" Savitch asked. "Don't we have to register, see about—"

Jake waved the questions away. "No need," he said, then pulled a walkie-talkie from his shirt pocket and extended the antenna. "Jake to front, come on!"

"Yeah, Jake," the radio crackled back.

"Billy, how about y'all bring them clubs over to number one, copy?"

"No problem. Where're their shoes?"

"Mine're in the golf bag," Aronica said.

"Me, too," Perrault added. "I think."

Chelovek frowned. "Think I packed mine in the suitcase."

Before Savitch could say anything, Jake spoke into the radio again. "Jus' bring it all on over, Billy. We'll get it sorted out here."

"Copy. They want caddies or carts?"

Chelovek spoke first. "I want to walk it. And carry my own bag. That okay?"

"You bet," Jake answered.

Aronica nodded excitedly, but Perrault said, "We'll need a vehicle for Deke."

"How about we bring up a four-bagger, you can put 'em all on one cart, not have to lug 'em around." Jake radioed the instructions, then put away the walkie-talkie and said, "Might wanna stretch after all that sittin' on the plane. Stuff'll be here in two shakes."

"What do we need to know?" Chelovek asked.

Jake stepped past them and pointed toward the water. "Whole place slopes toward the ocean. Kind of a optical illusion, there, on account'a you got no perspective. Green that looks dead flat, it's gonna break toward the water. . . ."

They did their best to concentrate as Jake described the nuances of the course with the expertise of a tour professional and the twang of a Tupelo truck driver, but the almost palpable pull of the first hole was too distracting. Each hoped that among the four of them they were catching enough to pool their memories later and reconstruct everything they were being told.

On the other hand, this was going to be a practice round to get familiar with the track, and so they really didn't much care.

Chapter 10

::

LESS THAN TWENTY MINUTES AFTER Jake radioed the hotel, the boys had their shoes on and their clubs at the ready. They took their time getting out the various specialized accoutrements of the game—tees, markers, gloves, divot repairers, groove cleaners—so that Jake and the valet would have the carts and themselves gone before the first of the foursome teed off.

When the crunching of coral beneath the wheels of the two carts finally died away, Aronica said, "Usual bet?"

Perrault shook his head. "As we're going to be here for a week, what I'd prefer is to get acquainted with the lady without being concerned about making shots. Doubt I'll even keep my score."

It was a good plan. "What do we need to clear the trees?" Savitch asked Chelovek, who was looking at the yardage book the valet had brought out for them.

"Hard to say," Chelovek answered, "on account of the downhill. Give it some fade, you can blast away and still stay on the fairway when it bends. Otherwise you're in the rough on the other side."

"Huh. Driver's too risky, then." Savitch took a two-iron and stepped up to the white markers to plant a tee and ball. He twisted the club's grip in his hands a few times and took several practice swings, paused, and drew a deep breath. "Air tastes like wine," he said quietly.

"That it does," Aronica agreed.

"Go for it, Deke," Perrault said.

With one last look out toward the beckoning jade fairway, Savitch settled in over the ball, set the clubhead behind it and willed his body to stillness.

A WORD ABOUT THE SWITHEN Bairn golf course.

In my business, top course designers are treated with almost as much reverence as chefs are in Los Angeles, the difference being that golf courses are designed for the ages rather than for this Sunday's review. Another difference is that there are more objective criteria one can use in critiquing a golf course than in evaluating a soufflé.

As you might imagine, I've played just about every notable golf course on the face of the planet, and I don't think there's another quite like Swithen Bairn. It's about as close to perfect as a course can be.

What makes for a good golf course? For one thing, it should be pleasing to the eye. One of the elemental joys of the game is being out of doors and walking around in an environment that is visually arresting, that smells good, where the air is clean. Swithen Bairn is certainly all of that, but the vistas are nowhere near as spectacular as, say, those at the Kona Country Club in Hawaii or Desert Canyon in Washington state.

The physical condition of the course is very important as well. Swithen Bairn's fairways look like they get cut with a ruler and nail clippers. It's at least as good as Augusta, maybe better, but that's still not it.

Swithen Bairn's perfection comes from the way the holes are laid out. Whoever the designers were undoubtedly had instructions to do whatever was necessary to get the best course possible, which meant no expense spared in doing away with natural imperfections that others would have been forced to work around and incorporate.

It was about the *fairest* course I'd ever be likely to see. What that means is a little difficult to describe, but the main idea is that good shots are rewarded, not penalized, and bad shots are punished in an amount appropriate to how bad they really are. That's not to say that it's an easy course; far from it. But its difficulty lies in its length, the types of shots required, and the risks it invites on many holes, rather than malicious caprice.

Here's an example of what I'm trying to say. At my home club there's a hole with a fairway bunker just before a slight dogleg left, and a eucalyptus tree just beyond. When the course was first designed, the idea was to tempt a good player to cut that corner by going over the bunker and past the tree. If you missed and landed in the sand, it was still possible, though difficult, to get up and over the eucalyptus and onto the green.

However, in the intervening years since the course was built, the tree grew so much that it is now impossible to get past it out of the bunker and onto the green. So instead of that errant tee shot resulting in the reasonable penalty of a very long approach out of the sand, it now holds the double whammy of limiting your options to a safe placement back on the fairway with a tricky sand shot, and you still have a long way to the green. Hitting into that trap makes par next to impossible.

The members think this is terribly unfair. For one thing, they say, the course designer didn't intend it that way.

Personally, I think their whining is unjustified. First of all, it isn't as if the designer was unaware that large trees from little trees grow. Second, all that really happened over time is that the risk of cutting the corner was increased. So what? If you don't want to take the chance, hit safely to the center of the fairway, from where you'll still have a decent second-shot opportunity.

What *would* be truly unfair was if there were simply no way to get to the green in two. But there is, and it's not all that tough, and birdies are quite possible, so I can't sympathize with the grousing. The only reason I'm even telling you about it is to illustrate not only what is meant by an "unfair" hole but the fluid nature of that designation.

Here's a better-known and less debatable example. On the evening before the second day of the U.S. Open when it was last played at the Olympic, USGA staffers setting the location of the pin on the last hole took a few dozen putts to make sure it was a reasonable placement, as they always do. Well, it wasn't reasonable, because the slope around the flag was too extreme. But it was the only patch of grass on the green that hadn't been badly beaten up, so with great reluctance they left it there, instructed the grounds crew to keep it soaking wet to make it as slow as possible, and crossed their fingers.

The next day was a disaster. Player after player who failed to get the ball into the hole on a downhill putt watched with varying degrees of fascination (the guys who were already out of the running), dismay (the guys who had a fighting chance at winning), and outright horror (the leaders, as each watched his ball, rather than slow down, pick up speed as it slid past the hole). In some cases those with uphill putts had to jump out of the way as their balls *reversed direction* and came right back at them. The most memorable piece of video of the entire event was of Payne Stewart, who had missed the hole by less than an inch, standing with his arms folded and watching in helpless revulsion as his ball traveled an unbelievable thirty-five feet past the flag and rolled right off the green.

Now, *that's* an unfair hole. Swithen Bairn didn't have any like that. Hit a great shot and you got a great lie. Hit one reasonable and you were in reasonably good shape. A poor shot might cost you a stroke, either because you had to punch out of trouble or because you had to make up distance. A really lousy shot might be unplayable and cost you a penalty, and a truly terrible one could knock you out of bounds or into water. But in every case it would be your own fault, and not the result of some ridiculous quirk of the course.

There were no flower-bed drops either. One of the banes of the good golfer when visiting resort courses is these professionally landscaped botanical gardens all over the place. Put a ball into one of these and you get a free drop, just to make sure maniacs don't start swinging at the foliage to try to save themselves a penalty for dropping from an unplayable lie. I know plenty of courses where the best play is to smack a ball right into the petunias, which is often much easier than stopping it on grass with some backspin. In you go and out you come with a free drop and a better lie than you were likely to get legitimately.

But those museum displays don't belong right next to the greens or where doglegs take their turns. At Swithen Bairn there is beautiful landscaping complete with all manner of exotic flora, but it's off to the side and not in the course of normal play. Hit into one of these and it's an automatic drop-with-penalty. As Eddie Caminetti said to one of my playing partners who claimed that was unfair, "So don't hit into them."

Oh, wait a minute. I haven't really told you anything about Eddie yet. Sorry. We'll get to him later.

Chapter 11

❖

THE SWEET CLICK OF SAVITCH'S tee shot was amplified slightly by the enclosing greenery boxing in the teeing area, making it sound as though the ball had been struck harder than it actually was.

"Good one, Deke," Chelovek said.

"So you think it's okay?" Savitch asked, the club still poised at the end of his follow-through. "You don't think I hit it through the fairway?"

They watched as sunlight glinted off the ball and saw it darken into silhouette as it receded. Savitch's controlled shot had imparted very little sidespin, and it traveled straight, touching down and continuing forward before rolling to a stop well short of the far rough, although not past the palm trees at the bend forming the dogleg. Just as Savitch had intended, which is the very definition of a great golf shot.

"Nice," Aronica said in approval as he knelt to tee up a ball. "What do you figure?"

"About two thirty-five. My shot was around two-twenty, and the downhill did the rest. I shoulda gone another ten yards."

Aronica, ignoring Savitch's typical display of insecurity despite the fact that he was the best golfer of the four, kept his own shot shallow and knocked it a few yards past Savitch's. As the others praised his shot, he held his club out so they could see the bottom of it. And held it there. Waiting.

"What?" Perrault finally asked, knowing full well *what*.

"It was only a five-wood," Aronica said.

"Well, thank you for sharing," Perrault said sarcastically. "Now we're even more impressed. Step up and give it a go, Jerrold."

Chelovek chose a two-iron and kept the trajectory even lower, managing to roll his ball to a good position. Perrault also hit five-wood, hoping to show Aronica something, but didn't catch it clean and was too short. "I came through it too early," he explained. "Didn't have my right shoulder in good position and blocked it out a touch. My thinking was, with the five-wood I'd have to—"

"Yeah, yeah," Savitch said, climbing into the cart and releasing the toe brake.

"Hang on a second," Chelovek called to him. "Any'a you guys in a hurry?"

"No," Perrault answered. "Why?"

"Show you why." Chelovek put away the iron and drew out his driver, stepped back to the box, and teed up another ball. "Might as well give it a whack. We got nobody pushing from behind."

He waggled the big club a few times, addressed the ball and whaled away with happy abandon, grunting with effort as the club came through the ball.

"Holy Hannah!" Savitch exclaimed. "Good one, Jerry!"

"I like it." Chelovek watched as the ball started out straight but soon began biting into the air. It looked good for about a second, but then they all could see that he'd overswung and given it much more spin than he'd intended. The fade gradually metamorphosed into a slice taking dead aim for the trees.

But he'd hit it so hard that it looked as though it might be a close contest between spin and forward momentum, a race to see whether it would be past the trouble when its flight path eventually crossed the tree line.

The ball disappeared somewhere in the vicinity of the fairway bend. "Gee whiz, you think it cleared?" Savitch asked.

Before anybody could answer, Aronica had pulled out another club and was bounding toward the tee box. "I'm gonna give it a try!" he announced, throwing in "This is a three-wood," so in case he hit one as long as Chelovek's, everyone would know that he hadn't needed a driver to do it.

"What the heck!" Savitch said with a grin, getting back out of the cart and nearly colliding with Perrault, who was also heading for his bag and a driver.

NEEDLESS TO SAY, THE BOYS had a ball. They simply couldn't get over how lush and well maintained the course was, as though it had just opened for the first time that very day. And they had it all to themselves, hitting multiple balls, replaying shots, replaying *entire holes* and playing them out of sequence whenever it struck their fancy to do so.

After about two hours of that, they took a break, Chelovek and Aronica breaking out cigars and lighting up. Looking around at the breathtaking scenery, Aronica said, "Don't remember the last time I hit this good."

"I quite agree," Perrault concurred. "I say, look at that!"

A peacock, eyeing them warily, stepped smartly across the tee box less than thirty feet away. Iridescent ripples of deep blue, green and yellow sparkled off the tail feathers hoisted aloft in full display.

"Not sure I've ever seen one'a those outside a zoo," Savitch said.

Chelovek took a step forward and raised his hands aggressively, letting out a growl at the same time. The peacock stopped and stared at him, with no sign that it was the least bit perturbed. Chelovek took a few more steps forward.

Without warning the huge bird tucked back its feathers and lunged toward Chelovek, unleashing an earsplitting screech at the same time. Chelovek, alarmed, stumbled backward and fell over the planter holding the white tee-marker orchids. As he lay sprawled on the ground, the peacock stopped, cast him one last, supremely derisive look, and proceeded calmly on its way, tail feathers once more proudly unfurled.

"Fuckin' piece'a-shit bird," Chelovek muttered, but he couldn't be heard over the laughter coming from behind him. He picked himself up and began brushing dirt from his pants.

"I've an idea," Perrault said when they were finally able to pull themselves together.

"Kill that shit-ass bird?" Chelovek spat, which only started them laughing again.

"No," Perrault said. "Let's return to number one and play a real round."

Chelovek stopped brushing. "Now you're talking."

With Savitch driving, Chelovek in the passenger seat and the other two standing on the back hanging on to the bag rack, they headed up the hill to number one.

Chapter 12

■

USUAL BET?" ARONICA ASKED.

The "usual bet" was thousand-dollar skins. Each of them would put a thousand dollars into the pot. They'd play hole by hole, and the winner of each hole would be awarded a skin. If two of them tied, or "halved," for the best score on a hole, no skin would be awarded.

At the end of the round the total number of skins won would be added up and divided into the four thousand in the pot, which determined how much each skin was worth. For example, if there were a total of ten holes that were won outright, each skin would be worth four hundred dollars, and any individual would receive that amount for each skin he'd won.

I like this format, because it sets a limit on how much any individual can lose but still lets you win more the better you play.

They flipped tees in the air to determine the order of play, Savitch coming up first. "Okay, boys," Aronica said, then performed the foursome's traditional opening ceremony, an idea he'd lifted from a story he'd heard about a tour pro. Taking Savitch's ball, he threw it to the ground on the tee box and said solemnly, "No mulligans, no gimmes, no bullshit. Let's play golf."

Amid answering murmurs of "Amen" and "Hear, hear," Savitch picked up his ball and took the tee.

"Mulligans on the first?" he said as he bent over to tee up.

"Absolutely," the others answered as one.

·

BY THE TIME THEY GOT to the fifth hole, not a single skin had yet been awarded. Even two birdies, one each by Savitch and Chelovek, couldn't get a win. Aronica got handicap strokes on both those holes and made pars, making sure the others knew that he had needed only three-wood, seven-iron to reach the green whereas they'd all used at least driver, five-iron.

"Look over there," Perrault said, pointing to another fairway visible beyond a hedge of honeysuckle and jacaranda. It ran parallel to the one they were on, and a group of golfers was just in the process of teeing off.

"You suppose any of them are the owners?" Savitch wondered.

"No way to know," Chelovek replied, keeping his voice low. "One guy there . . . the shortest one? Kind of looks like somebody."

Perrault fetched his laser rangefinder from a pocket in his bag and used it like binoculars to get a closer look. "I'd venture that's because he looks rather like *everybody*," he concluded after studying the man. "Watch—they're going to hit."

Each of the four had nice technique, although it was difficult to tell from that distance how their balls flew. The shortest guy, hitting last, had the most fluid and relaxed swing of all.

"They're looking this way!" Perrault rasped, quickly lowering the rangefinder and scratching at a nonexistent itch on his head as he turned away. The others tried to look nonchalant as they picked up clubs and took practice swings.

"Maybe they're trying to get a handle on how *we* play," Savitch mused as he took the tee.

"So hit a shitty one, Jerry," Aronica suggested amiably.

"Yeah, right. Four grand on the table and you want *me* to be the sacrificial lamb?"

"Okay, hold up a minute, then. Looks like they're walking off."

"Good." Chelovek kept his back to the other fairway. "See if you can tell how far they hit."

"Certainly are walking a considerable distance," Perrault said after about a minute.

"Oh, yeah?" Savitch stepped up to his ball. "Well, watch this."

"Hold up, Deke!" Chelovek's voice was harsh. "You gonna whup it, do it after they can't see."

"You serious, Jerry? If they're the owners, they're not gonna play us any-way, Carlos said."

"Well, fuck Carlos. I guaran-goddamn-tee we get a game with them. Now hold up."

"Doesn't look like more'n maybe two-twenty, two-thirty to me," Savitch said with some peevishness when the other group finally stopped walking.

Perrault took up the rangefinder again and zeroed in on the player getting ready to hit. "News bulletin for you, Deke: It's a lady."

"You're shitting me," Chelovek said, abandoning all pretext of inattention and grabbing the rangefinder out of Perrault's hands.

"Sure as hell is," Aronica said. "Don't need the Hubble to see *that* from here."

Chelovek watched as the woman took her stance and swung away. "Great balls'a fire. Broad can hit."

The three of them whirled around as a loud *c-r-aaaa-ck* sounded behind them, just in time to see Savitch up on his toes following the flight of his ball.

"Goddamnit, Deke!" Chelovek snarled.

"Rats!" was all Savitch had to say in return as his ball took a vicious hook and sailed over the tops of some low-lying bushes.

"Serves you right, asshole," Chelovek pronounced. "Hope those guys were watching."

"This is kind of a gas, isn't it?" Aronica said. "Spying on the enemy, like?"

"Club's a piece of garbage," Savitch said, staring disgustedly at his driver.

"Lemme try that," Chelovek said. Savitch handed it over as though it were covered with raw sewage.

Chelovek teed up, took a few warm-up swings and then leaned into it full-bore. The ball shot off like a mortar shell, dead straight and longer than anybody had hit that day so far. Chelovek turned to rub it in Savitch's face.

"Nice shot. How we doing, gentlemen?"

None of them had heard Jake approach, and they shuffled awkwardly as he offered them drinks and sandwiches, wondering how much of their conversation he'd heard.

"Woulda thought y'all'd be further along by now."

"We, uh, kind of skipped around a little," Savitch confessed. "Hope that's okay."

Jake shrugged it off. "Long as nobody's behind you, you can play one hole all day, all anybody cares. How'd you do on that number two?"

"Went over the green with a driver and a three-wood," Aronica bragged.

"Really." Jake loaded a cooler and jug into the four-bagger. He seemed impressed with the feat, as Aronica had intended, then asked, "How'd you end up?"

"Bogey," Savitch answered for Aronica.

Jake smirked slightly, or so it seemed, and said, "Next time try laying up and going in with a sand wedge. Get on instead'a over and make yourself an easy par that way." He got back into the service cart. "Give us a call from seventeen, we'll be out to pick you up."

THEY DID THEIR BEST TO catch glimpses of the other group as they played on, their excitement rising steadily at the prospect of a serious money match, and they continued to shoot well all afternoon.

Putting on eighteen, they spied the valet waiting for them about fifty yards away. As soon as the last ball was in, Chelovek took the scorecard out of his back pocket and started doing some quick addition. "Don't want to tell the guy our scores," he explained surreptitiously, " 'case he reports back to anybody."

"Don't you think you're going a tad overboard here, Jerrold?" Perrault chided him. "It's golf, not Desert Storm."

"Yeah, well, you shot a seventy-six, Joe—"

"I know that." Low handicappers don't need a scorecard to know where they stand; they just keep track of how far over or under par they are.

"I know you know, but I didn't. First day out on a strange course, you gonna flash a seventy-six up on the big board and then try to convince them you're really a seven?"

That quieted Aronica down, and Chelovek turned to Perrault. "You shot even, Pete, and I got a seventy-five. Only one didn't beat his handicap was Deke, with a seventy-seven." Savitch was a three. "I don't know about you boys, but I'd just as soon not show up and right out of the box let anybody know we were overachieving, you get my drift?"

Chelovek put the card back in his pocket and stopped walking. "Unless we want to spend the rest of the week twiddling our own schlongs while everybody else here in Swizzle Barn—"

"Swithen Bairn," Savitch corrected him.

"What the fuck ever. While everybody else is out here slurping adrenaline and having some real fun." He crossed his arms over his chest and regarded his friends defiantly.

"Man's got a point," Aronica said after a few seconds. He also got the subliminal message: *Try to hold off bragging to everybody about how well you played.*

Chelovek saw the contrite looks on everybody's faces, nodded in approval and resumed walking toward the cart.

"How'd it go?" the valet asked as they approached.

Everybody assured him it had been a lovely day and the course was fine.

"How'd you shoot?"

Savitch started to answer but quickly deferred as Chelovek interrupted. "Tell you the truth—Whud you say your name was?"

"Billy, sir."

"Billy. Okay. Tell you the truth, Billy, we were mostly just trying to get a feel for the course, know what I'm saying?"

The valet grunted knowingly. "That's good thinking, seeing as how you got the whole week. Most guys, one look at this course, they try to tear it up on the first day and never do get it figured out. How about one of you drives your cart, rest pile in with me here."

Chelovek motioned for Savitch to drive the four-bagger, then said, "We put a couple bucks on a few holes here and there, you know. Keep ourselves motivated."

"Just follow me, sir," Billy said to Savitch as he got back into the larger cart. "So who was the big winner?"

"Came out pretty even," Chelovek answered, keeping his voice casual. "Think maybe Joe here won around a grand or so, that right, Joe?"

"Something like that." *No big deal at all,* he tried to communicate, following Chelovek's cue.

Billy turned around to glance at these guys who thought nothing of dropping a thousand dollars on a few holes. "Izzat so?"

As he faced forward again and pulled the cart out slowly, waiting for Savitch to follow, Chelovek winked at Aronica and Perrault and touched the side of his nose.

Chapter 13

∷

DINNER THAT EVENING WAS A wonder. There were fewer than two dozen people in the dining room, if it could even be called a dining room. It looked more like a lanai, mostly open on two sides to the mild night air and with a magnificent bar of teak and mahogany filling one of the two walls.

The first question they'd been asked upon arriving was where they'd like their table.

"Don't seem to be any available," Perrault had replied, looking around and seeing that there were very few seats to begin with and all were filled.

What the maître d' had meant, though, was quite literally where would they like to sit. Aronica pointed to a spot on the perimeter overlooking the water, and in short order a new table had been brought out and set up, exactly where they'd requested.

Check-in had been equally confusing at first. When they arrived at the main building, Billy had begun escorting them to their rooms. "Mustn't we register?" Perrault had asked.

"Register for what?"

"You know, check in. Let them know we've arrived, sign in, provide a credit card . . . ?

"We know you're here," Billy had said as a second valet arrived to take their clubs to storage. "We flew you here, remember?"

"I suppose so," Perrault had conceded halfheartedly. He and the others noted that there was no registration desk in the lobby, just a woman in a sundress seated at an elegant writing desk.

Billy had paused, seeing that one of his guests was a little disoriented and perhaps upset. "Um, if you'd like, Doctor, we can go over to Kerry and introduce you. Make it official, you know? Maybe write down your credit-card number?"

By that time Perrault had seen the absurdity of his discomfort and laughed it off, prepared to follow the valet to his room, but Chelovek had said, "That's a good idea, Billy. Why don't you introduce me?"

"Can't you give it a rest, Jerry?" Aronica had said with some annoyance.

"Fuck's it to you, Joe? Go take a shower and mind your own business!"

They'd waited while Billy dutifully took Chelovek over to meet what seemed to be the concierge. When the valet returned, they passed by the desk just in time to hear her say to Chelovek, "If I throw a stick, will you leave?"

There were some equally uncomfortable moments at dinner when Chelovek began harassing their waitress, a stunning brunette, or at least her face was stunning, because the rest of her was swathed in loose layers that kept well hidden whatever treasures lay beneath. Perrault went after him angrily. "Damnit, Jerrold . . . you're really beginning to annoy me!" He stood up and threw his napkin onto his chair. "It's not my intention to waste my entire holiday gritting my teeth while you behave like a farm animal and embarrass us all!"

He started to walk away and passed by the waitress. "Sit down," she whispered.

"What?"

She hissed at him forcefully. "Sit down, Doc!"

Perrault went back and did as he was told. Several seconds later the waitress returned with a carafe of fresh coffee. As she set it down, Chelovek said suggestively, "I hope that's good and hot. I like it hot, know what I mean?"

The waitress put a hand on her hip and turned to Chelovek. "Tell me something," she said.

Perrault felt himself go tense all over, and exchanged nervous glances with Aronica and Savitch as Chelovek grinned lasciviously.

The waitress leaned down and looked directly at Chelovek. "Your parents have any kids that lived?"

Aronica almost spewed water through his nose, while Perrault stared at the waitress in wonderment. Chelovek was frozen.

She reached two fingers into the top of her uniform and pretended to pull something out. "Are these your eyeballs?" she said, frowning in puzzlement. "I found them in my cleavage."

Savitch heaved with laughter as Aronica wiped water from his chin. Chelovek, turning red, looked at Perrault, eyes pleading for some help, but found none.

"Hello?" She snapped her fingers in front of his eyes several times. "What'sa matter . . . aliens forget to remove your anal probe?"

The other three were helpless now, and under that onslaught Chelovek had little choice but to be graceful, especially since the waitress's voice had been completely devoid of any malice. "Okay, okay . . . I'm not that bad a guy, you know."

"A guy who's nice to his friends but rude to a waitress? That's not a nice guy."

"I can change. I'd change for you . . . ?"

"Sorry, buster," she said as she gathered up empty wineglasses, "but a hard-on doesn't count as personal growth."

She winked at Perrault as she left, and it took them all a while to compose themselves afterward.

"Seems to me," Chelovek said as he waited with exaggerated patience for the laughter to die down, "a place like this, goddamned staff oughta be a bit more respectful."

"Gentlemen," the maître d' said as he came up, "care to take brandy outside?"

THEY SAT ON A PAIR of crouches at right angles, with a low rattan table between them. The maître d' brought over a large humidor and set it down, then lifted the lid, revealing a wide assortment of cigars.

Perrault immediately recognized the distinctive black-and-yellow band on the cigars in one of the interior bins and his eyes went wide. "Are those—"

"Cohibas? Yes, Doctor," the maître d' affirmed. "Ever had one?"

"Only the Dominicans. I take it these are genuine Havanas?"

"Indeed they are. What do you usually smoke?"

Perrault told him, rattling off several brands and sizes. The maître d' listened carefully, then said, "Might I offer a suggestion?" He pointed to a different bin. "You might enjoy these more. The Cohibas may taste too harsh, given what you're used to."

Perrault shook his head. "You may be right, but I feel compelled to try them once."

"By all means." The maître d' lifted out a double corona and took a silver clipper from his pocket, neatly snipping off the entire end of the cigar. He produced a simple butane lighter, lit it, then held it to the tip of the Cohiba, turning the cigar to precook the end. He handed it to Perrault, who immediately put it in his mouth and began drawing on it as the maître d' held the lighter. In short order the tip was alight with an even red glow.

"I'd have thought you'd use one of those cedar strips to light it," Perrault said as he sat back.

"And why is that, sir?"

Perrault took the cigar out and blew a thick cloud of smoke up into the air. "Avoid the butane taste? Cooler flame doesn't overheat the tobacco, that sort of thing?"

"Yeah," Savitch agreed. "Like in fancy restaurants."

"All show," the maître d' assured them. "Butane has no taste, and how can you overheat something that burns on its own? Now, then . . ."

Chelovek asked for the cigar the maître d' had suggested to Perrault, a Partagas, and Aronica and Savitch went for Montecristos. A waiter wheeled up a trolley containing a variety of brandies and a rack of large snifters. The maître d' described some of the more exotic brands, and soon the boys were alone, happily sipping brandy that had been laid down before World War I and watching smoke drift lazily off into the night. Perrault was slumped down in his seat, eyes half closed, the picture of utter contentment.

"Hey, isn't that the guy from the other bunch today?" Savitch said after a few minutes, pointing toward the bar.

Aronica turned to look. "Hard to tell. Not much to distinguish him one way or the other."

"Then it's probably him," Chelovek said.

"I think he's heading our way." Aronica sat back and swirled the brandy around in the goblet.

"Evening, gents," the man said as he walked up. "Name's Eddie. Everything okay so far?"

"You work here?" Perrault said, rousing himself partway from his slouch.

Eddie laughed. "Manner'a speaking."

"You own it!" Savitch blurted without thinking.

"Piece of it, yeah. Like it so far?"

Chelovek looked down at the cigar in his hand, then at Eddie. "What's not to like?" He tried to throw a subtle, cautionary look to his friends: *Let me handle this!*

Eddie looked at Perrault sprawled haphazardly on his seat and said, "You're looking pretty useless and unproductive there, Doc."

"It might appear I'm doing nothing," Perrault answered lazily, "but at the cellular level I'm really quite busy."

Eddie laughed and pulled over a wicker chair. "How'd it go out on the course?"

"Good," Chelovek said. He knew that Eddie would smell it immediately if they started right in sandbagging. "Real good. It's a damned beauty, but you already knew that."

"I don't think I've ever played on anything quite like it," Perrault added. "Fairways are absolutely exquisite, the ball sits up like it was on a tee . . ."

"Not a bad lie on the whole track," Savitch threw in.

"Even the sand is amazing," Aronica enthused. "What is that, like ground-up coral or something?" Eddie confirmed that it was, and Aronica shook his head in wonder. "Clubhead glides right under it, easy as pie."

Taking this all in, Eddie wore an expression somewhere between pride and arrogance, as though he was used to hearing people extol his course and felt deserving of all the homage.

In fact, he was silently gritting his teeth and doing his best to bear all the praise without gagging. Truth was, Eddie hated the course and had nothing but contempt for those who adored it. Including me, I have to admit. Swithen Bairn represented everything he despised about modern golf, especially as it's played in the United States, and *especially* on the PGA tour.

I'm not entirely sure what his racket is these days—you'll see why later on—but back when Eddie was a pure hustler, the Swithen Bairns of the world were his working office. Their utter predictability were to Eddie what T-bills are to a conservative investor: boring as hell, to be sure, but safe and reliable.

On those rare occasions when he played for fun—and fun to Eddie meant serious money with serious golfers, straight up with no bullshit—he flew himself off to the U.K. and those classic courses like Royal Troon or Birkendale or Carnoustie, where the track did everything to bite you in the ass while the wind howled in malevolent glee and chilly rain purposefully worked its way down your back. He told me many times that all you had to do to play well at courses like Augusta or Pebble or the Stadium at PGA West was plan for them, which was easy because you could predict with great precision what you'd be up against. You could practice the handful of shots you were likely to need and ignore the rest, even tailor your clubs just for that course, and that's why savvy sportscasters could predict a year in advance and with 99-percent accuracy which clubs every pro in a tournament would be hitting from every tee. "Derek will use a four-wood on number seven so he can get it just left of the fairway bunker to the smooth grass and go seven-iron to the first tier back of the flag."

Commentary like that always made Eddie gag. "Jesus H," he'd fume, "you call that golf? It's a goddamned video game, is what it is!"

He cackled in delight every time he saw a tour pro go ballistic because his ball rolled into a divot or complained about a tree that he felt shouldn't have been there. Eddie would shake his head and say, "But it *is* there, you fucking moron, so why'd you hit there?"

At a place like Birkendale you brought every shot in your bag and could end up using all of them on the front nine alone. Depending on the wind, a hole could play three-iron, sand wedge one day and driver, three-wood the next. A green that let you stop an eight-iron within inches of where the ball landed when it was drizzling could easily send a soft sand wedge skittering into the gorse when it was dry. A single course could look like a dozen different layouts depending on the weather. Was a place like that fair? Hardly; it was an evil, scheming witch and the only kind of track Eddie had any real respect for.

He had a set of clubs that were ideally suited for Swithen Bairn, and on those days when the wind was up or there was humidity in the air, maybe he'd change one or two irons, but that was about it. There was barely a lie on the entire course for which he couldn't simply go into autopilot, and the only real question on any given hole was how close he could get his approach shot so he could one-putt instead of two. Swithen Bairn, candidly, bored the hell out of him. He might as well have been processing accounts receivable in a back office somewhere or stacking stereos in a warehouse.

The only thing that kept him motivated on a course like this was the people he was playing against. Like a poker player shilling for the house against a busload of Midwestern assembly-line workers, Eddie was less concerned with the mechanics of the game, which were firmly burned into his neural pathways and required little in the way of conscious attention, than he was with the dauntingly complex nuances of personality that presented themselves with every load of fresh meat that stepped off the jet. Each new mark, complete with his own tangled web of frustrations, insecurities, skewed self-perceptions and unfilled yearnings, represented a Rubik's cube of pathologies, which, however seemingly infinite in their variations, could always be reduced to a manageable set of recognizable and categorizable characteristics that, to a keen and cynical observer of the human condition like Eddie, were nothing less than the combination to the locks on their souls.

And it didn't hurt whatever purpose he had in mind that as soon as the door on the plane opened, the dazzling jewel that was Swithen Bairn struck his guests speechless and rendered them all the more vulnerable. After all, they reasoned, how could one entrusted with the care of such a treasure be less than trustworthy himself?

I, of course, was in love with the place. I make my living playing golf, and as anyone who is a professional athlete can tell you, there is nothing more unfair than an arena in which the ugly element of chance is allowed to intrude. Who wants to bet a couple of hundred grand on a lousy bounce or an errant twig? We pros want the fairways to look like pool tables and the greens to be bikini-waxed. We want the trees where God intended them to be—the hell out of our way—and the only downside to being in the rough should be hitting off grass that's five millimeters high instead of three. The sand in the bunkers should be perfectly uniform and freshly raked, and no matter what the rest of the green looks like, the area around the hole should be free of any debris, organic or otherwise, that is large enough to be seen without the aid of a microscope, and dead flat, too. Who wants to stand there, like Payne Stewart did at that Open, and watch a slow putt roll right off the green?

To me, that's just not fair. To Eddie, that was golf, and "fair" didn't have a damned thing to do with it. You want fair? Go bowling. Swithen Bairn was nothing but a tarted-up, bump-and-grind bimbo hiding secrets not worth concealing, while a good golf course was a bar hussy, rough and raw and dangerous and irresistible, rubbing up against your thigh and telling you point-blank that, one way or the other, you were going to get fucked.

But he listened to the boys politely and smiled benignly as they went on praising in detail everything about the course he couldn't stand, until he finally couldn't take it anymore. "How d'you like that Cohiba?" he asked Perrault.

"Quite delicious."

"So how come you make a face every time you hit on it?"

Perrault, not wishing to be impolite or critical, was caught off guard and at a loss for words. Eddie waved to the maître d', miming a box in the air with his hands, and soon the big humidor was back on the table.

"Bit harsh, Doctor?" the maître d' said smoothly and without a trace of I-told-you-so.

Perrault looked uncomfortable. "Seems rather a shame, though, wasting such a—"

"So what do you figure to do instead?" Eddie asked amiably. "Smoke your throat raw so you don't hurt my feelings? Here . . ." He picked an Upmann out of the humidor and handed it to the maître d', and in short order Perrault was happily puffing away.

"Say, Eddie," Aronica said during a lull in the conversation, "where the hell are we anyway?"

Eddie looked around as if to make sure they weren't being overheard, then leaned forward and said, "Tell you the truth, Joe, I'd as leave not say. Last thing I need is the world discovering our little hideaway. Next thing you know we got choppers circling overhead with long-range cameras. We do get a celebrity or two in here once in a while."

"Carlos said you had Ted Turner once," Savitch said.

"Did he," Eddie responded frostily, causing Savitch to wonder if he'd spoken out of school.

"So, Eddie," Chelovek jumped in smoothly, "how about your own game? What kind of handicap you carry?"

"I play off two," Eddie answered, using the British expression for describing a handicap.

"Pretty good," Chelovek said. "I'm—"

"A seven," Eddie finished for him. "I know."

He knew a lot about a lot of things, but mostly he knew how to listen, and as the night sky deepened and the sounds of crickets and cicadas grew louder than the diminishing bustle in the dining room, he listened a great deal, drawing the boys out easily, playing off how flattered they were that the proprietor himself was ignoring all the other guests in order to spend time with them.

They swapped a few stories about great courses and great players and great wine and cigars, they compared philosophies about the game, they commiserated about the vicissitudes of the real world that interfered with golf. They talked about a lot of things.

What they didn't talk about was a money match. Eddie never mentioned the possibility, and, as instructed by Carlos, the boys never brought it up to him. By the time he excused himself and left, they were surprised by the depth of their disappointment and at how his absence rendered the prospect of further conversation among just themselves wholly unattractive. Within a few minutes they began rousing themselves to leave.

ON THE WAY OUT, ARONICA collared a busboy and asked for a pencil and paper.

"What's Joe up to?" Chelovek wondered out loud to Savitch.

"Who knows? See you guys in the morning."

When he and Perrault had gone, Chelovek went back in and found Aronica out on the veranda where they had been sitting with Eddie. The engineer looked out toward the ocean, then at his watch, then wrote something on the piece of hotel stationery he was holding, then looked at the ocean again.

"What're you doing?" Chelovek asked.

Aronica didn't answer right away but looked at his watch and wrote something down again. "Finding out where we are," he said when he'd finished. "Position of familiar stars when they come up over the horizon, exact time they appear—that's all you need to nail your location."

"You can do that?" Chelovek asked, impressed.

"I'm a scientist, remember? Ah . . . Betelgeuse. Perfect!" He made some more notes.

Chelovek's admiration evaporated. "Scientist. Hah! What kind of scientist lugs around a set of lucky clubs?"

"They work, don't they?"

Chelovek snorted and dropped onto the chair Eddie had sat on earlier in the evening. "They're all the same, and you know it. Hell, I write ad copy for a lotta those bullshit 'innovations,' so nobody knows better'n me it's all bullshit. You of all people!"

Aronica took no offense—indeed, appeared not even to have noticed Chelovek's sarcastic blast—and patiently made a few more notes before turning around to face him. "Jerry, let me ask you something." He received only a snort by way of permission to proceed but did so regardless. "You know anybody less likely to fall for pseudoscientific bullshit than me?"

"What about those lucky—"

"I'm asking you a serious question here."

Chelovek had to admit that, no, he doubted he knew anyone else who placed more faith in logic and reason than Aronica or who hewed more passionately to the principle that if something couldn't be proved scientifically, it wasn't worth believing. "So how come you got this thing with lucky clubs?"

"What makes them lucky, Jerry," Aronica explained, slowly and patiently, as if to a backward child, "has nothing to do with luck. The reason I hardly ever use them isn't because they're lucky and I might break the spell or something. They're lucky *because* I hardly ever use them."

"Meaning . . . ?"

"Just this: Anytime you pick up an unfamiliar club, you're going to hit it better than your own. It's the only reason people ever buy new clubs, even though they don't realize it."

"I don't know what you're talking about."

"I'm heading out, gentlemen," the busboy announced from the entryway. "You need something, just help yourselves."

"Thanks," Aronica said impatiently, anxious to get on with his lecture. When the busboy had gone, he said to Chelovek, "You ever take a practice shot with another guy's club in the middle of a round?"

"Of course." Chelovek got up and began walking toward the entryway. "Today, matter of fact."

"Right. You hit one with Deke's driver. Good shot."

"Best I hit all day," Chelovek called from inside the dining room. He lifted the lid on the humidor and looked over the stock. "Thinkin' about getting me the same club."

"Then you're an asshole."

"Why?" He pulled out a Primavera and walked back out to the veranda. "I hit the damned thing near three hundred yards!"

"That's because it was new to you. Don't you get it? But if you buy one, three holes later you'll be hitting it exactly like you hit your own now."

Chelovek thought about that as he bit off the end of the cigar. I happen to know that he'd bought his present driver after trying another guy's a year ago, but he didn't see fit to tell Aronica that at this particular moment. "So what you're telling me, those lucky clubs are lucky because they're unfamiliar?"

Aronica nodded, pleased that Chelovek had caught on. "Golf shops have these little indoor hitting ranges set up. You grab a nice expensive club, it feels new, there's no pressure because there's no hole and no game going on, you whack a couple of monsters while the salesman stands there going 'Holy shit!' and 'What a whack!' and you buy it."

Which, of course, was exactly how Chelovek had bought all his irons. Same way as two years before, when he'd gone for the new cavity-backed, perimeter-weighted, tapered-hoseled and foam-inserted technological marvels, and two years before that, salivating after some equally stupendous scientific breakthrough in club design. Aronica knew all that. He also knew that Chelovek's handicap had dropped exactly seven-tenths of a stroke in the last six years. Not wanting to make his point by blatantly insulting him, Aronica thought it best not to mention at this moment his personal opinion that in the entire history of the sport no one had ever lowered his scores by buying new equipment.

"All I'm doing," he said instead, watching as Chelovek sat down, grabbed a candle, and lit up, "is simulating borrowing another guy's clubs."

"Huh." Chelovek picked at his lower lip as smoke streamed past his fingers. "I got this friend, he's a three? He's got a boatload of clubs, like five sets worth. Every time he feels a club 'going stale,' is how he says it, he puts it aside and uses another one for a few weeks. When that one starts to go, he gets another, puts the first one back in his bag. Says it keeps 'em fresh."

Aronica closed his eyes and nodded as Chelovek proved his point. "What he's doing, he's keeping *himself* fresh. Just what I'm sayin' here."

He turned back and made several more observations, occasionally waving away cigar smoke that obscured his view of the sky.

"Okay, you're so freakin' smart," Chelovek said amicably after some time, "where the hell are we?"

"Beats me," Aronica said without turning around. "Won't know till we get home and I get my hands on some charts. But I'll tell you one thing."

"And that is?"

"Now we know the real reason there weren't any windows on that airplane."

Chapter 14

✠

Day Two

CHELOVEK RAN HIS EYES OVER the teeing area, then smiled. "Carlos was right, boys. Look at these markers."

"Way up front," Perrault said.

"Exactly. Make us think it's a cream puff, then set 'em back when we play for dough."

"He also said the owners wouldn't play us," Savitch argued.

Perrault nodded glumly. "Think last night proved him right."

"Horseshit." Chelovek pointed back toward the blue-orchid planters. "We'll get a game, so let's hit from the back and get used to it."

"What's the distance there?" Aronica asked.

"Bugger the distance," Perrault said. "Is there enough light yet?"

"Seven thousand something." Chelovek peered intently at the scorecard clipped to the steering wheel of Savitch's cart. He could barely read it in the predawn light.

Savitch picked up his ball and tee, and they marched back to the blue-orchid planters forward of the thick wall of bamboo. When they arrived, Chelovek pointed behind them and said, "Forget the markers; let's go right to the tips."

Savitch dutifully teed up as far back as he could and still leave himself room for his backswing. "So what am I looking at to clear the bend?"

Chelovek did a quick calculation. "Figure two-sixty. But . . ."

The "but" was that, from the back tees, the luxuriant foliage on either side of the teeing area formed a kind of tunnel, and it was immediately obvious that there was more to the back tees than just distance. In order to get the ball past the stand of palm trees at the dogleg, you couldn't just aim directly for the ideal landing area. Instead, you had to send the ball straight out to exit the tunnel cleanly, and have enough fade dialed in to get it curving to the right once it was out over the fairway. Not enough and you could hit past the fairway and into deep rough.

Seeing that, and not trusting himself to pull off the shot, Savitch said, "So, maybe two-thirty, two thirty-five to play it safe?"

"You're starting to sound reasonable, Deke," Chelovek replied. "Must be time to up my medication."

Savitch exchanged his driver for a three-wood before re-teeing his ball. "Now we're using our heads," Perrault said excitedly. "Getting brighter out, too. Go ahead, Deke."

Savitch hit a good one, a conservative shot that kept him in contention without needlessly escalating the risk. "I don't know . . . you guys think that was okay?"

"It was fine," Perrault said, unable to keep the exasperation out of his voice. "You know it was fine."

"Seems maybe a little short," Savitch said as he started to leave the tee.

He stopped when Chelovek tossed him another ball and held out his driver. "Smack the big dog, Deke. See if he'll hunt."

Savitch teed back up and leaned into the driver with everything he had. It sliced badly and disappeared among the trees on the right. "Again," Chelovek ordered.

Savitch gave it three more tries but wasn't able to improve on his first shot. Finally he put everything he had not only into the swing but into his concentration on his form. The ball sailed out of the tunnel beautifully, bit into the air and curved gently to the right, landing nearly forty yards past his first shot and in perfect position to reach the green easily. He turned with satisfaction to find Chelovek shaking his head.

"Percentage is too low, Deke. Stick with the three-wood."

Aronica was up next and hit his driver with everything *he* had. It was a prodigious shot but hooked badly and sailed off to the left, out of play. He hit twice more, with equally dismal results, although they could at least see where his last ball had come to rest.

"Hey, Joe," Chelovek said crossly, "we all know you can drive it four hundred yards, okay? You're a real stud. So why don't you quit trying to hit the thing so goddamned far and just put it in play?"

"Fuck you, Jerry," he spat back angrily.

Perrault replaced Aronica on the tee. He had a three-wood in his hands. "If I swing a little outside in and aim left, daresay I ought to be able to bring it back a touch so I have a second shot. All that's required, close the clubface down somewhat and take a weaker grip so I get the right amount of spin."

He topped the ball, and it dribbled about forty yards, stopping at the forward tees.

"What happened there, I didn't come through the ball, rather quit on the swing because I figured if I could keep my shoulders square I wouldn't block it out to the right, but what I ought to have done instead, I should have—"

"Jesus Christ, Pete, who gives a flying fuck?" Aronica took a ball out of his pocket and threw it to the ground in front of Perrault. "You're so goddamned smart, put it on the fairway!"

It went on like that through all eighteen holes, testing different clubs and trajectories, discussing probabilities and cooperatively determining the optimum combination of risk and reward. It was new to all of them, even though Chelovek, the self-appointed head coach, tried to make it sound as if he did this all the time.

If they'd asked me, I would have suggested they spend a little of that time on their heads as well, and try to stanch the effluvia of Savitch's whining lack of self-confidence, embarrass Aronica out of smashing the ball huge distances and constantly bragging about what clubs he'd hit how far, let Perrault know that his endless descriptions of every single one of his shots were not only insufferable and tedious but laughable, and make known their growing hostility toward Chelovek's casual assumption of the role of guru, mentor and team captain.

Those kinds of ongoing irritations might be ignorable on Sunday mornings at the club when they were competing against one another, but if they were to play together as a team, little annoyances heretofore suppressed could come bubbling up in a damned hurry and scuttle whatever advantages their physical skills might otherwise have afforded them.

SOME SIX HOURS LATER ON the eighteenth green, Aronica picked his ball out of the cup, then arched his back to relieve some of the strain. They'd each taken enough shots to have played fifty-four holes.

"Carlos was right," he said, grunting as he stretched sideways. "It's a whole different course from the back tees."

"But now we know what has to be done," Chelovek pronounced. "We can

concentrate on hitting the ball instead of wasting time and energy trying to figure out what shot to hit."

"At least from the tees," Savitch cautioned. "Still no predicting what's
gonna happen once the hole is under way."

"True enough," Perrault replied. "But were I to hazard a guess, there's
likely to be a good deal fewer surprises than there might have been."

"So who's up for a real game?" Aronica proposed. "It's only noon."

Savitch craned his neck back and forth a few times, working the kinks out
of his shoulders. "Gettin' kinda hungry . . ."

"We can take care of that easily." Perrault stepped over to the phone normally used to summon a valet for a ride back to the main house. He spoke for
a few minutes before meeting the others at the two carts Chelovek had insisted
they ride: "Don't want us getting tired, and don't want any caddies watching
us," he'd said.

Perrault dropped his putter into his bag and got behind the wheel.
"They'll meet us on number one straightaway."

WITH COOLERS FULL OF SANDWICHES, fruit and beer tucked
into the carts, the foursome set off on their usual money match, thousand-
dollar skins, playing from the back tees. Despite the sizable bet, they cajoled
each other to produce their best games, freely offering advice, reading each
other's putts and openly discussing shot strategies.

At the end of eleven holes they'd each won exactly one skin. If it kept up
like that, no money would change hands. They were having the time of their
lives, and playing as well as they ever had.

The sound of excited laughter wafted over from behind a patch of
bougainvillea somewhere to the right. "Thought we were the only ones on the
course," Aronica said.

Perrault walked up the edge of a high bunker to see what was going on.
Once at the top he stared without reporting back, so the others soon followed
and saw that he had a commanding view of the last half of number seven.
There were about a dozen people loosely assembled some 130 yards from the
green.

The laughter ceased abruptly, and one of the group, a young man no older
than twenty, hunkered down over a ball. He looked from the ball to the flag
and back again a few times, then swung smoothly and sent his shot sailing
high into the air, where it seemed to hang for an inordinately long time before
starting back down. Once it did, it became very apparent that the ball was

heading directly for the pin, and the rest of the bunch began a tentative swooning cry that grew louder as the ball continued downward, ending in delighted shouts as it hit the flagstick with an audible clang and bounced backward a few feet before coming to rest.

"Heck of a shot," Savitch remarked needlessly.

As the people on number seven applauded, the young man held up the club as if it were a rifle and aimed it at Eddie, who clasped his chest and staggered backward, causing the laughter to start up again.

Perrault turned and walked back down the edge of the bunker. "It's a money match!" Aronica exclaimed, a little too loudly.

Chelovek hissed at him to be quiet lest their covert observation be discovered, and they watched Eddie take his shot from the same location. He elected to land well short of the flag and let the ball release and run forward a little, but he didn't pull that shot off as well as the much younger man had his own, and he ended up about ten feet away. Two of the men began hissing and booing theatrically as Eddie stood there, head hanging down.

When they all began trooping up toward the green, our boys could see that the group consisted of eight players, four riding carts and four using caddies, plus a beverage cart. They all seemed relaxed and casual and having a grand time. One of the caddies was Carlos.

"Hard to imagine it's a money match," Chelovek observed, "everybody so damned cozy and cheerful."

Perrault returned, carrying his rangefinder. "How do you field eight players at one go?" he wondered out loud, training the glasses on the green. "The round would take all day."

"Is that money in that guy's hand?" Savitch asked, squinting.

"Certainly is." Perrault twisted the center ring to get better focus. "Several bills, in fact."

The guy pointed the money toward Eddie's ball. Eddie nodded and then knelt down to read his putt as everybody backed away.

"I only see four balls out there," Perrault said. "Where're the rest?"

After only a few seconds Eddie stood up and got in position over his putt. He glanced at the hole just once, then brought the club back and swung it smoothly. The ball sped away, ran out of steam just as it reached the hole, and dropped in. Eddie raised his arms in triumph as the man with the money groaned and handed it over. Then Eddie walked over to the younger man's ball, lying less than a yard from the hole, and kicked it away, conceding the putt.

"Goddamn right it's a money match," Aronica said dolefully.

Just like that, the wind went out of their sails. Here they were on this stunning course, playing their best and their smartest, only to be confronted with the sight of a bunch of happy people whooping it up, making wild-ass, spontaneous bets—having *fun*, is what it was—with Lord only knew how much riding on the overall game. Suddenly the same old wager among the same four longtime friends seemed more like a boring, useless formality than an occasion for real enjoyment. Just like that, the glittering jewel that was Swithen Bairn seemed to be mocking them: "All of this," it cried out piteously, "and all you pitiful hackers can do is play with yourselves? Gee, now *there's* a happenin' time!"

Nobody said much about it, and they glumly continued their game. What else were they to do?

On number fourteen Aronica hit a beauty to within twelve feet of the flag from 140 yards out. "Great shot!" Savitch said, grinning.

Aronica held out his club. "Pitching wedge."

Savitch's smile disappeared, and he shook his head as he walked away. "Woulda been a lot more impressive," he muttered to Perrault, just loudly enough for Aronica to hear, "he'da kept his mouth shut."

"Hey, guys . . ."

Startled, Savitch and Perrault stopped and looked to their right. The bunch they'd seen earlier playing on a nearby hole was on its way to another tee, and it was Eddie who had called out to them.

"How's it going?" Aronica said, coming up from a few steps behind Savitch and Perrault.

Chelovek, walking alongside, started to whisper sternly "Let me handle—"

"Oh, give it a fucking rest, Jerry," Aronica shot back, and hurried ahead to avoid any further conversation with him. "How you guys doing?" he said.

"Ah, lousy," Eddie replied, not looking at all lousy. He pointed back over his shoulder with his thumb. " 'Nother couple'a holes and I'm gonna be askin' these clowns to let *me* come down and visit."

"You're so full'a shit, Caminetti," someone in his group threw back at him.

"Just great," Perrault answered. "Say, Eddie, listen, we were kind of wondering . . ."

Carlos came up behind Eddie and threw Perrault the hardest, sternest look he could without actually running up and clamping a hand over his mouth. Eddie took a cigarette from his shirt pocket and patted his pants to locate some matches.

"Here you go," Perrault said, stepping forward and taking a lighter from his own pocket. He flicked it and held it up.

Eddie bent forward to take the light. "So what's up?"

Perrault glanced at Carlos, who was now shaking his head barely perceptibly but unmistakably, and said, "See here, we were wondering who designed this course? Doesn't seem familiar, you know, in the same way as, say, a Robinson or a Dye."

"It isn't." Eddie drew a lungful off the cigarette and turned his head to exhale it away from Perrault. "Was a bunch of guys. We asked 'em to design a course without worrying about what the terrain looked like to start with, just what's the best they could come up with if they could make it look any way they wanted." He waved a hand around. "This was the result."

"Interesting." Perrault knew that Eddie knew that it wasn't how the course was designed that he'd meant to ask, but neither betrayed that awareness.

"Deke," Eddie said with concern, "that cart helping you out? Don't want to put any strain on your ticker."

"Just fine, Eddie. No problems at all."

"Good. You can drive it right up to the greens if you want. Grass is firm enough to take it."

"Much appreciated. Thanks."

"You bet. By the way, Greg here"—Eddie waved at one of his playing partners—"he does something's got to do with securities, beats me 'zackly what. Greg, this here's Deke Savitch. I think he's in the same game."

"Oh, yeah?" Greg came forward to shake hands. "What's that?"

Savitch took his hand and said, "Stockbroker. I manage a retail division."

"Ah, good." Greg smiled conspiratorially as he shook Savitch's hand. "Least you're not one'a those program traders."

"Hell's that?" Eddie asked.

"Goddamned parasite, is what. Am I right, Savitch?"

"Uh . . ."

Greg let go and turned back to his own group. "Sumbitch who sits in front of a computer sucking up pennies by jumping all over little price differences."

"Isn't that what stock trading's all about?" Savitch asked as pleasantly as he could.

Greg waved a hand dismissively. "Idea behind the market, people invest in companies that do some real shit. They take a risk, the company raises capital so it can operate—mutual grease, like, and everybody wins, more or less. But a program trader?" He grunted and made an obscene, pumping motion with one fist. "Leeches, all of 'em. Making money off other people's sweat and not contributing a goddamned thing. Hell, some of 'em even got computers so automatic they do all the work for 'em, am I right, Savitch?" He threw his arm across Savitch's shoulders and squeezed him painfully.

"You bet, Greg."

"There you go! How long you guys gonna be around?" He removed his arm and walked away. "Maybe play a little, whaddaya say?"

"Yeah, get him off my tail," Eddie said. "Sure as hell hope I have better luck in the match I got tomorrow."

More pleasantries were exchanged, and as the two groups moved off on their separate ways, Carlos passed close to Perrault and Savitch and hissed "Patience!" at them under his breath.

Before he could get away, Chelovek grabbed him. "Did I hear somebody call him Caminetti?" he demanded.

"Yeah, Caminetti," Carlos answered. "Eddie Caminetti, that's his name. Didn't I mention?"

"Well, I'll be go to hell," Chelovek said when the other group was out of earshot.

"Caminetti." Aronica, brow creased in concentration, tapped at his chin. "How come that sounds so familiar?"

"I'll tell you why," Chelovek said, a smile beginning to crease his face. "He played on the U.S. Ryder Cup team, that's why."

"I knew it!" Perrault cried. "I knew I'd heard that name!"

Chelovek folded his arms across his chest and stared as the other group receded behind some trees. "A two-bit hustler from a dipshit muni course that whatshisface put on the team."

Whatshisface was me, of course. Like I said, another story.

"I recall now," Perrault said. "So that's the fellow, is it?"

Chelovek nodded. "Whole tournament came down to his last hole."

"Not to interrupt here or anything," Savitch interrupted, "but anybody feel like finishing our round?"

Chapter 15

WELL, AT LEAST WE KNOW we can get a match with that Greg guy." Savitch, anxious to put the best face on things, was trying unsuccessfully to cheer his friends up.

"You mean the one who called you a parasite?" Aronica asked, pushing away his half-eaten dinner.

"He didn't know what I do."

"And that makes a difference?" Perrault snarled. "See here, I don't wish to play with Greg, I've no desire to play with the bloody kitchen staff and I sure as shit don't want to play with nobody but you three assholes all week!"

I should have mentioned earlier: In times of great stress or acute agitation, Perrault was known to momentarily abandon his painstakingly acquired upper-crust manner of speech.

"We were good enough for you to play with all week when we were planning this trip," Aronica snapped.

"So what are you telling me, Joe?" Perrault waved off a busboy who was approaching with a pitcher of water. "You've no desire to play the owners, is that it?"

"Course I want to play them. The Big Swinging Dick over here"—he pointed to Chelovek—"said he could make it happen."

"Week's still young," Chelovek muttered halfheartedly.

"Well, I'll tell you this." Aronica tapped two fingers on the tabletop several times. "So far this isn't the most memorable vacation I ever had, and when we check out of here, I'm not paying them one red—"

"Hang on a minute," Savitch said furtively. "Here he comes!"

Indeed, as the others could see, Eddie was entering the dining area and heading for their table. He waved, and as Aronica and Perrault waved back, Chelovek leaned in and said quietly but forcefully, "Now I mean it: Don't say a fucking word!"

Perrault slumped back on his chair. "Oh, blow it out your—"

"Not one fucking word!" Chelovek growled with real menace. "I know how to handle this."

"Gentlemen!" Eddie said, slapping a hand on Aronica's shoulder and leaning the other on the back of Savitch's chair. "Hate to intrude on whatever plans you guys got for the rest of the week, but my game tomorrow fell through. You interested in a friendly match, maybe put a couple three bucks down to make it interesting?"

Chelovek leaned back and exhaled loudly. "Boy, I don't know, Eddie. We kinda had—"

Eddie straightened up and put his hands in the air. "Hey, no problem, no problem a'tall. Just thought I'd—"

"Well, I'd certainly welcome a game," Perrault said. "Was rather hoping you'd ask, actually."

"Really?" Eddie looked surprised, maybe even upset. "Well, whyn't you just say so, fer cryin' out loud! Don't have to twist my arm to get me to play."

"Didn't think it'd be polite," Savitch said unconvincingly.

"Polite! Jeez, Deke, what the hell'd you think goes on around here? So listen, eat up and let's meet out on the porch for a drink afterward, swap lies about our handicaps, see what we can set up, okay?"

Nearly choking with glee, Savitch said, "I'm an eighteen!"

"Yeah, my *dick's* an eighteen," Eddie said, then turned to walk to a table of other guests. "See you boys later!"

Grinning like an idiot, Aronica pulled his dinner plate back and said to Chelovek, "Gee, that was beautiful how you set that up!"

"Yes, you're the man, Jerrold." Perrault held up his glass to a passing waiter and signaled for some more wine.

"Ah, fuck the whole lotta you." Chelovek, too happy himself to take any real offense, reddened anyway.

They dug in to the rest of their dinners with renewed zeal, hoping that Eddie would finish his fast.

Chapter 16

∺

I'M NOT GONNA SANDBAG YOU guys," Eddie said once they were comfortably seated outside and had brandy and cigars in hand. "I'm a pretty good golfer."

"What's your real handicap?" Chelovek asked him. "You said you played off two."

"I don't really know."

Perrault let loose a derisive but utterly dignified hoot, as might befit a member of parliament rather than an aerobics instructor. "Did you think we hadn't seen you hitting out there today? How can someone who plays like that not know his handicap!"

Eddie laughed, too, as he blew out some smoke. "I'm serious!"

"You're full'a shit!" Aronica said.

They were all laughing now, and Perrault kept up the mock attack. "You weren't kidding when you invited us out here to swap lies!"

"Will you shut the hell up for a second and listen?" Eddie set down his drink on an end table and rearranged himself on the seat. "Problem is, Swithen Bairn's about the only course I play anymore, and it's never been officially rated or sloped, so how the hell can I figure my handicap?"

He had them there, but Chelovek had a comeback. "Okay, so what do you usually shoot?"

"Varies all over the place depending on how I feel, how the winds are blowing . . . Best I can figure, I really am about a two."

"A two," Savitch echoed. "I'm a three." Neither he nor his friends mentioned his reputation of almost always beating his handicap—by a healthy margin—during tournaments, which no rule of golf, written or implied, required them to do.

"I knew that already. So I gotta give you one."

"Whoa, hold it, hold it," Chelovek said. "You kidding us or what here, Eddie?"

"What do you mean?"

"I mean, every golfer in the world plays up and down depending on the weather and how he's feeling and all that other bullshit. That's why the handicap system only uses the ten best of your last twenty scores."

"That's true . . ."

"So forget your shitty rounds. Now, you know this course like I know my wife's ass—"

"And probably half the asses in Connecticut, according to my waitresses," Eddie retorted.

"Never mind, never mind," Chelovek shouted over his friends' raucous laughter. "Point is," he continued when it died down, "if you think you're a two, my guess is you're more like scratch, especially on your own course. Now, tell me I'm crazy."

Chelovek paused for just a second and, when no answer was immediately forthcoming, plunged ahead as though Eddie had agreed with him and that this part of the deal was already closed. "Meanwhile, you already know all of our handicaps because you contacted our club—now, don't look so surprised." Chelovek made sure to smile broadly, underscoring that he took no offense and saw only humor in the situation. "And you haven't even told us who else is on your team!"

"Matter of fact, I haven't contacted your club because up until now there was no match in the works, but . . ." Eddie thought about what Chelovek had said, then nodded slowly. "I got a couple people. They're good players."

"I bet," Savitch said. "What, probably off the Tour, right?"

Eddie shook his head emphatically. "Strictly amateurs. Not one of us has ever played for prize money other than in the same kind of twerpy little local tournaments you guys play in all the time."

"That a fact?" Chelovek asked.

"Absolutely."

"Eddie, Eddie . . ." Chelovek sat back and looked sadly at the ground. "Now, here we were, all of us trying to be honest, and you hand us a load of crap like that?"

Eddie's smile faded slightly as he detected a note of seriousness in Chelovek's voice. "You trying to say something, Jerry?"

"You think we just got off the boat?" Savitch said, delighted to have caught their host dissembling.

"Come on," Aronica said. "You're Eddie Caminetti. You think we don't know that? Think we don't know you played in the Ryder Cup?"

"So what of it?"

"What of—" Savitch looked around to see if his outrage was justified. "You just got finished telling us that nobody on your side ever played on the tour!"

"Which is true."

"The freakin' *Ryder Cup?*" Savitch nearly shouted.

Eddie shrugged. "Ryder's not on the Tour."

Savitch blinked a few times. "Okay, maybe not on the official tour, but are you trying to tell me—"

"And there's no prize money," Eddie added. "Prestigious, maybe, but no dough. Zip. Nada. Not one red cent." That was true, and the boys were well aware of it.

Chelovek sensed that his friends were in danger of ruining everything. "Eddie, what say we take a little break. Lemme talk to my buddies, see what we want to do here, okay?"

"No problem." Eddie stood up and kicked some wrinkles out of his pants. "Pro'ly ought to mingle with a couple other people anyway. See ya in a few."

"WE MUST BE MAD," PERRAULT said, "going up against a man good enough to play on the Ryder."

But Chelovek was not to be deterred. Speaking in a low voice, he said, "Don't you even remember what happened in that tournament, you dummy? Whole damned thing came down to that guy in there. Hell, the poor bastard dropped so far out of sight right afterward, everybody thought he was dead."

"Come to think of it," Aronica said, "*I* thought he was dead."

"That's what I'm saying here. Guy waltzes in, flips the whole Cup on its head, then he evaporates."

Chelovek was right, and who knew that better than I, three-time Player of the Year Al Bellamy himself? I was captain of that team, I was the one who put Eddie Caminetti on it, and I was the one who suffered the most because of it.

I was also the only person alive other than Eddie who knew that what he'd done, he'd done on purpose, having pretty much planned the entire thing out before he'd even shown up, but that's part of that whole other story I men-

tioned before. All you need to know for now is that he was the last golfer on
the surface of the earth you wanted to underestimate.

Aronica looked around the room. "Looks like he did okay for himself."

"Not necessarily," Perrault opined. "Quite possible his fellow owners
placed him here just to afford the establishment some color."

"Speaking of the other owners," Savitch said, "we don't know those guys
at all. At least with Eddie we know something. What if they're all like
scratch . . . or better?"

Aronica, Perrault and Savitch argued among themselves for a while, until
Perrault said, "What's with you, Jerrold? You're the one wanted to play them
worst of all. How come you're all mum now?"

Chelovek, who'd been silently chewing a fingernail, frowned. "I think I
know what's going on here."

"Oh?" Perrault said, sensing they were in for more condescension from
the master of all hustles. "And what might that be?"

Chelovek's brow was still creased as he concentrated on something, and
no traces of wiseguy smarter-than-thou-ness were evident in his expression or
demeanor. "I think we're being scammed. And I mean big-time scammed."

Perrault looked around to try to gauge everybody's reaction. "What are
you talking about, Jerrold? My word, you're the most suspicious human being
I've ever met!"

"Eddie's looking impatient," Savitch observed.

Chelovek stole a peek, and indeed, Eddie was standing up and checking
his watch. "Whole thing's starting to sound like not so much fun anymore,"
Savitch said.

Chelovek whirled on them. "Listen," he said, sounding frantic, "we gotta
take the bet!"

"Take it? You just got finished telling us we're being—"

Chelovek grabbed Aronica by the sleeve. "Trust me, Joe, let's just take the
fucking bet! I got a way we can make the handicaps less important, but we
gotta do this, we gotta play them!" He was grinning now, almost manic, and it
made the others smile as well.

"Hey, I think he's about had it," Perrault said, looking at Eddie grow
increasingly impatient.

"Okay by me!" Aronica announced to his friends.

"I'm in," Perrault concurred. "I'm in!"

"Come on, Deke!" Chelovek was practically begging. "I'll explain later, but
you gotta—"

"Okay, okay, I'm—"

"Eddie!" Chelovek called out, standing up so fast he almost knocked Savitch over. They all beckoned in as friendly a fashion as they could, and soon Eddie was coming back out to the veranda, looking mildly annoyed.

"I apologize, Eddie," Chelovek said solicitously, holding out his hand. "Really, I mean it. We, uh, we're not used to playing people we don't know with money on the line, and it made us a little nervous, you can understand that."

Eddie accepted the outstretched hand but said, "Listen, I don't know. You're our customers here, and I'd sure feel terrible if you felt any pressure—"

They all waved away the concern and practically forced Eddie to resume his seat. "Only thing is," Chelovek said, "the handicaps need to be fair, right? And you gotta admit, there's a little flake in yours, and your other guys', on account of ours are official and you're asking us to take your word for it. That's true, isn't it, meaning no offense here?"

"You gotta point, I'll admit."

"That's all I'm saying."

"Fair enough."

Chelovek and Eddie exchanged some comradely nods and some extrasensory handshakes as well. I know that feeling well, two old bullshitters respectfully, even admiringly, complimenting each other's well-honed brand of crapola, no offense taken because each acknowledges of his own free will that great handfuls of grade-A manure are flowing liberally in both directions.

The other guys sat quietly and let it happen, sensing that some kind of subliminal rapport had been established between the two and that things were best left in Chelovek's hands at this point. They were anxious, though, to know what the idea was to which he'd alluded, the one that would reduce the impact of handicap differences.

"What I'm thinking," Chelovek said, "is some kinda format, we don't gotta worry so much about who's a two or a three, see?"

"Like maybe, what . . . best ball, or something like that?"

"Best ball" is one of the most common betting games played by weekend foursomes, and us pros as well, when we're just out for fun. It's a team contest, two against two. On each hole a team's score is simply the lower of its two scores: If I shoot a 5 and my partner a 4, our team score is 4, our "best ball." We match that up against the other side's "best ball" to determine which team wins that hole.

"Just what I was thinking!" Chelovek exclaimed gleefully. "We're on the same wavelength here, am I right or am I right?"

"You're right!" Eddie responded with equal enthusiasm. "Now, this being eight guys altogether, gonna take us three weeks to play a round in the first place, so—"

"We needa cut it down," Chelovek finished for him. "But everybody's gotta play, or it's no fun. That's still the point isn't it? Have some fun, I mean? Otherwise—"

"Otherwise, might as well flip a coin and *fuck* the golf!"

"Just what I'm thinking!"

They were grooving along like two morning DJs who'd been working together for thirty years and could read each other's mind. The other three eagerly let themselves be drawn into the developing *Gemütlichkeit,* all of them bonding into a happy band of brothers.

"Here's an idea," Chelovek said. "What about we play two-man 'best ball.' On each hole it's our two best scores against your two best."

"That could work."

"What about handicaps?" Savitch asked.

"Ah, we're all probably about the same," Eddie said. "Whole point of 'best ball' anyway, it pretty much wipes out the little differences."

"You gotta be kidding!" Aronica exclaimed. "With you guys already knowing every square inch of the entire track?"

Eddie, clearly enjoying the process, waved Aronica's protest away. "We haven't even verified your handicaps, on account'a we didn't know we were gonna be playing. All I know is what Carlos told me. You wanna start fiddling with a stroke here and there, we gotta wait until we get that done. House rule, and we don't break it for anybody. That way nobody gets offended."

Chelovek looked around to get consenting nods from his friends, then turned back to Eddie. "Stakes?"

"Hang on a minute," Eddie said. "Still haven't figured out how to cut the time down."

"I got an idea," Aronica said hesitantly, not wishing to tread on Chelovek's turf.

"Shoot," Eddie said encouragingly.

"Okay. On every hole we all tee off. But as soon as we finish the tee shots, each side picks just two of their guys to play out the rest of the hole, and the best score of those two is the team's score."

Eddie saw the cleverness of it and was nodding in approval even before Aronica had finished. "Genius, Joe. Everybody gets to play, and we don't gotta take all day."

"Should be fun, too," Perrault threw in, "figuring out which two play out each hole." The implication wasn't lost on Chelovek, the self-appointed, de facto captain: *First thing we do is figure out* who *does the figuring out while we're playing.*

"So whaddaya want to play for?" Eddie asked. "Grand a man?"

"Sounds good to me, Eddie," Chelovek answered. "Blue tees, right?"

"Grand a man, how?" Savitch asked. "Overall, or three ways?"

By "three ways" Savitch meant a format called a nassau: a thousand for the team that won the most holes on the front nine, another thousand for the back nine, and another thousand for the team that won the most holes over the whole eighteen. "Overall" meant a single thousand-dollar bet for who wins the most holes out of eighteen.

"I'd say just overall," Eddie suggested. " 'Case we wanna jump around holes, makes it less complicated. We can do two thou a man, if you want."

"Two sounds agreeable," Perrault said, and Aronica and Savitch concurred.

"Great!" Eddie stood up and rubbed his hands together. "Always sleep better knowing I'm gonna be playin' with a bunch of good guys the next day. Eight o'clock good for you fellas?"

And he was gone, leaving the foursome bathed in tingling anticipation. The impending match, which was peanuts from a financial standpoint, wasn't as responsible for the elevation in their collective mood as was a new feeling of inclusion, of being a part of Swithen Bairn rather than just customers. The owners themselves would be spending most of a day with them, while the rest of the resort and its guests would have to fend for themselves.

They sipped their brandies quietly, aswirl in the genial camaraderie, and Chelovek was the first to break the cozy silence.

"You three are about the dumbest buncha assholes I've ever seen."

Chapter 17

■

"WHAT'S YOUR PROBLEM, JERROLD?" Perrault said with considerable resentment, at both the insult and the intrusion on the mood.

Chelovek held his brandy up to the light, peering at it as if it took only half his mind to explain to the others what was already clear to him. "The whole thing is such an obvious setup."

"That's our Jerry," Savitch said with a sigh, "always suspicious of other people, always thinking everybody's out to screw everybody else."

"You think so, Deke?" Chelovek put down the glass and took a deep puff off his cigar, pleased that nobody spoke while he took his time. He waved his hand, taking in the dining room, the veranda and pretty much the rest of Swithen Bairn. "A lavish vacation, background financial checks, old Carlos planted on the good ship *Bend Over and Spread 'Em* to soften us up and give us tips on how to deal with the owners . . . Hell, I bet the little spic owns half this joint himself!"

Chelovek took his glass and stood up. "A proposal for a modest little wager. Chrissakes, fellas, you'd have to be blind and brain-dead not to see what's going on!"

Sometimes things that you perceive one way can, with a slight alteration in mind-set, suddenly seem completely different, like when you struggle through some classic old novel and somebody tells you they thought it was a piece of junk and you realize they're right and can finally admit to yourself and everybody else that you just plain hate it without coming off like a philistine. The others knew that the supremely cynical Chelovek really was an expert on every kind of put-on ever conceived—he was, after all, in advertising, so bullshit was his stock in trade—so when he summed it all up as he had and it was too obvious not to be true, they were aghast and chagrined at how they'd managed to miss something that clear.

Which isn't to say that they were cowed by their gullibility vis-à-vis Chelovek's superior discernment. "So what do we do now, big shot?" Aronica demanded, electing not to point out the ethnic slur the man of the people had just used to refer to Carlos.

"Yeah," Savitch followed up. "Why'd you tell Joe to take the bet?"

"I believe I know why," Perrault said as a smile slowly spread across his face, thinking he had Chelovek's angle figured out. "The whole world knows what happened at the Ryder. If we can escalate the bets high enough, we'll compromise his resolve, is that your contention?"

Chelovek blew another cloud of smoke into the air. "Not even close, boychik, but I do like the way you think."

He pulled his chair closer to the others, took a look around, and leaned forward as he waved them in closer. "Forget about the Ryder," he said soberly. "I remember some of the stories that filtered out of there, stuff I heard from sponsors we did some ads for. Eddie's a world-class hustler, maybe the greatest match player ever. This is not a guy who slaps a couple'a dollars down just to have some yucks with a bunch of outta town yahoos. We're being suckered."

"You said that already," Perrault pointed out. "So what's his gambit? Are we going to find ourselves competing against people capable of shooting sixty-five?"

"Don't think so, on account of that's too easy to see through, especially with guys who practically live here and everybody knows how they play." Chelovek shook his head. "No, what I think, the owners are gonna try to make it look good, but what they're really gonna do, they're gonna tank this match and let us win, and probably let us win a lot more than two large each."

Perrault blinked a few times in noncomprehension. "And . . . ?"

"Then we play 'em again, and we win even more."

He let it sit there for a second until Savitch, not at all pleased with Chelovek's condescending attitude that forced the others to prompt him to keep going, said, "And this is a bad thing for us because . . . ?"

"Because," Chelovek said with a smug smile, "it's all a setup for our last day, when we're so full of ourselves we put the huge bucks on the line and they kick our asses from here to Pebble Beach."

"Ah . . ." It was breathtaking in its simplicity.

"So everybody play it cool and follow my lead here."

"Which is . . . ?" Perrault asked.

"Just this," Chelovek answered. "Let's take as much of their dough as we can and not play them on the final day."

He sat back and put the cigar in his mouth, immensely pleased at the looks on their faces and not happy when Savitch ruined his the-butler-did-it moment. "What about paying for the vacation?"

Chelovek sniffed in contempt. "Well, if it pricks at your conscience, Deke, you can just pay your bill, which is gonna be a fraction of what we walk away with. Hell, maybe we *should* pay"—he smiled broadly—"'cuz it *is* going to be our most memorable vacation ever!"

Unwilling to break up for the night, they sat around discussing tactics—like how they'd start to act cocky after they took the lead and would offer to bump the wager—and grew more and more excited about beating Eddie at his own game.

Eventually Chelovek suggested they all go off and get a good night's rest. "We still gotta play 'em, and play 'em good. Whole thing's down the crapper if it doesn't look kosher."

As the others reluctantly drifted off, Aronica went to the ledge bordering the veranda and sat down. He took a small leatherbound notebook and mechanical pencil from his pocket, unstrapped his watch and set it on his lap, and looked up at the brilliant night sky.

Chapter 18

✙

Day Three

HAVING HAD A CHANCE TO sleep on it, and with the heady effects of fine brandy and cigars no longer at work, our boys were somewhat subdued as they left the driving range and drove the verdant path to the first tee. I can imagine how they must have felt: Prior to a tournament I always pep myself up by slinging a lot of thinly veiled bravado at the media, gushing with respect for the opposing players, which really means that I'm so self-confident I can easily afford to be lavish in my praise.

But once my tee time approaches, a kind of nagging trepidation always scratches at me. It's not butterflies, which is different. This isn't nervousness but the fear that maybe I shouldn't have shot my mouth off, fear that I might have fallen for my own hype and inadvertently conjured up the wrong mindset. I start to replay every line of every interview I gave, fearful that I might have said something that would wind up in one of those supposedly hysterical, deeply hurtful little throwaway gags of which sportscasters and columnists, always desperate to distinguish themselves in a field from which cleverness and creativity have been thoroughly wrung, are so fond. "Al Bellamy started this contest saying he didn't want to have one three-putt this entire round, and he got his wish, all right, he didn't have *one* three-putt, he had *nine* of 'em, yuck, yuck, yuck. Back to you at the Shit for Brains Open, Roger . . ."

And so it was with the boys that day on their way to the first tee. What had they gotten themselves into?

"Sure hope you're right about this, Jerry," Savitch said for about the twelfth time since breakfast.

Chelovek slammed on the brake, Savitch nearly flying out of the cart and Aronica behind them narrowly avoiding a collision, yelling "Hey!" as he wrestled the cart to a stop.

Chelovek tore off his sunglasses and turned full-on to Savitch. "*Fuck you, Deke!* You don't wanna play, get the fuck out of the cart!"

"Hey, what the heck's got into—"

"Ho!" Perrault called from the second cart. "What's the rumpus, Jerrold?"

"I'll give you the fuckin' rumpus!" Chelovek, seriously asteam, jumped out of the cart and stepped back so he could see all three of them. "You bastards have been telling me for two goddamned days you want to play the owners, you're all depressed, this is no fun . . . I set up a game, and now you're all whining like a bunch'a faggots!"

"All he's saying—" Aronica began, but Chelovek cut him off.

"No, Joe, I don't give a rat's ass what he's saying! Whatever it is, you shoulda said it last night, not when we're two minutes away from playing! You guys are making it sound like I roped you into this, like you're doing me some kinda goddamned favor. Well, I got a hot flash for all'a you: I don't give a shit one way or the other, and if you're gonna dump this on my ass, then fuck the game and fuck you!"

The painful silence that followed was broken by a soft crunch as Mambo the vervet monkey jumped from a limb and landed expectantly on top of the front cart. Chelovek pulled a golf glove from his pocket and hauled back to throw it, but Mambo leaped away with a screech.

"All I'm saying, Jerry," Savitch began, "is what if you're wrong, what if you didn't read 'em the way—"

"That's it." Chelovek put his glasses back on and began walking down the path toward the main house. "I'm outta here. Do whatever the fuck you want, but leave me the hell out of it."

Aronica got out of his cart and called, "Oh, for shit's sake, Jerry, would you just hang on for a goddamned second!"

Chelovek waved once without looking back. Savitch sniffled and said, "I think maybe—"

"Shut the fuck up, Deke," Aronica commanded. "Not one more word outta you. Hey, Jerry, hold it a second!"

Chelovek, now about twenty feet away, stopped and turned. "I'm not kidding, Joe, I won't do this. I gave it my best shot, my best read, and whatever happens, I don't want you guys coming back and—"

"See here!" Now Perrault got out. "*All* of you quiet down! Jerrold, step over here, would you?"

Chelovek hesitated, then came back and stood with them defiantly, arms across his chest.

Perrault looked at each one of them in turn. "What in heaven's name are we arguing about here!"

The other three began talking simultaneously as Perrault listened, incredulous, then put his hands up. "Have you all gone mad? My God, it's only *two thousand dollars* . . . who gives a whip if Jerrold's wrong!"

Nobody moved until Savitch shuffled a foot, then Aronica scratched his nose, and Chelovek let his arms drop to his sides. Chastened and chagrined at their behavior in light of the perspective Perrault had provided, they tried to find a conciliatory way out of the unnecessary clash.

"You know, guys," Aronica said, "it's a gorgeous day, we're gonna play golf on a gorgeous course, we been eating and drinking and smoking like a bunch'a friggin' sultans—somebody gonna tell me this hasn't been worth two G's already?"

Perrault nodded supportively. "And who's to say we'll lose anyway, right?"

"What if I'm wrong?" Chelovek said, still concerned about the potential aftermath.

"Everybody seems to be forgetting something, my friend," Perrault said with a knowing smile. "Even if it isn't a scam, where's it written we can't beat these people straight up?"

That thought hadn't as yet occurred to any of them, and it brought them some renewed optimism. "You're right!" Aronica said happily. "We stop fighting like a basket of wet cats, I bet we could do it. C'mon, Jerry, get in. Let's go play some golf."

"You on board, Deke?" Perrault said.

"Yeah. Only . . ."

"Only what?" Perrault said, stiffening.

Savitch put his hands up defensively. "Don't get me wrong here: I'm in. Just one question, Jerry."

"Okay . . ."

"You said maybe we're gonna bump the bet. Then it's not two thousand anymore. So then what do we do?"

It was a good question, and Aronica answered it. "What I say, we leave it to Jerry. We follow his lead. If he fucks it up, we laugh it off, and that's all there is to it. Okay?"

The only appropriate response, given the mood, was to go along, but Chelovek still wanted to cover himself. "Anybody doesn't like a new bet, just say so, and we don't do it."

"Quite acceptable," Perrault agreed, and he got back into the cart. As the others followed suit, he said, "I've seen Deke spend more than that on a stereo system he still hasn't figured out how to turn on," which brought a gale of tension-relieving laughter.

"I just hope you're right, Jerry," Aronica called, then ducked as Chelovek turned and threw his glove at him.

It's worth noting here how cleverly Chelovek worked the little guilt trip that got his partners off his back and set them up not to blame him if things went south. I don't mean to insult your intelligence, but it escaped me at first, too. Fact is, the rest of them had *not* agreed of their own volition the night before to get into this match.

If you recall, it was Chelovek who, with scant seconds to spare before Eddie needed their final answer, grabbed Aronica's sleeve and frantically begged all of them to just trust him and take the bet, saying that he would explain later. Swept along by his enthusiasm and his authoritative conviction, they'd agreed, without knowing in advance why he'd suddenly come to the conclusion that they simply had to take the bet.

THE INSTANT THEY SAW THE tee box, they had a pretty good notion that Chelovek *had* been right.

"Well, I say!" Perrault exclaimed, eyeing the blue markers. They were set so far forward they might as well have been the middle tees. It was the easiest possible tee-off spot.

Savitch, anxious to smooth out any awkwardness he might have caused, clapped Chelovek on the shoulder. "Good call, bud. Think the whole course is gonna be laid out like that?"

"Guaran-damn-teed. Bet the flags're easy, too. So where are these guys?" The owners hadn't been on the range or at breakfast.

"Who might this be?" Perrault was looking down the fairway at two golf carts just past the dogleg.

"Looks like they're coming this way," Aronica observed. "Is that Eddie driving the front one?"

"Hard to tell," Chelovek answered. "I can hardly pick that guy out when he's two feet away."

Perrault had his rangefinder out and trained it on the approaching carts. "That's him, all right. Where do you reckon he's been? Wait . . . they're waving."

The boys waved back, and as the carts got closer they had their first, albeit distant, look at the opposition. Sitting next to the unremittingly nondescript

Eddie was a black man of very dark complexion, his head about half a foot closer to the roof of the cart than Eddie's. Behind them was someone dressed in long pants and a loose-fitting, long-sleeved pullover wind shirt, and the passenger seat was occupied by a ruddy-complected man with a brush mustache dressed in khaki shorts and what looked somewhat like a safari shirt, light tan with a lot of pockets.

"That's a broad!" Chelovek exclaimed.

"You're kidding," Aronica said. "Pete, is he kidding?"

Perrault moved his rangefinder to the back cart. "He most certainly is not. Good God, Jerrold! How'd you—"

"I can smell 'em a mile away, don't need no binoculars." If a voice could leer, his did.

"Try not to embarrass us, okay?" Perrault pleaded. "So help me, you harass one more waitress and I'm switching tables."

"Gee, *that'd* ruin my whole day. Now, put the damned glasses away; you're embarrassing *me*."

Eddie drove his cart past them and swung it around to get it facing in the proper direction. The other driver did the same, everyone smiling at everyone else as they went past and returned. The boys walked up as the others piled out of the carts.

Perrault leaned in toward Chelovek as they stepped forward and whispered, "You suppose the tees are up forward for the woman?"

Chelovek shrugged noncommittally. "Not sure what's up. We'll see."

"Morning, gentlemen!" Eddie called cheerfully. "Whatcha guys been up to all morning?"

"All morning?" Aronica replied with equal good humor. "It's only eight o'clock. Didn't see your lazy butt on the range!"

"Just played nine holes; who needs the range? Like you to meet some friends."

"You played nine holes?" Savitch echoed.

"You know a better way to warm up, *mon ami?*" the black man said, his accent a lilting, melodious mix of Paris and Roadtown. He hadn't so much gotten out of the cart as unfolded himself, much like an Indian fakir emerging from a small box. Towering above the others, he held out a hand. "I am Étienne Pensecoeur."

"Pensecoeur . . . the thinking heart?" Aronica took his hand and shook it. "Joe Aronica."

"Very good, *monsieur!* But, in fact, the restless heart."

"Really?"

"Not the French; my temperament."

"Trevor Blanchard," Eddie said, taking the khaki-clad gentleman by the arm and moving him forward. They could see that Blanchard, every inch the picture of a proper British military officer, was somewhere in his late fifties. "And this is Dr. Peter Perrault."

"Just Pete," Perrault said graciously.

"Just Sir Trevor," Blanchard answered austerely. His accent dripped with peerage and pedigree.

"Oh, sorry." Perrault's outstretched hand wavered slightly in indecision. "You're—I mean you've been—you're a *knight*?"

"No, my good man." Blanchard reached for Perrault's hand. "I'm a bull-shit artist. Trevor's the name."

As Perrault reddened beneath the hail of rowdy laughter, Blanchard beamed him a high-wattage smile and pointed to Eddie with his free hand. "If this weak-kneed scoundrel can agree to play without getting us any strokes, and do so absent any consultation with his mates, least I can do is tweak the opposition a bit, what?"

Perrault grinned back at him. "Okay, you got me a good one there. Now go easy on my prosthetic hand, will you?"

Eddie put a hand on the woman's shoulder. "And this is Selby Kirkland."

Chelovek stepped forward immediately. "Well, I'm very pleased to me you, Selby." Then he almost fell backward, and Perrault had to put a hand on his back to steady him. He'd anticipated that Chelovek might need some propping up as soon he noticed that Selby Kirkland had been their waitress the night before.

Seemingly having forgotten their little interaction at dinner, and further pretending unawareness of the more unsavory aspects of Chelovek's persona, Kirkland accepted the greeting graciously and extended her hand, which Chelovek, recovering with admirable suddenness, took in both his own. She was about five-nine, but other than her face, there was little else to see, because every inch of her was again covered with loose layers of fabric. The face, though, was a miracle. Kirkland's slightly narrow eyes gave her an air of exotic mystique, and her face was the kind that makeup could only mar. Her skin was somewhat pale and was offset by dark eyebrows and naturally dark lips. Her hair was pulled up, but a few wisps dangled tantalizingly at her longish neck. Chelovek was having trouble keeping his eyes off her.

Perrault stepped to her rescue. "Pete. Hello again."

He offered his hand, and it seemed to him that she had to pull away from Chelovek to get hers loose. "Pleasure," she said easily, no hint in her demeanor that anything was amiss.

"Gonna be awfully warm in all those clothes," Chelovek said.

"A mild skin condition. Direct sunlight isn't good for me."

"Feels warmer today, though," Chelovek persisted.

Perrault let go of Kirkland's hand and walked to his cart, brushing past Chelovek on the way. "Give it up, Jerrold!" he said in a raspy whisper.

"True enough," Eddie said. "Temperature inversion, fairly common around here. Seems to turn the whole atmosphere into kind of like a lens. Focuses the sun's rays and can make it pretty hot. So . . . everybody loose?"

The boys were so amped for this match there was no way they were going to get loose, but they did their best to suppress at least the appearance of their excitement. "Where's the girl gonna play from?" Chelovek asked of no one in particular, remembering that this was a money match and wanting his partners to know he was staying on the ball.

"Her name's Selby," Blanchard said as he dug around in his golf bag for something. "And you might ask her directly."

"I'll play the same as everyone," Kirkland answered, giving no indication that she'd taken offense and also giving no hint of the kind of wisecracking persona she'd worn the evening before.

"Is that fair?" Aronica asked, earning him a steely look from Chelovek.

"Probably not," Eddie responded, "but it wouldn't be fair to make her go back to the tips while we play up here, now, would it?"

"What I meant was—"

"Just kidding, Joe. Don't worry about it. We're gonna beat you either way."

"Is that so?" Perrault said affably.

"Take you to the laundry," Pensecoeur threw in as he pulled a fifty-four-inch driver out of his bag and began swinging it to warm up. The sound the clubhead made as it whipped through the air was like an F-15 on a strafing run.

"Cleaners, Étienne," Blanchard corrected him. "Take them to the cleaners."

"We'll see about that," Aronica piped in. "Who's up?"

"Makes no difference," Eddie said. "ET, you ready?"

"*Pourqouis non?*" The Haitian moved to the tee box and set up his ball, then took a few more practice swings, full range of motion this time. From the way he took up his stance and gave only one glance down the fairway to check his alignment, it was evident that he knew the layout so intimately that his course of action from the tees was a matter of habit requiring no analysis. He went completely still, then slowly took the club away, accelerated into a deep backswing and lashed the huge club forward, throwing his hips toward the target as his hands came down through the ball.

The sound as the metal head slammed into the ball was reminiscent of a sledgehammer being dropped on concrete. Everyone watched as the ball took off toward the trees guarding the right dogleg and quickly disappeared over them, leaving little doubt that they'd cleared completely.

"Okay, ET got us a safe one," Eddie said, as if there were nothing special about the shot.

"Safe one?" Savitch exclaimed. "He's darned near on the green!"

Pensecoeur shook his head. "Too much fade. Robs one of distance. Next?"

"I'll go." Aronica replaced Pensecoeur on the tee box. He was holding a driver.

"Sure you wanna do that?" Chelovek asked. The safe play, as they'd already determined, was a three-wood down the middle. *Is this really how we want to start out?* he was trying to convey to Aronica. *Abandoning our strategy on the first tee?*

Aronica, determined not to let Chelovek take over the top management spot, didn't even bother to answer but hauled away with the driver and placed his ball squarely into the trees, likely never to be found again.

Pretending to commiserate with him as he returned to the sidelines, Chelovek sidled up and said, "You gonna spend the whole fuckin' day showing off, or you gonna try to win this thing!"

"Don't remember asking you for advice," Aronica spat back, "and I don't remember appointing you captain either."

Kirkland stepped to the tee carrying a driver. Her setup wasn't easy and natural but looked to be the product of a lot of lessons from a drill instructor. Feet together, she set the clubhead down next to the ball, stepped back to let the grip fall into her hand, and took a few small steps to adjust the shaft to some predetermined angle. Then she moved her feet left and right to complete the mechanical stance and was equally meticulous about forming her grip on the club.

After all of that, her swing was much smoother and more relaxed than the boys would have guessed, and she hit a very sweet shot down the middle of the fairway, but not far enough into the dogleg to allow her a good second shot for the green.

"Nice one," Chelovek said.

"Thanks." Kirkland picked up her tee and walked back, allowing Savitch to take up his position.

He hit the exact shot they'd planned for, a beauty right down the middle and about fifty yards past Kirkland's, putting him in excellent position to reach the green in two. Blanchard and Chelovek did much the same, but Perrault pulled his left and had no realistic chance for the green.

Eddie stepped up last, carrying a driver. His movements were economical and completely at ease, his swing as classic a piece of poetry as you could imagine. He hit it about 250, with a bit of fade that set him down next to Chelovek but some 15 or 20 yards closer to the green.

"Well struck," Perrault complimented him.

"Thanks. I'll take it."

"You're such a bore, Eddie," Kirkland said as they headed for the carts.

"I know. Ain't it awful? Think it's gonna be me and ET, assuming we can find his ball."

"That's an easy call," Savitch said.

"Not really." Blanchard pulled a head cover onto his club and dropped it into his bag. "The big gent has the short game of an elephant."

"Let's see where he is first." Eddie waved Pensecoeur into the cart and pulled away slowly. "Even an elephant can get up and down once in a while."

Aronica, the only one of the bunch to have hit an unplayable shot, wasn't joining in on the good-natured joshing. He took up his place behind the wheel and slapped the seat next to him, irritated that Perrault wasn't in the cart yet.

SAVITCH AND CHELOVEK WOULD BE playing out this hole for their side, and they didn't need a formal decision to make that determination. Aronica was out of it and Perrault too far away. Chelovek was closest to the green and had the clearest shot. Savitch's approach wouldn't be that much harder, and he was the best short-game player of the bunch. The worst they ought to come out with was two pars.

The owners would undoubtedly go with Eddie, and it only remained to be seen where Pensecoeur had ended up; otherwise, it would be Blanchard.

Eddie's cart appeared from behind the trees up ahead. Pensecoeur got out and raised his arms in triumph, and Eddie made a gesture for Blanchard to pick up his ball. Kirkland had already retrieved hers. Pensecoeur grabbed some clubs and walked toward his ball, while Eddie drove the cart back up the fairway alone.

"Wouldn't believe where that sonofagun landed," he said as he pulled up. He braked to a stop and got out, reaching for a club without appearing to have gone through any analysis as to which one he'd need. "You're away, Deke."

Savitch found a fairway marker and figured he had about 160 or so downhill to the middle of the green, with the flag in the back. "Land it short and let it roll," Chelovek advised. "Green's too hard to stick it."

"If you do that, stay right," Eddie added. "Gonna break left when she rolls."

Savitch threw him a suspicious smile. "I bet."

"Trust me—I never lie. Least not on a golf course."

Savitch, allowing for the downhill and some roll, chose a nine-iron and walked to his ball. Chelovek was already there, eyeing the shot. "Got a hundred-and-forty-yard club," Savitch said. "Eddie says it's gonna run left."

"Then it's gonna run left."

"You believe him?"

"Of course I believe him! What's he gonna do, screw you up on the first hole? If he's gonna bullshit us, he'll build credibility first and do it when it counts."

"Makes sense. Move away."

Chelovek stepped out of his partner's sight line and kept still. Savitch lined up carefully and put an effortless swing on the ball, lofting it at only a modest angle. He groaned as it landed just short of the green, but it released well and began rolling, gradually swerving left just as Eddie had predicted, coming to a stop about fifteen feet before the pin.

"Good one, Deke," Chelovek said, and similar compliments came from the other onlookers.

Chelovek wasn't as delicate with his shot, sending the ball off at too shallow an angle. It landed on the green and kicked ahead, rolling past the hole and off the back, but only by about two yards. "You can par that," Savitch said.

"Guys're makin' it tough," Eddie complained. "Gotta get risky here."

He also chose a nine-iron, set the ball well back in his stance and took a full, hard swing. The ball shot up at a very steep angle and didn't seem to start down until it was almost directly over the green. It hit with an audible plop about eight feet past the flag and rolled barely a foot more before coming to rest less than four feet from the back of the green.

"That *was* risky," Blanchard opined.

Eddie put his club back in the bag. "Yeah, but at least in the air I can control the ball. Roll it along the ground and who knows what the hell's likely to happen."

They got back in the carts and headed for the green. As they passed the tree line, Pensecoeur came into view. Having successfully cut the corner, he was only seventy feet or so from the green, hunched over the ball. He took a half swing, which looked tentative even at a distance, and the ball landed short.

"*Merde!*" he cursed loudly.

"You're such a chickenshit, ET," Eddie called lightly as they drove by him. "*Hit* the freakin' ball!"

Pensecoeur pursed his lips and nodded at the fitting criticism as he began walking toward the green, swinging the sand wedge in simulation of how he should have struck it. Over where the carts were coming to a halt, Perrault said, "Rather imagine he was afraid of going over the green."

"So what?" Eddie got out and reached for his putter. "We're playing 'best ball,' he knows I'm good for at least a par, so what did he have to lose? His job was to go for an eagle or a birdie, go right for the pin, and if he screws it up, who gives a shit?"

Chelovek hung back with Aronica for a second as the others walked toward the green. "See how he thinks?" he said. "I told you, match play's in the man's blood." Aronica, already over his earlier pique with Chelovek, nodded in agreement as Pensecoeur putted from the fringe and blew past the cup.

It's a whole different ball game, match play. Your objective is to win holes, and individual scores at the end are irrelevant. After many a round with Eddie, I knew exactly what his attitude toward the game was: You win holes, and it doesn't matter how you look while doing it. If you shoot a miserable eight on a par-four, it's okay so long as your opponent shot an even more miserable nine.

If you're playing two-man "best ball" and your partner is sitting with a sure par and you're still off the green, you don't play conservative, because there's nothing to be gained by protecting your par; your partner's already got one sewed up for the team. You go for that birdie and do it aggressively, because the team still has its par even if you miss. It's just like hitting on a soft sixteen in blackjack—there's absolutely no way you can hurt the hand; you can only improve it, even though that may not be immediately obvious to the casual player.

"Pick it up," the two of them heard Eddie call to Pensecoeur.

"Pick it up?" Aronica said to Chelovek. "What's that all about?"

Chelovek took his putter out of the bag. "Man's out of the hole, so what's the point?" In the present situation there really wasn't a need for the Haitian to putt out. The best he could get was a par, and Eddie would get that at the very worst.

"But what about for his own score?" Aronica protested.

Chelovek began walking toward the green. "Eddie doesn't give a shit about his score," he said over his shoulder. "You comin'?"

"What for?" Aronica wasn't in this hole either.

"'Cuz it's rude not to," Chelovek said, pointing to the green where Kirkland and Blanchard, who also were out of the hole, were nevertheless standing and watching. "You're on a team, remember?"

Aronica didn't like taking orders from Chelovek, but he didn't want to look discourteous or self-centered either, so he followed.

Chelovek was off the green, but Savitch was farther away from the flag, so it was his turn. Taking a cue from Eddie's match-play style, Chelovek said, "Whatever you do, Deke, don't leave it short. One of us is gonna par, so don't blow a chance for birdie."

"Okay." Savitch had already cleaned and replaced his ball. He knew the break was to the left, a continuation of his approach shot had it not stopped short, so there was no need to bend down and get a new read. Planning to hit the ball with enough force to take it two feet past the hole if he missed, he knew that there would be less effect from the break and picked a target still to the right of the cup but closer than if he were trying to let it die in the hole.

He kept his head down as he hit and didn't look up until the ball was halfway to the hole. It looked promising at first, but then they could all see that it was going to miss. Surprisingly, it got close enough to wobble over the lip, which took some speed off, so it stopped less than eighteen inches away.

Eddie stepped up and kicked it back to him, conceding the next shot. "Nice par, Deke," Kirkland said. She turned to her left, saying, "I think it's you, Jerry," to Chelovek, who was staring at her and seemed to have forgotten where he was for a second.

"Just checking the green," he mumbled unconvincingly, momentarily flustered. He handed his putter to Savitch and walked to his ball with a seven-iron. It was a good lie, sitting well up on the grass, but his chip for a birdie was way short of the stick, and he picked up his now useless ball.

Savitch didn't say anything out loud as he handed the putter back, but a question was in his eyes nonetheless: *What's the point of leaving a birdie chip short!*

"Didn't mean to do that," Chelovek said defensively. "Just misjudged it."

"Well, let's see here." Eddie positioned himself over his twelve-foot putt and swung the club a few times to groove in an arc square to his intended line. Following one lingering look at the hole to gauge the distance, he fixed himself on some piece of grass about a yard away that he'd already decided was his aiming point, lined up the clubface behind the ball, then forgot about the hole altogether and swung.

His shot wasn't as strong as Savitch's had been but still enough to look like he'd taken out too much break. The ball skittered toward the outside edge of the hole, losing some speed as it encountered a few wayward blades of grass, and rolled to a near-stop just as it came up to the lip. It paused there for a heartbeat, seemed to lean over slightly, then dropped in with a satisfying rattle.

"I say, well done!" Blanchard shouted, as Pensecoeur chimed in with a "Bravo!" and Kirkland applauded.

"Nice putt, Eddie," Savitch concurred, as did his teammates, although with not quite the same enthusiasm as the others.

Eddie bent over to get his ball out of the cup. "Yeah, well, nothin' like a bird to get your day started."

The owners were up one hole. Perrault stared at the ground as they returned to the carts, but Savitch threw Chelovek a look that was half disgust, half warning, and half murder. Chelovek wondered if it was because of his lousy shot or his lousy read of the overall situation. At least he *would* have wondered that, had he been looking at Savitch instead of at Kirkland's rear end.

Chapter 19

✚

T HING OF IT WAS, THE boys weren't playing badly. In fact, they
were playing even better than they had on that magical first day. They were
just having trouble scoring birdies, and in a "best ball" match with low-hand-
icap players, birdies are what you need to win holes.

They halved the second hole, a par on each side, so it was still the owners
by one. They hadn't used Kirkland on either hole; she just didn't seem to have
the length, and it wasn't clear why they'd brought her along at all.

The third was a par-three, 170 yards uphill to an elevated green protected
front and sides by bunkers. The flag, only the top of which could be seen
looking up from the tee, was set well forward. Chelovek put his tee shot on the
very back edge of the green, Savitch was off completely, and Perrault hit somewhere in the middle. It was hard to tell from this angle, but it looked like he
might have about a twenty-foot putt.

Eddie and Blanchard were both on, probably about the same distance
from the flag as Perrault, but Pensecoeur sliced a six-iron wide and was out
of it.

Aronica stepped up and hit what looked like a beauty, a high arc and
straight for the pin. It surprised everyone when it sailed way over the green
and disappeared.

Aronica smiled and held out his club toward Eddie, who waited a few seconds, then looked up and said, "What?"

"Was a seven-iron."

Eddie looked back at the club, then at Aronica. "I don't get it."

"Hole's a hundred and seventy yards uphill. I used a seven-iron."

"Oh." Eddie nodded in understanding, then inclined his chin toward the green. "So what you're telling me, you used the wrong club."

"For God's sake, Joe . . ." Perrault said.

"I think," Kirkland said to Eddie, "his point is that he hit it very long."

Aronica pointed to Pensecoeur. "He used a six. I hit it *over* the green with a seven."

Kirkland, the last to hit, walked toward the tee box, which was still occupied by Aronica, who still had his club held out. She stood patiently until he got the hint and finally walked off, then bent to tee up. "Would have been a whole lot more impressive," she said as she made sure the ball was at the right height, "if you'd used an eight and put it *on* the green."

Kirkland seemed less casual than she had on the first two holes as she straightened up, quieter and more focused. She was holding a wood, but one with a very small head and a sharply angled face.

"What have you got there?" Perrault asked.

"Seven," she answered.

Kirkland's tee shot looked like Aronica's, except that the distance was more accurate. The ball had a very high trajectory and seemed to descend purely vertically, right for the stick, probably with very little roll once it landed.

"That's going to be close, *chère*," Pensecoeur said.

It was. As the carts climbed the hill and the green came into view, it looked like Kirkland had about a four-footer for birdie.

"Which other one are you guys gonna play?" Chelovek asked, pointing to Eddie's and Blanchard's balls lying about eight feet apart and equidistant from the hole.

"Probably neither," Blanchard said. "Selby, dear, why don't you go ahead?"

Kirkland got out, carrying her putter. "Anybody mind?" she said, and there were no objections to her going out of turn. She pulled the flag herself as she went by and never even read the green, just lined up and hit the ball firmly, thereby neutralizing what break there might have been and dropping the ball into the cup dead center.

"Aggressive putt," Chelovek commented as she retrieved her ball.

"That distance, it's the only thing that makes sense," she said as she walked by Perrault on her way to picking up Eddie's and Blanchard's balls.

The owners had a birdie, and now one of the boys had to make one just to halve the hole. Perrault, roughly between the pin and Chelovek's ball at the back edge of the green, marked his ball. "I need a read off you, Jerrold," he said as he walked over, "so don't leave it short."

Perrault walked all the way off the green and took up a position about fifteen feet behind Chelovek so he could watch the path of his putt. Chelovek correctly read some left-to-right break, but his speed was off and he missed the cup by a foot, a pretty good putt considering that it was about a forty-footer.

Perrault now had a good read, and less than a third the distance of Chelovek's attempt. He knew there was no sense babying the ball. He either got it in or they lost the hole, so it didn't make a difference if he overshot the cup, since there'd be no next putt to worry about. He lined up as if there were less break than there actually was and hit it firmly. The ball was dead on line for the hole, and he stepped aside as he watched, hand clamped in a fist ready to pump in triumph when it dropped.

The ball hit the front lip perfectly, banged into the back edge, popped up into the air and plopped back down about three inches behind the cup.

"Tough break," Kirkland said with genuine sympathy. "You had the line perfect."

The owners were up two after three holes.

As they drove off, Savitch said, "Now, don't go getting all defensive, Jerry, okay? But this doesn't seem to be going according to plan."

Chelovek didn't get his hackles up. "Maybe not. But it's possible this is just part of making it look good."

"You think?"

Chelovek shrugged. "Not sure yet, but one thing I do know . . ."

"And that is?"

"Far as I can tell," Chelovek said with only mild sarcasm, "they haven't done anything to stop us from scoring birdies. We haven't had one yet, and they've had two."

THEY HALVED THE NEXT HOLE, and the next, and then the owners won the sixth.

"How does a waitress get to be such a good golfer?" Chelovek asked, with little humor about it, on the way to the next tee. Several of the bunch walked, while the others drove.

"That's a tad nasty, Jerrold," Perrault admonished him. But he was curious about her as well.

"Wasn't asking you."

"It's all right, Pete. I'm not a waitress. I was just filling in. Eddie sometimes loads luggage, and Étienne's been known to work the switchboard."

"What about Blanchard?" Chelovek asked, a surly edge to his voice.

"What about him?"

"Hell of a golfer. What's his story?"

"He's a very good golfer."

"That's not what I meant."

"What did you mean?"

Chelovek veered off in a huff. "Forget it."

"Say, Joe," Eddie said, several steps behind, "how'd you come up with this metal of yours anyway?"

"I'll tell you, Eddie," Aronica answered. "After years studying covalent bonds and exotic substances like polymorphic fullerenes, I was trying to make one thing and made another instead."

"Sounds hard to believe."

"Happens all the time." Aronica lapsed easily into the kind of sound bites that his hosts used to introduce him during speaking engagements. "Many of the great discoveries in materials science were serendipitous."

"Like Post-it notes," Kirkland said, walking up beside them.

"Exactly!" Aronica said. "The guy was trying to invent a new super glue and came up with some stuff that would barely stick. It was a complete failure, way too weak, and then he realized it would peel off paper without tearing it."

"So all you do is walk in one morning and see this stuff lying there, and that's it?"

"I bet it still took a bunch of work, right, Joe?" Eddie asked smoothly.

"A lot," Aronica replied as they resumed walking. "Seeing it lying there was one thing, but bringing it up to commercial grade was a long haul."

"Commercial grade . . . what's that mean?" Kirkland asked.

"So it could actually be used. Taking it from a laboratory curiosity to a useful product. Convincing potential buyers that it could really do what I said it could do."

Number seven was a short par-four, just 350 from the middles, but absurdly narrow, with low trees lining both sides of the nearly nonexistent fairway. "Anybody mind if I go ahead?" Kirkland asked.

The owners had used Kirkland's ball only once, on the par-three third hole. None of her other tee shots had gone far enough to be useful. In fact, it looked to the boys as if she really hadn't tried to hit any of them particularly hard. Now she had a two-wood in her hands and that same steely-eyed look of concentration she'd had on the par-three.

Her partners hung well back, standing unusually still and silent. Kirkland took a long time over the ball, then pulled the club away very slowly and wound up into a deep backswing, staying in perfect control as she whipped the club back around.

The clubhead hit the ball with an almost musical pinging sound, and it took off as flawlessly straight as if it were a missile riding a laser beam to an enemy bunker. It went about 210 yards and landed smack in the middle of the fairway.

Aronica, standing back with the owners, looked at her respectfully and said to Eddie, "Where the hell's she been hiding that?"

"One of the best short-game players you'll ever meet," Eddie replied. "Tee shot like that, a par for sure, the big guy can just blast away. ET . . . give it a whack!"

"Après vous."

"Okay." Eddie went ahead and hit his usual boring tee shot, 250 and dead down the middle. The owners now had two great second shot set-ups, and Pensecoeur, grinning broadly at Kirkland, happily pulled out his driver and gave it a kiss, then began walking forward.

"What's that?" Chelovek asked acidly. "Some kinda voodoo shit?"

Pensecoeur laughed as he walked by. "No, my friend. Who would waste voodoo on something as trivial as golf?"

"Suppose I may as well relax," Blanchard said to Perrault as he restored his unused driver to his bag.

The Haitian practically leaped onto the tee box and set his ball up. He gripped the driver lovingly and gave it a few big practice swings, then took a long look out at the fairway to check his alignment. Once he was down over the ball, he never looked at the target again.

His take-away was as slow as Kirkland's, and the big man demonstrated extraordinary flexibility as his left shoulder came beneath his chin but his head didn't move nor did his left arm bend at the elbow. Pausing for a fraction of a second at the point where going any farther back would have pulled a tendon loose, he uncoiled in one, long, fully extended and fully accelerating swing, throwing his hips toward the fairway just when it seemed the clubhead couldn't possibly go any faster, so it looked like every cubic inch of his entire body had shot down the shaft and come exploding out right into the back of the ball.

As soon as he heard the sound of the ball being struck, Chelovek, who'd been feigning indifference, knew that something extraordinary had just happened and jumped out of the cart to watch the ball fly off. Unlike Kirkland's shot, Pensecoeur's was well left of the fairway but above the treetops, completely free to travel its own trajectory unhindered by any impediments attached to the earth far below. Once the ball began to shed the purely ballistic component of its flight and the dimples begin biting into the air, the spin it was carrying pushed it back to the right. Breaths were held in anticipation of that moment when they would know whether the ball had enough to clear the last bunch of trees and drop free or would clip a branch and disappear.

Finally succumbing to gravity, it started down, and its flight path steepened as aerodynamic drag grabbed at it. A leaf fluttered at the very top of the last good-size tree, indicating that the ball had hit it, but it was a mild collision and there was sufficient momentum left to get the ball out of trouble before it dropped to the ground, not quite on the fairway, but that was because there *was* no fairway that close to the green, which was less than twenty yards away.

It was a colossal shot, not just because of its distance but because of its astonishing accuracy. The Haitian had been whapping the hell out of the ball since they'd started, but not all of his shots had been usable.

"Do you realize what's going on here?" Chelovek asked. Even though Savitch was sitting right next to him, he'd asked the question of nobody in particular.

"Yeah," Aronica said, walking up from behind the cart. "We're losing our asses."

Chelovek ignored him, nodding slightly to himself and pointing surreptitiously at Eddie. "He custom-tailored that team to this course."

Perrault had joined them and caught the last bit of conversation. "What are you talking about?"

Chelovek stroked his chin and took his time answering. "He didn't just slap together four good players at random, see? He put 'em together knowing that as a group they'd win enough holes to beat us. I'll bet you anything their average handicap is higher than ours."

"You're talking gibberish, Jerry," Savitch said as he got out of the cart.

"Oh, yeah? Take the broad. I doubt she can hit a ball more than two-twenty, but she doesn't have to. Eddie said she was a great short-game player. So what he's figuring, all she needs to do is win them some par-threes and a couple short fours, and that's good enough."

The logic hitting him even as he spoke, Chelovek warmed to his thesis. "Don't you get it? The voodoo man, he hits like freakin' Godzilla—"

"But he sprays them as much as he places them," Perrault opined.

Chelovek whipped around to look at him. "That's the whole goddamned point, Pete, don't you get it? He doesn't have to hit 'em all good. All he's gotta do is belt the living shit out of the ball all day, and if he only lands safe five or six times and makes birdie only two or three times, he's done his job."

Aronica saw it, too. "Eddie and Blanchard, they're so steady, they're gonna rain pars all day, maybe get some birdies just on account of that's the way it is if you hit good."

"It's more than that, though," Chelovek said. "They're the backstop, the insurance policy. If all they do is get in position to par, the Haitian can take chances all day, and the broad is always there for the shorter stuff."

He rested his driver on the ground and leaned on it. "It's more like a baseball team than a golf team. Everybody's a specialist, and every position's filled."

"Nice analysis, Jerry," Savitch said, not quite as enamored of Chelovek as the others seemed to be growing, "but there's another thing."

"And what might that be, Deke."

"They're not sniping at each other like a bunch of kindergartners, that's what. They're playing golf, working their strategy, supporting each other . . . and, oh by the way, in case you haven't noticed, they're the only ones having any fun at this tea party."

"They're having fun because they're winning, asshole."

"That's what I'm talking about right there, Jerry. You jumping down my throat like that. That your head coach's method for drawing out my best game?"

"Didn't know you needed a baby-sitter."

"What I *don't* need is you playing chairman of the board, especially when you're the dumb jerk who got us into this in the first place."

"Listen, you sawed-off little—"

"Hey!" Perrault's shout was loud enough to have caused the owners' heads to turn, but he'd gotten his partners' attention and made them quiet down for a second.

He lowered his voice and turned away from the tee box. "That's the last bloody time I want to hear any of us taking out after each other. Now, Jerrold's correct on one point, and that's that those people over there aren't stopping us from making birdies. While they're playing smart and thinking about how to play each hole and behaving like a team, we're whaling away like it was Sunday morning at Connaught and each of us was out for himself."

"I thought the whole idea here was that they were gonna lose on purpose," Aronica said, knowing that Savitch wanted to say it but couldn't after Perrault's stern admonishment.

"It may still be," Perrault answered, "but that's not to say they're simply going to lay down and die. If they did that, their scam would be too obvious. We've at least got to give them some kind of a game that'll make it appear a genuine contest, instead of fighting each other when we should be fighting *them*."

It was too self-evidently correct for Perrault to be wrong, and they all knew it. "So you think Jerry's take is right?"

"I'm inclined to. And I'll wager that if we can start putting up some birdies, they'll start shooting pars. We're down three holes now, and if we manage to catch them, we can offer to raise the bet."

"You think they'd take it?" Savitch asked.

"You bet your ass they'll take it," Chelovek replied. "The more they lose today, the more they'll think we'd be willing to bet on a rematch. So we should get all we can right now."

"But how do we know for sure?" Savitch persisted.

"We get a letter from the Pope, Deke." Aronica turned and spat on the ground. "I'm starting to see why Jerry thinks you're such a douche bag."

"Let's have none of that, Joe!" Perrault warned sternly. "See here, Deke. One never knows for sure. This is just a best guess, and we've already agreed to bet on it. I was under the impression you were of the same mind."

"I was, until they started beating us."

"Okay, listen—" Chelovek started to say.

"Don't get started again, Jerrold!" Perrault snarled. "Things are bad enough as it is."

"Gentlemen?" Eddie called to them.

"Be right there, Eddie," Chelovek yelled back. "Just listen, Pete, here's the deal: Let's start using our heads and play with a plan on every hole. Now, if we still can't start putting up birdies, we lose two large each, and who really gives a shit, right?"

The others admitted that it wasn't any more than any one of them could lose on a Sunday morning. "But if we start draining birdies," Chelovek went on, "one of two things is gonna happen. A, they're gonna start shaving and we win some holes, or B, they keep playing like they have been. If it's B, we're out the same two grand, and we still don't give a shit."

"But if it's A," Aronica finished for him, "we raise the bet."

"Exactly. Even if they just keep it real close, we raise the bet."

"I'm for it," Perrault said. Aronica concurred.

"But what if it's just coincidence?" Savitch said.

"Then I personally beat the living shit out of you with a Nicholson until you're dead," Chelovek said evenly. By "Nicholson" he'd meant a five-iron.

"I'm for that, too," Perrault said. Aronica concurred again.

"Grab your three-wood, Deke," Chelovek commanded, and the thoroughly cowed Savitch obeyed.

"DEKE," CHELOVEK SAID AS THEY walked to the tee box, "I want you to hit the safest shot you possibly can, just like the broad. No heroics, just put one in the middle. Pete, you try to do the same."

"Everything okay?" Eddie said as the foursome came up.

"No," Chelovek said lightly. "We're losing, case you haven't noticed. Needed a little team meeting, get ourselves back in the game."

"Quite understand," Blanchard said. "Bit of an upsa-daisy, boost the old spirit, eh?"

"Yeah, whatever. You're up, Deke. Smooth one out there."

Savitch knew that his friends were now committed to the cause, and despite his misgivings, he didn't want to be the guy who let the team down, especially considering he was the best golfer of the four. He did his best to put aside all that had gone on thus far as he addressed his ball and neatly hit it about 230, not as perfectly dead center as Kirkland's, but about twenty yards farther.

"I say, fairly struck, Deke!" Perrault shouted, and Chelovek and Aronica joined in to chorus their approval, the first time that day any of them had shown any kind of spirited enthusiasm.

"Think that'll be okay?" Savitch said. "Wasn't quite dead center."

"Didn't have to be," Chelovek answered, trying his best not to let Savitch's insistent lack of self-confidence ruin the moment. "Pete, get on up there and do the same."

Perrault teed off with a three-iron, his safest club, and put one within twenty yards of Savitch. They now had two reasonable opportunities to stick one close to the pin and make a birdie.

"Okay, Joe," Chelovek said. "Might as well come right on out of your shoes."

And Aronica did, blasting a driver with everything he had. It didn't have the accuracy of Pensecoeur's drive and was also a little shallower and banged into a tree, but he got a lucky break and the ball kicked out onto the fairway.

"I think that woulda gone past Étienne's," he announced, "if it hadn'a hit that tree. I hit it as hard and it was lower, so it woulda run a lot. Look how far it got after it came off the tree."

Chelovek gritted his teeth. "No doubt there, Joe. Great shot."

"You dropped your shoulder a bit, is all," Perrault said. "Stay through it a touch longer next time, you'll be okay."

Chelovek was up last and tried to draw the ball in over the trees on the right, but it went absolutely straight and dove into the woods somewhere.

"No problem," he said as he came off the tee box. "We got three good ones out there."

Out on the fairway. Pensecoeur was a natural to play out the hole, and even though Eddie was about forty yards closer to the green than Kirkland, he picked up his ball so Kirkland could play hers. She hit a seven-iron but barely made it onto the green.

"Bit thick, Selby," Eddie called out, with not an iota of criticism in his critique.

"Yep," she responded. "Should have stepped back half an inch."

Aronica's ball was closest to the green, but Chelovek, arriving after fishing his own ball out of the woods, said that Savitch and Perrault should both play and Aronica should pick up. "Why?" Aronica asked. "I'm closest."

"Because you're all inside one-ten, and it doesn't make much difference who's closer, so let's just go with the guys who have the best approach shots, which is Deke and Pete."

"You're not even in this hole!" Aronica complained. "How come—"

"Let it rest, Joe," Perrault said, menace in his voice.

"But—"

"Nobody wants to hear it. Now, stand aside."

As Aronica got out of the way, Perrault pulled out a gap wedge and started to get himself lined up but then abruptly backed off and put the club across his shoulders, his hands dangling from either end. "Bloody hell, Joe!"

"Whud I do?"

"You put me off, that's what you did. Put me off when I need to concentrate!"

"Okay, no problem, take a blow, Pete," Chelovek said soothingly. "Deke, whyn't you go first?"

Savitch grabbed a sand wedge and took a full swing with it, lofting it high and straight, dropping it down barely ten feet from the cup.

"Don't you even think about bitching, Deke!" Chelovek said with a big smile. "That was a beauty."

"I'll take it," Savitch said. "Come on, Pete. Pull yourself together and put one inside'a me."

"Hey, I'm sorry, Pete," Aronica said, walking up. "Go ahead, knock one stiff."

Perrault easily shook off his annoyance in the face of that apology and got back down over his ball. His trajectory was shallower than Savitch's, but it wasn't hit as hard, landing well short and releasing beautifully to set up an eminently makeable five-foot birdie putt.

"Nice pair'a shots, boys," Eddie said. Pensecoeur had already walked up past the tree line and stood aside while the other had hit. He had a pitching wedge in his hand but bladed the ball slightly, causing it to hit low and hard and skitter past the pin to the back edge of the green.

He was the first to putt and left it nearly four feet short. Kirkland was next and had a perfect line but was also short, though only by about two feet.

"Pick it up," Savitch said to her, conceding a par to the owners, and Pensecoeur picked up his irrelevant ball as well. "Okay, Pete, one of us gotta drain this puppy."

"Do it," Perrault said. "Take the pressure off me."

Savitch knelt behind the ball and held up his putter to plumb the line. "Hers was dying left," Perrault observed about Kirkland's putt, which had been on the same side of the green as Savitch's but not on exactly the same line.

"C'mere and have a look at this," Savitch said. "I think she had a lot more right-to-left than I'm gonna."

Perrault looked over his shoulder and nodded in agreement. "I'd venture two cups, no more."

"Yep." Savitch stood up and positioned himself over the ball.

"And no sense risking it short either," Perrault threw in. Savitch didn't respond but looked straight down, took a deep breath and hit. The line looked good, but it was fast. If he missed, he'd shoot way past the hole, but he didn't care. Par was a given; what they needed was a birdie, so it didn't make any difference if a missed putt ended up past the hole, but leaving the birdie putt short would be a sin.

The ball shot over the lip, smacked into the back edge and dropped in.

"Hallelujah!" Aronica called from the sidelines. "Hell of a putt, Deke!"

Savitch walked up to the hole and bent over to get his ball. "Darned good thing you told me to hit it hard," he said to Perrault. "I think I woulda babied it."

Perrault slapped him on the back. "I saw the others come up short, so I assumed it was slow."

"Nice bird," Kirkland said. "Your hole."

Chelovek was grinning as Perrault and Savitch came back to the cart. He made a fist of one hand and held it out, and Savitch hit it with his own, then offered the same back. "Just one thing," Chelovek said.

"What's that?" Perrault asked suspiciously.

"You shouldn'a conceded that putt to the broad."

"You gotta be kidding, Jerry. She coulda nailed it with her eyes closed."

"Nothing to do with that." Chelovek pointed back to the green. "The Haitian was away, so he woulda putted first. He would have shown you the line, Pete, but once you conceded the broad's putt, his was dead, and he just picked up."

Aronica stared at him for a second, then said, "Jeez, you're right. Never even thought of that."

"What if she'd gone ahead and putted first anyway?" Perrault asked.

"We can insist," Chelovek responded.

Chelovek *was* right: If someone else's ball is lying along the same line to the hole as yours but is farther away, there's a huge advantage in having him putt first so you can see how his ball behaves on the way to the cup.

But the rules say that once you concede an opponent's ball, and his or her partner can't possibly improve the team score anymore, the hole is over for them. So there's no requirement to actually make the putt, and he simply picks up the "dead" ball.

Chelovek's insight was that, because conceding is a purely optional courtesy, they didn't have to concede Kirkland's short putt. That would have obligated Pensecoeur to putt before her, since he was farther away from the hole, and he would have shown Perrault the line.

However, Chelovek forgot a little something while he was pontificating on his knowledge of all things devious, but we'll get to that later.

"If we're gonna insist on stuff, then why didn't we make Blanchard tee off first?" Savitch asked. "He had the honors. That way they wouldn't have known Selby was going to hit safe, and maybe Pensecoeur wouldn't have taken the chance of walloping such a huge shot."

"Now you're thinking, Deke," Chelovek complimented him. "Except that honors on the tee is just an unofficial tradition; who putts first is a rule. We can insist on the rules, but otherwise . . ."

"Okay, we've gotten one back," Perrault said. "They're only up two now."

"Gentlemen," Aronica said as he got back into the cart, "I think the game is finally afoot."

"One thing you didn't include in your little list of possibilities, Jerry," Savitch said as he got in next to Chelovek.

"What's that?"

"That we could beat them straight up, no baloney. That we could just out-play them."

Chelovek sat with his hands on the wheel, not moving. "Anytime, Jerry!" Aronica called from the cart behind.

"You're right," Chelovek said as he pressed the accelerator, which released the toe brake with a clank. "That didn't occur to me. I wonder why."

"I don't know, but I think we can take 'em, if we hunker down and get back into our own game instead of worrying so much about what *they're* doing."

ON THE EIGHTH GREEN, EDDIE was eighteen feet from the hole and Pensecoeur less than twenty inches. They were both lying two. Eddie hadn't even gotten out of his cart, assuming our boys would simply concede Pensecoeur's birdie. The Haitian stood near his ball expectantly, waiting for the official word for him to pick it up.

But Savitch's ball was between Eddie's and the hole. If Eddie putted first, he'd show Savitch the line, which wouldn't happen if they conceded Pensecoeur's putt because that would end the hole for the owners.

Glancing slyly at Chelovek, who beamed approvingly from the cart, Savitch pointed to Pensecoeur's ball and said, "Mark it, please."

"You're kidding," Kirkland said from somewhere behind him.

Savitch shook his head. "It's Eddie's putt."

Before Kirkland could express some appropriate indignation, Eddie got out of the cart holding his putter and said, "Not a problem. I'll go."

Perrault and Aronica watched smugly as Savitch set himself off to the side to get a good preview of how his own putt would roll based upon how Eddie's ball behaved on its way to the hole.

Eddie, no trace of resentment on his face, didn't stop to read the green but took up his stance—at right angles to what it should have been—brought the putter up around his shoulder and whacked his ball off the green and about 130 yards into a small pond bordering an adjacent fairway.

"I missed," he said, then returned to his cart.

AFTER CONCEDING PENSECOEUR'S BIRDIE, BUT not without first casting Chelovek a murderous glance for having made him look like a complete jackass, Savitch made his own putt, and the hole was halved.

On the ninth, Chelovek sank his birdie putt and Eddie missed his. They were down only one at the turn.

Perrault felt himself getting stoked. "I must say, gentlemen, we're playing most excellent golf here." He pulled his cart up abreast of the other, tossed a banana to Chelovek and passed an orange to Aronica.

"Damned straight we are," Aronica agreed. "Nothing more we can do except do what we're doing."

"Only wish we'da gotten in the groove a little earlier," Savitch said.

"I think it's okay," Chelovek said as he negotiated the jungle path to the tenth tee, slowing down near one of the benches. Mambo the monkey appeared on a branch but hung back, unsure of the situation, until Chelovek whistled and held out what remained of his banana. Mambo hesitated for just a second, then jumped to the roof of the moving cart, reached down to snatch away the banana and jumped back into the trees. "We keep this up, I think it's in the bag."

"So what do we think?" Perrault asked. "Time to boost the wager?"

"Gee, I don't know," Savitch bleated.

"How about this," Aronica suggested, quickly, before Chelovek could turn on Savitch. "If we win the next hole, we offer to double the bet."

"Any problem with that, Deke?" Perrault asked.

"No, not—"

"Good. Then that settles it."

Chapter 20

⠴

T HE TENTH WAS A PAR-THREE, just 140 yards but tricky as
hell. The area in front of the green dropped off so steeply that anything
falling short would roll backward into a depression about fifteen feet down
and twenty yards back. Bunkers guarded the left and right sides, and behind
the green the ground angled sharply upward, so not only the green but all of
the area surrounding it sloped from back to front.

"Who should hit first?" Savitch asked.

"Doesn't make any difference on a par-three," Aronica surmised. "Does it,
Jerry? We all just try to get it close and go with the best?"

"I think it does make a difference." They were standing well off to the side,
allowing the owners to go first. "Somebody's gotta get on early and ensure at
least a par. Then the rest of us can try to stick it close."

"So we let Deke hit the safe one?"

"No." Chelovek flashed Perrault an enigmatic smile. "He goes last."

"Yep," Aronica concurred. "Because Deke's got the best chance of getting
close. If he plays the safe one, we waste him, so the rest of us are gonna buy
the insurance."

"Ah . . ." Perrault purred, seeing the wisdom.

"Watch these guys," Chelovek said, motioning toward the tee box.
Technically, the foursome had the honors and should have teed off first, but
by implied assent nobody on either side had been paying any attention to that
procedure since they'd started play. "Ten bucks says Eddie goes first, not the
broad."

And so it was, Eddie hitting a nine-iron onto the front of the green that released and rolled but did so a little fast, ending up about eight feet behind the pin.

"Damn!" they heard him mutter.

"What was the matter with that one?" Perrault asked.

"Downhill putt," Savitch replied. "Gonna be a bitch on that green. You gotta stay short."

Aronica scratched at his temple. "But you risk dropping down into that gully."

Pensecoeur hit next. His shot looked much too fast and shallow, but it hit just before the green and, instead of rolling backward, had enough momentum to pop up into the air a few inches and come to rest on the green. He was still twenty feet from the flag, but it was an uphill putt.

"They got their par in the bag," Chelovek said. "The Brit and the broad can go for it now."

"Wish you'd stop calling her that," Aronica said. "She really seems awfully nice."

"She's just another stuck-up broad."

"Meaning she didn't fall for your line of horseshit," Aronica said.

"Quiet down, the two of you," Perrault scolded. "She's hitting."

From the instant she struck the ball, Kirkland's shot looked like it could go straight into the hole.

"My word!" Blanchard exclaimed as the ball reached the top of its trajectory.

"That's all over the pin!" Eddie chimed in as it began descending.

"Fuck *me!*" Aronica whispered as it accelerated downward.

There was no doubt in anybody's mind that Kirkland was going to end up with a tap-in birdie. "Stick!" Pensecoeur commanded through gritted teeth, willing the ball to stay put when it finally touched down. All eyes left the ball and focused on the likely touchdown spot on the grass.

A fraction of a second before the ball was due to land, a sickening clang sounded, the flagstick shuddered, and the ball disappeared.

Nobody spoke for a second. Then Savitch called out toward the owners, "What the heck happened!"

"Hit the stick," Eddie said with a wide grin. "Bounced off into the bunker."

After it struck the flag, the ball had changed directions so suddenly that Savitch and a couple of the others who'd been focusing on the grass surface hadn't seen it streak away sideways and down, then plop unceremoniously into the sand trap on the left side of the green.

"Hell of a shot!" Eddie said to Kirkland, who'd dropped her club to the ground and was bent over, face in her hands.

She stood up and took her hands away. Laughing, she said, "Isn't that like a do-over or something?"

"Rub of the green, bitch," Chelovek muttered under his breath with undisguised glee.

"Damnit, man!" Perrault said. "Can we do without that?"

Blanchard hit last for the owners and made the green, but he'd pulled it slightly and was way to the left.

"Okay, boys," Chelovek said as he led his partners to the tee box. "Let's win one for the Deke. Everybody forget about the pin and just get on somewhere."

Aronica teed up first and hit a high, arcing shot that dropped down almost vertically and stuck to its landing spot six feet below the flag.

His friends erupted in happy shouts, and even the owners applauded and called out their congratulations, all of which ended as abruptly as it had begun when Aronica held up his club and announced, "Sand wedge."

Into the braggadocio-induced pall Chelovek said, "Now we can all go for it. *Fuck* hitting it safe."

None of them came close to duplicating Aronica's shot, but Savitch was the closest. Aronica never got a chance to putt, because Savitch made his birdie first. Then they stood away expectantly and hopefully, but to everyone's amazement, including his own, Pensecoeur sank his twenty-footer and got a birdie for the owners.

"No blood," Eddie announced, "but damned nicely played all around."

Chelovek threw his arm around Savitch as they walked off the green. "Outstanding Deke. Keep that shit up, we'll be fartin' in silk by dinnertime."

Exhilarated by his performance, Savitch said, "What the heck, guys—let's bump that bet up!"

"Thought you wanted us to win another—"

"Never mind. We're cookin' on all cylinders, we birdied the last four holes—who gives a hoot if you read 'em wrong? I say we can beat 'em anyway!"

"How 'bout it, boys?" Chelovek said.

ON THE ELEVENTH TEE CHELOVEK stretched his arms way over his head and leaned first to one side, then the other. "Took us a while to get cracking," he said to Eddie, "but we are most definitely in the groove now."

"You think so, huh?" Eddie responded with a grin. He tilted his head up and sniffled a few times. "So, Selby, whaddaya think?" He sniffled again. "You smell, uh—what is that now—a *proposal* of some sort in the air?"

Kirkland frowned, licked her finger and held it up as she looked around. "Why . . . I do believe you're right, Eddie. What do you suppose it could be?"

"What it could be," Chelovek said, looking at Eddie and doing his best to ignore Kirkland, "is a slight modification in the wager."

"Do tell."

"What say we double it?"

"My, my," Blanchard said as he walked up from the rearmost cart. "Is someone feeling his oats this fine morning?"

"We all are," Chelovek said brightly. "I think my boys here are gonna birdie their way in, and I think you guys are toast."

"You're down one now, Jerry," Eddie said. "If we birdie our way in, too, you're gonna lose."

"So let's start off even."

"You mean forget the one-hole lead?"

"Why not?"

"Why not?" Eddie stroked the bottom of his chin with his thumb. "Because right now we got two G's each in the bag, so why do we wanna forgive our lead?"

"Because you might win a lot more, but why would we agree to increase the bet if we start off one down?"

"Bird in the hand, Eddie," Pensecoeur said. "It's an absurd bet."

Chelovek attempted to look casual, even though his theory was starting to fall apart. He'd been certain the owners would try to lose a substantial sum to set them up for another match.

"No problem," Savitch said. "Let's just keep on going."

Disappointed, and sensing a shroud settle over the lightness he'd been feeling since the seventh hole, Chelovek turned away and started back toward his cart.

"Tell you what . . ." he heard Eddie say, and the shroud swirled away on a gentle breeze.

Chelovek winked at his friends and turned back again. "Whatsat?"

"If we give up the lead, we could be here all day playing off extra holes, everybody keeps dropping birds."

"So . . . ?"

"So let's play two best scores combined, instead of just the one lowest. That way we're less likely to halve so many holes, and it'll be a lot more fun."

Chelovek sensed a warm glow start in his chest and suffuse itself through-out his arms and legs. He could practically feel raw endorphins squirting their Prozackian geniality into every one of his cells. Eddie had just created the absolutely ideal method of the owners throwing the match without any hint that they'd be doing so on purpose. Just one hole out of the next eight on which the foursome scored two birdies and the owners only one, or birdie-par against two pars, and that was all it would take.

Chelovek pretended to think about it, but all he was doing was taking the time to make sure his voice would sound normal when he spoke. "Hmmm . . ."

He turned to his partners. "Whaddaya say, fellas?"

"Four grand?" Savitch asked.

"What the hell, let's make it an even five," Eddie said.

Chelovek held his hand in front of his chest and made a thumbs-up only his friends could see.

"Sure, why not?" Savitch said.

Chapter 21

∷

THE ELEVENTH WAS A PAR-FIVE, 520 yards from the middle tees. The foursome went first, and each of them hit well, aided by a moderate tailwind. Savitch laid down a safe three-wood of about 230 yards, Perrault did the same with his driver, Chelovek got to 250, and Aronica put everything he had into his swing and cracked a 285-yard monster cleanly to the middle of the fairway. It was their best combined performance off the tee since they'd arrived at the resort.

"*Sacrebleu!*" Pensecoeur cried out in mock alarm. "A few pennies are wagered and you become changed men!"

Smiling, Perrault walked back to the cart and put away his club. "Just took ten holes to get warmed up, is all," he said good-naturedly. "You folks played nine first, remember."

"Great shooting," Eddie said as he took the tee box. Nobody even needed to look to know he'd put his drive about 265 right down the middle with the tailwind. Blanchard did roughly the same, and then it was Pensecoeur's turn.

"Do we need ear protection, Étienne?" Perrault inquired amiably. "In case you go supersonic or some such?"

"My only hope, *mon ami*," Pensecoeur said as he bent over to tee his ball, "is that the cover does not burn from the friction."

He smiled at the guffaws and catcalls that came back as he straightened up. He worked the grip in his hands a few times and looked out toward the hole in the far distance, took a few big practice swings and then carefully got himself set up and aligned. The smile disappeared as he grew still over the ball.

Pensecoeur's backswing was quicker than usual, and his body swayed slightly as the club reached its apex. When he swung, he brought himself back to center and then past it as he seemed to throw his entire body down into the ball, shoving it forward with every piece of him that wasn't firmly planted on the ground. Watching, some of the onlookers got the feeling that he might literally fly right out of his shoes.

It seemed inconceivable that the ball could physically survive such an impact. With the sound of a brick dropping onto a steel rail, the ball rocketed away with such velocity that it seemed destined to visit another layer of the atmosphere on its journey.

But Pensecoeur had hit it too far to the left, and it was headed away from the fairway. "Uh-oh," he muttered.

"It should come back," Perrault said.

"How do you—" Pensecoeur started to ask but stopped as the ball indeed began to curve to the right.

"You came out of the shot a little," Perrault said. "Came across the ball and spun it right." *Good thing you lined up wrong and hit it to the left,* he didn't add out loud.

That they could have that much conversation while the ball was still in the air was remarkable in itself, but not half as remarkable as how this shot was turning out. Because of the enormous amount of hang time, the tailwind added some 30 yards to Pensecoeur's drive and set him down an astonishing 345 yards from the tee. At least that was the estimate, because none of them could actually see something as small as a golf ball at a distance of a fifth of a mile.

"Good one," Aronica said, not realizing how absurd that sounded until everyone else began laughing.

"Think I'll just kind of mosey on back to the cart," Kirkland said with her usual self-deprecating good humor, not bothering to take her own shot.

Eddie patted her on the head. "Too bad we're not playing scramble."

"You'd have to give us four a side," Perrault joked, but in reality it probably wouldn't have been an unreasonable proposition.

Aronica was sitting 235 from the green and was an easy call to play out the hole, but Perrault balked when Chelovek said Savitch should be the one to join him.

"I don't get it," he said. "I'm practically right next to Deke, so how come he's playing? In fact, how come he plays every time he's safe?"

"Because he's a better golfer than you," Aronica answered before Chelovek could.

"Well, perhaps, but that still doesn't—"

"What's your beef, Pete?" Chelovek asked. "I'm twenty yards ahead of both of you, and I'm not playing."

"So what's the implication here . . . he automatically plays every hole and I sit out?"

"Matter of fact, that's about the size of it. Bottom line here, Pete, our only job is to back Deke up."

"Might I ask why? No offense, Deke."

"I told you. He's the best golfer."

"Look at it scientifically," Aronica said, ignoring the resultant groan from Perrault. "If we had to pick just one guy to play for all of us and the rest had to sit out the whole round, who'd it be?"

Perrault shrugged rather than giving the obvious answer.

"Well, it's the same thing," Aronica went on anyway. "Statistically, Deke's got the best chance of getting low score on a hole if he's in decent position, so we always let him play if he can."

There was no escaping that logic, and it made no real sense to be retrospectively critical once a decision had been arrived at based on it, even when Savitch, made nervous by the interchange, chunked his next shot horribly and sent it wobbling toward some shrubbery on the right. The clump of dirt he'd dislodged flew farther than the ball, which, fortunately, hit something hard at the base of the bushes and dribbled back out into sight, but just barely, and still nearly 180 yards from the green.

"Well, Jesus still loves me," Savitch said.

"Maybe," Chelovek mused. "But everybody else thinks you're an asshole."

Perrault couldn't suppress a haughty posture as he turned to walk back to the cart, but Savitch didn't notice it. "Thing is," he said, "I just thought of something."

He and Chelovek walked toward Aronica's ball together as Perrault veered off to bring up the cart. "What'd you think of, when you weren't thinking about your shot?"

"This format?" Savitch said, pointing to Eddie, some thirty yards ahead. "It's very unforgiving of a bad shot."

Aronica caught up with them in the cart and drove alongside. "How so?"

"Before," Savitch said, "if somebody screwed one up, we still had another guy left to try to win the hole. But now . . ."

"You're right," Aronica said. "We gotta add up the two remaining scores, regardless. One guy screws up, it's pretty much lost."

Chelovek considered it. "The owners can screw up, too, you know."

Savitch shook his head. "One thing I noticed, Jerry: As a group we can pretty much hit as good as they can—"

"You bet, and that's what we been doing since—"

"But they make fewer mistakes."

There was no arguing with it, and just like that, their entire strategy was in serious jeopardy. "What you're saying," Chelovek concluded, "we gotta start playin' it safe?"

"What's going on?" Perrault said when they all met up. Savitch ran it down for him quickly, and Perrault saw right to the heart of it. "That's not gonna win it for us. Not against these guys."

"No, it isn't," Savitch agreed. "Rats!"

"Hang on a minute," Chelovek said. "Maybe it will."

"How do you figure?" Savitch asked.

"It'll work if they're planning to throw the match. All we gotta do, we gotta play it safe, score well and let them execute their strategy."

"What if you're wrong?" Savitch said, and this time nobody criticized him for it. They'd bumped the bet up to five thousand a man largely on Chelovek's read of the situation.

"Well, lemme put it to you this way," Chelovek said. "What's our alternative? If I'm right, we're going to win if we keep our heads and score two guys reasonably well on every hole. And if I'm wrong—"

"Then we're in a real match," Perrault said, "and we still have to play it safe so we don't get killed."

"I agree," Aronica added. "And I still think Jerry's right anyway."

Perrault did, too. "As long as we put on a good show, they'll let us win."

"I hope you're right," Savitch said, to the surprise of no one.

EDDIE HIT NEXT AND, PREDICTABLY, elected not to go for the green 255 yards away but laid up to excellent position with a 200-yard three-iron.

Aronica hesitated over his own shot. "I'm two thirty-five to the green, Jerry," he said. "I gotta go for it."

"I think you should."

Aronica pulled out a five-wood but dialed in too much fade. It blew wide of the green and landed about thirty yards to the right of it.

As his lips tightened and he looked down at the club ruefully, Savitch said, "What the heck's the problem, Joe?"

"What's the problem? I hit the damned thing too far to the—"

"So what?" Savitch said, smiling and slapping the side of Aronica's arm. "If you'da laid up, it wouldn't have been one darned bit better than where you are now!"

Aronica brightened immediately at this insight, then started to raise his club.

"I know, I know," Savitch said, spinning on his heel and walking away quickly. "It was a pitching wedge."

"You can still get a par out of this, Deke!" Chelovek called after him. "You got a clear shot to the green!"

Savitch waved without looking back. Up ahead, Pensecoeur was evaluating his shot. He was only 175 yards out, lying one. "Don't even think about the flag," Eddie said. "Just grab a six-iron and go for the fat of the green."

Pensecoeur nodded as Eddie stepped away and got his club for him. "Nice and smooth, ET."

Nice and smooth it was indeed. Our boys looked on with a mixture of awe and horror as Pensecoeur's ball sailed inexorably for the hole, ending up a very makeable ten feet away.

Savitch tried to shake off the earlier unpleasantness so he could do something useful with his ball, which was cozied up against the bushes. "I'd move heaven and earth to par this hole," he said somewhat wistfully as he analyzed his options.

"Well, you'd better move heaven," Perrault said, pointing back to the hole in the ground still visible from where Savitch had hit his last shot, "because you already moved the earth."

"Very funny. I'm going for it."

Savitch managed a heroic escape from the bushes. It didn't quite make the green but was an easy chip and a putt away from a par. Aronica got on safely as well, and would have about a twenty-footer for birdie, and things were starting to look up a bit until Eddie hit up and planted his ball less than two feet from the pin.

Too shocked even to make a pretense of sportsmanly congratulations, our boys simply stood there with their mouths hanging open. Eddie walked to his ball and stopped, looking around without picking it up. "You boys all got lockjaw or you really want me to hit this thing?"

Perrault was the first to swim back to the surface. "Oh, bugger . . . sorry, Eddie, wasn't thinking. Go ahead and pick it up."

Eddie looked inquiringly at Savitch and Aronica. There were no rules to cover this situation, since the unusual format they were playing under had just been invented that week, but it seemed reasonable that only the two players who were still in the hole should be the ones making a concession. Flustered as they caught on to Eddie's drift, Savitch and Aronica tried to make up for their momentary lapse and overdid it. "Sure, sure you kidding? Pick it up, g'wan, you shouldn't even'a waited . . ."

"Hell of a birdie there, Eddie," Chelovek said, and Eddie saluted his thanks.

Savitch was up next and chipped it splendidly into the hole from off the green for a birdie, to the amazement of everyone and the ecstatic delight of his partners. Inspired, Aronica concentrated intently on his putt until Chelovek, knowing how much grief he could be in for by stepping in at this crucial moment, said, "Hold it, Joe."

Aronica looked up, glaring, but held his tongue as Chelovek approached, hands up defensively. "Sorry, bud, really. But just to make sure . . ."

"What?" Aronica said icily.

"Don't leave it short."

"No shit."

"What I mean is, if you miss, we're gonna lose the hole, so there's no reason to worry about going past it and messing up your next putt. There isn't gonna *be* a next putt, get me? It goes in or we lose, 'cause there's no way in hell the Haitian's gonna three-putt from ten feet out."

Aronica looked down at his feet for a few seconds, then back up at Chelovek. "Got it."

"Atta boy. Now drain the fucker."

Chelovek stepped off to the side, and Aronica once again assessed the line and bent over his ball. He looked to the cup and back a few times, then the ball only. Making a perfect pendulum of his arms and shoulders, he brought the putter back and then didn't so much hit it into the ball as let gravity naturally swing the club down and forward so as not to lose the rigid triangular structure he'd created.

There was plenty of speed on it, and even though there was a very evident left-to-right break, it wasn't affecting the ball's path as much as it might have had Aronica hit it softer. More break kicked in as the ball slowed, but he'd read it beautifully, and just as the curvature began to increase even more, the hole was suddenly right there, and the ball disappeared straight down into it.

He raised his arms in triumph as his partners cheered loudly and with little regard for traditional decorum. There was a good deal of backslapping and high-fiving and fist-bumping and joking around and then Pensecoeur made his putt for an eagle and the foursome lost the hole and Chelovek's Theory of Scamativity disappeared right down the cosmic Porta Potti with all the dignity of a gnat splattering into a windshield.

Chapter 22

❖

"W E ' R E   S T I L L   G O N N A   W I N   T H I S , you know," Chelovek said.

"Stick it in your ear, Jerry," Savitch said.

"I'm already visualizing the duct tape over your mouth" was Aronica's contribution.

"What the hell did you numbskulls expect the Haitian to do!" Chelovek bellowed. "Purposely miss a putt for eagle? How many'a those you figure the sonofabitch gets in a year!"

"Like I said, stick it in your—"

"See here. Quiet down, will you!" Perrault admonished.

Nobody was rising to Chelovek's defense. "So what are you warriors telling me?" he demanded. "That you're giving up? You're quitting? You're just gonna let these guys walk away with it without even putting up a fight?"

"You screwed it up, Jerry!" Savitch whined. "You said—"

"I swear I'm gonna pop you one!" Chelovek threatened, looking like he meant it. "What the fuck difference does it make if I screwed it up . . . you can shoot me later, okay? Right goddamned now we're still playing golf!"

"But—"

"Jerrold is correct," Perrault said. "We've still got a match going here."

Eddie had called for a cigarette-and-soda break, summoning the beverage cart by radio. Our boys were sitting off by themselves in the cool shade of a banyan tree. They were depressed and gloomy out of all proportion to the money at stake, and it wasn't lost on any of them that the owners seemed to be behaving as if they were on a picnic rather than in the middle of a high-stakes contest. Blanchard sat in the cart happily sipping a beer, Eddie was stretched out on the grass smoking a cigarette, his back propped up against the wheel well, and Kirkland was trying to balance a four-iron on the end of one finger, lurching comically all over the place as the two men cheered her on. Pensecoeur knelt near some bushes, trying to get a pair of skittish chipmunks to eat out of his hand.

"Well, *they* certainly seem to be having a gay old time," Aronica said morosely.

"I daresay we would as well if we were winning," Perrault shot back.

"If you ask me—" Chelovek started to say.

"Nobody's asking you," Savitch spat.

"If you ask me, those guys would probably be behaving the same way even if they were losing."

The other three knew, without knowing how they knew, that Chelovek was right. That did little to enhance their affection for him, and despite his vaunted insight into the human psyche, he had no idea how fine a line he was walking at that moment, which happened to be the same moment he inadvisedly chose to endow them with yet another nugget of Chelovekian sagacity. "Trust me," he said glibly. "They're still gonna throw it away."

Perrault loudly slapped both his knees and swung his legs out of the cart. "You know something, Jerrold?" he said as he stepped out and walked forward to confront Chelovek head-on. "I'm getting mighty irritated with you, professing a Ph.D. in human nature with all this brilliant insight and keen instinct you claim to possess!"

Chelovek was taken aback but rallied quickly. "I know a thing or two, *Doctor*, shit they don't teach you in a fancy medical school while you're taking apart dead people! Shit, I learned watching live ones!"

"Yes, you're quite the student, you are." Perrault put one hand on his hip and the other against the roof of the cart, looking down at Chelovek. "You make a living selling second-rate bits of useless bric-a-brac to immigrants newly off the boat before they even have a chance to breathe and wake up to how you're exploiting them."

Chelovek, startled by the outburst, needed a second to find his tongue but fired before he was fully loaded. "First of all, buddy, I don't *sell* anything. My clients do. All I do is adver—"

"Well, now *there's* a truly striking distinction!"

"And second of all, nobody's ripping anybody off! My clients are the only ones who care enough about new Americans to take an interest, to address their needs, and—"

"Oh, spare me!" Perrault stepped away from the cart and flapped both hands dismissively at Chelovek. "Boat people risking their lives to buy cartoon images of Princess Di printed on a plate? Yes, I've seen some of those preposterous commercials. You confuse the devil out of those people so they barely know what they're buying or why!"

Now Chelovek got out of his cart and stood up so he could gesture more forcefully. "That's total bullshit, Pete! I got principles, so don't you—"

"Principles?" Perrault fairly shrieked. "What manner of principles are involved in cheating on your wife with anything in a skirt that comes within a seven-iron of you!"

Savitch winced and turned away. Aronica grunted softly, as if in pain, and did the same.

Chelovek folded his arms across his chest. "So let me ask you something, Pete. You mind?"

"No, you just go right ahead."

"Fine." Chelovek unfolded his arms and put his forefinger a centimeter from Perrault's nose. "What the fuck business is it of yours!" he shouted.

"You've no sense of decency, that's what! The reason we're even playing this stupid match isn't so we can go toe-to-toe and give it our all; it's because you thought you could boomerang their own scam back on them! The whole thing's a bloody charade!" He pronounced it "Sha-rod."

Chelovek, incredulous, stared at Perrault, then looked to Aronica and Savitch and back again. "You hypocritical sonofa—I don't remember hearing any *bloody* complaints when you thought it was working!"

"Never liked the whole idea to begin with," Perrault sniffed lamely. "It's like cheating them."

Chelovek laughed and turned away. "Y'hear that? Mister High-and-Mighty here feels bad about cheating people better'n they're trying to cheat him!"

"Goes against my principles, is all. Whole thing's dishonest."

"Ah." Chelovek scratched at a nonexistent itch on his chest and walked to the cooler sitting on the ground near the back of the cart. "Well," he said as he opened the lid and looked around inside, "that's pretty damned hysterical coming from a guy who spends most of his time stealing money from his patients."

Chelovek savored the sudden silence and the renewed attention he knew he was receiving from Savitch and Aronica. He put his hand into the cooler ice and stirred it around, pretending to look for something but really just making noise. "No snappy comeback there, Dr. Principles?"

"What are you talking about, Jerrold?" Perrault said quietly.

"Nothing much." Chelovek tapped his chin a few times, then reached farther down into the cooler and pulled out two beers. He snapped the top on one as he stood up. "You order up tests for your patients, then you send them to labs you own to get them done, except the labs don't have to do a goddamned thing except send back made-up results because there was no need to do the tests in the first place, except you get to bill the living hell out of the HMOs."

He took a long sip of beer and walked back to the front of the cart. "And you can't get caught, because you dribble a piece of the action back to everyone involved, so who's gonna blab that the tests never really got done?" He held out the second can. "Beer?"

Perrault stared dumbly at Chelovek, then reached forward without really thinking about it and took the can, then let his arm fall to his side without opening it. "And you come by this knowledge how?"

Chelovek grinned maliciously. "Focus groups, my friend. Focus groups."

"I don't get it," Savitch said.

"Nothing to it, really," Chelovek explained. "Those immigrants Pete thinks we're ripping off, we meet with them in groups and listen carefully to what's on their minds."

"So you can be sure your clients meet their needs, right?" Perrault sneered.

Chelovek laughed it off easily. "Just keep it up, Pete. One of the things they told us, see, was about this terrific deal they get from these great clinics up in Connecticut. Man, they say, those guys up there, they give us the works! No expense spared!"

His eyes narrowed with mirth, Chelovek paused to take another sip of beer, then wiped his mouth with the back of his arm. "What a country, this America!" he said with his arms spread wide.

"Where you going with this, Jerrold?" Perrault challenged.

"Well, I'll tell you, *Doctor*." Chelovek brought his arms back down. "Seems that the only ones getting all this incredible medical service are the ones who have jobs with large corporations. Mostly it's things like cleanup crew or parking attendants, but they're on the payroll. Full-time employees, every one of 'em."

"They have insurance," Aronica concluded for him.

"Indeed they do," Chelovek confirmed. "And who do you suppose runs those clinics and is only too happy to take these lowlifes in—you know, the same people he says *I've* been exploiting—and is so concerned about their welfare that he orders up MRIs and CAT scans for perfectly healthy people who just come in for a checkup?"

"Not our very own Dr. Perrault!" Aronica cried theatrically.

"His own self," Chelovek said, resuming his seat in the cart. "And then cooks the books so the IRS doesn't see all of that dough coming in."

"And everyone thinks he's a genius for making money in medicine when nobody else seems to be able to." Aronica looked down and shook his head. "You're some piece'a work, Pete."

Before Perrault could jump to his own defense, Savitch, sitting cross-legged on the grass, stepped in. "I wouldn't be so quick to get on the man's case, Joe. Not when your own hands aren't exactly clean as a baby's bottom."

"You're full'a shit, Deke."

"That so?" Savitch stretched his legs forward and leaned back on his hands. "I know a thing or two about your miracle metal, what the heck do you call it . . . ?"

"You know damned well what it's called!"

"Arondium, yeah. Sounds like a hip-hop singer, you ask me. Where d'you get your raw materials, Joe?"

"What's it to you?"

"To me? Nothing. Except you been trying to sell licenses to produce the stuff for Christ-only-knows how long, and the big boys can't figure out why nobody's biting. And part of it is, they're thinking maybe this guy is scoring second-rate materials in Third World stinkholes and passing it off to buyers as aircraft-quality. Now"—Savitch stood up and brushed off his pants—"that wouldn't be true, would it, Joe?"

"It's a complete crock of shit and you know it, Deke. I been fighting those rumors for years."

"Yeah, you been getting a raw deal, all right. Straight-shooting guy like you, it's a real shame."

"How do you know all that, Deke?" Perrault asked.

"Everybody on the Street knows it. It's the only reason Joe can't take his company public: Who wants that kind of risk in this day and age?"

"Well, who in the holy flaming hell are you to talk, Deke?" Aronica stepped over to Perrault and pointed to the unopened beer in his hand. Perrault, still somewhat stunned, handed it over mechanically.

"You got a problem with what I do?" Savitch asked.

"Do?" Aronica snapped open the top of the can and considered the trickle of foam that appeared in the opening. "What you *do*?"

"Yeah. You even know what I do?"

"I know what you do, Deke. I'll *tell* you what you do." He took a sip of beer and licked his upper lip. "You do *shit*, that's what you do!"

"That's what you—"

"You're a leech, Savitch." Aronica pointed at him with the can. "You sit in front of a bunch of computers all day long doing the same thing my blue-haired grandmother does in Vegas, which is basically pull the handle on a souped-up video-poker machine. You make bets on other people's companies, but you don't contribute a damned thing to any of 'em."

"There's not a thing wrong with—"

"You don't *do* anything, Deke! You didn't invent anything, you don't provide a service, you don't put capital into a business—you might as well just be shooting craps."

"So I take it all your dough's in a bank account, right?" Savitch argued back. "Don't own any stocks, no mutual funds—"

"Least I don't do it for a living," Aronica replied halfheartedly.

"Spoken like the hypocritical jerk you are. Who do you buy your investments from, Joe—elves?"

"I say, Deke," Perrault said, "you know what I've always wondered? That fellow Greg reminded me."

"Can't imagine. What about the *fellow*?"

"All of those financial talk shows . . . Why do they keep interviewing brokers all the time?"

"Who else is gonna know about investments?"

"But it's rather like interviewing a car salesman and asking him if this would be a good time to buy a car. Doesn't matter if the market's up, if it's down, if there's a war starting or one ending—these people will always tell you this is a great time to be in stocks no matter what's going on. So what's the point?"

"The point is," Chelovek said before Savitch could answer, "what kind of a schmuck who gets paid on commission would tell you not to buy?"

"I'm talking about the schmucks who ask the question, Jerrold. And aren't a lot of those broker chaps paid by companies to tout their stocks?"

"Deke sure as hell is," Aronica said.

"So how come you don't disclose that when you make a recommendation?"

"No law says I have to. What am I supposed to do, cut my own throat?"

"Sounds deceptive."

"It's perfectly legal," Savitch averred defensively.

"Legal!" Aronica crushed his now empty beer can with one hand and threw it into the cart, where it landed with a loud clatter. "Cheating on your wife's legal, too; doesn't make it right."

"And you're a big contributor to society, that it, Joe?" Chelovek asked, knowing full well the last crack had been aimed at him.

"At least I manufacture something. Whatever else you think of it, at least something comes out of what I do."

"You don't manufacture shit. You sub it out and somebody else makes it. Don't remember hearing any machines humming last time I was in your office."

"I invented it. And it's making airplanes safer."

By now Perrault had had about enough of this self-aggrandizement as well. "Safer?"

"You got it."

"Who do you think you're kidding, Joe? I heard that bit with Carlos, about building planes without windows."

"You got a problem with that?"

Perrault shrugged. "Depends."

Savitch looked up with interest. "On what?"

"On one's motivation. Now, the way I heard it—and correct me if I'm wrong here, Joe, because I've certainly no wish to impugn your integrity—but the way I heard it, the only reason Boeing even bought your miracle metal in the first place was because you agreed to lead the charge on windowless airplanes."

"That's horseshit."

Chelovek, ever alert to a good con, sniffed one in the air now. "What's this?"

"Oh, yes," Perrault said. "If Boeing itself ran such a campaign, everybody would suspect them. But our man Joe here, he doesn't make airplanes, so his heart is as pure as the driven snow. Right, Joe?"

"I don't get it," Savitch said. "If it's a safer way to make—"

"Because they'd save four million a plane on production, Deke, which is what this is really all about. And if they really cared so much about safety, then they wouldn't have used . . ."

Perrault's voice trailed off as Aronica, listening but staying quiet, got slowly to his feet. "Wouldn't have used what, Pete?" His voice was thick with menace.

"Ah . . ."

"What!"

"Hey, c'mon fellas," Chelovek said pleadingly. "Don't let's start getting—"

"How about it, boys!" they heard Eddie shout from across the fairway.

Aronica continued to glare at Perrault, who looked like he was awaiting permission to end this and get back to the game.

"Come on, Joe," Chelovek said again, and Aronica finally relaxed the tension that had overtaken his body and made him lean forward threateningly.

Perrault let out the breath he hadn't even realized he'd been holding. As he walked past the front cart to his own, Chelovek stepped into his path and said, "There's a limit, Pete," before letting him by.

Adversity in the face of a common foe often has a unifying effect, but not this time. Within the space of ten minutes the dam that had been holding back over a decade's worth of pent-up hostility and mutual distrust had burst open, leaving our boys shaken and confused. And there were still seven holes to go.

"You okay, Deke?"

"What?" Still distracted, Savitch glanced around before realizing it was Eddie who had spoken. "Uh, yeah. Course I'm okay. Why?"

"You were rubbing your chest. Sure you're feeling a hunnerd percent?"

Savitch quickly dropped his hand. "I'm fine."

"'Cause we don't gotta keep on—"

"I said—"

"He's quite fit, Eddie," Perrault said smoothly. "I'm keeping an eye on him."

"Okay, Doc. Just don't feel like you gotta, you know— It's just a game, right?"

"Understood. You needn't concern yourself."

Chapter 23

∺

THE BOYS WERE BARELY SPEAKING to each other. They even let Chelovek resume his captaincy, just so they could avoid extended conversations and reserve maximum mindshare to brood over the damage wrought by the sudden savagery with which they'd assaulted one another. The private hurts they nursed were mixed in with misgivings about the relative weight that ought to be assigned to the truth of what they'd each been confronted with versus the carefully nurtured rationalizations that had protected them for years.

It was hard to concentrate on their games at first, but then they realized that the only times they could get the unpleasantness out of their minds were when they were able to focus completely on the shot at hand. Giving themselves over to that became a kind of therapy, and after losing the twelfth hole because they'd been too busy wallowing in self-pity, they halved thirteen and won fourteen but were barely even aware of what that meant.

"Hey." Savitch was sitting in the cart at the fifteenth. "We're only down one with four to go."

"Just noticed that," Aronica said from the cart behind.

"Wasn't aware we were playing all that well." Perrault, still pensive and tense, reached for the scorecard clipped to the steering wheel. "Are we coming alive here?"

Aronica, in a subtle attempt to demonstrate some kind of reconciliation, quickly removed it and handed it over. "Sure are. We went birdie-par on the last two."

"And they just had par-bogey." Chelovek got out and stood up, waiting.

"Par-bogey?" Now Savitch got out. "They haven't put up a bogey all day!"

Chelovek didn't say anything but let it hang there, until Perrault finally got the message. "They're dumping it?"

"Gee, Pete, I don't know," Chelovek said sarcastically, but it was mild and might even have passed for amicable. "Why don't we find out?"

The best they were able to mount on this hole were two pars. The owners did the same, but, as Chelovek so aptly put it, what more could have been expected? The boys didn't really think they'd dare put up another bogey and make the whole thing too obvious, did they?

"We gotta do better," Aronica concluded.

It's hard to "do better" in golf. It's not like a footrace, where you can reach way down inside and find an extra burst of energy to take you over the finish line. Try to "reach way down" in golf or "give it everything you got" or "win one for the Gipper," and you'll blow your game completely, even though sports commentators liked to import such metaphors from strength and endurance sports.

Golfers know better. They know that you can't will yourself to putt straighter or judge the line better or stop the lob shot quicker or draw it more severely around the trees. Golfers know that the only way to bring it home is to utterly forget why you want to bring it home in the first place and just concentrate on this particular shot at this particular time and never mind why it's important.

So when Aronica said they had to do better, he didn't mean they should try harder. All he meant was that they should get back into their own games, the way they knew how to play already, and instead of finding ways to improve, simply remove the obstacles that were keeping them from playing their best.

Chelovek and Savitch both birdied the fifteenth for the win. The match was all square with three to go.

Walking away from the green, Perrault said to Aronica, "Don't mean to compromise our momentum, but I must ask: What did you mean when you said I was stealing from my patients?"

"Ah, shit, Pete, forget about it, okay? I was just pissed off on account'a—"

"No, it's all right. Just, what did you mean by that specifically?"

Embarrassed now, Aronica didn't really want to get into it very deeply. "I have to provide health insurance for my employees. The HMO says it lost too much money last year, they gotta raise my premiums, and now I can't give out the raises I'd promised. Some of my people, they made plans based on those increases, bought some stuff on time or had vacations planned—stuff like that."

"And?"

"And they all got together and decided to go with reduced coverage, on account of they'd pretty much spent the dough already. So I got my premiums back to where they were and gave them the raises, but now . . ."

He didn't have to finish. Perrault knew where he was heading because he heard it all the time: A good chunk of an HMO's losses came from scams run by unscrupulous medical practices. "You've a goodly number of immigrants in your place, right?" he said after a while.

"A few."

Perrault nodded grimly. "Were I to guess, it would be that a lot of that money they're spending goes for useless knickknacks that Jerrold's clients purvey."

They halved sixteen and seventeen, and it was all square going into the last hole.

Chapter 24

■

CHELOVEK SAW IT AS HIS job to keep the excitement level in check. He didn't think the owners would risk exposing themselves by posting another bogey if they needed it, so the boys needed at least a par and a birdie to bring the match in.

The eighteenth is a stunning finishing hole, a 580-yard par-five that starts out on a tee box sitting nearly a hundred feet in the air, which effectively takes 50 yards off the distance. The fairway far below is unbroken except for a creek running directly across it and feeding into a lake on the left that stretches right to the green, then drops off and runs down a spillway all the way to the ocean.

Eddie was standing near the tee box with them. "What do you need to clear the creek?" Aronica asked him.

"From here," Eddie said, noting the placement of the tees, "figure maybe two-fifty in the air."

"In the air. Huh."

"This format," Chelovek said, "we need to put out a couple safe layups and then let Joe try to whack it over the agua."

"We should do better," Aronica suggested. "Jerry and Pete, you hit two safe ones, then Deke, you get as close to that water as you can without going in."

"No," Chelovek countered. "Can't risk Deke getting it wet. I'll be the guy takes that chance."

"Well, then," Perrault said, "step on up and have at it."

Chelovek nodded and took a ball from his pocket. He walked over to the washer and spent a long time cleaning the ball, looking out somewhere else as he worked the handle up and down. When it seemed that he was in danger of washing the cover right off, he removed it from the holder and began wiping it with the towel hanging below. Slowly.

Eddie looked at Chelovek, then toward where he was staring, a spot that at the moment happened to be occupied by Kirkland, who was making use of the delay by performing some deep stretches to keep her back loose. Eddie walked to the ball machine and turned his back to his own playing partners.

"Listen," he said quietly, "I'd really appreciate it if you stayed away from the female visitors and staff. You get what I'm tellin' you?"

Chelovek looked as if he'd been punched in the stomach. He dropped the ball right out of the towel and began stammering out denials. "I wasn't . . . I was just . . . I don't know what you're—"

"Uh-huh." Eddie, his calm demeanor in stark contrast to Chelovek's flustered fumblings, bent down to pick up Chelovek's ball, then put it in the washer and gave it a couple of quick pumps. He wiped it off and reached for Chelovek's hand, turning it upward and dropping the ball into it. "You're that hard up, I'll provide a limo to the local cathouse, okay? Now go hit your shot."

It was like ordering a diamond cutter to make the crucial hammer blow five seconds after you told him he had a brain tumor. Nearly trembling, Chelovek thinned the shot and sent it shooting out parallel to the ground. It hit the fairway and ran all the way to the creek, where it dribbled over the bank and into the rushing waters.

It had been a mistake to let Chelovek go first anyway, without seeing whether Savitch and Perrault would have decently playable shots. Had he known what was going to happen, he would have gone for a safer layup rather than try to get it so close to the creek.

As a result of what had happened to Chelovek, Perrault got tentative on his shot instead of just hitting it. He pulled it badly, stopping just short of a rock wall, landing in the rough 100 yards shy of the creek, and that meant Savitch had to play ultrasafe. He put a two-iron down the middle but still had 320 to the green.

The pressure was all on Aronica now. Chelovek was out of it, and Perrault had nearly 380 left and a lousy lie to start with, and that meant Aronica had to hit a playable ball. Savitch could probably par, but a birdie would be difficult, so Aronica had two choices: play it safe and go for the par, which would probably mean two pars for their side and make it very difficult for the owners to tank the match without its being obvious, or try to smash one over the creek and give himself a birdie opportunity but risk blowing the shot and the match completely.

Aronica came to the only logical choice before the others did. "I gotta go for it."

Perrault was still eyeing his awful lie way down below. "Indeed."

"Don't worry about it, Joe," Savitch said. "Nobody's gonna give you any grief if it doesn't work."

Buoyed by the murmurs of assent from Perrault and Chelovek, Aronica took his driver and teed the ball while the others moved to his left to get out of his peripheral vision. The owners, some thirty feet away, stood still and watched.

Aronica took his stance and looked out at the fairway. "Gonna take it out left and let it come back."

Chelovek picked up some loose grass and let it drop. "Wind's pure left-to-right, Joe. All that hang time from up here, give it a little extra and you'll be all right."

Aronica nodded and shifted his feet so that his alignment faced a few degrees more to the left. He gave the fairway a last look, then put it out of his mind and beamed all his attention at the ball. Taking a deep breath and exhaling completely, he remained motionless for about two seconds, then brought the club back smoothly, much slower than usual, and visualized an iron bar from his forehead to the ground that made it impossible for his head to move even a centimeter left or right.

He took his backswing to the straining point, but not so far that it would pull him out of the shot, and kept his arms fully extended as he brought the club back around as hard and as fast as he could without losing his form. Just before impact he brought the right side of his body into the swing, as though providing an extra push that would ensure that his hands didn't bounce back but thrust every bit of his power irresistibly into the ball.

Chelovek caught his breath as soon as the sound of the titanium clubhead slamming into the ball reached his ears. Even before his eyes could pick up the ball in the air, he knew that Aronica had hit an immense shot, and done so with commensurate precision. He heard a very feminine and admiring "Oh!" escape from Kirkland but fought the urge to look at her and followed the ball instead.

As Aronica had intended, it took off left of the fairway centerline, and as

Chelovek had suggested, it did so alarmingly, crossing the rock wall just above where Perrault's ball was sitting far below. In short order, succumbing to both the spin imparted by the club and the strong offshore breeze, it stopped moving left and reversed direction, picking up speed until it was clear to everyone that it was going to be a feat difficult to surpass.

The ball was still fifty feet in the air as it crossed over the creek, its rightward drift running out of steam, and when it finally came to rest—reluctantly, it seemed—in the very middle of the fairway, it was barely two hundred yards from the green.

Applause erupted, from the owners as well, and Savitch held out a fist for Aronica to bang with his own. "You and me, fella."

When the clapping died down, Perrault let out a whistle and said, "Thank heavens I don't have to play that monstrosity I hit," and the applause turned to laughter as his partners, elated by Aronica's performance, surrendered the tee box to the owners.

"One hell of a shot there, Joe," Eddie said as they passed.

Chelovek started to take a wide berth around him, then mentally slapped himself in the head, thinking, *Why the hell am I letting this guy intimidate me?* "Hey, Eddie . . ."

When he'd caught up, Chelovek said, "What's with the staff in this place? How come everybody's so familiar?"

"Familiar?" Eddie kept walking as he spoke, so Chelovek did the same.

"Yeah. Like they got no respect. Calling us by our first names, actin' so casual. Like that Carlos guy on the plane . . . jeez, you'da thought he was coming on vacation with us. Where do you train these people anyway?" Chelovek had the feeling Eddie wasn't used to having his precious Swithen Bairn criticized.

Eddie stopped walking and turned to face Chelovek. "You call *them* by their first names. You call *me* by my first name."

It was one of the things I liked about the place, how everybody working there was a thoroughgoing professional and proud of it but none of them thought the paying customers were in any way superior. The service was truly incredible in every respect but didn't extend to simulations of medieval feudalism: Treat one of these staffers with anything less than the same respect with which they treated you, and you were likely to get an instant and unforgettable refresher course in the golden rule.

"Yeah, but I'm a guest!" Chelovek protested.

"So what? Your shit smell better'n theirs?"

"Seems to me, guests at a place like this, they got a right to be treated better."

"First of all, you're not a guest, you're a customer. And are you telling me somebody isn't doing his job?"

"No, but—"

"The service too slow? The food no good? Somebody spill coffee in your lap?"

Chelovek had to admit that the service was the best he'd ever seen, if you didn't count the attitude.

"Attitude. In other words, you want them to treat you like a maharaja instead of an ordinary citizen, which is what you are."

"I'm not an ordinary citizen when I—"

"When you what—stay in a hotel? Somehow you turn into a fucking crown prince or something? If they're doing the job, how come you need them to grovel and scrape, too, tell me!"

Eddie didn't wait for an answer but turned and continued walking to the carts, Chelovek in reluctant tow. "What the hell is it about people with money, they can't have fun unless everybody around 'em is pretending they're slaves." He shoved his club angrily into the bag. "That somehow enhance the experience for you?"

"I just don't expect to be insulted."

Eddie turned around to face him. "Who insulted you?"

Chelovek pointed off to the side. "She did. At dinner. Stood there and hurled insults at me in front of my friends."

"Why?"

"Why! What the hell difference does that make? I'm a guest, and she—"

"Listen: You just lodged a complaint, I'm investigating. Why did she insult you?"

"I have no idea!"

"So right out of the blue, she picks you out of everybody in the dining room and decides to give you a hard time."

"Well, not exactly," Chelovek said, backing off slightly. "But that's not the point, damnit! I'm a paying guest, and—"

"So she's supposed to stand there and just take it when you leer at her and make crude remarks and generally treat my daughter like a Seventh Avenue hooker, is that what you're trying to tell me?"

"Your daughter!"

Eddie didn't say anything at first. Then, "No, she's not. But she mighta been. For damned sure she's *somebody's* daughter."

Chelovek didn't answer. He'd expected Eddie to be chagrined and apologetic and to promise to get it straightened out, just like every other resort operator he'd ever encountered. He hadn't expected *this*.

"Let me tell you something, Jerry," Eddie was saying. "You got off easy. Was me, I'da gone after your nuts with a fork."

THE OWNERS PLAYED PREDICTABLY. EDDIE hit safely to within ten yards of the creek, the best layup shot so far on that hole. Blanchard's was almost as good, sitting some ten yards back of Eddie's.

The boys had assumed that Kirkland wouldn't bother to hit—she hadn't on several of the longer holes—but she did, and put her ball just between and slightly to the right of her two partners'.

Which left Pensecoeur, who bounded happily to the tee box knowing he could go hell-bent for leather without worrying if he screwed up. He belted a good one, not taking it out as far left as Aronica had but also hitting it lower, so that it wasn't as affected by the wind. It looked for a moment like it might not clear the creek, but it did, and its low angle kept it running after it touched down. It stopped about fifteen yards short of Aronica's.

"Nice one," Aronica said, with a smug glance at his partners over his having outdriven the Haitian.

"Thank you," Pensecoeur said simply as he walked off the tee box, and that looked like all he was going to say until Kirkland called out, "What the hell did you hit, Étienne?"

Aronica whipped his head around. "The hell's she mean, whud he—"

"Three-wood," Pensecoeur answered without elaboration.

"Three-wood!" Savitch echoed in wonder but let it go when he saw the grim set of Aronica's jaw.

Aronica's partners didn't know if he could hear what they heard Eddie say to Kirkland: "You can tell people how great you are, but if you really are, they'll tell *you*."

AFTER THEY ALL DROVE DOWN the hill, Perrault veered off to pick up his ball, then swung around to meet up with the other cart at Savitch's.

"That was a smart shot, Deke," Chelovek was saying when they arrived. "Mighta saved our asses."

Savitch took a three-wood and hit a beauty to within seventy yards of the green.

"It's a good man comes through when his chums are up against it," Perrault remarked as he got back into his own cart.

"Ain't that the truth." Chelovek slapped Savitch's knee and started moving up to watch the owners. They assumed that Eddie and Pensecoeur would be the ones playing it out.

Perrault suddenly slammed on the brake, causing Aronica to grab on to the side rail to steady himself. "What the—"

"What's she doing?" Perrault said pointing.

"Looks like she's hitting," Chelovek said as their carts pulled abreast. "But that's crazy. She's way over three hundred out."

Blanchard, stooping to pick up his own ball, held up a hand for them to be quiet, and they waved their apologies as Kirkland took her stance. She wound up into a backswing much deeper than any they'd seen her take all day, and there was some wincing as they doubted whether she'd even connect with the ball on the way back.

But connect she did, and with a beautiful follow-through that brought the club well over her left shoulder until it pointed at her right shoe, which was poised, toe down, as she held the position and watched the results of her shot. Her ball came to rest less than twenty yards behind Savitch's.

"Yikes," Savitch said softly.

"Seemed a bit risky," Perrault said.

Chelovek thought for a second and said, "She turned it into a hundred-and-thirty-yard par-three." They all knew that Kirkland was devastating on short par-threes. "All the Haitian has to do now is take it easy, and they'll have a good shot at a pair of birds."

They drove toward the small wooden bridge that would take them over the creek. "Hey, where ya going?"

Chelovek and Perrault both hit the brakes and glanced to their left, where they saw Eddie standing over the ball he hadn't yet picked up. Seeing non-comprehension in the two drivers' eyes, he pointed down and said, "We're playing this one."

The four of them turned as one in the other direction, just in time to see Pensecoeur pick up his ball and drop it in his pocket.

"He's gotta be kidding," Perrault said.

"If you think he's kidding about that," Chelovek said, "look what he's got in his hands."

Sunlight glinted from the ground at Eddie's feet. "An iron?" Savitch said, blinking against the glare. "He's hitting an iron?"

"It's not even a long one," Aronica added.

It was in fact a seven-iron, and Eddie hit it about 170 yards. Not even bothering to wait for it to drop, he put the club back in his bag and was sitting in the cart by the time it fell, landing about 100 yards from the green.

As his cart approached, Chelovek held up a hand and called out, "I don't get it."

"Get what?" Eddie replied, slowing to a stop and fishing a cigarette and lighter out of the driver's compartment.

"You hit a middle iron. Why not something longer and get closer?"

Eddie lit the cigarette and turned his head to exhale away from them. "Because I'm deadly with a sand wedge at a hundred yards."

What Eddie meant was that if you know you can't reach the green, getting as close as possible may not be as good a strategy as getting the ball to a point where you know you can take a full swing with your most accurate club.

Aronica jammed his foot down on the accelerator, and they took off with a lurch. "Well, fuck that," he said as they headed for his ball. "This one's going on the green."

It didn't, but it was close. A pitch and a putt, and he could grab a birdie.

Kirkland was up first and got out of the cart with an eight-iron already in her hand. She was just about to assume her stance when Blanchard called out, "Don't hit the flag this time!"

She backed away, laughing. "I'll just get it close, okay?"

"Don't get it too close," Eddie warned with more seriousness. "Flag's way back, and you don't want it rolling off."

Setting herself so the ball was well forward in her stance, Kirkland swung smoothly and lofted it high into the air. The shot took off slightly left, but the winds aloft began to move it back to the correct line.

"I don't believe this," Savitch said.

The ball didn't hit the pin this time but landed short, released and rolled to within four feet.

Nobody said anything for a few seconds. Then Eddie spoke. "You missed the hole."

Kirkland held her club up and looked at it. "Must have taken the wrong stick."

"Splendid shot, Selby," Perrault said, trying to look the good sport. Pensecoeur was on his knees bowing to her with exaggerated movements, and she did a little curtsy before standing by the cart to watch Eddie hit.

"Ain't no girl gonna outshoot me," he said loud enough for everybody to hear.

"Hundred bucks says you don't get inside," Kirkland proposed.

"I'd give her a hundred to get inside," Chelovek mumbled.

"Shut up, Jerry," Aronica scolded.

"That's a bet." Eddie waggled his sand wedge a few times and let loose, his shot an almost perfect replica of Kirkland's. As it started down, it looked as though he'd given it just the bit extra it might need to pull closer to the flag than hers had. It certainly looked as if it landed closer, but it also released more and was moving faster along the grass. It ended up past the pin and within inches of the back edge of the green.

Kirkland took a few steps to the side to get a better perspective, then stopped abruptly and began walking back, one hand in the air and rubbing her fingers together.

"Booger." Eddie reached into a back pocket and pulled out his wallet, from which he withdrew a hundred-dollar bill. As Kirkland reached for it, he pulled it away. "Double or nothing?"

"Nope," she answered and tried to grab the hundred, bumping hard into Eddie as she did so, causing them both to land in a heap on the ground.

Chelovek again said something, barely audible but easily guessed at, and his friends elected to ignore it. As the giggling Kirkland leaped to her feet and raised the bill in triumph, Eddie said, "Jeez, it was a hunnerd bucks, not a freakin' kidney."

She offered a hand and pulled him to his feet. "Never mind the hundred, Eddie—I beat *you*, that's what counts!"

"Knock down an old man . . . no respect . . ."

"I'm glad they're having so much fun," Savitch said. "I still got a shot to hit here."

Chelovek waved him and Aronica over as the owners regrouped. "Nothing fancy," he warned them. "Just get yourselves on clean. If you guys par, they will, too, and we'll have a playoff hole."

"But if one of us birdies, we'll win it!" Savitch objected.

"Can't take the chance of screwing up, Deke. Gonna be tough enough for them both to purposely two-putt. Force 'em to three and they won't do it. So just play it safe, and if you get a birdie opportunity, fine. But play it safe!"

Chelovek and Aronica stepped back to the carts as Savitch walked to his ball carrying a sand wedge.

"Right for the fat, Deke," Chelovek said encouragingly, Aronica and Perrault declining to join in support of what was essentially to be a cowardly shot.

Eddie and Kirkland had by now sorted themselves out and were standing by the carts with Pensecoeur and Blanchard. None of the owners said anything as Savitch hit safely to the center of the green, it being very apparent that he hadn't even attempted to get it back to the flag. Having set the ball down precisely where he'd intended and therefore assuming he could have been equally precise had he gone for the flag, Savitch cast Chelovek a mildly rebuking look as he came back. Aronica grabbed some clubs and walked to his ball, which was off the green to the right, while the rest of them drove to the path behind the green.

They stayed off and waited for Aronica to pitch up. Chelovek took a step forward as he noticed Aronica lining up directly for the flag, but Savitch grabbed his belt and held him back. Chelovek had no choice now but to keep perfectly still and hope for the best.

It was an excellent shot, hitting the edge of the green and bouncing to a stop about twelve feet from the cup, and this time Savitch and Perrault were vociferous in their appreciation. Savitch and Aronica were away and would putt before either of the owners.

Savitch took his time and plumbed the line carefully as Aronica came to stand behind him and help him with the read. "You see the speed on mine?"

"A little," Savitch answered as he closed one eye and sighted along the putting line. "Looked like it might be slow."

"Yeah. I'm seeing right-to-left here, maybe a foot."

Savitch stood up. "I'm going firm, though. Figuring maybe two cups right, tops."

Aronica, who'd caddied in his youth, was savvy enough to know that you didn't second-guess a final decision and disrupt a man's confidence. He waited a few seconds to show that he was giving it careful consideration. "Yup," he said definitively. " 'Zackly what I'd do. Uphill, so don't be shy."

"Okay." Savitch bent down and gave his putter a few practice swings as Aronica got out of the way. Then he took up his position and got oriented to the spot of brown grass about four feet away that he'd picked as his aiming guide. With one final look at the hole to confirm his distance and one last adjustment to the alignment, he put the line and the hole and the match out of his mind and concentrated only on bringing the club squarely to the ball so it would slide precisely over that brown spot, and swung.

He'd had to hit it hard, and the ball skittered at first, which meant it wouldn't really feel the break until it bit into the surface and began a true roll. Once it did that, though, the line looked excellent, as did the speed.

"Ho, ho!" Perrault yelled out as the ball continued on its way, and it looked as if the birdie was in the bag.

"Get there!" Eddie yelled in sportsmanlike encouragement.

He knew what he was talking about. Aronica and Savitch had both seen that it was uphill but hadn't taken into account how the slope increased closer to the hole. The ball was running out of steam more quickly than they'd thought it would.

Aronica saw it first. The ball might have enough speed to reach the hole, but Savitch's plan to hit it firm and take out some of the break was starting to look like a bad idea. It's difficult to use speed that way over a long distance, and now Aronica could see that as the ball began slowing dramatically, all of that break was kicking in and dragging it farther and farther left.

It missed by a good six inches but only went about two feet past. Blanchard walked up to it and kicked it back toward Savitch. "Fine par," he said. "Devilish putt, that."

"Good effort, Deke," Perrault called out, and it was Aronica's turn.

He waved Savitch over. "Way yours turned," he said, "mine's gotta be downhill from here."

"Definitely. But you sure as hell can't leave it short."

"Hmmm." Aronica bit a fingernail and thought it over. "What I'm thinking—"

"Just like your tee shot," Savitch guessed. "You gotta go for it. Never mind what's left if you miss."

He slapped Aronica on the back and walked away. Chelovek waved him over and said, "What's he gonna do?"

"He's gonna put it in the hole," Savitch answered curtly, "unless you got a better plan."

Not having to worry too much about speed or break, Aronica didn't leave himself extra time to get shaky. He lined up, got square and hit it.

Right into the hole.

Shouts of joy rose from his partners, as did admiring plaudits from his opponents. They had a birdie and a par, for a team total of 9.

Kirkland and Eddie both had birdie opportunities. If at least one of them two-putted, they'd have no less than 9 themselves.

"He's the one's gonna miss," Chelovek said confidently. "It's easier to swallow than if the broad blew it from four feet."

Eddie sank the putt.

"Okay, no problem," Chelovek said. "My guess, she'll leave it short. Broads, they do that."

Kirkland didn't even look at the break, just hit it aggressive and straight and right into the cup.

Chapter 25

▪

"HELL OF A MATCH, BOYS," Eddie said as he walked toward the foursome standing at the edge of the green. "Right down to the wire, way it's supposed to be."

Chelovek, dazed, took Eddie's offered hand mechanically. "Yeah . . ."

"Excellent handicapping," Blanchard joked as he came forward to shake hands. There had been no handicapping at all, no strokes having been given by either side, and yet the entire match had come down to a single putt.

Savitch, not behaving much more alertly than Chelovek, somehow managed to get through the traditional handshaking ceremony without betraying his anxiety at having just lost five thousand dollars. The part of his brain that was still on patrol couldn't help noticing that the owners didn't seem to be thinking about the money; they were just happy to have won.

Aronica didn't see it that way. It seemed to him that they were happy just to have played well in the clutch, which they had. "Were you guys really on today, or was that, uh . . ."

"For myself," Pensecoeur said, pulling the leather glove off his left hand, "I must say this was a good day. An excellent day, as it were. My only wish, I had played a true round and kept my own score. Now I will never know."

"Same here," Eddie said. "At least about playing well. Couldn't care less about my score, though. If I had, I wouldn'ta hit so good. How about you boys?"

"Oh," Chelovek said quickly, "I think that was probably above normal for me."

His partners mumbled agreement. Now they were all on the record as having played better than they usually did, essentially neutering handicapping negotiations for the rematch and ensuring that once again no strokes would change hands.

"Can hardly wait to play you all again," Chelovek said as they began walking off.

Savitch pulled him away as discreetly as he could. "Are you nuts?" he whispered forcefully. "They cleaned our clocks!" He judiciously desisted from pointing out that Chelovek had misread the whole situation completely.

"They didn't clean anything," Aronica said, having overheard as he caught up to them. "They beat us by one stroke." When they arrived at the carts, he jammed his putter back into his bag. "And I'm not letting them walk off with my five grand and not get a chance to win it back."

"I feel the same." Perrault pulled tees and ball markers from his pocket and began stowing them in his golf bag. His mustache looked like it was twitching. "You ready to simply walk away, Deke?"

"Sure don't feel good about it. Feel a damned sight better if we get some strokes out of them, though. I think we may have got a little sandbagged there."

Chelovek had his ball poised to drop into a pocket on his bag and held it there. "You sayin' I didn't negotiate right?"

"You did fine, Jerry," Aronica said before Savitch could respond and start another battle. "You did fine with what we knew then. Now we know better."

"He's right." Perrault leaned against the cart and wiped his brow. "They were really good."

"That's all I'm saying." Savitch dropped into his cart and slumped against the back of the seat.

"How about a beer?" Eddie called out.

"Let's do it," Perrault said softly. "We can begin setting up the rematch."

"Sounds good!" Chelovek answered back.

"And, Jerry," Savitch added, no longer intimidated into holding back his opinion following the complete disintegration of Chelovek's theories, "no baloney this time. Let's just assume they're gonna show us their best game."

Aronica, quiet the past few minutes, was sitting in the rear cart holding a scorecard and making notations. He took away his pencil and sat back. "I'll tell you what," he said, flapping the scorecard in the air. "Way I figure it, these guys were playing pretty much to the handicaps Eddie told us they had."

"That's what I'm saying." Savitch was nodding vigorously. "Carlos was right."

Chelovek, feeling they were starting to gang up on him, said, "Right how?"

"He means," Aronica said, still holding up the scorecard, "that the owners were completely honest. There wasn't any kind of scam going on at all."

Chelovek turned away and pretended to make some adjustments to the straps on his bag. "Who says they didn't sandbag us today? How do we know we saw their best game?"

Perrault threw up his hands and let them drop to his sides. "Oh, for—"

"Follow us, lads!" Blanchard yelled out as the other two carts began pulling away.

Perrault noticed that Eddie was talking into a two-way radio.

THEY HERDED UP IN FRONT of the main house, where valets were waiting to gather their equipment. As the eight of them walked up the stairs, a short man wearing a business suit and a practiced smile greeted them. He raised his eyebrows questioningly at Eddie, who pointed to our boys and said to Chelovek, "This here's the Piper, Jerry."

"Nice to meet you, Mr. Piper."

Pensecoeur laughed. "Not Mr. Piper . . . *the* Piper. The one you pay."

"Oh . . ."

"Name's Saunders, actually. This way, gentlemen?" The Piper was holding a manila envelope and gestured with it, in a direction away from the bar.

Bewildered, the boys looked at Eddie, who said, "See you in a few minutes. We'll keep 'em cold."

They followed Saunders into a small but elegant office containing a conference table, a personal computer and a bank of telephones and fax machines arrayed against one wall. When they were seated, Saunders opened the folder and took out a sheaf of papers, from which he separated one and put the others aside. "What was the amount of the wager?" he asked.

"Um . . ." Chelovek looked at Aronica, who only shrugged in resignation. "Five thousand."

"Each, I presume?"

Chelovek nodded glumly. Saunders, smiling dryly, wrote something on each of what turned out to be four sheets and then began passing them out.

"What are these?" Perrault asked.

"Wire-transfer instructions. All properly filled out and awaiting only your signatures."

Perrault pointed to the sheet Saunders had set aside. "And that one?"

"Instructions to transfer money from Swithen Bairn into your accounts, but we shan't be bothering with that, eh?" His smile hadn't changed.

Aronica gave his sheet a cursory glance, took a deep breath and signed. Perrault and Chelovek did the same.

"Everything quite in order, Mr. Savitch?" Saunders inquired of the only one who hesitated.

"Sure. No problem. Only, uh . . ." Savitch looked around uncomfortably. "Can you send this tomorrow instead of today?"

Saunders, heretofore the bespectacled picture of accountant wimpitude, metamorphosed before their eyes into a menacing, powerful beast capable of snapping up grown men and chewing them into pulp without breaking a sweat. It was nothing any of the boys could actually put their finger on; before-and-after photos would doubtless have been identical even under a magnifying glass. Even the mirthless smile remained unchanged as Saunders sat there, motionless, hands folded patiently on the table in front of him, just as he had been doing. "Nothing amiss with the funds, I trust?"

Savitch gulped and wiped a trace of sweat from his upper lip. "No, no, of course not, nothing like . . . it's just . . ." He sighed heavily. "Today's the last day of the interest period, is all, and I figured, well . . ."

"Ah." Saunders half closed his eyes and reopened them as he nodded in approval. "Most astute of you, Mr. Savitch. Only too happy to comply."

"END OF THE INTEREST PERIOD," Chelovek sneered at Savitch on the way out. "Gimme a freakin' break."

"What's the point of—"

"What are we talkin' here, like thirty bucks, a month's worth on five lousy grand?"

Savitch turned away. "A week, actually," he mumbled.

"A week?" Chelovek threw back his head and laughed. "Eight bucks!"

"Lay off 'im, Jerry," Aronica said.

"Yes, by all means," Perrault said sarcastically. "His whole livelihood depends on small spreads, so what would one expect? There's Blanchard."

"Why don't you go to work, Jerry?" Aronica said. "Start setting things up before we go into the bar."

Chelovek, still chortling over Savitch's penny-pinching, tried to force himself to look serious as he veered off toward the Englishman. "See you guys inside."

"Ah, Mr. Chelovek," Blanchard said amiably. "Painful bit over, is it?"

"Wasn't so bad," Chelovek replied, waving it away as no big deal. "Besides, we're gonna win it all back and then some when we pull out our 'A' games and rake you guys over the coals." He gave Blanchard a big grin and swatted him on the back.

"A rematch, yes." Blanchard smiled gamely and took a step backward. "But, ah, I'm afraid there won't be a rematch, you see. Terribly sorry."

Chelovek frowned. "The hell you mean, no rematch?"

"Just that, actually. We shan't be playing again, hmm?"

Chelovek eyed the Brit suspiciously. "You're kidding me, right?"

" 'Fraid not, old boy."

"Well why the hell not!"

Blanchard looked around uncomfortably to see if anyone else had noticed Chelovek's blustery retort, then stepped in closer to try to keep things quiet. "You lads don't make a good team, you see. At each other a bit too much." He raised his eyebrows and shrugged. "If we can't see your best games, we'd as soon not take your money."

Chelovek, unable to think of anything to say, could only stare at him.

Blanchard dabbed the end of his mustache with a forefinger. "Enjoy the rest of your stay, what? Splendid place, this."

Like the mule who starved to death, unable to decide between two bales of hay, Chelovek remained rooted to the spot in the lobby, unable to decide between the equally odious alternatives of going after Blanchard to plead piteously for a rematch or facing the certain wrath of his friends who were waiting in the bar.

Eventually he chose the latter path. At least there'd be alcohol in the bar.

Chapter 26

⊞

(A depressingly short one)
Day Four

THE BOYS TRUDGED BACK OUT to the course the next day. What else was there to do?

Their play was desultory and laconic. Although still upset with each other, they couldn't even muster up the energy to continue the vicious disparagement they'd begun with such ill-considered timing the day before. Besides, having cranked that activity up to such a destructive level once, there really wasn't any way to scale it back to a more civilized level of sniping, so it was just as well they left it alone.

I could have warned them. Playing for big money with your friends as partners is like entering a road rally with your wife: If there were tethered mines hovering below the surface of the relationship, the pressure of prolonged competition would set them off as surely as if they'd been rammed broadside by an aircraft carrier. And even if there hadn't been any lurking ordnance to begin with, there would be by the time the day was over. I knew that from playing in the Ryder Cup, where one of the formats was "alternate shot," in which you and your partner play a single ball, taking turns hitting it until it was holed out. If one of you played well but the other kept screwing up, it might be years before you repaired the damage, if ever.

In the case of our foursome, a dispassionate outside observer would easily see that none of them could claim blamelessness for the juvenile behavior that likely had been the culprit in the loss of a sizable wager, not to mention the resultant, even more sizable humiliation: They were convinced that the entire resort knew the whole story and that the other guests were laughing at them.

But despite their insistent entreaties, the owners had remained steadfast in their refusal to play them again, intimating that their lack of sportsmanship had no place at Swithen Bairn.

Each such refusal lent credence to Deke Savitch's contention that they had not been the victims of any kind of scam, which of course only intensified their desire for a rematch. Savitch, not in possession of self-esteem to any great extent to begin with and therefore not overly preoccupied with its diminishment, was primarily concerned with the money he'd lost. For Jerry Chelovek it was more the loss of his stature as the worldly-wise, street-savvy, nobody-gets-the-better-of-me leader of the bunch. Joe Aronica nursed a very private pain at his inability to have played the hero at the crucial moment, and Pete Perrault, the pedagogical egotist of the group, was mortified at his failure to have stepped in and nurtured his weaker charges to a victory despite their collective shortcomings.

They went around the course with little zest, feeling like outsiders, emasculated not necessarily by their defeat in the previous day's match but by their inability to establish themselves as worthy opponents with a legitimate entitlement to have competed in the first place.

Earlier in the day Perrault had underestimated the hair-trigger mood of his friends. "Life is like photography," he'd tried to tell them at breakfast that morning. "Use the negative to develop."

It had almost cost him his life.

Chapter 27

✠

Day Five

THE FOLLOWING DAY WASN'T MUCH better.

"We lost control," Chelovek said as they slogged their way to the seventh tee. "That's what happened. We let ourselves be goaded into going after each other 'steada going after *them*."

"And how, exactly, did they do this goading, Jerry, hah?" Savitch was determined not to let Chelovek get away with unchallenged philosophizing. "What was it they did, got us all PO'd at each other?"

Aronica, finding the topic of their spiteful outbursts acutely uncomfortable, veered off slightly, as if to remove himself from the conversation Chelovek seemed bent on instigating. "Short par-four here."

"We know it's a short goddamned par-four, Joe." Chelovek threw his ball to the ground between the white tee markers. "Think any of us don't remember every last shit-ass chuckhole on the whole goddamned track?"

"Perhaps Jerrold's right," Perrault said. "Not about their having made us play poorly, but, damn it all, there we were so intent upon thrashing each other, we didn't even pull any of the usual shenanigans." The "usual shenanigans" being a scraped spike during someone's backswing, an equally well-timed cough or twitch while in their line of sight, a barely discernible derisive roll of the eyes after a bad shot and a solid dose of well-choreographed irritation following any similar tactics on the other side's part. Intimidation, humiliation, distraction . . . often effective and rarely provable.

"We weren't supposed to need the usual shenanigans," Savitch said. "A win was supposed to be in the bag, remember?" He looked at Chelovek unflinchingly, feeling confident and brave in his conviction. "Congratulations on *that* brilliant read of the competition from the self-proclaimed Marquis of Malarkey."

Perrault and Aronica braced for a strong reaction, but Chelovek merely stared back at Savitch and shook his head with mild contempt. "It's exactly that kind of unproductive, irrelevant, childish prattling," he said, flaunting his condescension by betraying not a hint of personal offense, "that got us into this mess in the first place."

As Savitch's face told the story of his instant reversion to slughood, Chelovek added, "I don't know about you, buddy, but I for one don't like being told by some faggoty-ass, limey soldier boy that I'm not good enough to play golf with him and his hoity-toity goombahs."

"Thing is," Perrault said, "whether they intentionally goaded us or not, there wasn't a blessed thing they could do to us that we didn't permit them to do. It's that simple, really. All we had to do was ignore them, stick together and just play the game.

"And what we did instead," Aronica finished for him, "we played like shit. They were good. We were shit. End of story."

They lapsed into glum acceptance of that simple analysis, and then Chelovek sighed and halfheartedly bent to pick up his ball and tee up.

"We can do better," Aronica said.

"Yeah, how?" Chelovek stood up and sighted down the fairway as he settled his hands around the club.

"Get off'a there," Aronica replied, pulling a club out of his bag.

"Huh?"

"Off the tee box. Take your ball with you."

Chelovek glanced at the other two. Perrault was looking in Aronica's direction and said, "Oh, pulling out the lucky clubs, are we?" He laughed loudly. "Yeah, boy, *that* ought to terrorize them mightily!"

"Gimme a break and cut the shit, Joe," Chelovek said, turning back to his ball.

Aronica strode up from behind him and kicked the ball off the tee. "Move over."

Something in Aronica's voice made Chelovek vacate the teeing area. Aronica put a ball on the tee he'd left behind and worked the club in his hands a few times.

"You're gonna hit an iron?" Chelovek guffawed, even as Aronica set up and got ready to hit. "Who the hell do you think—"

Ignoring him, Aronica took the club back and brought it down with his usual swing. The ball shot off the tee with a crack and streaked away, easing into a gentle arc before landing cleanly on the fairway nearly two hundred yards away.

"Nice shot," Perrault said laconically. "And what might your point be?"

"It was a seven-iron."

"Horsepucky," Savitch said, at the same time as Perrault said, "Oh, sure."

Aronica tossed the club at them without warning. Savitch winced and ducked, but Perrault caught it just before it would have hit them. He turned the clubhead up and looked at it, disbelieving. "What the fuck . . . ?"

"Gimme that!" Chelovek demanded as he strode over and yanked the iron away, only to confirm what Perrault already knew. By then Savitch had straightened up, and the three of them turned to Aronica, standing on the tee box with his arms folded across his chest.

"It's made out of Arondium," he said. "Same stuff I sell for tennis rackets bike frames, airplane rudders . . ."

Wordlessly, Chelovek walked to the tee box holding the club. Aronica gave way as he teed up a ball, took a few practice swings and hauled off. He landed more than twenty yards past Aronica's ball, but in the center of the fairway.

"It's slightly springy," Aronica explained, "but snaps back into place faster than any other substance known to man. So not only does the ball fly off the clubface faster, it goes the way your swing path goes, even if the face is a little open or closed."

As Chelovek stared dumbly at the club, Aronica turned to the others. "Just finish your swing toward the target, and that's where it's going."

"Is that legal?" Savitch asked.

Aronica laughed. "Hell, no, it isn't legal! Are you kidding? They'd have to build whole new golf courses if this club ever—"

Perrault, eyes growing wide, suddenly pointed behind him, and Aronica turned just in time to see a red-faced Chelovek screaming his way in his direction.

"You sonofabitch bastard!" the adman roared, choking in rage as he raised the club over his head. "I'll crack your goddamned skull, you no-good, lyin'—"

"Jesus Christ, Jerrold!" Perrault stumbled backward as Chelovek rushed past him, then recovered just in time to jump up and get his hands around the club that was about to come crashing down on Aronica's head.

Savitch quickly jumped to give Perrault a hand, finally leaping onto Chelovek's back in an attempt to slow him down. They fell in a heap, three pairs of hands now struggling to obtain sole possession of the club. Perrault finally won out, and rolled away from the other two.

Panting heavily and holding his chest, Savitch said, "What the hell got into you, Jerry!"

Out of breath himself now, but no less incensed, Chelovek sat up and pointed to Aronica. "That piece of shit's been cheating us for years!"

Realization now dawning, Perrault glanced back and forth from the club to Aronica and back again, his face growing dark. "Why, you—"

"Hey, hold it!" Aronica said forcefully, thrusting his hands out as if to stave off impending blows. "I never cheated you guys, okay? I only brought them out in tournaments!"

"Tournaments *we* were playing in!" Savitch countered, now catching on.

"Yeah, well . . ." Aronica cleared his throat. "Probably none'a you woulda won 'em anyway, right?"

"A man who cheats at golf," Perrault growled, "there's no telling what kind of deceit he's capable of. Or toward whom."

"You dumb chuckleheads are missing the point," Aronica said, sensing a lessening in the tension. "You wanna give me shit for conning pennies, fine, go ahead. But what I'm telling you here, I can give us the edge."

"Lemme see that," Savitch said to Perrault, who reluctantly handed over the club. Savitch looked it up and down and said, "You step up and hit a seven-iron one-ninety, one ninety-five, they're gonna break our thumbs."

"That one's a demo," Aronica replied. "To show you what it is. My full set, they're all mislabeled. That one there, that'd be a five in my bag. So nobody catches on."

"Won't they notice the loft angle's off?" Chelovek asked, his breathing almost back to normal now.

"What are they, carrying around protractors? Who the hell notices a thing like that? Shit, I bet the six in *your* bag's really a five!"

"That's true," Chelovek confirmed. "Clubmakers do that so you think their sticks hit longer."

"You'd know, wouldn't you, Jerry," Savitch said.

"Cut that shit out!" Aronica commanded. "Let's talk some business here!"

"What I fail to see," Perrault said, "is what the benefit is if it's simply mislabeled. Wouldn't it just be the same as using a longer ordinary club?"

Aronica shook his head. "I told you: not just farther, but straighter. Like with a seven-iron, you don't have to swing as hard, so you can concentrate on the path of the club and not worry about the distance. Only you don't want the other guy to see you hit a seven that far, so . . ."

"Huh." Chelovek reached for the club, and Savitch handed it over. "We can't all use 'em. Would give away the whole deal."

"Just me," Aronica affirmed. " 'Best ball' format, we only need one of us to do better, and then just a little. Hell, I gotta purposely mis-hit most of the time as it is."

"Huh," Chelovek grunted again, appreciating a great scam when he saw one and willing to put aside his suddenly petty outrage when his greater self-interest demanded it.

"What do you estimate you could shoot with those?" Perrault asked.

Aronica shrugged. "Scratch. Maybe better."

Chelovek felt the bile rising again but fought it down. "You better not."

"I know that." Aronica came forward and squatted on the ground. "But I don't have to in this format, don't you see? I don't even have to be *in* most holes. All I gotta do is, once in a while, I gotta score a winner when we need it."

Perrault agreed. "Joe carries a seven, so one would expect birdies out of him here and there. All he'd need do is—"

"Just get 'em at the right times," Savitch finished for him.

"And all I'd carry is a couple of these puppies: the seven for sure, a three-wood that looks like a driver . . ."

"Huh." Chelovek was staring at the club.

"On top of that," Perrault said, growing excited, "the way we played the first time, we're sure to get some strokes. So he might even win us a few just with pars, right?"

"You got it," Aronica said. "But we gotta concentrate on the match 'steada trying to murder each other, okay?" The others nodded, even Chelovek.

"One problem, though," Savitch said.

Perrault nodded dolefully. "How do we convince the owners to play us again?"

They stayed quiet for a few minutes, thinking, and gradually they all looked at Chelovek.

Lost in thought, he was tapping a finger against his lip.

"Huh" was all he said.

■■

Chapter 28

THEIR RESOLVE TO ENTER THE dining room that evening with heads held self-confidently high lasted about the time it took them to get ten feet past the door, at which point Aronica stumbled slightly and his friends came to a halt behind him.

Unable to stop staring at Eddie's table even though people soon began staring at *him*, Aronica finally said, "That can't be—"

"It can't be, but it is," Chelovek confirmed.

"Sam Coolidge?" Perrault ventured.

Savitch jabbed two fingers into Aronica's shoulder. "They're waving at us, Joe. What the hell do we do now!" Indeed, Eddie was half out of his seat, gesturing across the room for them to come over.

"Whaddaya think we're gonna do, Deke?" Aronica said without turning around. "Ignore him?"

Aronica tried to smile as best as he could and wave back. Then he took what he hoped was an unnoticeable deep breath and advanced purposefully, not exhaling until he heard the sound of the others following.

"Sam!" he said amiably as he approached the table, his hand out. "What in the holy hell . . . !"

"Hiya, Joe," Coolidge answered warmly, seizing Aronica's outstretched hand and pumping it eagerly. "Been too long."

He was equally affectionate with his other three old friends, even his former medical partner Pete Perrault, not a hint in his demeanor of any hard feelings over the subtle ostracism that had separated him from what used to be a happy fivesome.

"How'd you—" Savitch began before catching himself. "I mean, I didn't think you could—" *Afford this kind of place,* he almost said.

Coolidge appeared to take no offense and was about to answer when Eddie said, "Sam's my guest." Étienne Pensecoeur and Selby Kirkland nodded approvingly; Trevor Blanchard wasn't at the table.

"So how're you liking it so far?" Coolidge asked, receiving mumbled variations of "Fine," "Great," "Swell" by way of reply.

A minute or two of very uncomfortable and totally vacuous pleasantries ensued, until Eddie said, "Well, enjoy your dinners."

Gently affirming the dismissal, Coolidge added, "Yeah, I'll catch up with you guys a little later."

DAZED, THE BOYS ELECTED TO eat out on the veranda, out of sight of Eddie's table.

"So that's how they found out about us," Savitch said after his second glass of wine.

"Why d'you suppose he did that?" Aronica wondered out loud. "What, you figure he gets a cut of our losses or something?"

Savitch dropped back against his chair in surprise. "Cryin' out loud, Joe . . ."

"No, sir." Perrault shook his head and reached for the wine bottle. "Impossible. You fellows don't know him like I do." He poured some wine and set the bottle down, then idly twirled the glass. "Or did, anyway. Sam is truly one of the nicest guys one could ever hope to meet. Not an ounce of guile in him, which is why . . ."

He didn't have to finish. It was why Coolidge hadn't made as much money as the others, couldn't afford a membership in the Royal Connaught Golf & Country Club and couldn't swing the cost of their increasingly expensive annual trips.

"So I don't get it," Savitch said. "Why'd he set this up for us?"

Perrault took a sip of wine and appeared not even to taste it before swallowing. "Probably because he thought we'd enjoy it."

They went quiet for a few moments. Then Aronica said, "So, Jerry, what's your brilliant scheme for getting us a rematch?"

Chelovek, who hadn't said a word since they'd sat down, glanced over his shoulder and then back again. "Whatever it was," he said, lifting his napkin from his lap and throwing it down on the table, "I'm switching to Plan B." He pushed away his chair and got up, then turned and headed back into the dining room.

The others exchanged glances, then did likewise, pausing at the entryway as Chelovek continued into the room and right for Eddie's table.

"As a matter of fact, Sam," they could hear him say in a voice slightly louder than normal conversation would have required, "how we're liking it so far is not too damned much."

Coolidge turned in his seat to face Chelovek. "Yes, well," he said, in a very low voice intended to convey that any higher volume was inappropriate, "I heard you boys lost a real squeaker the other day. Hope it didn't ruin your whole trip."

"What's ruining this trip," Chelovek said, as loudly as before, "is that your pal and his cronies here"—he waved a hand at the table without looking at the others, then bent in close to Coolidge—"dragged us down here, took twenty large from us and refuse to give us a rematch!"

"We weren't under any obligation to play you again, Jerry," Eddie said, in a voice as low as Coolidge's.

"Sure you were, buster. It's how gentlemen play."

"Now, what would you know about how gentlemen play?"

Chelovek bristled and straightened up. "We break any rules?"

"Something you need to understand." Eddie stood up. He was a good four inches shorter than Chelovek but somehow seemed taller, or at least more imposing. "We play for fun. We play because we like it. And we don't play with people who don't know how to relax and enjoy themselves. Now, you're welcome to—"

"Don't bullshit me, Eddie!" He could see that the smaller man was becoming angry at this disruption to the quiet serenity of his beloved Swithen Bairn, which was just the effect Chelovek wanted.

"Mr. Chelovek, I'm going to have to ask you to—"

"Ask me to what!" Chelovek bellowed, then turned around and indicated the rest of the dining room with a sweep of his hand. "The rest of your guests know how they're being scammed, hah? They know you're a professional con artist?"

The rest of the room had gone quiet, all movement had ceased, and all eyes were on the developing confrontation. Eddie looked around and didn't like what he was seeing. "You want a rematch?" he asked softly.

"We want a rematch!" Chelovek spat back.

Eddie declined to raise his voice; if anything, it got even softer. "If we play again," he said with pointed deliberation, "you're gonna lose."

I hate it when he does that! I'm sorry to interject a purely personal matter here, but I just hate it. The first time Eddie taught *me* a lesson—a painful one, both physically and financially—he told me in advance that I was going to lose. I chalked it off to the usual psych-out blarney, but he was right. Every time I've ever heard him say it, he's been right.

What's even more galling is his standard disclaimer when making a bet: He tells everybody that if they think he cheated them, or misled them, or was unclear about the rules, or if they think he did anything else that wasn't strictly on the up-and-up, they could call it off, anytime, right up to and including the eighteenth hole. I've seen only one person ever take him up on it, a pro golfer the day before the Ryder Cup I captained, and he had no right to do it. What made that whole incident truly memorable was that I came unglued at how calmly Eddie took it and asked him how come he wasn't monumentally pissed off, and he answered that he only would have been pissed off if it had come as a surprise; turned out he'd engineered the whole bet just to show me the true nature of that pro's character. It was that kind of eerie insight into human nature that made it entirely understandable how even such a logical, appropriately skeptical scientist like Joe Aronica could let himself get freaked into entertaining all sorts of absurdist fantasies for what happened to his friends and him at Swithen Bairn.

Getting ahead of myself again, but I want you to know that, interestingly, this match I'm telling you about now was the only time I'd ever heard of where Eddie hadn't extended his customary you-can-call-it-off offer, knowing as he did that these boys were likely to be as honorable about that as they would be about paying for their indisputably memorable vacation. In any event, they were the ones pressing for the match, not Eddie, so he was under no obligation to offer them an escape clause.

Chelovek didn't know all of this about Eddie, but something in the man's voice made him falter slightly anyway. Then bravado reasserted itself, and he said, "Says who!"

"Listen to me, Jerry," Eddie warned again. "You're gonna lose, you understand? I want you and your friends to be real clear so you don't come back with any more accusations later. You're gonna lose, and I'm giving you the chance right now not to play."

But Chelovek had heard only one thing. "So you'll play us?" He could practically feel his friends at the entryway holding their breaths.

"Maybe." Eddie looked at him for what seemed like an hour. "I'm willing to discuss it."

Mission at least partially accomplished, Chelovek suddenly found himself at center stage with klieg lights illuminating him before an unappreciative and hostile audience. "Well, uh, okay then," he stammered, unsure of what to do next.

Eddie gestured to a waiter, who immediately hurried over to the table and turned out to be the same guy who'd greeted them when they'd stepped off the plane. "Find the Piper, Jake," Eddie said to him. "Tell him I need the numbers for the Aronica group, 'kay?"

"What numbers are those?" Chelovek asked.

"Your handicaps," Eddie answered as Jake ran off. "Now, if you'll return to your table, we'll meet later and see what we can work out."

"Yeah, sure." Chelovek nodded dumbly and shuffled his feet. "Sounds real good. We'll, uh—"

"I said *later*."

"Right." Chelovek turned quickly and tried to get out of the dining room without looking around at any of the other guests.

Chapter 29

⚏

THE BOYS WERE IN A grand mood, enjoying their cigars and brandies and joking lightly among themselves, when Eddie walked onto the veranda and changed the atmosphere in an instant. It wasn't anything he said or did, but it was easy to sense that some serious fury was smoldering beneath the placid exterior. It wouldn't have surprised any of them had he pulled out a gun, shot Chelovek through the heart and calmly gone back to finish his crème brûlée.

But he didn't mention the adman's boorish and sophomoric display during dinner. He had more important things on his mind.

"Basically, I got one serious problem with playing you guys again."

"Look," Savitch said, "we got a little angry at ourselves, okay? Maybe the pressure, being strangers here when everyone else seems to—"

"Won't happen again, Eddie," Aronica said quickly. "Scout's honor, we'll be on our best—"

"That's not it." Eddie pulled up a straight-backed chair, tugged at the knees of his pants and sat down. "What I want to know is, how come none'a you told me about Deke here having a heart condition?"

Chelovek recovered from the *non sequitur* first. "Why should anyone tell you that?"

"Why?" Eddie signaled to a waiter. "You guys lookin' to see your friend collapse in the middle of a money round on account'a his bum ticker couldn't take the strain?" The waiter started to approach but turned around as soon as he saw Eddie wiggle a little finger at him. "You can try to embarrass me all you want in front of my customers, but I'm not about to stand by and watch a guy go into cardiac arrest over a stupid game of golf."

"It's *my* ticker," Savitch protested. "Why do *you* care so much?"

"Why do I—Hey, do I *look* like a fuckin' people person? It may be *your* ticker, but it's *my* club, and I don't need that kind of news showing up in our brochure."

"You don't have a brochure, remember?" Again it was Chelovek who refused to be intimidated, by either their host's demeanor or his staking out of the moral high ground. "Deke's right: His health isn't any'a your business. What do you do, check out everybody's medical records along with their financials? Somebody's got a sinus condition, you don't let him have a mask and snorkel down at the beach?"

To his own surprise, Chelovek realized that Eddie didn't have a packaged answer, so he pressed the advantage. "Thought you said we were gonna discuss this. Some discussion, you come in here and tell us you're not gonna play."

It was a bad move, putting Eddie's back up against a wall like that. Aronica saw it immediately and needed not only to repair the damage but move things forward. "Pete here's a doc, Eddie. Something happens to Deke—"

"Quite right," Perrault said. "I can take care of it."

Eddie saw past that one immediately. "With what, a nine-iron? You're a family physician, not a cardiologist, and even then all you done the past ten years is run a business, not heal the sick."

"I still see patients!"

"Fine. Man gets a hangnail, maybe you got a fighting chance, but a heart attack?" The waiter reappeared and handed him a tumbler of scotch, neat.

"Now look here . . ." Perrault began indignantly as the waiter took off, but then he stopped. Looking past Eddie, he pointed toward the dining room. "You've a board-certified cardiologist sitting right there!"

Eddie turned around to follow Perrault's finger. "Where?"

"Hey, he's right!" Savitch chortled. "Sam Coolidge himself. Best darned heart guy in the Northeast!"

Eddie turned away and took a sip of his scotch.

"What'll it take, Eddie?" Chelovek asked. "Let's cut the bullshit and peel this onion. You're still talking to us, so don't tell us you don't want to play. What's it gonna take?"

Eddie shook his head and took another sip. Licking his lips, he said jokingly as his eyes crinkled up, "Sam and a portable defibrillator walking right along with us."

"Done." Chelovek slapped his thighs and sat back on the couch.

"Whaddaya mean, 'done'?"

"Just what he said," Aronica explained. "You got a deal." He turned to Savitch and Perrault, both of whom were nodding their agreement.

"Unless you were just jerking everybody off when you agreed to discuss it," Chelovek challenged. "You laid down a condition, we accepted . . ."

Eddie, cowed by having been taken by surprise, found himself with little choice. "You guys are serious?"

He could see that they were. He took a deep breath and blew it out noisily, just as the waiter came back with a piece of notepaper in his hand. "Thanks," Eddie said, taking the paper from him. "Now go ask Sam Coolidge could he come by, wouldja?"

"He's left the dining room, Eddie," the young man said. "Want me to go find him?"

"Yeah. Ask him does he wanna have a drink with his old buddies."

"Same format as before?" Eddie had barely finished his sentence before Aronica, anxious to seal the deal by getting down to the fine points, dove right into it. "Everybody tees off, and we pick two on each side to play out the hole?"

"Sounds fair," Eddie said, "except let's total the two scores on each side again, like we did the last time, instead of going with just the one best ball."

"Why?" the genetically suspicious Chelovek asked.

"So it's not just our best guy against your best guy, and it doesn't make the tee shot more important than it should be. Use two scores combined, everybody gets involved, and it brings out your best game."

"Makes sense," Aronica agreed.

Eddie couldn't help smiling in reaction to the glee so evident on the faces of his guests. "Never saw a bunch'a guys so happy about losing money."

"Not after you give us four a side," Chelovek said.

The smile left Eddie's face like a bank robber leaving Dodge. "Four a side! Whadda you, nuts?"

"Come on, Eddie! You're fielding at least two guys're probably scratch, probably *better'n* scratch, against a bunch'a fives and sevens!"

"Fuhgedaboudit! First off, your team as a whole is no worse than the best guy!"

"That's true . . ."

"And that best guy's got three other guys to cover his ass. So the way I see it, your gang is probably two *under!*"

"Well, you got a point there, Eddie . . ." Chelovek agreed again.

"Betcher ass."

" . . . but that makes your gang about *six* under!"

Aronica smiled knowingly at Savitch and Perrault, appreciating how Chelovek had Eddie hoist' by his own petard.

But Eddie wasn't buying it so quick. "First off, where'd you get the idea about I got two scratch guys?"

"Okay," Chelovek continued, warming to the fray, "so let's say you're close. You still got yourselves one hell of a home-court advantage, my friend. Way it looked a couple days ago, you're on a first-name basis with every blade'a grass on the entire layout. Local knowledge like that is good for a lotta strokes."

Eddie scratched his chin a little more, then said, "Maybe. So what we'll do, we'll give you one stroke off your team score on the four toughest holes. Two a side."

"Two . . . ?"

" 'S'what you asked for, right? So what's the complaint?"

"I asked for *four* a side!" Chelovek protested.

Eddie held out his hands in a gesture of supplication. "You agreed you were about two under as a team, you said we're like six under—that's four altogether, so it's two a side."

Trapped, and not wanting to look like a camel trader, Chelovek said, "I never agreed we were two under as a team."

"And I never agreed we were six under. So let's agree that we were both flinging the crapola equally and play it as it lies. We'll give you two a side, which, I gotta tell you, is highway freakin' robbery, but I'm feeling generous, what can I tell you?"

"Generous, yeah." Chelovek knew it was a done deal. "Gonna count my fingers when I leave this place, make sure you didn't steal 'em right off my hand."

Aronica did a quick calculation. "Don't think that's gonna work, Eddie," he said while trying to ignore Chelovek's threatening glare at being interrupted. "I think we should just play with full individual handicaps."

"Makes no sense at all. You can get two strokes off on a hole just by playing your two highest-handicap guys if they hit decent shots."

"But like Jerry said, your guys know every single—"

"Hey, listen! I already told you: We don't want to play you at all, remember? We'd just as soon you all got the hell out of here, so—"

"Wait just a bloody minute!" Perrault set his drink down and leaned forward on his chair. "That's not cricket, Eddie. You agreed to play us, so don't make it sound like you're doing us a favor, okay? If you're going to play, play, but don't presume to hold your initial reluctance over our heads, because it's no longer relevant. If it were, we might as well flip a coin for ten thousand dollars and forget about playing at all."

Perrault's partners held their breaths as they waited to see if Eddie would decline the challenge to his honor and call the whole thing off.

Eddie stared at Perrault, who stared right back at him. "Point taken," he said finally.

Perrault nodded his acceptance of the apology and sat back.

"But what's the sense of getting greedy," Eddie continued, "when you got a scratch golfer on the team?"

The foursome exchanged puzzled glances. "Who's a scratch golfer?" Chelovek asked.

"Listen," Savitch said nervously, "maybe Eddie's right. Maybe we should—"

"We don't have a scratch golfer!" Chelovek insisted. "What the hell are you . . . ?"

"You see what I'm saying?" Savitch went on, the words falling all over themselves as he tumbled them out hurriedly, gesturing with his hands. "Let's just take the four strokes, or just play 'em straight up, and—"

"Right there," Eddie said, pointed at Savitch. "You talk about sportsmanship? What the hell are you trying to pull!"

"Savitch?" Aronica said. "He's a three!"

"Fellas!" Savitch persisted, almost pleading now. "Wouldja just . . . can we just keep this simple and get on with it? What's the point of—"

"Not according to Rusty Tremmel, he isn't a three," Eddie said, ignoring Savitch's pitiable bleating as the others seemed to be doing.

"And just who in the flaming hell is Rusty Tremmel?" Chelovek demanded.

"Head pro at Mystic Cove," a voice said from the entryway, and they all turned to see Sam Coolidge walking in with Jake. "How's about a Lagavulin neat?"

"Sure thing."

As the waiter went off to get the drink, Aronica looked at Savitch, who was slumped back on his chair. "Mystic Cove?"

"That's the most exclusive club in the whole Northeast," Perrault answered.

"I know what it is," Aronica said in confusion. "What I'm asking, what—"

"What the hell does it have to do with Deke?" Chelovek finished for him.

Into the silence that ensued, Eddie held up the piece of paper he'd gotten from the waiter and said with offhanded innocence, "Well, according to this, he plays at Mystic Cove, and his handicap is zero. I take it this is some kind of surprise to you boys?"

"Surprise?" Aronica answered, catching on slowly but definitely catching on. "That Deke's got a secret membership at another club and is really three strokes better than we thought? Now, why would that constitute a—"

"Listen'a me!" Savitch whined. "You don't—"

"You slimy sonofabitch!" Perrault shrieked as he abandoned all deportment and shot out of his chair, lunging across the coffee table and sending drink glasses and ashtrays flying. His hands, poised like a high diver's, were aimed straight at Savitch's throat.

Jake had just walked in and handed Coolidge his drink. "Hey!" he yelled as he launched himself at Perrault, knocking the enraged physician sideways just as Savitch pulled his knees to his chin and tried to slither up the back of his chair and out of the way.

"Get him off me!" Savitch squealed as Jake wrestled Perrault away.

"He's not on you, you miserable piece of shit!" Aronica growled. "Personally, I'da let him choke you to death!"

"How could you cheat your own friends!" Chelovek thundered at Savitch.

"I never cheated you guys," Savitch moaned pathetically. "It was only—"

"I'll kill you!" Perrault screamed, trying to get away from Jake so he could get at Savitch. "I'll hit you so hard it'll kill your whole fucking family, you fat, pasty prick . . . !" He finally realized it was Jake who was holding him back, and began pounding ineffectually on the waiter's broad back.

"Hey, what about his heart?" Eddie asked.

"*Fuck* his heart!" Perrault gurgled, still trying to break free of the waiter. "I'll tear it right out of his—Goddamnit it, would you let me—"

As Perrault began to run out of steam, Chelovek reached down and squeezed Jake's shoulder. "Let him go, will ya?"

The waiter turned his head to look at Perrault, who was red-faced and wheezing. "You gonna take it easy?"

With one last murderous look at Savitch, Perrault closed his eyes and nodded. Jake relaxed and patted him on the arm. "Okay, then." He disentangled himself and got up, then offered a hand and helped Perrault to his feet, pointing him to his chair once he was up.

As Perrault dropped heavily onto the cushions, Aronica looked at Savitch, who was lowering himself back onto his chair, and shook his head. "Man who cheats in life, maybe he'll cheat at golf. But a man who cheats at golf?"

"He'll fuck you every time," Chelovek responded.

Assuring himself that Perrault had been rendered benign, Savitch took out a handkerchief and began mopping his face. "I never cheated you guys," he said limply. "I just—"

"Every time we played in the same tournament," Perrault said, still heaving slightly but already starting to resurrect his manufactured persona, "you cheated us. Everybody always thought you just got especially motivated in the heat of competition, how you always beat your handicap, but what was really going on, you were just holding back the other times!"

Eddie signaled to Jake that it was in hand and he could leave. "So what was it?" Coolidge asked Savitch. "Couldn't have been the money. Hell, you had a membership at Mystic, you sure didn't need the chump change."

"I don't know." Beaten and humiliated, Savitch shrugged disconsolately. "Just . . . I guess . . ."

"Just an overweight toad trying to elevate yourself above the rabble," Perrault muttered savagely.

"Seems to me holding a scratch handicap woulda been enough," Aronica observed.

Chelovek picked up his dead cigar and a book of matches. "We'll take the four strokes, Eddie." He tapped the tip of the cigar straight down in the ashtray to compress the end, then struck a match and started to relight it.

Eddie, who'd remained mostly silent through the altercation, looked up in surprise. "You still want to play?"

Chelovek shrugged as he puffed and tried to get the tip glowing again. "Not gonna let this low-life scumbag ruin my trip." He shook the match out and blew a cloud of blue smoke into the air.

Eddie looked around to see that Perrault and Aronica, after being startled by Chelovek's pronouncement, had seen his logic and were in agreement. Then he looked at Savitch.

"I'll play," the stockbroker said. "Least I can do, I guess."

"Well, thank you very much," Perrault snarled. "Too bloody right, you'll play. And you'd better bring your Mystic Cove game with you, too."

"Way to really pump up his motivation there, Pete," Aronica said sarcastically. "Anybody want to talk about stakes now?"

Chapter 30

❖

WELL, YOU GOTTA AT LEAST give us a shot at winning back our twenty large," Chelovek opened.

"Good by me," Eddie replied, and started to get up.

"Just a minute." Perrault waved Eddie back onto his seat and addressed himself to Chelovek. "Breakeven, that's the height of your ambition, Jerrold?"

"Yeah." Aronica stuck a finger in the air and twirled it. "Some typhoon of excitement that's gonna be."

Eddie sat back and looked at each of them in turn. "All the fuss you guys raised, I'da thought you might have had this little discussion in advance."

"Why don't we make it ten thousand each?" Savitch suggested quickly, not wishing to let Eddie know they'd spent all their time just figuring out how to get him to agree to a rematch, which Eddie knew anyway. "At least make it interesting."

"Why don't you quiet down, Deke," Perrault snapped.

"Why don't *you* quiet down," Savitch shot back at him. "This is my money we're talking about, too."

"Fine," Chelovek said. "Let's make it twenty-five grand each and satisfy everybody."

"I like it," Aronica answered. Perrault looked a little uneasy.

"Jeez, guys," Savitch said. "Isn't that a little steep?"

That was all it took to vaporize Perrault's discomfort. "So, Deke, you turn yellow when you have to play fair?"

"Yellow? Okay, make it fifty, fathead!"

Aronica gulped. "Fifty *each*?"

"Well, what the hell've we been talking about here!" Savitch barked.

"Fine by me!" Perrault declared, his voice trailing ever so slightly on the last syllable, so he cleared his throat of something nonexistent to dispel any perceptions of hesitancy he might have created.

"Okay, okay, everybody calm down a minute here!" Eddie held up both hands and waited for quiet. "Don't let's get our dicks in the way of our heads. I think fifty large is a little out of your league, so why don't we come up with something more reasonable?"

Which, of course, planted their collective dicks even more squarely in the way of their heads. "Out of whose league?" Chelovek challenged. "You afraid to play for that kind of dough?"

"We'll play you for anything you want," Eddie replied, "but we'd rather not see you fall apart again because you can't take the heat."

"Who says we can't?" Aronica said huffily. "I got no problem with fifty—"

"That is kinda high," Savitch protested.

"Ha!" Perrault shouted triumphantly. "You *are* a worm—fifty was your idea!"

"I didn't really . . ." Savitch squirmed and scratched at his ear. "What I meant . . ."

"Listen, this is getting us nowhere." Eddie leaned forward and put his elbows on his knees. "Maybe there's another way." He brought his hands together and touched his fingertips to his chin as he thought it over.

"I got an idea," Sam Coolidge said.

COOLIDGE WALKED OVER TO A bookshelf just inside the entry-way to the dining room. None of the others had noticed before, but in addition to a selection of books, it held several dozen board games. Coolidge pulled one out, opened the box, took something from a smaller box inside and left the rest of the game behind as he returned to the veranda.

"What've you got there, Sam?" Perrault asked his old medical partner.

"Doubling cube," Coolidge answered, tossing what looked like a large die on the coffee table. "From a backgammon set."

Checking first to see whether Perrault would go after him again, Savitch reached tentatively for the cube. "Got only numbers on it," he said. "No dots."

Aronica nodded. "Smallest one's a two, then there's a four, an eight and so on up to sixty-four."

"Way it works in backgammon," Coolidge explained, "at any point in the game one player can offer to double the original bet. Let's say that was a buck." He took the cube from Savitch and set it down with the number two facing up. "Now it's raised to two bucks. The other guy either accepts the offer and they keep playing for two bucks or he declines and pays up the amount of the original bet, one dollar, and the game is over."

"Like a raise in poker," Aronica said. "You either see it or you fold."

"What about the rest of the numbers?" Savitch asked.

"If they keep playing, the other guy—the one who accepted the double—now has the right to do the same thing back." He turned the cube so the number four was now facing up. "He offers to double the current bet, so now it's up to four bucks. The other guy either accepts and they keep playing for four dollars or he declines, pays up the two bucks and the game ends."

"So if he accepts," Savitch said, "he can then double it again, to eight?"

"Right. Except one guy can't offer two doubles in a row. It has to alternate back and forth. As soon as your double is accepted, the right to offer the next one goes to the other guy."

Eddie pointed to the cube. "So what you're saying, we do that in our match? Start off small and let each side offer doubles?"

"Sounds like it might solve this problem here, Eddie. Of course, the whole team would have to decide together whether to offer a double, or whether to accept one that's been offered."

"So they'll probably end up with the same dilemma they got here. Can't make a decision."

Coolidge curled his lip and thought about it for a few seconds. "You're right. Oh, well . . ."

"Wait a minute," Aronica said, reaching for the cube and rolling it around in his hand. "What if, ah . . ."

"What if what?" Savitch prompted him hopefully.

Aronica stopped playing with the cube and set it back down with the two showing. "What if three guys want to accept a double and one guy doesn't, but the other three agree to cover the whole bet themselves?"

The wisdom of that solution was self-evident. "Can't see any problem with that," Eddie agreed. "Why should the other team care, so long as the bet is covered?"

Chelovek looked at Coolidge admiringly. "That is one clever piece'a work there, Sammy!"

"Sure is," Aronica concurred as Coolidge smiled sheepishly. "That way, Eddie's people can get out early if things are looking hopeless for them."

Eddie laughed at the jibe, then said, "So what's the opening bet . . . figure a hundred bucks?"

The suggestion was greeted with undisguised derision. "A hundred?" Perrault bellowed. "Pathetic, Eddie! Start off with a thousand. I mean, after all!"

"Yeah," Savitch said enthusiastically. "That'll at least make it interesting if somebody wimps out early."

Eddie shrugged. "Whatever you say."

"Just so we understand." Chelovek looked at the tip of his cigar, then at Eddie. "That's a thousand a man."

"Of course. And just so we all understand"—his voice grew serious, and he waited until he had everybody's attention—"each side is responsible for the team's losses as a whole."

"Meaning . . . ?" Savitch inquired.

"Meaning, nobody wants to be stuck going after individuals for payment. If one member can't cover his loss, the others have to cover it for him."

"But what if—"

Eddie cut Savitch off. "That situation you mentioned before? About how maybe three guys could cover a fourth if he didn't want to continue?" He held up his hands. "Don't even want to *hear* about it! You work that out among yourselves. The team speaks as one and pays as one, because there's just no other way it makes sense."

He didn't wait to get agreement but turned around to Coolidge. "Forgot to mention, Sam: How about walking with us, case something happens to Deke?"

Relighting their cigars and pouring fresh brandies, our boys were unprepared for Coolidge's reply. "No way, Eddie. What the hell kind of vacation would that be, walking around waiting to see if an old friend has a heart attack on a golf course?"

Eddie, chagrined, turned back and frowned just as Jake returned. "Phone call, Eddie. Mr. B., and it sounds important."

"Be there in a second. Sam, look—"

"Deke's never had a heart attack," Coolidge said stubbornly, "and he doesn't have a doctor on call when he plays at home, so why's he need one here?"

"Doubt he plays for this kinda dough. Stress might—"

"Then he shouldn't play," Coolidge said. He held up a hand as Eddie seemed ready to try to persuade him further. "I can't even afford to play with these guys anymore, so I come down here for some golf and I'm supposed to spend a whole day just waiting for Deke to code?"

Eddie sat back and appeared to give in. "Ah, you're right, Sam. All those hours you put in at the clinics . . ."

"It's not that, Eddie. If I could do a useful service, I'm there, you know that. But this?" He waved a hand toward the foursome. "It's like being standby physician at a game of Russian roulette. Deke, you telling me you'd bet your life against a few bucks?"

"That's my business," Savitch answered defiantly.

"Fine, but it isn't mine. Just doesn't make any sense, Eddie, and I'll be damned if I'm gonna be a willing participant. You guys are on your own."

And he was gone.

Eddie looked crestfallen. "Shouldn't even have asked him. Sometimes I don't think."

Jake stepped uncomfortably from foot to foot. "Eddie . . . ?"

"Shit. 'Scuse me, guys." Eddie went into the dining room to take the phone call.

"I THINK THIS IS BULLSHIT," Aronica said, "using Savitch's heart as an excuse not to play us."

Chelovek lit his cigar again and took a long, contemplative puff. "Then why'd he go through all that negotiating?"

"To make it look good?" Perrault ventured. "So we wouldn't throw another fit and embarrass him?"

"Maybe. Here he comes."

Eddie's lips were tightly drawn as he came back out onto the veranda. "Well, it's all academic anyway. Blanchard's been called home, some kinda emergency. Guess the match is off."

"Hey, wait a minute . . . !" Savitch barked.

"What?" Eddie spread his hands, as if helpless before the circumstances. "Whatever rematch rights you thought you had, we no longer got our foursome, so . . ."

"That's a crock, Eddie!" Savitch looked almost desperate, probably because he had only one chance to resurrect himself in the eyes of his friends, and that was to be an integral part of a victory in this match. "Get another player to fill in!"

"Can't do it. Most everybody's got matches lined up, and I doubt too many of 'em would be up for stakes that could get cranked this high anyway."

Perrault angrily stubbed out his cigar, jamming it repeatedly into the glass ashtray on the coffee table. "I feel compelled to tell you, Eddie my good man, that again this doesn't sound terribly cricket."

"What do you suggest?"

"I don't know. But I thought we had this matter all sewn up, and just like that it falls apart. Hardly the hallmark of a gracious host."

"But what can I do? There's not—"

"You could try a little harder." All eyes turned to Chelovek, who'd been silent through most of this latest interchange. He calmly turned his brandy snifter in his hand and watched as the amber nectar dripped down the sides of the glass, then looked at Eddie. "You could try to make this happen, instead of finding a hundred reasons why it can't." He took a slow sip and savored the vapor expanding in his mouth. "It's a matter of attitude, see? You set a weirdo condition, we accepted it, and now shit just keeps bubbling up to sabotage it, and you don't seem to much give a rat's ass. Now, I ask you . . ."

He set down the glass and leaned forward, eyeing Eddie intently. "Is that how you typically set up money matches here at Smith fucking Barney?"

The two stared at each other for what seemed like an hour. Then, without taking his eyes off Chelovek, Eddie said, "We'll take Sam Coolidge on our team."

"Ah, whaddaya talking about, Eddie?" Aronica said gruffly. "Man hasn't got a pot to piss in! How's he supposed to back his losses?"

"I'll cover him myself," Eddie responded, still face to face with Chelovek, who turned slightly but without taking his eyes off their host.

"You'll cover him?" Chelovek said suspiciously, rodent odor wafting into his hypersensitive nostrils.

"Uh-huh."

"Now, why would you want to do that?" Aronica asked. "The man's no player."

"I'll tell you why, Joe." Eddie finally turned away from Chelovek. "Because the way I see it, I think we could beat you without a fourth player at all. So if Sam can get a few bucks out of you guys for his clinic, maybe I'll go to heaven."

Savitch either ignored the insult or didn't get it in the first place. "You think he'll play?"

It was a dumb question, and Perrault shot him an appropriately disgusted look. "Of course he'll play!"

"How do you know?"

"Because," Chelovek answered, giving Eddie a knowing look, "he's got everything to win and squat to lose. We still get our four strokes?"

"Your funeral, Jerry. But the match can't go past sundown—"

"Well, obviously," Savitch said, trying to regain some ground.

"—and nobody makes any phone calls out of here tonight."

"The hell's that all about?" Aronica asked.

Chelovek smiled appreciatively. "So we can't yank money out of our accounts beforehand."

Rather than confirm Chelovek's observation, Eddie signaled to Jake. "What say we seal it with a fresh round?"

When the drinks were served, Eddie took one sip of his, bade them all good night, and left.

"Let's do the same," Perrault advised. "No sense playing hungover."

"You're a real jerk, Joe," Savitch said to Aronica out of nowhere, his voice tinged with anger.

"What the hell are you talking about?"

"Giving me all that guff when you've been using a set of illegal clubs. In front of Eddie, too."

"I told you, I never cheated you guys. It was only—"

"You can kiss my rosy wrinkled behind, bud. I said the same thing, but that wasn't good enough, so who are you to—"

"I wonder if maybe Eddie was right," Chelovek interrupted. "About your heart, I mean. This isn't some friendly weekend bet, you know. This could get into some serious shekels, and I wonder if—"

"Well, thanks a heap for your heartfelt concern, Jerry!" Savitch was trembling with rage now "You think if I croak it's an automatic forfeit? Where the hell was all this concern when Pete was trying to beat the—"

"Okay, so I was mad! But now—"

"Just mind your own gosh-darned business, okay!" Savitch was on his feet. "Okay? I don't want to hear any more bull from you! From any of you!"

"All right, already!" Chelovek waved him back down as Perrault said, "Just take it easy, will you?"

Savitch's eyes darted back and forth a few times. "You guys are a whole lot worse'n me," he said, then slowly sat down again.

"Izzat so?" Chelovek said.

"Darn tootin'. Starting with Joe's magic friggin' clubs."

"So how come you didn't rag on him when Eddie was here?"

The two of them stared at each other, and then a tiny smile began playing itself around Chelovek's mouth, and soon Savitch was grinning back at him as they both remembered that Aronica's magic metal clubs were going to be working in their mutual self-interest.

"Y'get right down to it," Chelovek said, patting Savitch's knee and gesturing for Perrault to join in the conspiratorial camaraderie, "we're all a bunch'a pricks at heart, am I right?"

Aronica, ignoring the commotion and the at-least-temporary reconciliation, had angled his chair toward the water in the distance and was staring at the sky.

"This place is really starting to give me the creeps," he muttered, but declined to elaborate.

Chapter 31

＃＃

Day Six

"COOLIDGE WON'T PLAY."

Eddie's words hung about them like unexploded grenades. The sun had only been up for about twenty minutes, but already the humid air was giving off the first intimations that it was going to be a muggy, stifling day.

"What do you mean, he won't play?" Perrault asked.

"Says he won't play against his friends." *Even if you are a bunch of shit-heads who treated him like crap,* he didn't have to add.

Our boys stood around, idly scratching their clubheads in the dirt adjoining the first tee, unable to think of some way to make this look like Eddie's fault and therefore something that he should be endeavoring to do something about.

Chelovek looked over at the three owners, their bags loaded onto two carts, Jake in a third cart with some kind of machine sitting in the back. It looked something like a large cooler, only metallic, and with half a dozen auto batteries slung underneath. A phone was affixed to its closed lid.

Chelovek pointed to it with his driver. "What's that?"

"Portable defibrillator," Eddie answered. "'Case Deke's heart acts up. Had it flown in last night."

Perrault bit his lip, trying to hide his disappointment. Aronica turned away to look longingly down the first fairway.

Savitch was still looking at the carts, and at Étienne Pensecoeur and Selby Kirkland holding clubs by their ends and stretching, Kirkland dressed as usual in loose-fitting clothes from neck to toe. "Call me crazy, but how come you guys look like you're ready to play?"

Eddie stepped back and took a few big swings with his three-wood. "Thought we'd go it alone. You game?"

Aronica turned back around. "You serious?"

"Possibly. Only problem is Deke here."

Perrault stepped forward. "I'm still perfectly capable of operating one of those," he said, pointing to the defibrillator.

"This here's kinda new," Eddie said skeptically, motioning for Jake to pull the cart around. As the waiter did so, several controls became visible on the front panel. " 'Course, Selby here used to be a nurse of some kind, and I got somebody standing by on the other end of that radiophone, can tell you what to do if—"

"I said I know how to operate it."

"Your sure, now?"

"What do you mean, 'go it alone'?" Chelovek asked. "You mean the three of you against the four of us?"

"Sound okay to you? I'll cover two bets myself. Naturally, we won't be giving up any strokes . . ."

"How come—" Savitch started to say, but Chelovek pulled him roughly to the side.

" 'Scuse us a minute, will ya, Eddie?" When he had Savitch out of earshot, Chelovek drew Perrault and Aronica in as well.

Aronica, an engineer at heart, said, "Am I hearing this right?"

"I heard the same thing," Chelovek answered.

"Hear what right?" Savitch looked confused. "No strokes?"

"Are you completely brain-dead, Deke?" Aronica looked back to make sure they weren't being overheard. "You got any idea what they're giving up, only three balls to choose from 'steada four?"

"But Sam is like a twenty handicap," Savitch argued. "Hardly makes a difference, they don't got him on their team!"

"Makes all the difference in the world, even if he's a forty!" Aronica whispered hoarsely. "Guy hits two good tee shots on two par-threes and he earns his tamales for the day!"

"He's right, Deke," Chelovek affirmed. "Or Sam could rescue them from two shitty tee shots on a couple of par-fours. The more guys you got on your side in best ball, the better your chances. No way another guy can hurt, only help."

Savitch and Perrault both saw the logic, which only made the stockbroker suspicious. "Then I don't get it. Why would they do it?"

"Beats me," Chelovek said, "but we were ready to play them with Blanchard or Coolidge on their team, and now they got neither . . ."

"And we can call it quits if it gets too expensive," Aronica added.

Perrault nodded eagerly. "So let's have at it."

Savitch was still troubled. "But—"

"I said let's do it."

Aronica tapped the face of his club lightly against Savitch's. It made an odd, almost tinkly sound, like two crystal champagne glasses being clinked in a toast. "What else do we need, Deke: balls with onboard radar?"

"I'll even let you guys set the tees," Eddie called out, "only let's not waste this beautiful day."

RIGHT FROM THE FIRST, THEY were at each other.

"Place them way up front," Perrault insisted. "That'll take the Haitian's long ball out of play."

"But then the broad gets a realistic shot," Chelovek countered. "And she's got more accuracy."

"She'll still never hit long enough for a good second shot," Aronica argued back.

"Okay, look." Eddie slung his driver over his shoulder and approached the foursome. "You guys got one minute to make a decision on each tee, or we play 'em from right in the middle. Agreed?"

Chelovek pointed back toward the bamboo wall. "This one from the tips," he announced, then turned back to his partners. "Anybody got a problem with that?"

Eddie threw a tee into the air; it landed pointing toward his group. "We're up first. Selby, give it a whack."

Cocking her head with a theatrical sneer at the futility of it, she dutifully stepped up to the very back of the tee box as Pensecoeur said to her, "Might as well whip the *merde* out of it, *chère*."

"Yeah, sure." Straining to elongate her backswing without coming out of the shot, Kirkland leaned into it with a grunt and overswung, catching the ball clean but imparting some vicious spin that sent it arcing to the right. Although she'd anticipated the slice and compensated by aiming left, the curve was too extreme, and the ball quickly disappeared into the trees.

"Don't drive angry, sweetie," Eddie said with a grin. "Any'a you guys ready?"

"Don't you want to finish your side?" Aronica asked.

"Let's alternate on this one, whaddaya say? Or do you guys really want to stand on honors and hobble us completely?"

Chelovek took the tee and hit a beautifully controlled driver down the middle past the dogleg, setting up perfectly for a shot to the green. Aronica used a three-wood, as did Savitch, and both came up playable, albeit a lot farther away from the green than Chelovek.

Eddie hit his usual, boring 250-yarder down the middle, about halfway between Chelovek and Aronica, and then Pensecoeur was up. The big Haitian took a much slower backswing than he had on the same hole a few days ago but came back much farther over his shoulder. Staying fully extended and with his head as still as a cheetah's, he brought his big driver down in a huge arc and slammed it into the ball with a loud bang, blasting it off the tee with a sharply angled trajectory.

As everyone else stared in amazement, the ball rose into the morning sky and almost seemed to accelerate instead of slowing down, then began to drift rightward as its cratered surface bit into the air. Before long it was over the trees and out of sight.

"Dumb shot, ET," Eddie said. With only one playable ball on the team thus far, he should have played it safe.

"You think it cleared?" Aronica asked in wonder.

Pensecoeur reached down to retrieve his tee. "One hopes so, or it might be bread and water for the dining tonight, *non*?"

With three good shots on the fairway by his partners, Perrault was free to take a driver and swing out of his shoes, but his shot wound up somewhere in the neighborhood of Kirkland's.

The boys elected to play Chelovek and Savitch. As Aronica picked up, Savitch hit a sweet six-iron to within fifteen feet, then watched as Eddie, lying about twenty-five yards closer, did roughly the same with an eight. Chelovek hit a pitching wedge to the very back of the green, and then they all trooped up to see if Pensecoeur was playable.

He was, but hit too tentative a sand wedge and ended up a few yards short of the green. His chip up from there still left him a twenty-five-foot putt.

Chelovek putted first, reading the green perfectly and coming to rest about eighteen inches from the cup. "Pick it up," Eddie called, and then went down in two himself, leaving Savitch and Pensecoeur.

Savitch bent down behind his ball and held his putter up by the end with two fingers, sighting down the line to read the break. "Miss it on the high side," Aronica said amiably.

Savitch smiled as he stood up. "Miss it, my eye. This one's going in the heart."

Poised over his ball, Savitch took one last look at the hole to nail the distance in his mind, then focused in on the tiny brown spot three feet away he'd decided would take the ball right to the hole. Keeping his eyes straight down, he took the putter back and brought it forward smoothly, following the ball with the clubhead as it sped away as though sweeping it toward the hole.

It was a fifteen-footer, and he'd hit it hard, so it took a few small bounces at the beginning before settling down and riding the contours of the green. It was barely a second before the others realized he'd hit it perfectly, and, as predicted, it hit the middle of the hole and dropped cleanly into it.

"Bird!" Perrault cried gleefully. Savitch's birdie and Chelovek's par gave the team a combined score of 7. Eddie and Pensecoeur already had 7 between them, and Pensecoeur still wasn't in, which meant the best they could do was an 8.

"Yikes," Eddie said as he stepped forward to pick up Pensecoeur's now-irrelevant marker. "Nice start, boys. You're one up."

"And you're doubled," Chelovek shot back.

Kirkland and Pensecoeur exchanged glances, but Eddie merely shrugged. "Two grand a man?"

"Yep. You accept?"

Eddie tossed the marker to Pensecoeur and said, "You don't really think we're gonna quit after one hole because dum-dum here played like an idiot, do you?"

Pensecoeur laughed as he scrambled to catch the tiny piece of plastic.

Chapter 32

O N T H E P A R - F I V E S E C O N D H O L E , the boys elected to put the
tee well forward, figuring Pensecoeur's distance wouldn't be that big an
advantage, given his short game, but they might have a better chance at birdie
if the distance were reduced. Once again Pensecoeur whacked one into obliv-
ion, and again he failed to reach the green in regulation, but he managed a
one-putt par anyway. Eddie made a brilliant birdie, but Aronica squeaked one
in as well. With Savitch's effortless par, each team had a combined score of 9.
The hole was halved, and the foursome remained one up.

On the par-three third, they went back to the tips again, fearful of
Kirkland's deadly accuracy. The hole played close to two hundred taking
into account the high elevation of the green. Using a five-wood, she hit a
high, breathtaking shot that took off and descended almost vertically before
landing on the green. Due to the height of the green, however, the surface
wasn't visible from the tees.

"I'd say a little toward the back," Chelovek guessed.

"I'd say three feet from the hole," Kirkland said as she stooped to pick up
her tee. If she knew that Chelovek's eyes were glued to her largely hidden
behind, she didn't show it.

Pensecoeur put his tee shot safely on, and then it was Aronica's turn.

"Whud you hit there, big guy?" Aronica asked.

"Seven-iron," Pensecoeur answered.

Aronica tried as discreetly as he could to return a six-iron to his bag and
get a seven instead.

"Don't start that shit again, Joe," Chelovek warned.

Ignoring him, Aronica teed up and took a few practice swings, then hauled off and hit, making a much larger turn than he normally did.

"I can't watch," Savitch said, putting a hand over his eyes.

But the sound of a fingernail flicking a crystal decanter made him look upward, just in time to see Aronica's ball soaring gloriously toward the green. Just as he was about to say something complimentary, Perrault blurted out, "It's too low!"

As they watched, it was evident that although the ball had plenty of momentum, its trajectory was so shallow that it wouldn't stick to the green where it hit but would likely skitter off the back. Chelovek's lips went tight, and he folded his arms across his chest, wondering how harshly he should berate Aronica for allowing a testosterone surge to get in the way of business, when the ball hit a few inches short of the green, popped up in the air and disappeared over the lip, the landing having short-circuited its forward speed.

"Oh my, oh my, that could be good!" Aronica said, still poised in his follow-through.

"Maybe those are indeed the clubs of luck," Pensecoeur ventured.

"Luck is right, fella," Eddie said dryly. "The shot sucked."

"Was hoping nobody would notice that." Aronica smiled sheepishly as he walked off the tee. "Ah, well, y'get more bad luck than good in this game, so might's well enjoy it, right?"

"Damned straight," Eddie agreed. "No sense 'pologizing."

He hit a sloppy shot that landed off the green, then Savitch and Chelovek did the same, but Perrault put one on safely. As they drove up the path and topped the rise near the green, they gasped audibly at Kirkland's ball lying less than two feet from the hole.

"No sense getting out of the cart," Perrault said to her, conceding her birdie.

"I *like* to see her getting out of the cart," Chelovek whispered to him with an oily leer.

"Looks like you and me, Pete," Aronica said. His ball was about eight feet away, and Perrault's was roughly the same distance as Pensecoeur's, about twelve feet. Eddie turned out not to be on the green at all but off the back about three feet into the rough.

"I think you're away, Étienne," Aronica said.

"No." Eddie had a sand wedge in his hand and was walking toward his ball. "We'll play mine."

"Are you serious?" Perrault asked, incredulous. "Étienne's on the green!"

"Yeah, well," Eddie replied casually as he dropped his putter onto the grass, "I got a feeling, what can I tell you? Wanna mark yours?"

"If you say so."

When Perrault's ball was out of the way, Eddie examined his lie carefully, then took a quick look to verify his memory of the green's topography. He swung the wedge through the grass several times, getting a feel for how the club would move through it, then hunched down over the ball. Arms and back locked into an unyielding triangle, clubface opened up at a large angle almost parallel to the ground, he took an alarmingly big backswing and hit the ball hard.

As the club slid underneath, the sound of it connecting could barely be heard, but the ball popped high and straight into the air, so high that it seemed impossible that any accuracy at all could accrue to the shot. Seven faces turned upward to watch it disappear as it crossed the path of the blinding sun and quickly reemerged, seemingly right above the flagstick, dropping with a thud less than four feet from the hole.

"Jesus H., what a shot!" Savitch exclaimed.

"Thanks," Eddie said. He was already bent over to pick up his putter and hadn't even watched it land. Perrault putted to within a foot, and Kirkland conceded the par. Aronica lined up carefully and drained his for a birdie, and that gave the foursome a team score of 5. Now Eddie needed his putt to halve the hole.

Aronica, somewhat uncomfortable, said, "Think we gotta make you hit it."

Eddie, who'd been checking his line, looked up. "What're you, kidding me? Who gives away four-footers?" He sank the putt anyway, and it was no blood on the hole, the foursome still one up over the owners.

ON THE PAR-FOUR FOURTH, EDDIE, Pensecoeur, Savitch and Chelovek were all on in regulation. Eddie and Savitch two-putted for par, and it was now up to Pensecoeur and Chelovek, their balls less than a foot apart and ten feet from the hole.

"I believe it is you, *monsieur*," Pensecoeur said.

Chelovek putted first, a valiant effort, but he'd struck too hard, and the ball rolled through the break. "Hope you learned something there, big guy," he said after Pensecoeur had conceded his par putt.

"Perhaps." Pensecoeur set his ball down and didn't bother to read the green, having seen how Chelovek's ball rolled. "If I hit same as you, but not as hard . . ."

Which is exactly what he did, sinking it and winning the hole for the owners, their birdie-par 7 against the foursome's par-par 8.

"That's the ticket, ET!" Eddie said happily, and Kirkland, much to Chelovek's dismay, planted a big kiss on Pensecoeur's arm.

"Nice bird," Aronica said from the edge of the green where he'd been watching.

"Glad you liked it," Eddie said. "You're doubled."

Chapter 33

✠

"FOUR THOUSAND A MAN," ARONICA mumbled half to himself as they approached number five. "Gettin' right up there, aren't we?"

"It's still less than what we played them for the first time," Perrault said. "And we're doing better now."

Chelovek wasn't thinking about the bet. "You waste another'a them so-called lucky clubs," he said to Aronica, his even tone belying the genuine threat in his voice, "I'm gonna shove one of 'em up your ass."

"*Waste?*" Aronica stopped dead. "I made a birdie!"

Chelovek stopped as well, and put himself in Aronica's face. "You didn't need that shot to do it!" he rasped. "You coulda taken a six-iron 'steada comparing dicks with the *schvuggie!*"

"*Schvuggie?*" Perrault echoed with some merriment. "This from the champion of the downtrodden immigrant?"

"What was the fucking point!" Chelovek demanded.

"Lay off him, Jerry," Savitch said as he selected a club. "Man made a birdie. Get off his case."

"He didn't know he was gonna make a birdie," Chelovek retorted. "You see those guys looking at him, how far he hit that thing?"

"He duffed the shot, Jerrold," Perrault pointed out. "He hit it thin, practically bladed it. Like Eddie said, it was luck. They didn't see anything amiss."

"That's not the point," Chelovek said, a bit more subdued now. "Point is, why take the chance? And before the bet gets any higher, tell me in advance just how stupid you all plan to get!"

"You're so smart," Savitch said, "how come we started this round five grand in the hole to begin with?"

Chelovek whirled to face Savitch, who'd balled up his hands into fists. Perrault folded his arms across his chest and regarded them both. "Say, I've got an idea!" he said eagerly. "With four thousand each on the line, why don't we take a break and kick the daylights out of each other, okay?" He unfolded his arms and rubbed his hands together. "Come on, it'll be fun! We can throw insults, a few cheap shots"—the smile left his face and was replaced by a cross between disgust and fury—"and then we can all hold hands as those three pains in the asses take all our fucking money and we look like four douche bags handing it over!"

Chelovek looked down at the ground as Savitch let his hands relax and Aronica turned to the cart.

"There, now," Perrault said, satisfied. "Let's all play nicely with our neighbors, shall we?"

"Yeah," Chelovek agreed. "But Joe holds back on those Arondi-what-the-fuck-evers until we need 'em."

"He's right, Joe," Perrault said before Aronica could protest. "None of us cares a tinker's cuss if you can hit it farther than Pensecoeur. It's just another way for them to provoke us into doing less than our best."

THEY HALVED THE NEXT THREE holes, and the match was still all square going into the eighth.

"I got an idea," Chelovek whispered to his partners. "Hey, Eddie!"

Eddie looked up from behind the wheel of his cart.

"You're doubled!" Chelovek said with a grin.

"Jesus Christ, Jerry!" Savitch squealed. "What the hell are you—"

"Ah, relax, Deke. Time to put a little juice in this sag-ass of a golf—"

"And we'll double you back!"

Chelovek froze, and Savitch reached reflexively for his heart.

"What was that?" Perrault gasped. "What did he say?"

Aronica, blinking in disbelief, gulped loudly. "I think he said he's doubling us back."

"Can he do that?" Savitch began sweating profusely. "He can't do that, can he? Can he do that?"

"Why the hell not?" Aronica answered. "It's their turn."

"How the hell come he never consults with his partners?" Chelovek asked. "How come he makes all the decisions his own self?"

"What do I care!" Savitch choked out desperately. "What the hell is that . . . sixteen thousand a man? Oh God oh God oh—"

"Will you for Chrissakes shut up!" Chelovek spat at him, the vehemence a transparent cover for his own anxiety.

"This isn't funny anymore," Perrault said. "But I frankly don't see where we have any choice, when you think about it."

Aronica nodded. "We give in now, it's eight large a guy."

"Eight?" Savitch burbled. "How do you figure it's eight? It's four!"

"That's what I would have thought," Perrault agreed.

"Nuh-uh," Aronica corrected them. "Went to eight as soon as Eddie accepted our double."

"So what's the problem here?" Chelovek asked with feigned casualness. "How come everyone's so freakin' morose all of a sudden? We're playing good, all square after seven holes, and we haven't used Joe's magic clubs but once yet . . ."

"True." Perrault cupped his chin with one hand and tapped the side of his nose. "Besides, what's the sense of throwing in the towel at this point? Were we so inclined, we ought not to have begun the match in the first place."

"Also true," Aronica agreed.

"But sixteen thousand . . ." Savitch whined plaintively.

"You're on!" Chelovek shouted to Eddie, then turned to Savitch. "And you can relax, now that the decision's made."

"Relax!" Savitch exclaimed incredulously. "Did he say 'relax'?" The paunchy stockbroker was looking closer to catatonic than composed.

"Think of it as a test," Chelovek said easily, Savitch's anxiety somehow helping to mask his own, like a soldier hunkered down under a fusillade who bolsters his courage by ridiculing his cowering buddies. "Anybody can shoot scratch on the driving range. Let's see what you got under fire."

Deciding that Chelovek was being too much of a hard-ass, Aronica threw an arm across Savitch's shoulders and gave him a comforting squeeze. "You got the best short game I've ever seen, Deke. With the tees up front, this hole is tailor-made for you."

From the middle of the tee box, which was where the markers were now, it was a straightforward, 160-yard par-three. Straightforward if you didn't count the scale model of the Grand Canyon separating tee from green, the latter lying twenty feet below the level of the former, with bunkers falling away on both sides and an oak tree guarding the back, and did I mention that the green was only slightly larger than a business card?

It was a classic target hole, demanding nothing in the way of strength or the ability to steer the ball in the air, just pure accuracy: Play it as 150 yards, hit it straight, and stop it cold, and there was nothing to it. Kirkland and Savitch, with more finesse between them than the rest of the players combined, were the ones to watch on this one.

Just sizing up the situation and assessing the challenge made Savitch calm down. Aronica was right: It truly was his kind of one.

"What are you going to use?" Kirkland asked as the foursome made their way to the tee box.

"Depends where we put the tee," Chelovek answered before Savitch could respond. "But you're not supposed to ask." He sneered at her openly, gleeful over having caught her in a rules violation.

"Joe asked Étienne on the second hole," she replied, "and we didn't object. So what do you say we not get petty about it, okay?"

Chelovek, his normally full lips now tightened into a thin line, started to pick up the plant used for designating the tee, but Savitch held up his hand. "Right where it is."

Chelovek was bent over with his hand stretched out. "How come?" he forced out between clenched teeth.

"Because he said so," Aronica told him.

Chelovek stood up, both hands held high in whatever-you-say position, and moved away as Savitch replaced him on the tee box.

"You mean you he-men aren't going to force the wee lady to hit long again?" Kirkland asked cheerfully as she and her partners walked up to the markers.

"Now, why would we wish to do an unneighborly thing like that?" Perrault replied in kind.

"I want you, Selby," Savitch said as he flicked some grass in the air to confirm the speed and direction of the nonexistent breeze. "You're all mine."

"Oh, I am, huh?" Kirkland smiled brightly. "So show me what you've got."

Chelovek, instantly jealous of the suggestive repartee that passed so easily between Kirkland and a man other than himself, gestured impatiently for his partner to hit. Savitch, aware of the irritation he was causing Chelovek, leered at Kirkland, who answered by kissing the air in front of her and aiming it at the tee box. With one last look at the flag beckoning invitingly in the distance, Savitch turned his attention to the ball.

His swing was so relaxed and fluid it looked like a gentle practice shot. The ball, apparently pleased with the purity of how it had been struck, lofted skyward lazily and obediently hugged its line.

"Oh, my," Kirkland breathed as the perfection of the shot became progressively more apparent. The ball got bored at some point and decided it might as well descend, veering not an inch as it did so, landing toward the front of the green, bouncing a few times and rolling right for the stick.

"Get in the hole!" Chelovek yelled, unmindful of how much he sounded like the you-da-man schmucks that staked out professional tournaments.

Without realizing it, nearly all of them had taken a few steps forward, as if to get a better view of what was shaping up as a hole in one. They were so well aligned with ball and flag, though, that it was nearly impossible to detect the ball's forward motion, so Savitch and Pensecoeur crabbed sideways to try to get some perspective.

"It stopped," Pensecoeur said. "Difficult to tell, but it does indeed look like a tap-in."

"Truly superb, Deke," Eddie said admiringly. "Looks like you really wanted that one."

"Mongo like," Savitch said as he finally took his club off his shoulders and, reluctantly it seemed, gave up the tee box.

As he passed Kirkland and showed her as a courtesy that he'd used an eight-iron, she kissed her finger and touched it to his cheek. "Awesome, Deke. Now, get out of my way."

"What you got there?"

"Six," she said. "Weaker sex and all."

"Oh, come on, already!" Chelovek muttered.

"Leave them be, Jerrold," Perrault admonished.

"Well, it's getting late," Chelovek said, making no effort to hide his impatience. "Shit, we been out here for hours already."

That part was true. The "two best ball" format they were playing was still time-consuming with seven players despite how they'd modified it, and they hadn't done anything else to speed it up. With this kind of money on the line, nobody was about to feel rushed.

"Gonna get right inside'a you, Deke," Kirkland said as she banged her club into the dirt, making a little mound for her ball rather than using a tee.

"I'd like to get right inside—"

"Can it, Jerry," Eddie warned. "I told you once."

Chelovek's faced plunged rapidly to crimson, but if Kirkland heard the remark, she didn't show it, so intently was she concentrating on the shot.

"Not a breath of wind," Savitch said.

Kirkland nodded. "Saw that."

Her swing showed considerably more effort than had Savitch's, but it was no less graceful or accurate. In fact, were it not for a shallower angle, it might have been a mirror image.

Kirkland sensed the impending trajectory before the ball had even left the clubface. "Damn."

"Line's good," Savitch said encouragingly. "It could hold."

"What the hell's with this mutual-admiration society all of a sudden?" Chelovek asked Savitch irritably. "You remember we're playing for a lot of money."

"Too hot," Eddie observed. "Hope you got some backspin on that thing."

Pensecoeur, already well off to the side, looked quickly back and forth from Savitch's ball on the green to Kirkland's plummeting toward it, then ran sideways, keeping his eye on the flagstick.

The ball finally landed, slamming into Savitch's with a loud slapping sound. One of the two—it was impossible to tell which—shot sideways to the left as the other planted itself in place.

Eddie threw his hands into the air like a ref calling a touchdown as Pensecoeur, Aronica and Savitch whooped in delight. Kirkland hung her head comically and leaned on her club. "No offense, Deke," she said, "but I really hope that was yours that popped off the green."

"My kind of luck, it probably was." They both knew that if it was his that had skidded sideways, he could replace it as close to its original position as could be estimated. Kirkland's however, would have to be played wherever it landed. "Either way, you owe me big time." Had she not hit his ball, hers likely would have run off the back of the green.

"Forgot my manners: Thank you, Deke."

"Whaddaya think?" Eddie asked Pensecoeur, who was some forty feet away now.

Pensecoeur rocked his head back and forth a few times. "About a meter, perhaps." He was estimating the distance Savitch's ball had lain from the pin before it got hit.

"Sounds about right," Savitch agreed.

Chelovek, somewhat disoriented and distracted, shanked his shot badly. Aronica came up short, but Perrault was safely on, as was Eddie.

When they got to the green, they discovered that it had been Savitch's ball that went off the green, Kirkland's having taken up residence in its place. "Let's just play 'em from the same spot," she offered as Savitch approached carrying his ball.

Surveying the situation, Savitch knelt to replace his ball, then looked up and said, "Good-good?" meaning, *I'll give you yours if you'll give me mine.*

"Done." Kirkland retrieved her marker, the two of them having conceded birdies to each other. Perrault and Eddie both putted to within inches, conceded each other's pars, and the match remained all square.

"Am I the only one who hungers?" Pensecoeur asked.

Perrault blinked in surprise at the Haitian's unexpected philosophical inquiry, but Eddie said, "He means it literally. Who's for lunch?" He fished a two-way radio out of the cart and pressed the call button, then gestured for Jake to head off toward the main house.

"No cell phones?" Aronica asked.

"Here? Lucky we got electricity." When his signal was answered, Eddie spoke into the radio for a minute or so, then put it away. "Let's finish the nine, and we'll eat at the turn."

Chapter 34

■

THEY HALVED THE PAR-FIVE NINTH hole as well, but what with all the consulting and analysis, it took nearly half an hour, which gave Jake and two assistants ample time to set up lunch near the first tee of the tenth.

"Good God!" Savitch exclaimed, his eyes the size of silver dollars.

"Now, that's what I call lunch," Aronica concurred. "Hey, Pete, you're on the food committee at Connaught. Take a lesson here, will ya?"

"Certainly," Perrault answered, nearly salivating at the cornucopia that had been laid out. "If you're willing to have your dues trebled."

Chelovek was already at the tables and seemed to be experiencing greater anxiety about where to begin than he had about any shot on the front nine. There were trays artfully displaying eight kinds of sliced meat and as many types of bread and rolls, all baked within the previous hour. A triangular tray sported a riot of exotic-looking cheeses framed by crackers arranged in S-curves. A four-tiered display held a variety of pickles, relishes, mayonnaise, four kinds of mustard, ketchup, several types of lettuce and tomatoes, and onions sliced so thin they were nearly transparent.

A second table held a warming bowl of thick soup, above which rose wisps of fragrant steam. Surrounding it were bowls of papayas, mangoes, bananas, honeydews and one other fruit the boys didn't recognize, but which was sliced in half exposing bright red seeds the size of corn kernels.

"It's a pomegranate," Kirkland said as Aronica picked one up to examine it. "You eat the seeds. Here . . ." She dug one out with a fingernail and touched it to Aronica's lips.

"Delicious!" he said as he bit down and chewed.

Chelovek, looking on, grew weak in the knees. "Which part?" he said under his breath, and reached for one of a dozen wine bottles resting on a bed of ice in a large silver bucket.

"Gotta save room for some'a these," Savitch said, nearly swooning as he surveyed a pyramid-shaped display of finger-size pastries. There were cubes of angel food, lemon cake and brownies; one level devoted to cannoli and other traditional Italian delicacies, another containing home-baked chocolate-chip cookies that sprouted macadamias, walnuts and pecans in addition to the morsels of chocolate whose surfaces still glistened wetly from the heat of the oven. Next to the pyramid was a large cherrywood humidor inlaid with ivory mosaic, and next to that a plain cardboard box filled with candy bars.

Perrault, contemptuously disdaining years of health lectures he'd delivered to community groups, had already finalized construction of an elaborate sandwich that would have given Dagwood Bumstead pause and was filling the remaining space on a large china plate with dollops of potato and macaroni salad that were sprinkled with red, green and yellow flakes of dried peppers. When finished, he needed a second plate to hold the pretzels and potato chips that would provide an occasional break from the effort it would take to consume the central sandwich and its satellite delights.

Jake and one of his assistants wrestled an enormous cooler off a golf cart and onto the ground. "Drink up," he said as he opened the lid. "Hot day and gettin' hotter."

Aronica walked up and bent over the cooler, trying to decide among the standard sodas, bottled iced teas and a variety of fruit juices he didn't recognize. He was about to inquire as to the apparent absence of beer when Jake opened a cabinet on one of the food carts, revealing a spigot with a wooden handle in the shape of a ram's head. "Home brewed," he said as he withdrew a frost-covered glass mug from another cabinet. "Anybody?"

"Right here!" Aronica replied.

"Ditto!" Perrault said. He'd gotten back into his cart, his culinary treasures arrayed on the passenger seat next to him. One of the waiters came by with a beer and also a large knife, which he held inquiringly over Perrault's sandwich, cutting it neatly into quarters once he got the nod.

"Eat up, boys!" Eddie called out. "Might could be the most expensive lunch you ever ate!"

"Gonna eat *your* lunch too, Eddie!" Savitch answered in kind.

Perrault picked up one of the sandwich sections and held it in front of his face for an admiring moment, then opened wide and got ready to bite into it when he saw Kirkland walking away from one of the tables with nothing more than some oriental chicken salad in one hand and a bottle of iced tea in the other. *Watching her figure,* he assumed, then looked to her left, where Pensecoeur was leaning against his cart.

The big Haitian was holding a pathetically thin sandwich, and only half of one at that. A few pretzels and a papaya were the only other things on his plate.

Perrault glanced over at Aronica, following his friend's eyes to the farthest cart, where Eddie, who hadn't visited any of the buffet tables, was reaching into his golf bag. They watched as he withdrew a foil-wrapped, store-bought granola bar, then walked over to the beverage tub and pulled out a large bottle of plain water.

Perrault turned to find Chelovek and saw him standing with a full glass of wine in his hand but not drinking any. Savitch was a few steps away, his overflowing plate untouched.

As the others watched, a slow smile spread across Chelovek's face. He walked over to Perrault's cart, and the others followed him. When they were gathered together and out of earshot of the owners, he said, "So just how serious are we?" and overturned his wineglass, spilling the pale yellow-green liquid onto the grass.

Perrault did the same with his beer, and Aronica immediately followed suit.

Savitch looked longingly at his plate, then cast one last covetous glance at the pastry tray lurking malevolently on the closest table before setting the plate aside. "You suppose they'd wrap this stuff for later?"

Perrault laughed and patted Savitch on the shoulder. "If Eddie comes over all hurt and tries make us feel guilty for spurning his largesse," he said, pointing to the lavish spread and dismissing all of it with a single wave of his hand, "just—"

"Just nothing," Chelovek interrupted. "Enough here for the Yangtze Division of the Chinese Army, and *they* didn't touch any of it."

Aronica nodded his agreement. "We're supposed to worry about some conniving SOB who wants us to gorge out on a couple hundred bucks' worth of sandwiches so we can puke sixty-four grand into his lap?"

"I'm going to get some chicken salad and a soda," Perrault said, "and then let's get this show on the road."

"You mean you guys aren't going to eat any of this stuff?" Jake said as he watched Perrault dump the contents of his untouched plate into a small garbage can.

"We're playing golf, son," Chelovek said, "case nobody told you." He opened the lid of the humidor and quickly selected two large cigars. Holding them up, he said, "All the nutrition I need right here."

Aronica came up behind him and took a Snickers bar from the cardboard box sitting next to the humidor. "All four major food groups in one itty-bitty package," he said. "See ya later, Jake."

KIRKLAND SAUNTERED OVER TO WHERE Eddie and Chelovek were lighting up cigars.

"Smoke bother you?" Chelovek asked.

"Nah," Eddie said, "she loves it. That's the real reason she came over."

Chelovek was trying to get some X-ray vision going as he surveyed Kirkland, then caught her looking at him and dropped his eyes to her hands. "Nice rock. What's that . . . about two carats?"

"Good eye. One and a half."

Chelovek munched on his cigar before blowing out a thick cloud of smoke. "Greatest triumph in the history of advertising. Wanna bet me a grand straight up you couldn't tell a real one from a piece of glass?"

"Ah . . . I don't think so."

"Right. Now, what I regret?"

"Yeah . . . ?"

"I wasn't the guy who got everybody thinkin' a good rule of thumb for what to spend on a diamond is two months' salary." Chelovek tapped the side of his head with a knuckle. "I'd give back my Clio, I knew how the hell he got anybody to fall for that. It's better'n Beanie Babies, Princess Di memorial plates and the Swoosh all rolled into one."

"As good as the lottery?"

Chelovek smiled at Kirkland's insight. "Nothin's as good as the lottery, but gambling's old news. Diamonds? That's genius from scratch." Chelovek could afford to smile, given how good a job he'd done of making Kirkland feel like two cents.

"Missed yourself a golden opportunity there, didja, Jerry?" Eddie said sympathetically.

"Ah, one'a these days my time'll come," Chelovek replied.

Then he stood up, grabbed a club and aced the tenth hole.

·

I COULD GO ON AND try to wax eloquent about what a gorgeous shot it was, but it really wasn't. A hole in one is always a matter of luck, of course; it's difficult enough to hit a four-inch target 420 feet away with a rifle, never mind a golf ball. While it certainly takes skill to hit a ball somewhere close to the pin, putting it in the hole is 100 percent pure happenstance, and while being an accurate hitter certainly increases your odds, there's simply no such thing as doing it on purpose. If there were, the best golfers in the world would be raining aces all the time, and they don't.

But there's luck and then there's luck. The kind you see on a televised tour event is generally some terrific golfer planting one close and draining it, which may be more about the laws of probability than skill but still requires plenty of the latter, and the result is a special reward for a well-struck shot.

Then there's the kind Chelovek had on the tenth at Swithen Bairn, a 140-yard teaser fronted by a valley, backed by a mountain and flanked by bunkers. Chelovek bladed a nine-iron badly, sending the ball shooting straight forward, where it smacked into the very bottom of the depression, popped into the air and landed on the front of the green. It had picked up so much topspin from the bounce that it shot forward as soon as it landed, heading for high up on the hill behind the green, until it was intercepted by the flagstick.

Shuddering from the impact, the stick gave just enough for the ball not to bounce back off of it, instead climbing straight up, *whuffing* softly into the pennant and dropping straight back down and into the hole, out of which it bounced right back up and right back in.

There was a moment of dead silence on the tee box, jubilation on the part of our boys being constrained somewhat by the sheer awfulness of Chelovek's shot. For their parts, the owners were a little stuck for what to say, feeling that to congratulate their opponent for the rare ace might prove embarrassing in light of the absurd manner in which it had been achieved.

Chelovek himself broke the ice. "Like Joe put it," he said, eyes still on the flag, "the golf gods taketh away often enough . . . they can freakin' well give one back once in a goddamned while."

"Amen, brother," Eddie acknowledged, as Perrault threw his hands up and Aronica gave Chelovek a high five.

"We're in trouble, boys," Kirkland said to her partners. She aimed her club at Chelovek. "How do I set this to stun?"

Savitch clasped his hands beneath his chin. "Can I touch you, mister?"

"Sorry, son, my powers can only be used for good." Chelovek held a hand out toward the tee and said to Kirkland as he leered at her, "Top that!"

"Tell you the truth," Kirkland said as she walked past him, "I don't think that can be topped." Chelovek's smile faded as he tried to figure out if he'd just been insulted.

"Don't give up yet, *chère*," Pensecoeur said.

"Yeah," Eddie added. "Couple'a birdies from us and a par from one'a them, ace won't mean a thing."

"Hold this," Kirkland said, taking off her ring and casually tossing it to Pensecoeur.

"Hey . . . !" Chelovek cried out instinctively.

"Don't worry," she said. "It's fake."

She took an especially long time sizing up the shot and hit a good one, wisely going for the fat of the green rather than a heroic attempt to nail the front of it. Eddie did the same, and they had two safe ones, although Eddie looked at his pitching wedge strangely and remarked that it didn't feel right. "Grip's a little off."

Pensecoeur's try was a valiant one, but it landed too short and the terrific backspin he'd put on the ball dragged it backward and off the green, where it rolled uselessly down into the depression.

For the rest of the foursome, Savitch's was the best shot, as expected, with a fifteen-foot putt for birdie.

At the green, Kirkland was up first. She took her time reading the line from various angles, and as she went back to her ball, Eddie said, "Whatever you do—"

"Don't leave it short, I know." If she didn't sink the putt, they were dead, so it wouldn't make any difference if she missed it long or short. Therefore, there was nothing to be lost by hitting it extra hard and making sure it at least reached the hole, whereas coming up short would be an unforgivable sin.

"And miss it on the pro side."

A good piece of advice to any golfer on any putt with a break in it: Always favor the side of the hole that faces uphill. There the ball always has a chance of falling *down* and into the hole, especially if it runs out of steam at the end, but it's never going to fall *up* from the low side. About 90 percent of amateur putts that miss do so on the low side. For the pros the percentage is more like half that.

"Hey, Socrates . . ." Kirkland stood up from her surveying and held her putter out toward Eddie. "You want to take the putt?"

As Pensecoeur sniggered loudly, Eddie whirled in feigned embarrassment and walked a few steps away before turning back to watch.

Eschewing practice swings, as was her habit on the green, Kirkland settled the club in behind the ball before taking up her stance. She had her beginning line picked out and carefully aligned square to it. With little further preamble beyond letting her breath out slowly, she brought the club back and swung it forward, same speed in both directions, not looking up until the ball was well on its way.

"Uh-oh," Pensecoeur said, sensing that it was moving much too slowly.

"But I belted it!" Kirkland insisted.

It was just a very slow green, and being the first to hit, she'd had no way to assess the speed based on somebody else's putt. The only good news as the ball decelerated rapidly was that she had in fact hit it on the high side, because the lack of momentum was causing the ball to respond to every bit of break and curve dramatically to the left. It was headed dead for the hole; one more millimeter per hour of clubhead speed and she'd have popped it right into the heart of the cup.

As it was, the ball had turned at almost right angles, losing the last of its gas at the exact moment it reached the very right edge of the cup, hanging on the precipice with such tantalizing tenuousness that a single dimple more of roll would have dropped it in for sure.

As Kirkland finally stood up straight and exhaled loudly, Chelovek walked to the cup and extended his putter in preparation for knocking the ball back to Kirkland and conceding the par, but before he could touch it, she screamed "Leave it alone!"

Startled, Chelovek yanked his putter away and stood there, wondering what her problem was. Kirkland strolled slowly to the cup as Eddie clapped his hands and said, "Shadow it in, baby!"

She had ten seconds from the time she arrived at the cup following a reasonably paced walk to see if the ball would drop in, and the longer she took, the better the chances. But even when she got there, she wasn't about to just stand idly by and wait.

As soon as she got to the cup, Kirkland stepped around it to put her shadow over the hole, then checked her watch. Chelovek, still somewhat shaken, looked at his partners in puzzlement.

Kirkland kept her eye on her watch. Meanwhile, the ground in the vicinity of the ball was cooling slightly, robbed of the sun's direct heat as she blocked the light. The contraction of individual blades of grass underneath was vanishingly small, but the weight of the ball was vast in comparison, and some eight seconds later the delicate balancing act that was holding the ball fast to the lip collapsed, and it dropped in with a startlingly loud and enormously gratifying clatter.

This time it was Pensecoeur and Eddie's turn to celebrate, which they did with something that looked like a cross between a Senegalese battle dance and the Funky Chicken, while our boys tried to muster up the good grace to mumble congratulations. Chelovek didn't at all like the hug Pensecoeur gave Kirkland, or the butt-wiggle she effected while his arms were around her.

When the merriment died down, it was Savitch's turn. He took a moment to tamp down the grass at the edge of the cup closest to his ball with his putter. "Don't think my poor heart could take it," he said to Kirkland, "if I had to stand over a lipper like yours and wait for it to go in."

"Strike it firm, Deke," Perrault called out to him.

"Never up, never in," Aronica added.

Savitch hit it too firm. It was a beautiful line, maybe a half inch left of center, but the ball's momentum was enough to send it careening around the inside edge and right back out again.

"Pick it up," Eddie said. With an ace and a par, the foursome had a combined score of 4. If Eddie could sink his putt for a birdie, the owners would also have a 4, and there would be no blood on the hole.

He wasn't about to be intimidated by what had happened to Savitch's putt; hitting it solid to the hole was the right thing to do in this situation, and that's what he did, missing dead center by the same margin as Savitch, and suffering the same result. His par gave the owners a 5, and the stalemate was broken, the owners down by one with eight holes left.

Our boys, abandoning all notions of sportsmanship, cheered lustily at their opponent's error, and it was Savitch, pecuniary greed lighting up his eyes like dollar signs, who grabbed Chelovek's collar and said, "Hit 'em, Jerry! Hit 'em hard."

"Do it, buddy!" Aronica and Perrault encouraged him. "Sock 'em one!"

"With pleasure, gents." Chelovek turned toward the owners, shuffling off the opposite side of the green. "You're doubled!"

All three of them stopped dead, looking at each other before turning around. "Thirty-two big ones each?"

"You got a problem with that?" Chelovek answered, barely able to keep the excitement out of his voice.

The owners huddled together and resumed their walk back to the carts. The boys could see Pensecoeur shaking his head, but it communicated doubt more than refusal, as if he was telling Eddie and Kirkland that he didn't know if he could keep up his end.

Eddie gave him two slaps on the back and then twisted his head around. "Accepted!" he cried without breaking step.

"Yes!" Aronica exulted quietly with an arm-pump.

THEY HALVED THE ELEVENTH, SAME thing on the twelfth and were still up by one with only six holes to go.

They tied yet again on number thirteen, and all seven of them ambled off the green together, Aronica, Eddie and Kirkland eventually walking as a threesome away from the others. Eddie was carrying the pitching wedge he'd complained about earlier.

"How'd you get into this game, Selby?" Aronica asked.

"That a question you ask your male friends, too?"

Aronica, blushing, tried to stammer something back, then stopped as Kirkland touched his arm lightly and flashed him a dazzling smile that could have warmed a small planet. "Just teasing."

Eddie pulled a pocketknife from his back pocket and before Aronica could react, opened the blade, laid it against the shaft of the pitching wedge and stripped off a large chunk of the grip.

"I used to play basketball and soccer," Kirkland said, totally oblivious to the damage Eddie was wreaking on one of his most reliable weapons. "The better you get," she said as Eddie continued to hack off the grip, "the more distasteful nonsense it takes to stay on top. Sportsmanship becomes this act you put on for the press, because for damned sure nobody who actually plays at the highest levels expects it from anybody else."

The grip now completely gone, Eddie folded the blade back into the case and extended a rasp, which he ran along the top of the shaft to smooth away the last remnants of the departed rubber.

"Thing about golf," Kirkland went on, still ignoring Eddie, "there's no way to interfere with your opponent's game. You can't block his shot, steal his ball, obstruct his vision or shove him or tackle him."

Eddie put away the knife just as they came up to the waiting carts. He reached into his bag, pulled out a small tin can with a screw top and opened it. There was a brush attached to the lid, and he used it to spread the clear liquid inside onto the naked metal of the club shaft. A powerful odor of acetone hit Aronica's nose and made him shy away.

"There's no defense," Kirkland said as she sat down in the cart, "so the only way to beat the other guy is to play better yourself, and that's what makes it the most civilized and sublime of sports. Don't you think so?"

"Um, definitely," Aronica agreed, still distracted. Eddie took a new grip from another pocket of his bag, slipped it onto the shaft and pressured it all around with his fingers.

"Much better," he said, dropping the club into the bag and getting into the cart. "Selby's right about golf, y'know. It relies more on honor than it does on rules, rewards finesse more than strength, and it's the only game that lets people far apart in skill compete head to head on an equal footing."

Kirkland leaned out of the cart and looked at Aronica. "So long as they don't cheat on their handicaps," she said as the cart moved forward, leaving Aronica standing in bewildered disbelief at Eddie's having casually regripped a club in the middle of a round.

THEY RECONVENED AT THE next tee box, still talking about the last hole.

"Nice putt," Perrault said to Pensecoeur.

"Good tee shot," Savitch said to Kirkland.

"You're doubled," Eddie said to nobody in particular.

Chapter 35

■

"I GOTTA SIT DOWN," SAVITCH said, and indeed he looked a little pale.

"I say, give us a moment here?" Perrault said to Eddie.

"Take all the time you want, boys."

Savitch's partners sat with him just off the green, so it wouldn't look to the owners like their portly friend had fallen down rather than voluntarily sat.

"Hells'a matter with you?" Chelovek asked without a trace of sympathy.

Savitch had his head between his knees, or as close as he could get to that position given the amplitude of his belly and the paucity of his flexibility. "I think I'm gonna be sick."

"Swell." Chelovek threw his hands into the air and let them slap loudly to his thighs. "Couldn'ta gotten sick when we were playing for a grand? You hadda wait till we were up to sixty-four large?"

At the mention of the size of the wager, Savitch groaned and wrapped his arms around his knees, as if to curl himself into a ball small enough to disappear down an ant hole.

"What do we do now?" Perrault asked, a tremor evident in his voice.

"What the fuck did you think we were gonna do?" Aronica answered tightly, suppressing his own fear by ridiculing Savitch's. "We're gonna take it."

"And then we're gonna double 'em right back," Chelovek threw in.

Savitch toppled over in a dead faint.

.

PERRAULT MANEUVERED HIMSELF AROUND SO the owners wouldn't see one of their opposite number stretched flat out on the grass, limbs akimbo and doubtless harboring no burning desire to be revived, which the physician nevertheless dutifully attempted.

Pinching a bit of skin on Savitch's forearm between his thumb and fore-finger, Perrault let go and observed how slowly it resumed its former shape, a white mark clearly indicating where he'd applied pressure. "Asshole's dehydrated," he announced, perhaps not in entirely appropriate medical terminology but nevertheless communicating the problem quite clearly. "Joe, be a sport and find out if Jake has any Gatorade or something similar in the ice bucket."

Chelovek regarded the prostrate stockbroker with clinical detachment. "Thought once you got this far, drinking can't do it any longer. Doesn't he need like an IV or something?"

"Would if he were badly dried out." Perrault lifted one of his patient's eye-lids, forgetting for a moment they were outdoors. The sun high overhead lanced into Savitch's eye, and he winced slightly, Perrault watching as the pupil quickly contracted. "But I rather suspect it was more the thought of playing golf for a hundred and twenty-eight thousand. My word, Jerrold . . . !"

Savitch weakly swatted Perrault's hand away, the doctor having forgotten to let his eyelid close, then rolled onto his side and tried to sit up. Chelovek got a hand under his arm and helped him into a sitting position, just as Aronica returned with a cold bottle of some greenish liquid.

"Eddie says this'll do the trick," he reported, holding it out to Perrault. "Says it's got potassium, and, uh—"

"Yeah, I'll bet," Savitch said softly. "Pro'ly more like strychnine."

"So you don't want it?" Perrault asked.

"Gimme that." Savitch, his strength returning, reached for the bottle. "Wish it *was* strychnine."

His friends laughed as he took a few tentative sips before eagerly downing half the bottle, but it faded quickly.

"You're serious, aren't you?" Aronica said to Chelovek.

"Betcher ass."

"That's exactly what I *am* doing!" Aronica threw back, and they laughed nervously again.

"It's a psych job, pure and simple." Seeing that Savitch was going to be okay, Chelovek leaned back on his hands. "We're up a hole, and they haven't won one since number four. We're playing great, all the marbles are in our court—they got no choice but to try to rattle us."

Perrault flicked a finger at Savitch, urging him to keep drinking. "Did a bang-up job, let me tell you." The only difference between Perrault's and Savitch's anxiety levels was that one of them hadn't fainted. Other than that, they were both in danger of turning to pudding.

"That's my point," Chelovek said, leaning forward to take the weight off his arms so he could gesture with his hands. "The best way to shake somebody up is by doing something that'd shake *you* up if they did it to you. Listen, their shit stinks same as ours. You think if we threw another double in their faces right now it wouldn't freak 'em out? Come on!"

"Well, thank you, Mr. Chelovek," Aronica said. "We're all refreshed and challenged by your unique point of view."

"Why don't we just accept their double and 'freak 'em out' that way?" Perrault asked, ridiculing Chelovek's mode of speech just as the adman liked to ridicule his. "Why inflate it all the way to . . ." He couldn't even bring himself to say the number.

"Who says we have to accept at all?" Savitch said, wiping his arm across his mouth and laying the empty bottle on the grass.

His partners looked at him incredulously. "You'd quit now and pay up thirty-two large?" Aronica asked in astonishment. "We're up a hole on 'em!"

"What if we lose?" Savitch asked.

"Fellas, fellas . . ." Chelovek got to his knees and grew even more animated. "You're not thinking! It's not just about accepting or doubling 'em back, it's also about making good and damned sure we win!"

"We're playin' pretty good," Aronica observed.

"Oh, yeah?" Chelovek pointed toward where the owners were sitting. "You willing to bet a hundred thousand bucks one'a those shitheads won't blow a shot on eighteen and accidentally sink the fucker anyway, like I did?"

Enjoying the silence he received by way of reply, Chelovek let it go on for a few seconds, then said, "I say we go high or go home. Only way it makes sense to keep playing is to throw it right back in their faces and let *them* be the ones shittin' their pants!"

He could see in their faces that they'd made the decision, and years of negotiating experience told him to stay quiet.

"Only one small problem with that theory, Jerrold," Perrault said at last as he wiped his hands and prepared to stand up.

"And what might that be?"

"Just because they're going to be soiling their trousers doesn't mean we won't be soiling ours." Perrault stood and took a deep breath as he looked over toward the owners, then let it out with a what-the-hell sigh. "Do it."

As soon as Chelovek got nods from Aronica and Savitch, he rose to his feet and whistled to get the owners' attention. He then leaned down and clapped a hand onto Aronica's shoulder. "Time to pull Excalibur out of the stone, Joe."

Aronica looked over at his special clubs and slowly nodded. Chelovek left quickly to accept the double and offer another back to the owners before his friends had a chance to reconsider.

Chapter 36

❖

CHELOVEK MOVED THE TEE MARKERS on the long par-five back as far as they would go. "That takes the broad out," he said quietly to his partners, "and maybe the voodoo man'll try to come out of his shoes and fuck it up."

"I like it," Savitch said. As Perrault invited Kirkland to hit first, Savitch went through half a dozen mind games to try to keep the size of the bet out of his mind, and settled on trying to sound as if he didn't care, thinking that might help him believe it. Eddie had proposed making the new bet an even $125,000 instead of $128,000 because, as he'd put it, "It makes the math easier." Savitch wished that it had stayed at 128, because he didn't want the math to be easier; he wanted those gigantic numbers to be cloudy and indistinct in his head.

"Just hit it safe," Eddie said to Kirkland. He looked slightly troubled, the acceptance of his double apparently having come as a bit of a surprise and the redouble as a total shock.

Kirkland, too, chose to forgo one of her usual acerbic comebacks and, nervously, it seemed, teed up and swung her three-wood a few times to loosen up after the long hiatus since they'd played number thirteen. She eyed the fairway, but it was purely habit; the flag was well over a quarter mile away, and her job was just to lay it down somewhere in the middle and keep it in play, a contingency in case one of her partners blew his tee shot.

Forcing herself to relax, she took up her stance and tried to focus solely on the job at hand. Her swing was tentative and unfinished, shooting off the toe of the club and alarmingly off-line, heading straight for a stand of palm trees to the right.

Dropping the club, she covered her eyes with her hands and bent over, waiting for the groans to tell her how badly she'd blown it. A sharp knocking sound was followed by exclamations of surprise behind her, and she popped up again and looked backward and then out toward the fairway. "Where'd it go!" she demanded.

"Directly in the fairway," Pensecoeur responded.

Not trusting his English, Kirkland searched frantically to see what he meant, then gasped as she spotted the ball dead center in the fairway and about two hundred yards out. "How the—I hit a tree?"

"Sure did," Eddie said. "Good thing, too, 'cuz I was about to put you over my knee and spank you."

Chelovek let out a low moan at that but cut it off when Eddie turned to give him a threatening look. Kirkland sighed deeply, rubbed her eyes hard with both hands and bent over to pick up her club.

Chelovek stepped up next. "Safe, safe, safe," Aronica reminded him, and so it was. Without the necessity to play a heroic shot, Chelovek used a two-wood, backed off the swing slightly and smoothly set it down 240 yards out and a little to the right. Savitch did roughly the same, which left Perrault free to go to hell with himself.

"Oh, joy!" he said as he hopped onto the tee box with his driver. For all practical purposes his shot was essentially superfluous, so he whaled away happily with everything he had.

It was a masterpiece, perhaps the best drive he'd ever hit in his life. He'd come so far out of the shot that he was twisted around and not even facing the fairway when he finished.

"Jumpin' Jesus!" Savitch cried out, watching in fascination as the ball flashed into the sky and seemed to wink out of existence altogether.

"I didn't even see it!" wailed Perrault, who knew by the sound how well he'd hit it.

"Just look out about three hundred yards," Eddie advised.

"But I can't hit anywhere *near* three hundred yards."

"That's what you think."

While the others ooh-ed and ah-ed over the wonderful shot, which was actually more like 290 than 300, Aronica smiled to himself. Things couldn't have been set up more perfectly. He'd been worrying about how to get away with an overachieving drive using his miracle-metal club without arousing suspicion, and Perrault had just handed him the key.

Returning to his bag and pretending to switch clubs, he came back with the driver still in his hands. "Was gonna use a safe three," he announced, "but with my buddies burnin' it up like they did, well . . ."

"Want us to hit?" Eddie asked.

"Nope." He hefted the driver and took a few big, fully extended swings, the sound of the clubhead moving through the air not unlike a powerful hair dryer being switched on and off. "I wait too long, I'm gonna chicken out."

That wasn't it. Aronica wanted his team to have four superb shots sitting on the fairway, two of them well in excess of halfway to the green, before the two remaining owners hit. Eddie and Pensecoeur would then have no choice but to overdo it and try to crush their own tee shots. It would be risky for them, but probably not as risky as opening a door wide enough to let Aronica and Perrault through.

"Best step back, folks," Aronica said. "I may break the sound barrier here."

Half of a good golf swing is mechanics, but a bigger half is the degree of confidence with which you approach the shot. The best chance at a great shot is knowing for a dead certainty that it's going to be great, and Aronica knew with religious conviction that this one would be. It didn't matter if he turned his wrists over or had his shoulders square or his hips properly aligned. All that mattered was making sure his hands followed through toward the target after impact, and Aronica had his swing plane so burned into his muscle memory that it was completely automatic.

ARONDIUM WAS ARONICA'S ONE MAJOR triumph, his only real accomplishment, and he knew it. He lived as though his whole life were a sham and it was only a matter of time until the rest of the world found out. Exactly *why* it was a sham wasn't precisely clear to him but probably sprang from the same deep-seated self-doubt that had plagued him ever since stealing home in the bottom of the ninth in a Little League game some forty years ago.

Running the bases, he'd gotten ready to hold up at third but noticed that a fortuitous little dust sprite had swirled sand into the eyes of the catcher, who was therefore in no position to shag the ball thrown in from center field. That allowed Aronica to swoop in on home plate without even the sportsmanlike concession of a feigned slide to at least show that the game-winning run had taken some effort. The poor catcher was still clawing at his stinging eyes as Aronica's teammates hoisted him onto their shoulders, hailing the hero who had given new meaning to "stealing" a base. The celebration had rung a little hollow at the time, Aronica knowing quite well how he'd accomplished his feat, but the subsequent adulation quickly dimmed that annoying memory, and the lesson was well learned: If you can't dazzle 'em with brilliance, baffle 'em with bullshit.

Aronica naturally went into sales, but not before earning a master's in engineering, largely by specializing in metallurgy at a time when that department at the university was in danger of being phased out owing to lack of interest among the students. By promising the anxiety-ridden professors that he could recruit students to the department, and by recruiting those students with assurances that grading would be absurdly lenient because the professors were too skittish about frightening anybody out of the program, a Faustian bargain was struck in which the department was saved by foisting upon an unsuspecting corporate world a graduating class consisting largely of lapsed English and philosophy majors who had found a neat way out of spending the next eight years of their lives uttering the line immortalized by generations of previous liberal-art graduates: "You want fries with that?"

Thus had Aronica saved the department the same way he'd saved the baseball game, via an uncanny ability to perceive opportunity where others perceived only failure. The eternal gratitude of the metallurgists was expressed with a *cum laude* designation on Aronica's diploma and a set of personal references that would have been excessive even had he invented Teflon.

Had Joe Aronica been as adept at introspection as he was at self-deception, he might have understood that part of his constant free-floating anxiety stemmed from the semiconscious realization that much of what he'd achieved had arisen from guile rather than skill, that his escalating quest for validation was doomed to failure because the one thing he'd never chosen to do to manifest his achievements was actually *work* for them.

Instead, his practiced denial had led him to the conclusion that his midlife ennui was the result of some Michael Jordan–esque notion of completion, that he'd achieved all he could in his chosen profession and without some new challenge he was forever doomed to the boredom and discontent that were the bane of all great men who'd done what they'd set out to do but hadn't taken the time to think beyond that point. That he hadn't had the slightest advanced notion of what he'd "set out to do" was beside the point, his official corporate profile making it sound as though the creation of the Arondium dream metal had been the result of superhuman effort expended over years in pursuit of a childhood dream.

He was the true scared rabbit of the bunch, more fearful of life itself than Savitch, and hadn't even had the stones to start his own manufacturing company for Arondium, choosing just to license it out to third-party manufacturers instead.

But he truly loved the stuff—even liked the ring of its name—and he was standing with a carefully machined piece of it in his hand right now.

ALL THAT REMAINED WAS TO swing as hard as he possibly could, normally the biggest mistake in golf and a guaranteed blown shot.

But not with this club.

I won't bother to describe the swing; it was too damned ugly to immortalize in text, Aronica stumbling at the end because of the momentum he'd generated. His right foot came completely off the turf, and he had to set it back down in a hurry to keep from falling over completely, but he finished with his elbows high and the club down between his shoulders facing his right foot.

The onlookers were so startled by the sound, which was like a powerfully hit cue ball slamming into the rack in a small room with cinder-block walls, several of them blinked and thought they'd missed the sight of the ball coming off the tee, which was understandable because the only thing that could actually have seen that would have been a high-speed camera like the ones used to photograph atomic-bomb explosions.

Kirkland could have sworn she saw condensation trailing from behind the ball as it rocketed upward, like what you see coming off airplane wings during takeoff on a humid day. Chelovek gulped and wondered if Aronica had overdone it. Pensecoeur's mouth was agape, and Eddie seemed lost in wonder at how anything hit that clumsily could travel so perfectly straight.

"I lost it," Aronica said as he straightened himself out. "It go okay?"

"Don't think you got all of it," Eddie replied, and the others might have laughed, except that the ball still hadn't started descending and at least two of them began to wonder if it might actually achieve escape velocity and head directly for Jupiter.

"I can't even see it anymore," Kirkland said.

"It's in the middle," Savitch said helpfully. "How far, I have no idea."

"There it is," Pensecoeur finally said. He was somewhat farsighted and was able to make out the ball on the fairway.

Chelovek squinted and nodded his head. "Yeah, I got it. Near that cypress tree."

"Bullshit," Eddie said. "That cypress is the two-hundred mark."

Aronica turned to him, his face full of surprise and amazement, all of it just to hide the guile below. "You telling me I hit it three-forty?"

"Either that or your buddy's hallucinating."

Aronica looked back down the fairway, searching in vain for his ball. "Damn!" he said with childish delight.

Pensecoeur walked slowly toward the tee box. "We are in the *merde* now, *mon ami.*"

"Man still has to put it on and putt," Eddie said encouragingly. "Your job, don't get crazy. Safe one in the middle, savvy?"

"*D 'accord.*"

Pensecoeur was too rattled to do anything but follow Eddie's instructions, and he did so brilliantly, laying a 270-yarder just to the left of the centerline, about 20 yards short of Perrault's career shot. Eddie's drive was a yawn, his standard 250 down the middle, and now that the big hits had been accomplished, this hole was about the middle and short games.

EDDIE HIT FIRST, USING A three-wood to put himself within pitching distance of the green. As per his advice, Pensecoeur used a four-iron to do the same.

Perrault was not as disciplined. From 250 out, he hit a three-wood too hard and shanked it. Luckily, it was still playable, but from nowhere near as good an angle as he would have liked, and much farther from the green as well.

As they resumed their walk up the fairway, Chelovek veered off from Aronica and called out so the owners could hear, "Whatcha gonna use, Joe?"

"Five-iron!" Aronica yelled back. He set down his bag and took the arondium seven-iron out, stepping up to the ball quickly so the owners would stop some forty yards away instead of closer, where they could get a look at the club. This time his swing was back to his classic, relaxed form, and indeed it would have looked to the casual observer like a perfectly reasonable five-iron shot, if by "perfectly reasonable" you included a trajectory that looked as though a rail had been laid down in the sky for the ball to follow.

The miracle-metal club could help you hit it very straight and very far, which was why it was illegal, or would be if the governing body of golf knew about it, but the one thing it couldn't help you do was fine-tune distance. That didn't make a difference on most long tee shots, where all you cared about was straight and far, but on approaches it was still a critical factor, and Aronica had misjudged this one. The ball waved hello and good-bye at the flagstick as it passed by, and only a soft surface kept it on the green at all instead of letting it fly off the back.

It was still a nice shot. "Good one, Joe," Eddie called generously, then said softly to Pensecoeur, "You see how the grass gave on that one?"

"*Oui.*" That meant he didn't have to be as concerned about exaggerating the loft on his pitch to the green, a shot the Haitian wasn't particularly good at. If he had decent height, the soft grass would help to stop his ball.

Eddie, on the other hand, was a master of the lob, and hit a sand wedge almost straight up and to a dizzying height. It plopped onto the green about eighteen feet from the pin, coming to rest less than a hand's width from the inch-high, muddy pitch mark it had raised.

Pensecoeur hit conservatively, landing near the very front of the green and letting the soft surface restrain the release. He ended up about fifteen feet away, then Perrault wisely went for the fat of the green and put his ball a foot from Pensecoeur's and an inch or two closer to the pin.

Now it was a putting contest. The two owners and Perrault lay three, and Aronica two. If everybody two-putted, our boys would have another one under their belts and be up by two holes.

But Aronica was still over thirty feet away, and he had to putt first, with no opportunity to assess the speed or break based on somebody else's shot.

Savitch, the best putter in the bunch, walked Aronica to his ball. "Way whatshisname's released, I think you're looking at a pretty slow roll here."

"Yeah, but it's a downhill." That made for a deadly combination, fiendishly difficult to judge.

"True, but for darned sure you want the second one to be an uphill, so you need this one to be past that cup."

Neither of them was planning on Aronica's first putt going in the hole. That wasn't something you needed to account for. As long as your intention was to miss it past the cup, draining it was an eventuality that would take care of itself.

Aronica moved back and knelt, aligning himself with the hole and the ball and holding up his putter by two fingers at the end of the grip. Lining up the bottom of the club with the ball, he saw that the top was to the right of the cup, which gave him the general direction of the break: right to left. But it told him little about the amount and nothing about where most of it would occur, so he walked to the other side of the hole, Savitch in tow, and checked things from there.

"Looks to me like most of the bend is near the ball," Savitch observed. "Gonna flatten out near the hole."

Aronica nodded his understanding. Since the ball's speed would be great-est at the beginning, the break wouldn't have that much effect on it, and it would have to be perfectly aligned with the hole by the time that break ran out. It was a tough one to judge.

There is no way for one golfer to communicate to another how hard to hit a putt beyond some relativistic expression describing the result rather than the method, such as *Put it three feet past* or *Go for the back edge* or *Just get it started and let the slope do the rest,* so Savitch patted Aronica's arm, said, "Be aggressive" and stepped well out of his sight line.

Aronica returned to his ball with a good idea of what had to be done, knelt once again to confirm his direction and then stood up. He took a few practice swings to try to nail down the speed and remind himself to stay square, then set up over the ball.

It came off the clubhead hot, as he'd intended in order to compensate for the mushy surface, but for a split second he thought he might have over-done it. The ball skidded instead of rolled and was affected by the break even less than he'd anticipated, heading straight off and barely turning at all.

"Bend, you sonofabitch!" Chelovek screamed at it, but by the time he fin-ished, the ball was slowing dramatically and starting to follow the topography as it was supposed to. More than it was supposed to.

"Hey . . ." Savitch began, startled by the ball's eccentric trail.

By the time the sloping part of the surface ended, the ball was heading wildly left of the hole and decelerating rapidly, petering out to a humiliating and anticlimactic stop some three feet short of the cup.

Aronica raised up his putter and looked at it. "Thought I hit the shit out of it!"

Savitch was down on his knees peering at the green. "What the heck is this stuff?" he said.

"Bermuda," Eddie answered, setting down his ball and picking up his marker.

"Bermuda?" Savitch looked up, surprise and confusion on his face, then returned his gaze to the surface to confirm Eddie's answer.

"Whaddaya mean, Bermuda!" Chelovek bellowed. "The rest'a this place is *bent!*"

"This one was redone," Eddie explained as he started to line up his putt. "Something the trees do to the drainage, beats me exactly what. It was either cut down the trees or change the grass, so . . ."

"Would have been sporting had you mentioned it," Perrault muttered, looking over Savitch's shoulder. He saw right away that Aronica had been putting dead into the grain of the Bermuda grass, which was why his ball had slowed so severely.

"How many times you guys play this hole since you been here?" Eddie volleyed back. He knocked his putt to within a foot and, receiving no concession from the suddenly mute foursome, tapped it in for a par.

Pensecoeur was now away, and as he replaced his ball, Perrault took up a position behind him but a respectful twenty feet back. With his ball only a foot from Pensecoeur's, he'd have an excellent read of the line by watching how the Haitian's ball behaved on its way to the cup.

"Can't stand there, Pete," Eddie admonished lightly.

"Pardon? Étienne, have you got a problem with it?"

"Doesn't matter if he does or not," Eddie said. "Rules say you can't."

Perrault looked over at Savitch, who nodded his agreement with Eddie's ruling, and then moved reluctantly out of Pensecoeur's line. "Wasn't aware we were standing on such formalities," he said, with a trace of petulance despite Eddie's lack of rancor in invoking the rule. "We've been teeing out of order all day."

"Honors aren't in the rule book," Kirkland explained. "With these kind of stakes, do we really want to make them up as we go along?"

"She's right," Aronica said. "Let's do it by the book."

"Actually," Eddie said, "honors *is* in the rules."

Chelovek blinked in surprise. "It is?"

"Yeah. But I don't give a shit about who hits first if you guys don't."

"I've no problem with that," Perrault agreed, Chelovek not being in the best position to speak for the team right now.

"Green's another matter, though."

"How so?" Perrault asked.

"Team that's away can go in any order it wants. You can't insist one guy putts first."

Chelovek, now totally chagrined, wanted to ask the obvious question— why had Eddie not said anything in their first match, on the hole on which the foursome had insisted he putt before Kirkland?—but he already knew the answer: Eddie was only too happy to go first, just so he could purposely crack his ball into a lake and set up for a later tutorial on how, if you're going to use the rules to your advantage, you'd damned well better know them cold to begin with.

·

PENSECOEUR'S LINE TO THE CUP was at right angles to what Aronica's had been, which told him that even though the green seemed perfectly flat, the grain of the Bermuda grass would be dragging him to the left. Breaths were held as his putt began shaping up as a beauty, but at the very end it took a final dive and missed by about two inches.

Pensecoeur spat some obscure Creole epithet and stomped to the cup, where he extended his putter and prepared to knock the ball away until Eddie yelled "Hold it!" and stopped him dead.

The putt hadn't been officially conceded.

"Think you can make that, ET?" Savitch asked mockingly.

"A difficult call," Pensecoeur said, then picked up the ball with the back of his putter for a par.

Perrault, standing off to the side, had watched the path of Pensecoeur's putt carefully and thought he knew what he had to do. Chelovek started to say something, but the physician held up his hand for silence and walked to his ball.

He hit it along exactly the same line as Pensecoeur had, but with a touch more force. That slightly neutralized the effect of the grain, and while the ball was moving much faster when it neared the cup, it was better aligned and dropped right in.

"Bird!" Savitch yelped as Perrault threw his hands up in the air.

"Beauty, Pete," Eddie said. "Yours is good, Joe."

Aronica would have needed only a two-putt from three feet to seal the foursome's victory, so Eddie had conceded it.

Our boys were two up with four to go, and totally unable to hide their jubilation as they walked off the green together.

As they neared the carts, Chelovek said, "How much do you guys trust me?"

The question instantly cast a pall over the heretofore ecstatic bunch. "Don't you dare tell me you're going to offer another double!" Savitch rasped.

"We can't," Chelovek said. "It's not our turn. But *they're* going to."

"A quarter million a man?" Aronica exclaimed. "No goddamned way in the world they'd do that!"

"Have you taken leave of your senses, Jerrold?" Perrault chimed in. "They're down by two—that'd be total insanity!"

"What if they do?" Chelovek insisted.

"They won't!" his friends chorused in unison.

"But what if they do!"

What, indeed?

Savitch, mystified, eyed Chelovek closely. "Why'd you ask if we trusted you?"

"I'll tell you later. Let's go."

"SORRY ABOUT THE DELAY, FOLKS," Chelovek said amiably as they drove up to the fifteenth tee. "We were just talking about how much beachfront property we were going to buy in Lauderdale when we took your money."

"Why Lauderdale when there's so much available in Monterey?" Eddie suggested. "We're doubling you."

"Ah. Well. Give us a moment, wouldja?"

"Take your time," Eddie responded affably. "Take your time."

CHELOVEK DROPPED ONTO THE PASSENGER seat of his cart after they'd driven back to the vicinity of the last green. "I think we got 'em. We do nothing but hold even the next four holes, or even lose one, and we got 'em. So we gotta decide right now."

"Do we take it or don't we," Perrault mused tremulously, almost afraid to say the words out loud.

"No." Chelovek tapped his palm on the steering wheel. "Do we double 'em back."

Savitch groaned and threatened to fall over again.

"This is a joke, right?" Perrault asked, but he could tell from Chelovek's face that it wasn't.

"Why don't we just accept and leave it at that?" Aronica suggested. "We beat 'em, we get a quarter meg each and go home."

"We double and we get half a million. And the fact that we doubled back helps us win."

"I'm having an awful feeling of déjà vu about this," Perrault said, holding on to the cart with one hand and getting ready to prop Savitch up with the other. "They sure don't look rattled to me right now."

"They do to me," Savitch said, causing three heads to snap in his direction in surprise. Color was already coming back to his face.

"What?" Perrault asked.

Savitch sniffled and shrugged off Perrault's hand. "I said, they look a little rattled to me. Look at 'em: Where's all that joking around and hardy-har friendly baloney?"

Savitch was right. Kirkland stood stonily by the next tee box while Eddie lit a cigarette and Pensecoeur chipped balls nearby.

"I think Jerry's right," Savitch said.

"And that's why I asked if you guys trusted me."

"Because if they offered it," Savitch said, realization dawning, "that means you were right. And if you were right about that, then you're right that we should hit 'em back."

Chelovek folded his arms across his chest and stayed silent.

"I refuse to discuss this," Perrault said with finality.

"It'll shake 'em up more if I hit 'em right back without waiting," Chelovek said.

"I wouldn't bet a half million dollars on a Treasury bond," Perrault shot back at him heatedly. "Do you seriously think I'd bet it on some childish mind game that only you can see?"

He whirled on his other two partners. "What in blazes is going on here, guys? This isn't Monopoly money we're dealing with! Three days ago we were ready to kill each other over a five-grand bet. For heaven's sake, Deke, you were already planning how to get out of paying the hotel bill!"

"Pete . . ." Chelovek started to say.

"Fuck it, Jerry!" Perrault looked completely horror-stricken. He took a few steps backward. "Fuck *you!*"

He put his hands to his head and stepped even farther back, looking frantically from side to side as if seeking an escape route. "Jesus Christ, what the hell have we gotten ourselves into! Half a million—I can't—Sweet Jesus, we're going to—"

Chelovek flew out of the cart and grabbed Perrault by both shoulders, shaking him so violently the hapless physician couldn't even hold his head straight. "Goddamnit, don't you fold on me now, you sniveling sonofabitch!"

Savitch and Aronica each leaped at one of Chelovek's arms and tried to drag him away from Perrault, but Chelovek wouldn't let go, and it took all their strength to finally pry his arms away.

"Okay!" Chelovek flipped his hands up in a gesture of surrender. "Okay!"

As Perrault staggered backward, they slowly let Chelovek go, staying close to make sure he wouldn't go after Perrault again.

But there was no need. Perrault took a few deep breaths and steadied himself, running a hand through his rumpled hair in a futile attempt to straighten it out.

"You gonna be okay, Pete?" Aronica asked solicitously.

Perrault nodded and gulped a few more breaths. "It just hit me suddenly. My apologies, Jerrold."

"'S'okay, Pete." Whether he meant it as sincere forgiveness or it was just a tactic to settle Perrault down, nobody could tell.

"I don't see the point of rushing it, Jerry," Aronica said. He seemed to be pleading. "If we take their double, the ball's in our court and we can hit 'em back whenever we want. Why do we have to do it right now?"

"I told you already: We do it right away and it's gonna strike terror into their—"

"There's another reason," Savitch said.

Perrault looked at him quizzically. "What's gotten into you, Deke? An hour ago you passed out when it went to thirty-two thousand, and now you're ready to—"

"What's the other reason?" Aronica asked.

Savitch looked at Chelovek, his eyes requesting backup, and said, "If we double them back right now, they'd take it, right?"

Chelovek played his part. "No question about it."

"But if we hold up through another hole and offer it, my bet is they'll forfeit the quarter mil and quit."

The thought of that was so tantalizing that Perrault had to grab the cart again to steady himself. "And the problem with that would be . . . ?"

Savitch, suddenly steely-eyed and in complete control, said, "We'd be throwing away another quarter mil apiece because we were too chicken to double back right now."

The force of Savitch's simple logic swirled around them like a shroud. "What if they turn us down right now?" Perrault asked, so addled he didn't even realize what a stupid question it was.

"Then we go home a quarter of a million dollars richer," Chelovek answered.

"What if we lose?"

That was a much better question.

And Savitch had an equally meritorious answer. "They'd have to win three of the next four holes to do that, Pete."

Which was something none of them had stopped to consider before. A slow smile began creeping across Savitch's face, and then it spread to Chelovek's.

"Well, gentlemen." The adman stood up and stretched from side to side, shook out one leg and then the other. "Shall we?" He started to get back into the cart, and Savitch did the same.

"Jerrold."

Chelovek turned at the sound of Perrault's voice.

"Jerrold, I can't do it."

Now it was Savitch's turn to stop and turn around. "Whaddaya mean, you can't do it?"

"I couldn't cover it if we lost."

"Neither can I, Deke." Aronica, this time.

"Everything okay?" Eddie's voice rang out from the fifteenth tee.

Chelovek and Savitch stared at Perrault and Aronica without speaking.

"Guys . . . ?"

Chelovek shook himself loose, walked in front of the carts and called out, "Couple minutes, okay, Eddie?"

He turned back. "Seems we got us a little problem here," he said so only his partners could hear.

Chapter 37

PERRAULT POURED HIMSELF SOME WATER from the pitcher mounted on one of the golf carts. He drank a few sips, cleared his throat and drank some more.

"Quite frankly," he said, flipping the plastic cup to one side and watching as the remaining water flashed into the sunlight and onto the grass, "I can't afford the loss."

He held up his hand as Chelovek's eyebrows rose. "Don't misunderstand, I have sufficient funds. It's just . . ." He cleared his throat yet again. "It's just, I can't get at it."

"And that's because . . . ?" Savitch prompted him.

"If I take that much money out of my business, somebody might wish to have a look at my books."

The rest didn't need to be said out loud. None of them knew the specifics, but all of them had long suspected that Perrault's medical empire rested on a financial house of cards that couldn't stand up to scrutiny from a mail-order accounting student.

"And what's your problem?" Chelovek asked Aronica.

"My problem is I haven't got it."

"You haven't got it?"

Aronica shook his head, and Chelovek buried his in his hands. "I don't fucking believe this!" he moaned softly.

"Are you telling me *you* could handle a half-million-dollar loss?" Perrault challenged.

Chelovek picked up his head. "I'm not gonna have to handle it, because we're gonna win, if you assholes can hang together long enough!"

"You do have the money, don't you?" Aronica pressed.

"Yeah, I got it."

Perrault wasn't buying it. "Where!"

Chelovek stood up belligerently. "I said I got it, and it's none of your damned business where!"

Savitch stepped between the two of them. "Actually, it *is* their business, Jerry. Mine, too."

"How do you figure that!"

Savitch looked over toward where the owners were waiting, ignoring the signs of growing impatience he saw. All he could focus on was Eddie, and all he was thinking about was how prescient the canny hustler had been.

"The deal was that we were all liable for any losses as a team," he explained. "If one of us can't cover, the rest of us have to make it up."

He tore his eyes from Eddie and turned them on Chelovek. "If you come up short, we're all gonna suffer."

Perrault broke off Chelovek's embarrassment without intending to. "It's all academic anyway, Deke. Joe and I can't do it either."

"Can you at least handle the quarter mil, Pete?" Aronica asked, and Perrault nodded. "And you said you have it, right, Jerry?"

"If I could do a half, I can sure as shit do a quarter. But we're not—"

"I know, I know: We're not gonna lose." Aronica heaved a relieved sigh. "Well, that's it, then. We take the double, but that's it."

"How 'bout it, fellas?" a voice rang out.

They all turned to see Eddie pointing toward the sun, which was surprisingly low in the sky, and then at his watch. Aronica looked at his own and said, "Holy shit, it's four o'clock already!"

"Let's hop to it, then," Chelovek said, getting ready to get into his cart for the third time.

"Hold it," Savitch said.

"Oh, for the love'a . . ." Chelovek hung his head but held on to the steering wheel. "Now what?"

"I'll cover the losses," Savitch said. "Let's double them back."

Chapter 38

✖

"WHAT'RE YOU TALKING ABOUT, DEKE?" Aronica asked suspiciously.

"Simple. I'll cover any of your losses in excess of the two hundred and fifty large you all already agreed to."

Perrault, mouth agape, dropped back against the side of the cart. "Are you serious?"

"Dead serious. Anything we lose over a quarter mil a man, I'll pay. Anything we win above it, it's mine."

Deke's proposal stunned them all, but it was Chelovek who jumped right to the bottom line. "What good's that do *us*, Deke? That's the same position we'd be in now if we didn't double 'em back."

"Man's got a point," Aronica agreed.

"No he doesn't," Savitch said. "He's the one trying to convince us that doubling them back is what's gonna *make* them lose. And I'm the only one can make that happen, so you wouldn't just be in the same position if you take my deal, you'd be in the *best* position."

"Except that I for one haven't bought into that little theory," Perrault countered.

Savitch thought it over, pretending none of this had occurred to him before. "Tell you what, then: I'll cut you in for ten percent of whatever extra we win. Now you got no downside, only upside, so whaddaya say?"

"I say there most certainly is a downside," Perrault said darkly. "What if you can't really cover it and we get stuck with the tab!"

"I said I can cover it."

"Oh, yeah?"

"Yeah!"

"Well, bugger the ten percent," Perrault said. "It's not worth the risk!"

"Goes for me, too," Aronica said.

"What about you, Jerry?" Savitch demanded.

"I'm for it. We're gonna win if we scare 'em, and who am I to throw an extra twenty-five large down the crapper?"

"You can't do it if we don't agree!" Perrault persisted.

"You'll agree, all right," Savitch said.

"Yeah? And why's that?"

" 'Cause I'm throwing my badge on the table. I'll quit right here and now, and you can either pay up the quarter million each or take the double and worry about half a million later. But you'll be playing the last four holes without me."

"WELL," CHELOVEK SAID TO EDDIE as they got back to the tee, "Monterey's nice, too. You're on, but why not move farther down the coast, say, uh, Malibu?"

"Meaning . . . ?"

"We double you back."

Eddie blinked, but otherwise his features didn't change. "You sure your guys are up for it?"

"You see any of 'em objecting?"

Eddie flicked his eyes to the left and saw the other three staring right at him, then looked at Kirkland, who was drumming her fingers on the seat and not paying any attention, and at Pensecoeur, who was still chipping balls. Eyes back on Chelovek, he said, "Half a million apiece. Seems to me there might be a little difficulty—"

"I can cover it all if necessary." Savitch stepped out from behind Chelovek. "You've seen my financials . . ."

Eddie *harrumphed* noisily. "Seen Pete's, too, and we all know what a—"

" . . . plus you know my cash accounts."

The sounds of fingertips on vinyl and golf balls being lightly struck ceased. Eddie, motionless, regarded the boys carefully.

"You're on," he said, waving toward the tee box. "And you're up."

When they should have been thinking golf, all Aronica, Chelovek and Perrault could think about was how quickly Eddie had acknowledged that Savitch had two million dollars—*at least* two million—in cash at his disposal.

Chapter 39

◫

PERRAULT, PRESUMPTUOUS PEDAGOGUE THAT he was, had actually done a fairly good job of restoring cohesion to the foursome following Savitch's ultimatum. Appealing to everyone's self-interest, he netted it down to a simple business decision: Was it worth $250,000 each to show the corpulent stockbroker that he couldn't get away with being a bully?

He admitted that his own objection—that they were screwed if Savitch couldn't really cover the excess himself—was a niggling non-issue, and therefore there truly was no downside to doubling the owners back. As an added bonus, Savitch's greed had finally gotten the better of him, the scent of easy money being more alluring to a degenerate day trader than sex, drugs or cheese danish, and at least they wouldn't have to listen to any more of his obnoxious whining.

So they'd agreed to get on with it but, without actually meaning to, Perrault had left the vague impression that once this was all over, he was going to tear Savitch's head off and shit down his neck, a subliminal message that wasn't lost on Savitch.

"You're looking a little pale there, Deke," Kirkland said, frowning in concern.

Chelovek snorted contemptuously. "Gee, isn't that a surprise for somebody who sits in front of a buncha computers that do all his work for him."

Eddie was watching as they came up to the tee box. "No, Selby's right. You feelin' okay, guy?"

"I feel fine!"

"You look like shit." Eddie waved to Jake, who jumped into his cart and drove it over.

"Don't even think about it," Chelovek said. "You're not going to call it off on—"

"Relax, Jerry." Eddie pointed to the defibrillator mounted on the back of the cart. "Pete, you know how to turn this thing on?"

"Of course I do, but we don't—"

"I got it!" Jake hopped out of the cart and ran around to the back. "I read the instruction manual. Hell, I could pro'ly zap the guy myself if—"

"Yeah, right. Just power it up, 'kay?"

"Sure, Eddie." Jake twisted a dial, waited for an indication from some kind of meter, then flipped a large black switch mounted near the power cord. A low hum began, whined upward in frequency, then quieted slightly as the pitch stabilized.

Jake looked up, smiling. "Anybody needs a jump start, I'm your man!"

"Pray to God everybody stays healthy," Eddie said. "Hope I don't see *you* reading the instruction manual, Pete. Okay, who's up?"

"I'll go," Aronica said, as he and his partners had agreed before arriving at the tee.

Chelovek had already moved the markers as far forward in the teeing area as possible. If Aronica hit another blast like he had on fourteen, eyebrows were going to be raised, so they'd decided that the accuracy aspect of his illegal clubs would have to be their competitive edge. The forward markers would give Aronica the opportunity to hit three-wood to the only spot on the fairway of this relatively short but tricky par-four from which there was even an outside chance of getting on in two. By letting him go first and Savitch second, the remaining two would be available to play for safe bogeys if something went wrong.

Even at that, Aronica would need to hit that three-wood close to 240 yards. Of course, his three-wood was really a mislabeled five, which would let him exert some appropriate effort and make the whole charade look good.

Trying to appear as nervous as possible, Aronica took some deep breaths, worked the grip in his hands a few times, rolled his shoulders to chase away some nonexistent kinks and at last assumed his stance. "This hole's been givin' me the heebie-jeebies all week," he said forlornly.

"I know what you mean, *mon ami*," Pensecoeur said sympathetically.

"Well, here goes." With one final, puffed exhalation, Aronica set the clubhead behind the ball, forced himself to stillness, hauled way back and let it rip.

The club plowed into the ball with a sickening *splat* not unlike the sound of a baseball hitting an apple pie. It looked like it wouldn't go 150 yards, but there was no way to tell, because the slice was so acute that the ball cleared a jungle of bougainvillea that was never even intended as a course obstacle and headed for a pond that *was*, except on a different hole entirely.

So stunned were our boys that they kept staring at the last known position of the ball despite its having slipped out of sight eons ago. The only sound was the whine of the defibrillator, Eddie suddenly looking downright prescient for having ordered it turned on when he did.

"Next time anybody sees that ball," Kirkland said, "its picture is going to be on a milk carton."

Aronica picked up the club and stared stupidly at the face, which beat by a long shot the thought of looking at his partners' faces, where he would have seen the same kinds of expressions as those displayed by earthquake victims who'd just watched their homes slide off a cliff.

"Musta been the heat," Eddie suggested, but when Aronica turned slowly toward him, he said, "Just kidding. Jerry, whaddaya say?"

Chelovek, thunderstruck and thoroughly paralyzed, at least managed to shake his head. "Not ready."

Perrault, despite struggling to get his heart rate down and keep the over-burdened organ from leaping out of his chest, volunteered to go. He prided himself on the ability to drive extraneous thoughts from his head when it was his turn to hit, and if he ever needed to focus, it was now. He had no idea what the hell had happened to Aronica but had enough wits left to know that if he didn't do something to restore hope to his team, they were dead.

Ignoring the consequences attendant to various outcomes and thinking only of the shot, Perrault came up with a superb drive that was deliriously close to the ideal target area. Turning to silently thank Chelovek for placing the tee markers at perfect driver distance for him, he was gratified to see relief washing over the adman in near-visible waves.

Perrault motioned for Savitch to take the tee. As they passed each other, he said, "Bugger the par, Deke. Keep it safe and play for bogey."

"Way ahead'a you, brother."

But Savitch, more flustered and bewildered than his cocky reply to Perrault was meant to convey, and not used to backing off, tried to hit an easy three-wood instead of something like a five-wood or three-iron flat out, and misjudged it completely, topping the ball and sending it dribbling off to the left. It was the kind of shot that caused onlookers to avert their eyes in deferential embarrassment.

Which put the foursome's fate entirely in Chelovek's hands. Contrary to what you might have expected, he wasn't averse to being in that position, needing as he did some way to vault himself to hero status in the eyes of friends who'd had ample cause to denigrate him over the past few days.

"Speaking of heat . . ." Kirkland said, mopping a light sheen from her brow.

Pensecoeur looked up and surveyed the sky, pointing at the sun low against the horizon. "Same as in Port-au-Prince," he said. "In the late afternoon the, ah, moisture . . . ?"

"Humidity," Kirkland said.

"Yes. The humidity seems to be more, so one feels more the heat."

Four-wood in hand, that being his most reliable club, Chelovek approached the tee box, affecting a confident stride just short of a swagger but enough to heighten the impression later that the splendid shot he was about to hit wasn't an accident.

"Sun that low, I bet the UV isn't so bad, right?" Kirkland asked.

"Next to nothing," Eddie assured her.

"See if I can lay this four-wood right next to yours, Pete," Chelovek said, emphasis on the *four*-wood to distinguish it from Perrault's driver.

"Do it, Jerrold," Perrault replied. With half a million dollars on the line, he wasn't about to get sucked into doing battle with Chelovek's ego and risk their last hope for survival on this hole.

"Ah, what the hell . . ." Kirkland said.

Chelovek bent over to tee up, carefully adjusting the peg to the perfect height, setting the ball on top with the logo pointing toward his target.

As he straightened up, he chanced to glance sideways just in time to see Kirkland start to strip off her loose-fitting pullover. He might just as well have looked at Medusa and been turned to stone altogether.

Even before the thin fabric was fully over Kirkland's head, and even though she was turned away, it was evident that hiding what lay beneath was classifiable as a mortal sin. The tight-woven mesh shirt she had on was damp with perspiration and clung to her like a bodysuit, revealing a broad upper back that narrowed beckoningly to a taut waist.

The pullover got stuck in her hair, and Pensecoeur came to the rescue, slipping both hands between her shoulder blades and up into the outer shirt. He then grabbed her hair and held it down, shrugging the pullover upward with his hands acting like a shoehorn to gently slip it off. As she worked it to the ends of her upraised arms, Pensecoeur kneaded her neck for a few seconds, and she groaned with pleasure.

So many chemicals were injecting themselves into Chelovek's bloodstream that he didn't know what was making him giddier: her exquisitely proportioned, alabaster arms or the sight of those ebony hands touching her with such easy intimacy. Every feature, even the light wisps of hair falling across her forehead, stood out in relief so bold he thought he could count individual atoms. Chelovek fought gamely to keep it together, but the hormonal tsunami washing over him was not to be denied.

Perrault and Savitch, puzzled at the delay, followed Chelovek's eyes to the other side of the tee box, just in time to see Pensecoeur back away and Kirkland, seemingly oblivious to the havoc she was wreaking, turn around.

Her arms were still raised high, but even that stretched position couldn't hide the knee-weakening swell of breasts that jutted straight outward from above a flat abdomen. It wasn't that they were especially large—they weren't—just *full* in the fullest sense, beckoning and irresistible, in the way that a feather bed at the end of a fifty-mile forced march would be, begging to be caressed and rendering even the strongest-willed man perfectly agreeable to being smothered to death in their comforting embrace.

Kirkland finally freed the pullover and dropped her arms, sighing in relief with her eyes closed and a grateful smile on her face. "God, is that good!"

Chelovek swallowed painfully, the first physical movement he could recall since a safe had dropped on his head from ten stories up.

Perrault wasn't completely inert, enjoying as he was the smorgasbord of treasures being revealed mere steps away, but neither did he fail to appreciate the poisons lurking within the delicacies. "Are you planning to hit anywhere in the near future, Jerrold?" His voice intruding on the sensual idyll being played out nearby was jarring.

"Huh?" Chelovek did his best to turn away from the tableau. His deep disorientation was manifested in a pallor singularly unhealthy in such a sun-drenched locale, dazed eyes more befitting an irredeemable crack addict and an ungainly posture symptomatic of the kind of complete loss of coordination normally attendant to victims of a massive stroke. "Yeah, sure. I'm uh—"

He looked down at his hands. Something was wrong, but he couldn't tell what. It finally hit him, and he bent clumsily to retrieve the golf club he'd unconsciously dropped at some point, Lord only knew when.

He stood back up just about the time Kirkland yanked the drawstring on her workout pants preparatory to shimmying out of them.

That her rear was narrow and athletic came as a surprise to no one, nor was the elegantly defined musculature of her thighs and calves. Pensecoeur again stepped forward to help her, this time to get the pants over her shoes so she wouldn't have to take them off. Kirkland sat down and put her feet up in the air, and the sight of the Haitian kneeling between her legs in an attitude of impending and invited violation twanged several sets of strings that ran taut between Chelovek's insatiable longing and his pathological jealousy.

He'd never been anywhere near this close to a body that could easily drive a eunuch to tears. Even as the neurotically driven, sexually defenseless side of Chelovek's character surfed to the fore on waves of toxic hormones, so did the golfer within him disappear into the black hole of his fragile psyche.

"For heaven's sake, Jerrold!" Perrault hollered. "Will you hit the bloody ball!"

Startled, and with one leg still in the air, Kirkland whirled her head to look at the source of the noise, then turned again to look at the apparent cause of Perrault's exasperation, which was standing on the tee holding a four-wood. By the head.

Trapped and mortified, Chelovek managed to tear his eyes away and attempt some semblance of setting up for a golf shot. Seeing him literally tremble yet still sneaking sideways glances, Perrault felt bile rising in his throat, and when he saw Chelovek take a few desultory swings with all the concentration of an anesthetized ground sloth, something in his brain snapped.

"Jerry, you slimy piece of shit!" he yelled. "Isn't Deke's wife enough for you!" Perrault slammed his club into the ground, took a ball out of his pocket and threw it at Chelovek as hard as he could, only his extreme distress making him miss and avoid inflicting a serious injury. "We got *money* riding here, for fuck's sake!"

It took Perrault a second or two to realize that the ambient temperature had plummeted to absolute zero before he'd gotten to his last sentence. It was a deep Arctic freeze that seemed to stop even light, and at that moment he would gladly have forfeited the match and all the money it involved in exchange for rewinding the entire universe back by just ten seconds. For an insane moment he envisioned his words as he might a croquet ball, something tangible that, were he fast enough and nimble, he might outrun and thereby retrieve before they struck an unsuspecting victim. He closed his eyes, but even through the tightly shuttered lids he could feel the full force of the shock he'd engendered and the impending carnage he was powerless to prevent.

"Wh-what?" he heard Savitch say, the voice tremulous and filled with dread, as though the request for repetition might result in something entirely different from what he thought he'd heard originally. "Pete . . . what did you say?"

Discarding childish notions of escape, Perrault sighed, opened his eyes and turned to face his friend. "You heard me right, Deke. He's been carrying on with Binky for two years."

Pensecoeur looked as though he'd been stung by a bee but was afraid to move for fear of angering the rest of the hive. His eyes darted back and forth, but other than that, he might as well have been in late-stage rigor mortis.

Kirkland looked at Eddie, hoping for some sign of what might constitute appropriate behavior at this point, but he, too, could only stand and stare, so she did the same.

Bottom line, nobody had any notion of what to do, so nobody did anything, until Chelovek got it into his head that they were all waiting for *him* to do something. So he did what he did best, which was to start flinging bullshit at the walls and hope enough of it stuck to save his ass.

"Wo—" Stammering would only make him look weak and apologetic, so he started again, strengthening his voice to communicate that he had nothing to apologize for even while he was apologizing. "Woman had needs, Deke," he said with a strong note of defiance. "What with your bad heart, well . . ."

Savitch's built-in defense mechanisms had clicked into overdrive, erecting filters between his ear and brain at the command of whatever part of him bore primary responsibility for self-preservation, but Chelovek's patently insane bravado helped to dissipate some of the resultant giddy confusion. "My heart— You were—" He shook his head in a vain attempt to clear it enough to articulate in words what was so clear in his mind. "You were doing her a *favor?*"

"No, no, Deke, no . . . !" Chelovek's breath was labored and hoarse as he struggled to defend himself against the indefensible. "I was only— I mean—"

Earning Chelovek's eternal gratitude, Perrault put an arm across Savitch's shoulders and turned him away, whispering urgently in his ear as he did so.

"Listen to me. Deke, are you listening to me?"

Savitch nodded dumbly, but it was more of an autonomic reflex than a conscious movement.

"You can't go 'round the bend on us now, Deke, you simply cannot!" Perrault's voice was awash with desperation and fear. "He's a cad, we both know it, the world's biggest, but for the love of Christ, our *lives* are on the line here!"

Perrault thought he detected some glimmer of awareness in Savitch's eyes, but it was just that, a glimmer, and that wasn't going to do it. Not by a long shot. "You've got to be a man about this, Deke," he pleaded. "Be a man!"

Perrault thought that some microbial bit of his challenge might have succeeded in burrowing beneath the multifaceted armor of Savitch's battered ego. He could see the pudgy little man's facial muscles twitch slightly as he struggled to compose himself into the image of what he assumed someone more self-possessed might look like under similar circumstances, as though appearing in control and on top of things might actually help him to achieve that state.

Once he had run through the entire menu of possible expressions, Savitch took a deep breath, hoping the shuddering wasn't apparent to the rapt onlookers, and let it out as he nodded his understanding of what was required of him at this moment. Mouth and eyes set in grim resolve, he turned away and strode with purpose and determination to his bag, three-wood still in hand.

"That's the spirit!" Perrault rasped out in relieved admiration as Savitch raised his hand to put the club back. Perrault was momentarily mystified as to why it was necessary for Savitch to lean so far over to the side in order to get the club into the bag but was soon enlightened as the portly stockbroker, with perfect form if you didn't count the somewhat horizontal swing plane, hauled back and took an immense whack at a nonexistent ball, electing to let go of the club in the middle of the swing and thereby launching it with horrifying accuracy on a path apparently intended to remove the head of one Jerrold Chelovek.

The involuntary yelps that erupted from the assembled golfers barely drowned out the sickening *whap-whap-whap* of the deadly club as it scythed its way toward the tee box. Chelovek had barely a microsecond to gape in disbelieving astonishment before flexing his knees in an attempt to drop below what he'd quickly gauged to be the zone of lethality, the club helicoptering in with such velocity that gravity itself was barely strong enough to get him down in time. Later he would swear that he'd felt something actually brush his hair before it whirled off into the distance.

His relief at having escaped grievous injury was short-lived, however, because he'd barely managed to catch his breath before it was knocked back out by the force of some 250-odd pounds of raging Savitch slamming into him at a speed he would have bet wasn't possible for his ex-friend to have achieved without the aid of a NASA rocket-sled. In contrast with Perrault's attack on

Savitch the previous night, when his fake handicap had been revealed and which, while genuine in some respects, wasn't truly intended to cause great bodily harm, the current assault was in every respect quite serious in its intent to terminate every one of Chelovek's life functions simultaneously. The sound Savitch was making, which several of the witnesses tried to duplicate for me later, is difficult to phoneticize, but think of the noise that might result if you touched a red-hot poker to the anus of a wild boar.

Stunned by the fury of the enraged stockbroker's pummeling of their playing partner, Aronica and Perrault hesitated, fearing that to intervene at this moment might be too risky to their own persons, but Pensecoeur had already assessed the seriousness of the situation and leaped forward to try to do something, which galvanized the rest of the men into action as well.

Buoyed by each other's presence, the four of them set about trying to get the choking, sobbing, utterly berserk Savitch off of Chelovek, who was doing only a moderately effective job of simply staying covered and trying to absorb the blows with minimal damage. They soon sorted themselves out, each claiming a flailing limb while trying to avoid getting hit by it, but were amazed at the effort it took to keep the overweight and out-of-shape hellion from pounding Chelovek into steak tartare.

For somebody for whom flossing his teeth was an intensely aerobic activity, Savitch had acquitted himself admirably, but as the surges of rage-induced adrenaline played themselves out, he eventually began succumbing to the fatigue that inevitably followed the energetic use of muscles long unaccustomed to activation. The four men who had hold of his extremities and were gasping from the exertion soon dared to relax their grips, until Savitch shook them off with one last, mighty heave and rolled away to try to suck in enough oxygen to keep from blacking out.

Chelovek looked up from under the arms he'd been holding protectively around his head and took in the scene around him, which resembled a rodeo in which a ferocious bucking bull lay panting and exhausted after having just thrown off four laughably inadequate riders. Savitch struggled to a sitting position and, without turning his head, lifted an arm and pointed at Chelovek. "Soon as I . . . catch . . . my breath . . . I'm going to kill you . . ." It looked to the others like he was going to have enough trouble just opening his eyes. The worst of it apparently over, Perrault and Aronica exchanged anxious glances. "You okay, Jerry?" Aronica asked.

Chelovek took the opportunity to check himself for damage. "Gonna be a little black-and-blue tomorrow, but otherwise . . ." He looked up and jerked a thumb at the beached whale heaving ineffectually and showing few signs of any willingness to be revivified, then looked questioningly at Perrault, who sighed and crawled over to Savitch.

Perrault drew up his knees and leaned forward, looking directly into the face of his thoroughly humiliated and dispirited friend, whose breathing had begun to slow down and become less throaty. He put his hand on Savitch's shoulder and waited until he was sure he was listening, then said, "You're personally looking at a million-two down the shitter, Deke!"

It was like a hundred CCs of lidocaine during a cardiac arrest. Savitch's eyes popped wide, he blinked several times to bring the world back into focus, and finally he roused himself enough to knock Perrault's hand off his shoulder.

"I'm cool," he announced, and Perrault could see that he was.

Savitch's painful return to the land of the living presented an opportunity to restore some semblance of normalcy to the whole entourage, and Eddie leaped on it without delay.

"Kinda stick you got there, Joe?" he said to Aronica who, amazingly, still had it in his hand. Not yet fully recovered from shock following his last attempt to use it, he had not only allowed Kirkland's inadvertent performance to go unnoticed but was also only partially aware of what had precipitated the imbroglio between Chelovek and Savitch.

"Huh?"

"Your club," Eddie said. "What's it made of?"

Aronica wasn't prepared for the question and had a moment of panic wondering why Eddie had asked it of him. But then he remembered how it had sounded when he'd hit it, which made the question perfectly reasonable, and now he had to think fast. "Composite alloy." He winced inwardly at the absurd redundancy unworthy of a metallurgist. "Copper, titanium, some nickel—not really sure, tell you the truth. Guy made it for me."

That seemed to satisfy Eddie's curiosity, at least for the moment, and Aronica looked around him for the first time in many minutes, seeing Chelovek still on the tee box and looking like an asylum inmate after a particularly severe psychotic episode, Savitch trying to sit up, Perrault pale and shaking and staring at Savitch as though trying to will him back to life and into the game.

"Is it legal?" Eddie asked.

"'Course it's legal!" Aronica retorted in indignation, even though a golf club made out of Arondium was about as legal as a golf ball made out of Flubber. "Got the head out of a catalog. It's no better than a normal club."

"So why'd he make it?"

"Supposed to last longer," Chelovek grunted, rubbing one shoulder painfully and eyeing Savitch warily. "Doesn't get banged up as much, knocking around in your trunk. I got a couple at home."

Aronica eagerly picked up the creative thread. "Matter of fact, I originally got the whole set for Jerry."

"Good trade," Kirkland muttered. Chelovek was about to fire back something equally insulting but probably far less clever when he saw Aronica glowering at him and got the subliminal message: *Don't put their minds back on these clubs!*

"Good thing one doesn't make airplanes of it," Pensecoeur said jokingly, picking up on Eddie's cue to try to steer things clear of the lethal situation that had erupted without warning between Savitch and Chelovek.

Eddie grinned and said, "Hey, ET, didja know Joe here *does* make airplane parts?" He turned to Aronica. "Although I guess not out of that stuff you invented, not anymore, right? What was it called? Do-ron-ron or something?"

Unable to absorb even an amiable knock at his beloved creation, Aronica drew himself up to full height. "It's called arondium, and I *still* make airplane parts out of it," he said with some prickliness. "And damned good parts they are, buster!"

"Really?" Eddie said in puzzlement. "I thought—trying to remember now . . . Wasn't there something, some problem a while back? Damn, I can't think of it."

Perrault was far too agitated to allow things to drift off track once again. "Anybody happen to remember that we've got a golf game going?"

Eddie snapped his fingers. "Now I remember! Rudders!"

He held the club out to the side as he looked at Aronica. "It was rudders, right? For airplanes, I mean!"

"Yeah, that's right. We make—"

"All those seven thirty-sevens kept crashing on account'a their rudders fail, am I right?"

"No!" Aronica shouted. "It's got nothing to do with the rudders, goddamnit."

He grabbed the club out of Eddie's hand. "I invented that stuff myself! There's not a goddamned thing wrong with it!"

"Gee." Eddie, not intimidated in the slightest by Aronica's passionate defensiveness, frowned in concentration. "I coulda sworn . . . Wait, I know! Something about magnetic fields! Yeah, that was it!"

He turned toward Kirkland and Pensecoeur, who were only now beginning to dare relaxing in the hope that an aftershock was about to be averted. "Don't you guys remember? Generators mounted in the tail section gave off all kinds of, uh, electromagnetic what-the-hell-ever . . . ?"

"Yes, yes," Pensecoeur said. "And this was failing the rudders, I do seem to recall—"

"Nobody's ever proved that!" Aronica roared. "They put my metal in front of the most powerful goddamned microwave transmitter in the Northern Hemisphere, and not a fucking thing happened!"

"Way I heard it," Eddie said, "wasn't about power, it was about frequency. Who gives a rat's ass about microwaves? Ain't no microwaves in an airplane. The right frequency, that was the problem, way I heard it."

"You some kinda engineer, Eddie?" Aronica challenged. "You all of a sudden like a Caltech professor, you know so much about physics?"

"Nah, not me." Eddie waved away the implied insult without seeming to take any offense. "Just only know what I read in the papers, and I was thinking . . ."

"Thinking what?"

Eddie shrugged and walked behind Jake's golf cart. "Now, you take this defibrillator here, for example. Guy who loaned me this, he said it's got this particular frequency, vibrates in, uh, something-or-other with a lot of common stuff."

"Sympathy," Aronica said. "Vibrates in sympathy."

"That's it!" Eddie cried. "Sympathy! Now, what the hell does that mean?"

"It means," Perrault stepped in, at last willing to step away from Savitch, "that when it's on, anything with the same characteristic frequency is going to start vibrating right along with it."

"No kidding?"

"No kidding. Like one tuning fork that sets another one going if they're close enough."

"Well I'll be go to hell. Like what, f'rinstance?"

Perrault looked at him oddly. "What is this, a physics lesson? We're supposed to be playing golf!"

"I'm just curious, Pete. Indulge me. Like what?"

Perrault looked around, then pointed to Eddie's wrist. "Like your watch there. Is that one of those old Accutrons?"

Eddie held up his arm. "Present, years ago. Can't seem to give it up. Got a transparent case, you can see all the little—"

"It uses a tuning fork," Perrault said. "And a coil. How's it running?"

"You kidding? This baby hasn't lost two seconds in— Hey!" Eddie had the watch up to his face. He shook his wrist and looked at it again. "It stopped!"

Perrault nodded. "The defibber's got a powerful magnet in it. Charge it up and it starts spewing fields all over the place, enough to grab hold of the coil that powers the tuning fork and throw it off-kilter."

Nobody had noticed that Aronica had been growing angrier by the minute as this completely absurd and irrelevant conversation was taking place. "Am I in the goddamned Twilight Zone," he said, "or is there a golf match going on here? And since when the hell did you get so damned smart about electro-magnetism?"

Perrault looked down and scratched a toe back and forth in the crushed coral of the cart path. "Sam explained it to me once."

"Sam Coolidge?" Eddie asked in surprise.

Perrault nodded. "When we got a defibber in the clinic. He said all kinds of equipment was going to go haywire whenever we used it. One of our orderlies had a watch like yours. Did the same thing."

"Great." Aronica licked his lips nervously. "Wonderful story there, Pete, and thanks for sharing." He pointed his club at Jake's cart. "Now, shut the fucking thing off, Eddie!" His voice was shrill, and he seemed to be on the verge of hysteria.

"Shut it off? How come?"

Aronica walked rapidly toward the back of Jake's cart, reaching for the machine as he got within arm's length. "The humming's driving me nuts, that's why!"

Eddie caught Aronica's arm and held it in a powerful grip. "Come on now, Joe . . . a little humming? Seems a small price to pay for your friend's health, doesn't it?"

Aronica, his pupils darting back and forth crazily, eventually nodded his acknowledgment but said, "I didn't really think he was that bad off, though."

Eddie let go of his arm, and Aronica backed off a few steps. "Isn't that right, Pete? I mean, he's never actually had a heart attack or anything. What was it, two, three squiggles on a cardiogram?"

"Something like that."

"Didn't know you were his physician, Pete." Eddie came out from behind the cart. "You write the note to his boss, he didn't have to go into the office?"

"That's right."

"Well, I guess I owe you an apology, then." Eddie looked around, making sure everybody could hear his contrition.

"Apology for what?"

"For insulting you, that's what!" Eddie laughed, taking off his cap and running a hand through his thinning hair. "There I was, asking you could you run a defibrillator, and all the time you were treating a heart patient!"

He put the cap back on and shook his head. "Jeez, but I can be an asshole. No hard feelings, right?"

Perrault didn't look the slightest bit insulted. "No. No hard feelings." In eight kinds of lingering shock, perhaps, but not insulted.

"Guess you and Sam haven't seen each other for a while."

"How do you figure?"

"He didn't say anything about you doing any cardio stuff. Guess it's tough to keep up with a guy, you kinda drift apart. Really sorry, buddy."

"Forget it already. Are we ready to resume play? Who's up?"

"Jerry was," Savitch said, standing and brushing himself off. He had made up his mind to defer any further physical actions against Chelovek but was unable to suppress the venom that laced his voice. "He was on the tee, just before . . ." His voice trailed off pathetically.

"I need a minute," Chelovek said as he stood up gingerly. He walked to his cart, pulled a plastic cup out of the holder and held it beneath the spigot of the water bucket mounted on the back.

"It is good, a physician who maintains his training," Pensecoeur said as he walked away from Kirkland and went to get a drink himself. He avoided looking at Chelovek, having noted with total astonishment that the adman was already shaking off the memory of Savitch's assault so he could get busy ogling Kirkland again, this time over the top of his cup as he drank at the rate of three molecules a decade.

"Étienne lost his grandmother last year," Eddie said. "Some funny stuff with a medical clinic, wasn't it, ET?"

The Haitian's normally sunny expression clouded up as he drew a cup of water. "Very sad. She was a saint, my *nonna*, a blessed woman with too much trust."

"What happened?" Aronica asked.

"She lived in Brooklyn. Legally, I assure you, and she got a job. She was so excited . . ." Pensecoeur turned away and drank some water.

"They required a medical exam," Kirkland filled in, coming over to join the others. As she walked, tiny ripples from the force of her steps appeared on various locations of her skin, further augmenting the impact of her physical presence. Gulping sounds could be heard coming from Chelovek's cart.

Kirkland began pulling her sticky shirt away from her body and shaking the material to try to cool herself down. "So she went to a clinic, an outfit the company had a deal with, and they did a bunch of tests and didn't like what they saw."

"Cancer, they said." Pensecoeur had turned back and seemed to have composed himself. "Or they suspected, and it was necessary to do more tests. She dropped to her knees and thanked the Lord Almighty when it wasn't cancer, but they then thought perhaps it was diabetes, and they tested for that, and then for heart disease, a brain tumor . . ."

"So what was it?" Aronica asked, so curious he momentarily forgot about his own little, potentially very expensive, problem.

"It?" Pensecoeur's face darkened even further. "There was no *it, monsieur!* There was no *it!*"

"It was just a scam," Kirkland explained. "The company's insurer paid for the exams, so this clinic, they'd run up a battery of the most expensive tests possible on people who were perfectly healthy."

"Why? How'd they make money doing that?"

"Because these doctors themselves," Pensecoeur explained, "they owned all the laboratories and the specialized testing centers."

"Extremely profitable," Kirkland said. "You run an MRI or something like that, bill it at full bore to the insurer . . . you make a fortune."

"So what's the objection?" Perrault had stayed quiet as Pensecoeur and Kirkland spun the tale, but he didn't understand why everybody was so engrossed and outraged.

"What's the objection?" Kirkland echoed. "They treated ET's grandmother like she was going into the astronaut corps or something!"

"And I ask you again, so what?" Perrault became animated, uncowed by Pensecoeur's forlorn look or Kirkland's indignation. "His grandmother got a free, world-class physical she couldn't have afforded in her wildest dreams. Okay, so the clinic was being a touch too diligent. It's damned near impossible to make a decent profit in medicine these days, so you bend the rules a little and overdo it on occasion. And besides, half the time that you *don't* go a little overboard, you get sued."

"Man's got a point," Chelovek said, daring to put a toe back into the social water. "You do too much, you're accused of cheating. You don't do enough, some asshole drags you into court and you have to explain everything you didn't do. Either way you're screwed."

"Damned right," Perrault snapped. "So Grandma gets herself checked out from top to bottom, she gets the job—tell me what's so bloody terrible!"

"What's so terrible, Doctor, is that she took her own life before the job begins."

Puzzled, Perrault asked why she'd do a thing like that. "They just got finished telling her she was perfectly healthy. I don't get it."

"She was terrified," Kirkland said. "Every other week she was faced with the thought of living with a dread disease, and every time she thought it was okay, she was faced with a different one."

"You must remember, Peter," Pensecoeur said, "she had only just come from Haiti. There, as most places in the world, many illnesses are death sentences. The thought of being a burden on her family . . . well, it was more than she could bear, and she did what she thought was honorable."

"Why didn't she just wait until all the tests were completed?" Perrault, genuinely disturbed by the story, seemed to be searching for a way to lessen the culpability of his fellow healers. "What was the point of jumping the gun?" He instantly regretted that choice of phrase, but it went unnoticed by the others.

"Because," Pensecoeur explained, "she assumed that if so much was suspected, then surely at least one thing must be true."

"She was an immigrant from a backward country, Pete." Kirkland put a hand on Pensecoeur's arm as she spoke. "She didn't know that people in the West run to doctors for tests all the time and that there are things that can be done even if you do come up positive. Thing is, those docs, they probably have no idea at all what their little racket does to people."

Eddie was shaking his head. "This one time, a guy says maybe I got cancer or something, we gotta do some tests . . ."

"I didn't know that!" Kirkland exclaimed. "What was it?"

"Gas. But it was the longest goddamned week in my whole life, waiting for the results. I was ready to . . . well, whatever."

It was an awkward moment, nobody willing to be disrespectful of Pensecoeur's grandmother by bringing up something so gauche as the golf match under way.

Savitch felt Chelovek sidle up beside him and stayed still as his traitorous friend whispered in his ear.

"We'll settle this between us later, Deke, but right now Joe's got it in his mind that the humming from that goddamned machine is lousing up his game."

Savitch nodded, and Chelovek stepped away. "Speaking of heart problems . . . you know, I think this business about my ticker's really been overdone, Eddie."

"Izzat so?"

"Ah, heck, yeah. It's not that big a deal, see? Just trying to be a little cautious, is all."

"I don't know . . ."

"Look, I'm telling you! I play six rounds of golf a week—" Savitch winced and bit his tongue. Literally.

Chelovek looked quizzically at him. "Six?"

"Man's a scratch golfer, Jerry," Eddie said. "Shouldn't be a surprise he plays that much."

"You only play twice at Royal," Aronica mused out loud, "so . . ."

"Must be four at Mystic." Chelovek shook his head in amazement. "Some life you lead, buddy."

"What the—what the heck is going on here, *This Is Your Life* or something?" Savitch demanded. "Since when does everyone care so much about—"

"Hey, Pete . . ." Aronica was scratching his head in confusion. "You know guys at Mystic."

"So?"

"I thought they didn't have carts over there. Doesn't everybody have to take a caddie?"

Perrault didn't answer, but Eddie did. "Now you mention it, you're right. I've played there a couple, three times. I remember because those caddies, jeez, a bunch of Cuban guys, not one of 'em had a handicap over five. Thursdays they could play the course, and I swear to—"

But nobody was listening. Chelovek, rapidly getting over his discomfort at being within spitting distance of Savitch, turned to face him head-on. "You telling me you *walk* four rounds a week?"

The humming from the defibrillator seemed to be getting louder. Aronica was right, Savitch thought, it really was a teeth-grating pain in the ass. He reminded himself of how much he had at risk here, and it occurred to him that leaving that thing on was probably just another one of Eddie's sophomoric mind games, except for the fact that this one was working. "The machine, Eddie . . . really, how about shutting—"

Nobody was listening at that point, but Kirkland picked up on the developing thread Aronica and Chelovek had started. "How does a guy with a heart condition walk four—"

"*I don't have a goddamned heart condition!*" Savitch screamed. "Now, will you for the love'a Christ shut that fucking thing off!"

.

YET ANOTHER OF THOSE AWKWARD silences set in, this one caused as much by confusion as by shock.

"I don't get it," Aronica said at last.

That broke the ice for Pensecoeur, who looked oddly at Chelovek before daring a question to Savitch. "And you let your wife believe you were ill?"

Chelovek caught the implication immediately; after all, it was in his best interest to do so, his current standing among the assembled group being roughly akin to that of pond scum. Now it would emerge that his diddling of Binky Savitch was in fact her husband's fault, because the hard-hearted sonofabitch had let her think he was ill, which worried her so that she couldn't bring herself to make love to him lest he suddenly seize up and clutch at his chest and maybe even die right there on top of her and she might not be able to get him off and she'd be stuck there for who knows how long with a dead guy smothering her, so Chelovek wasn't such a bad sort, see, and maybe you could make it out that he really *was* doing her a favor, because at least she was being serviced by someone other than the guy who helps her out of the Sack 'n' Save with her groceries . . .

"She knew I wasn't really sick," Savitch said, any possibility of reversing his total emasculation via something so déclassé as beating up Chelovek now on a par with his winning the lottery and getting struck by lightning on the same day.

"Oh, dear," Kirkland said, and turned away. Pensecoeur, who'd posed the key question in the first place, surreptitiously crabbed his way sideways to the other side of the tee box and resumed practicing his chip shot.

Savitch tried to force himself to the business at hand, to remember how all of this had come up, to remember not to get sidetracked into losing just about everything he had. "So now you can turn it off, okay, Eddie?"

Eddie stepped closer to Savitch. "Tell you the truth, Deke . . . I can't."

"You can't." It was the most Savitch could muster as his bowels jellified, which was only a pale imitation of what Aronica's were doing at the same time.

"No." Eddie put his hand on Savitch's shoulder and gave him a sly look. "Fact is, I kind of knew maybe there was a little"—he put his other hand in the air palm down and rocked it back and forth—"a little of that good ol' golf-match ka-ka going on, you know what I'm saying? Some'a the ol' razzmatazz?"

He took his hand away from Savitch and waved Aronica in closer. "Not above a little'a that myself, now and again, but here's the thing." He leaned in closer and jerked a thumb to his right. "The machine's really for ET. He's the one really needs it, 'cept he's too proud to spend a whole round of golf being shadowed by some contraption lets everybody know he's not a hunnerd percent, see?"

He stepped back and laughed. "So I just jerked your chain a bit, Deke! No hard feelings, right?"

Aronica and Savitch stared at the machine, a giant Africanized killer bee poised to sting the four of them to death. "'Course not, Eddie," Savitch managed to croak.

Chelovek had no idea how he was supposed to feel now. Was he an asshole for betraying his friend or a jackass for having been deceived by his friend's wife? Was he supposed to be embarrassed now for their affair having been outed?

And there was the small matter of a half-million-dollar bet still to be decided.

Eddie began walking away, and Perrault followed him. "How come you know Sam Coolidge anyway?" he asked.

"Jesus, are we ever gonna get back to playing again?" Eddie stopped and turned around, pulling a cigarette out of his pocket at the same time. "Been here a couple times."

"How in blazes could he afford it?"

"I invited him. Like I told you before, he's my guest. Smoke?"

"No. You *invited* him? How come?"

"Because I like the guy, what can I tell you? Met him on some dumpy course in Florida, couldn't play golf worth a shit, but I never saw a guy so happy just to be out there bangin' away. We got along, I own the joint, I invited him down . . . What, you thought this place was only for the likes'a you guys?" Eddie blew out some smoke and resumed walking to his own group. "Besides," he called out over his shoulder, "this trip's kind of his finder's fee. He's the one recommended you guys."

When Perrault returned to his own cart, he found Chelovek and Aronica glaring at him, Savitch having retreated to one of the other carts.

"How come you faked his diagnosis for him, Pete?" Chelovek demanded. "Why would you do that for the little peckerhead?"

It was not a day for hiding secrets, as something in the air of Swithen Bairn was making quite plain. "Because I hit his carrier for a hundred and eighty thousand worth of every test and diagnostic procedure in the annals of modern medicine, that's why." *And pocketed damned near all of it,* he chose not to add.

"Well, isn't that swell," Aronica squeezed out between clenched teeth.

"How was I supposed to know he'd go off and fake his handicap!" Perrault angrily shoved the club he was still holding into his bag. "Just thought the little slug was going to stay home with his computers."

"Come to think of it," Chelovek wondered, "when the hell *does* he work?"

"Say, Jerry," Aronica said, "you think maybe it'd be a good idea you got up and hit about now?"

"Definitely," the adman answered.

"Are we actually gonna play?" Kirkland called out when she saw Chelovek returning to the tee. She picked out a club and walked over, directly in his line of sight the whole trip.

"Hit it already!" Aronica said impatiently, so Chelovek hit it while Kirkland was still moving.

It wasn't pretty.

Chapter 40

■

I'M NOT SURE HOW TO fully describe how badly our boys screwed up the rest of that hole, so I'll just tell you that they conceded it to the owners before they even got on the green. Their lead was now down to one, with three holes left to play.

As everyone was getting out of their carts at the sixteenth, a chime sounded. Eddie, greatly annoyed, cursed and reached into his cart for his radio, answered it curtly and threw it back in after a short conversation.

"Something wrong?" Chelovek asked, unable to keep completely out of his voice a note of hopefulness that some catastrophe had occurred that would require calling off the match.

"Nah, just the Piper. Where you gonna put the tees this time?"

"Don't know yet," Chelovek answered. "Fellas?"

"Doesn't make much difference," Savitch advised, apparently winning his battle to behave normally during the remainder of the match. "Even Pensecoeur's not gonna cut the corner on this one."

"Fine. Let's put 'em back and take the broad out of play again."

"The hell you got against that woman!" Aronica asked in annoyance.

"Got nothin' against her. Just pisses me off, is all."

"On account'a she's all over whatshisname while the great cocksman here isn't gettin' any?" Savitch said with undisguised malice. "That it?"

"Cut it out, Deke!" Aronica commanded. "You trying to get us to self-destruct on purpose? We got three holes left to save our asses!"

"Is that what we're about now, Joe?" Perrault asked quietly. "Not losing? Isn't anybody in this sorry crew even thinking about *winning* anymore?"

"Just get up there and hit the fucking ball, Pete!" Chelovek said. "Sick and tired of you acting like my eighth-grade guidance counselor!"

Perrault started to take a step toward Chelovek, but Aronica blocked him. "Come on, guys. Can't we hold it together for a couple lousy holes and *then* try to kill each other?"

Perrault looked toward the cart for some sign of a temporary truce, but Chelovek just grunted and waved his hand dismissively, so Perrault grunted, too, then turned and walked to the tee all square in the grunt match.

"Everything okay back at the ranch, Eddie?" Kirkland said as Perrault eyed the fairway.

"Yeah, just the Piper gettin' his skirts in an uproar."

"What's up with him?"

"Usual kinds of accountant bullshit."

Perrault finalized his grip and his stance and slowly brought the clubhead into position behind the ball. He was feeling loose and confident, getting into some kind of a groove here, ready to show that schmuck Chelovek who had the biggest brass ones, and he just knew he was going to hit the best shot of the day.

"He forgot to get everybody's Social Security number," Eddie said. "I told the anal twerp we'd do it later."

Aliens from Neptune drove electric spikes into Perrault's brain and turned on the juice. "Social Security numbers?" he said in a voice so feeble it seemed to come from a great distance.

"Yeah. He likes to get this shit done before the end of the day, and . . ." Eddie pointed upward, where streaks of purple were already beginning to replace the bright blue of late afternoon. "But forget it. Not a big deal."

"Why does he want Social Security numbers?" Perrault persisted.

"For when we report to the IRS, of course. Can't do that, you don't got Social Security numbers. Hit it smooth, Pete!"

"Report to the IRS?"

"Certainly."

"Report what?"

"Your wins and losses, what else are we gonna report? Give it a nice rip there, bud!"

"Wins and losses? Why are you doing that?"

"It's the law."

"But nobody could possibly know what goes on here! These are private bets!"

"Still gotta report 'em. Hell, you don't believe me, ask the IRS commissioner. Man plays here three times a year, and believe me, the guy's no dummy. Now, let's see you put a good one right on out there, Pete!"

A report of a gambling transaction to the IRS would be to Perrault like a jewel thief carrying an air horn during a second-story job. The only open question would be who would get to his books quicker: government auditors, insurance-company lawyers or the assistant U.S. attorney for the Southern District of New York clutching a briefcase full of blank indictment forms.

Perrault chunked the shot.

So did Savitch. Walking to the tee box, he'd had a premonition of hitting a good one and then hearing someone—probably the woman—say something like *Well, at least he can still hit a golf ball, the dickless wonder*. So he ended up chunking it.

"Jeez," he heard Kirkland mutter, "the dickless wonder can't even hit a golf ball!"

As he crawled miserably off the tee, he could see that Kirkland was too far away for him to have heard anything she might have muttered, so it had only been in his head, and now he could add to his sea of woes that of wondering if he was going insane altogether.

With the squishy sound of Arondium hitting a golf ball still rattling around in his brain, Aronica knew he couldn't trust those clubs anymore, that he'd have to forgo the miracle sticks and play straight up, and with no three-wood or seven-iron available either. In the same way that he had total confidence that he would hit the Arondium clubs perfectly, so did he now know for a dead certainty that he couldn't hit the standard ones if his life depended on it, which, in a not entirely figurative way, it did.

He was right, of course. But then Chelovek, who through a monumental effort of self-control that was all the more amazing considering how alien a concept it was for him, managed to ignore Kirkland for the few seconds it took him to hit a pretty decent tee shot.

They lost the hole anyway, and it was all square with two to go.

Chapter 41

∷

CHELOVEK WAS THE ONLY ONE of the four with the presence of mind to do a little advanced planning on how he was going to get himself out of bankruptcy, should that unthinkable eventuality eventuate. (Not my phrase, that; it's how Chelovek put it when he recounted this to me. I apologize for it anyway.)

"Let's you and me walk to seventeen, Eddie."

"Sure, why not? Cigar?"

As they paused to clip the ends and go through the ritual of lighting up, Chelovek waved his hand in the direction of the main house. "You know, with a little advertising you could be filling this joint up every weekend."

"You think so? Here, hold still." Eddie held his lighter to Chelovek's cigar, waving it around to cover the entire tip.

"Definitely!" Chelovek pulled back and blew out a cloud of smoke. In the still air it hung around until they began to walk again, then tried to follow in the draft their movement created before dissipating. "I know exactly what it'd take, too. Not a big deal, if you've done it before."

"And you have."

"You betcha. Nice smoke . . . Havana?"

"Nicaraguan."

"So whaddaya say? Ready to talk some bid'niz, see what we can do to kick this place in the ass a little?"

The carts coming from sixteen caught up to them. "How you guys doing?" Kirkland said, leaning out of the passenger side as Pensecoeur slowed the cart, her posture stretching the fabric of her shirt tight across her right breast, accentuating the shape of it as if the blouse had been spray-painted on.

"Hey, you all right?" Eddie said to Chelovek as he pounded him on the back to try to quell a sudden coughing fit.

Chelovek nodded as he turned away and continued to hack and fight off Eddie's useless ministrations at the same time.

"We'll catch you at the tee," Eddie said, urging Pensecoeur and the others to keep moving.

"Jesus!" Chelovek choked, the heaves finally beginning to subside.

"You're not inhaling that, are you?"

Chelovek shook his head, hauled back and let loose one more explosive gurgle that seemed to clear the last vestiges of smoldering gunpowder from his throat. "Whew! Somethin' down the wrong pipe, I guess."

"Come on." Eddie slapped him gently on the arm, and they began walking again.

"So like I was saying . . ." Chelovek prompted.

Eddie snorted and took a light hit on his own cigar. "You're supposed to be a salesman?"

"Damned good one, too."

"Seems to me anybody can sell in a narrow enough field."

"Narrow?" Chelovek was too arrogant to be insulted; he needed only to set this putz straight. "Listen, bud, I've sold advertising for hair spray, shoes, cars, beer—"

"Like I said: narrow. All you sell is advertising. You know exactly what all your customers want, because you're the one taught 'em to want it. Outside that envelope you'd be dead meat."

"Oh, you think so, huh?"

"Yep."

"I could sell a guy his own goddamned desk!"

"You couldn't even sell me advertising!" Eddie said, laughing.

Chelovek knew better than to get into a pissing contest with a potential client. The only thing that counted was the sale, not ego points. "Can't help it, you got your head up your ass," he said amiably.

"That what you think of anybody doesn't buy from you? That it's their problem and not yours?"

"Let me tell you something, Eddie: You can't sell a man's got his mind made up not to buy."

"Who says my mind's made up not to buy? But I sure as hell ain't buying based on that piece'a shit speech you gave me."

"Why's it a piece'a shit?"

"Listen, Jerry." They rounded a corner formed by the edge of a thick stand of jacaranda and could see the others waiting about forty yards ahead. Eddie stopped and turned to Chelovek.

"One time I wanted to buy one'a those sport utes, I forget which. I'm in L.A., someplace up in the Valley's supposed to be the biggest dealer in California. This salesman, I barely got my name out, he starts right in selling. Tells me how terrific it is for kids, 'cuz it's got these sidebar something-or-others, separate headphone jacks in the back so we don't gotta listen to that shit music they like . . ."

"So what's wrong with that? Sounds like the guy was playing heads-up ball."

"What's wrong? I don't have any kids, that's what's wrong!"

"Well, how was he supposed to know that?"

"He was supposed to *ask!*" Eddie searched in Chelovek's eyes as if trying to see whether the guy could really be that thick. "Here he was, trying to sell me based on shit I didn't need, and all he had to do was ask! Just like you, starting right in trying to get me to buy something, and you didn't take even two seconds to find out what I *need*. You assumed everything, you asked nothing. You don't know our operating structure, you don't know the local rules and regulations, you don't even know if it's *possible* to run this place at capacity."

Eddie leaned back and regarded Chelovek probingly. "Worst of all, you have no idea what I think's important, why I do what I do, what motivates me."

"Hah!" Chelovek pointed to the hotel, clearly visible from their vantage point even in the dying light. "You telling me you don't want to get butts in those beds, fill this place right up to the rafters and get the revenue up?" He stuck the cigar back in his mouth, his eyes twinkling.

"That's exactly what I'm telling you."

That was a surprise. "Then, what the hell *do* you want?"

"Well, I don't think you'd understand, Jerry. Besides, you're too late. If I have to tell you how to do your job, what the hell do I need you for?" Eddie began walking again, and Chelovek had to trot after him for a few steps before catching up.

"I understand plenty, buster! I'm damned good at what I do, and I make a lotta dough doin' it!"

"Doing what, Chelovek? Selling trinkets to immigrants?"

Chelovek faltered slightly but caught himself quickly. "My clients provide a lot of very valuable products and services to new Americans."

By now they'd caught everyone else at the tee, and heads turned to catch the latest installment of what was fast turning out to be a most bizarre round of golf.

"Valuable, right," Eddie said as they pulled up next to the ball washer. "Like what? Electric can openers and hair-coloring kits for Nigerians fresh off the boat without a pot to piss in? Business-interruption insurance for Vietnamese getting minimum wage washing dishes?"

Eddie pulled two balls from his pocket and lifted the handle on the washer. "Concerned citizen like you, you're probably gonna get a special bronze plaque on the Statue of Liberty."

He dropped a ball into the slot and began pumping the handle, looking at Chelovek as he did so. "You take cheap shit you can't sell to people who were born here, dress it up and double the price, then tell the huddled masses that if they don't buy it, they'll never be real Americans." He stopped pumping while the handle was in the up position and pulled his ball out. "Regular fuckin' saint you are."

"That's horseshit! What I do—"

"Face it, Jerry!" Eddie said harshly. "What you do, you help your clients bilk defenseless people out of millions! You challenge their manhood if they don't buy useless hunks of crap jewelry for their wives, you tell the women they're gutter trash if they don't buy the right underwear, you tell 'em both they're rotten parents if they don't spend the food money on shoddy gadgets for their kids—your whole business is preying on people's inadequacies, which they didn't even know they had until you told 'em they did!"

"That's a total load of horseshit, Eddie, and you don't—"

"Oh, give it a rest, Jerry," Kirkland said in a bored tone. "Are you seriously defending what you do?"

Pensecoeur tried to turn his head before Chelovek could catch him giggling. Savitch, less charitable, began whistling as he walked to his bag to get a club, while Aronica just scratched at his chin.

"*Chelovek*," Eddie mused out loud. "Kinda name is that anyway?"

"What do you mean?"

"I mean, I don't remember seeing it on the passenger list of the *Mayflower*, so what is it? Cherokee? Sioux?"

As Perrault (né Piernowsky), Aronica and Savitch began to snicker at

Chelovek's discomfort, Eddie silenced them with a glance that intimated that their derision was misplaced, coming as it did from snooty members of the Royal Connaught Golf & Country Club whose parents had arrived from Latvia, Hungary and the Ukraine.

"Very funny. It's Eastern European."

"Ah. So your parents came over, when . . . the thirties, maybe?" Chelovek's silence was all the confirmation Eddie needed that he'd guessed correctly. "Damned shame, you ask me."

"What's a damned shame?" Chelovek asked, walking right into the trap.

"That *they* didn't have somebody like you waiting to lend them a helping hand when they stepped off the boat. A goddamned wonder they survived here at all."

AS WAVES OF NIGERIANS, HAITIANS, Filipinos, Vietnamese and uncountable others stepped off the boats, even minimum-wage jobs paid them more in a month than some of them had seen in their entire lives. Having no experience of banks or savings accounts or even rainy-day cigar boxes, and painfully sensitive to the fleeting nature of sudden good fortune, they couldn't get rid of all that money fast enough and squandered it in an alarmingly haphazard manner.

At least that's the way Chelovek saw it. "Meaning," he liked to say to his clients, "they're spending all that dough on the other guy's stuff instead of yours! Why? Because they're getting zapped with the same advertising you guys smear all over America at large, so they got no way to discriminate. There are people out there just waiting to have your brands tattooed on their foreheads forever, and you're not going after them!"

Chelovek believed that people had to be taught how to spend money, otherwise why would they pay companies to let them display corporate logos on their kids' T-shirts instead of demanding payment for doing it? Young mothers thought nothing of buying up the entire collection of intrinsically worthless Beanie Babies so their little darlings wouldn't have their precious self-esteem compromised because everybody else at kindergarten had the whole set. Half the population was buying homeopathic remedies even though most contained nothing but distilled water, and damned near everybody in America was fiercely loyal to single brands of cigarettes or cola or beer or motor oil or aspirin even though there were only nine people in the whole country who could tell any of them apart, and then only with fabulously expensive lab equipment.

White Americans were used to that, Chelovek argued. Not only that, they didn't give a shit. Hell, they were willing to pay thousands for a tiny piece of crystal that had no use whatsoever and that they couldn't tell from a chunk of glass if you gave them a goddamned electron microscope to look at it with.

The problem was that this target audience was so saturated with advertising already that real strokes of brilliance in cracking it anew were getting farther and farther apart. How long had it been since someone successfully convinced people to fork over billions for ordinary water from France, for cryin' out loud?

No, coming up with new stuff was too hard. But coming up with new people to sell all the old stuff to was easy. And it may not seem like a very large market, but once your beer is emblazoned on their asses, they're yours for life.

Chelovek knew what he was talking about. He was the guy who'd put Y2K COMPATIBLE stickers on can openers and came up with the name "Internet 700" for a line of light switches, so it was a no-brainer for him to figure out that eye drops could be "Specially Formulated!" for people who came from humid climates like Vietnam to the arid air of Los Angeles, that razor blades could be "Honed Precisely!" for the beards of Nigerians and that shampoo could be "pH Balanced!" for the uniquely structured tresses of Albanian women. You really didn't have to come up with anything new except for the labels. Once you got your old stuff into new packages, all you had to do was convince the new immigrants they weren't real Americans unless they bought it. And if you got in there quick enough, you didn't even have any competition to worry about.

It was all legal, completely ethical—who the hell was twisting anybody's arms, after all?—and insanely profitable. In fact, the only time Chelovek had ever gotten into any kind of trouble was when he ran a gag ad in an April 1 edition of *The Wall Street Journal* soliciting investment for a new company whose purported objective was to allow people to auction off their organs to people awaiting donors. It might have gone unnoticed by all but his friends were it not for the U.S. Postal Service complaining to the Securities and Exchange Commission that the nonexistent post-office box mentioned in the ad was getting huge amounts of mail, including not only offers from some three dozen medical outfits to contract for the transplant procedures but checks totaling over $9 million from people wanting to invest because the company was going to be called *e.bodyparts*.

CHELOVEK, ALONE AND UNARMED, STRUGGLED in the whirlpool of a truth he couldn't face. It wasn't about his job—hell, he might not have liked to hear it from somebody else, but he'd never kidded himself that he was some kind of critical asset to the world at large. So it wasn't that.

It wasn't about being humiliated in public either. That came with not only the job but his habit of self-aggrandizing preening, which, if you do it often enough, carries with it the inevitable certainty of the occasional backfire. About two months after Chelovek joined the Royal Connaught, he walked into the clubhouse for dinner with some friends, swaggered up to the valet guy and roared, "Son, what's the biggest goddamned tip you ever got!"

"Uh, fifty dollars, sir," the startled young man replied.

"Oh, yeah?" Chelovek pulled out his money clip with a flourish, peeled off a bill and handed it over. "Well, here's a hunnerd!"

As the guy stammered out his profuse thanks, Chelovek looked around at the growing number of onlookers, smiled broadly and said, "So who gave you the fifty, kid?"

The valet looked around, helpless, and said, "You did, Mr. Chelovek!"

So it wasn't the embarrassment per se that was the proximate cause of his present distress.

It was being stripped bare, forced spread-eagle onto an examining table, pummeled, trampled and beaten by a *woman*.

And not just any woman, but this woman. Beautiful, smart, self-possessed—raw sexual power poured out of Kirkland and couldn't have overwhelmed Chelovek more completely if she'd been made out of plutonium. His whole life he'd feared that power, the kind of irresistible force so lethal that kings, presidents, houses of parliament and titans of industry with the ability to change the world could be reduced to simpering, quivering, submissive and often criminal morons because of the merest baring of a few square inches of skin. Women like Selby Kirkland pierced to the very heart of his fragile masculinity and held aloft, as a superior warrior holds aloft the heart torn out of his enemy's chest, every deeply embedded insecurity that drove him to spend his entire life proving that he was bigger, stronger, smarter—*better!*—than any goddamned piece-of-shit slut broad that dared to think he couldn't reduce her to a cinder if he wanted to, and just like *that*, too.

In Chelovek's tortured mind, if he could bed them, the victory was his. He had no idea that the mere act of engaging in such battle was a sure sign of his defeat.

Kirkland sniffed contemptuously at Chelovek and stepped out of the cart, flashing him a slight hip toss as though daring him to see if he had the stuff to tangle with *this* particular piece of ass.

Of course, that was all in his mind, Kirkland having done no such thing.

Chelovek remained rooted to the spot, paralyzed by a primordial dread far worse than if he were being chased by a wounded lion or hanging by his fingertips over the side of an erupting volcano. He wanted to kill Kirkland right there—*needed* to kill her, in fact, to neutralize the effect she had on him—but doubted he could get past the Haitian.

"Y'know," he heard Savitch say from somewhere behind him, "I've always kinda thought the same thing."

Chelovek blinked himself out of his murderous fantasy and turned slowly toward Savitch.

"Advertising. I mean, gimme a break." Savitch was grinning broadly, drinking in Chelovek's distress as if it were a fine wine. "You hit it right on the head, Eddie, my man. Just like—"

"What you do is worse," Eddie said, and the grin dropped from Savitch's face as though by a remote command from a puppeteer.

"No it isn't."

"Oh, yeah. It is." Eddie motioned for Pensecoeur to get on up and hit but kept talking as his partner got ready.

"Every other job in the world, it's a kind of exchange. Somebody gives you some money, you give 'em back something. Might could be something you made, or a service you perform, or a piece of advice—we can argue about the value, whether the price was right, but at least something moved in both directions. Even Jerry here, the advertiser? He works. Somebody pays him, and he does something for it."

He paused while Pensecoeur wound up and hit. "Nice one, ET!"

Then he turned back to Savitch. "But you, Deke? What you do? You sit at a computer or on the phone and you grab off pieces of something that somebody else accomplished as it streaks by you. You do nothing of use, you manufacture nothing, you provide nothing . . . there's not even another *person* involved! All you do, you take. As much as you can, whenever you can, from wherever you can, and give absolutely nothing back. Now I ask you . . ."

He stretched a club across his shoulders and twisted his trunk back and forth. "Is that any kind of way to make a living?"

Savitch, dumbstruck, had a few choice replies he might have voiced but couldn't seem to get any of them out. This was Eddie's turf—it seemed as if the entire world were Eddie's turf—and Savitch was too fearful to tread upon it.

Chelovek, watching him, understood all of this instantly, and he was no Deke Savitch. "Hey, Eddie," he said from off to the side. "I got an idea."

"Yeah, what's that?"

"Why don't you go fuck yourself? Okay? How's that for an idea?"

Eddie stopped twisting.

"Oh, I'm sorry," Chelovek said with mock contrition. "Nothing to say? Thought you could insult the living shit out of us and all we'd do is stand there and take it, like you were some kinda nun smacking a ruler across our knuckles?"

Chelovek looked around, pleased with the reaction he was getting from his partners, even more pleased with the stunned look plastered across the broad's face. "Well, fuck that, fuck this place, and fuck *you!*"

Eddie let the club down, rested it on the ground and leaned on it. "Seems to me, Jerry," he said after an uncomfortably long interval, "that there's some bad blood in the air."

"Well, don't look at me, bub. You started it! I don't remember any of us insulting *your* sorry ass. Speaking of which, what the hell makes you so much better'n us, hah? What in the freakin' hell do you do that's so goddamned vital to society!"

Eddie cocked his head to one side. It was not an unreasonable question. "I give lessons," he finally said. "Just like it said on your invitation."

Chelovek heard a partially stifled chortle from one of his partners. *"Lessons?"* he said, drawing the word out. "You give *lessons?"*

Eddie nodded.

Chelovek turned toward his boys. "Now, can you beat that? Mr. God's-gift-to-the-world here teaches golf!"

The four of them laughed, a little too loudly and just a bit too forced.

Eddie smiled in kind and waited for them to settle down, then said, "I didn't say golf lessons, Jerry."

As I told you before, I've pieced together this whole story from various accounts, so even though I might have had to fill in a little dialogue here and there or guess at some details, I'm fairly convinced I got most of it right. This little snippet of conversation I just quoted I'm pretty sure is just how it happened, word for word, but what I've never been able to get a straight answer to is why not a single person who'd heard Eddie say it wasn't golf lessons he'd been talking about bothered to ask what he'd meant by it. For the life of me, I can't understand why they didn't, but the more I've thought about it, the less it surprises me.

"Becoming dark, Eddie," Pensecoeur said.

"You're right. So whyn't one'a you boys go ahead and hit?"

"Hit?" Chelovek began nodding vigorously, striding quickly to his cart and reaching into his bag for his driver. "Goddamned right we'll hit. And how we'll hit! You ready, fellas?"

"Fuckin' A!" Aronica cheered, as Perrault and Savitch scrambled to get set up and show this supercilious shithead of a resort operator just what kind of men he was dealing with.

Chelovek gathered them all together for a quick huddle. "Now look, and don't argue with me: He's counting on us getting high on adrenaline and fucking this up, see? That was the reason for all'a this bullshit, so don't anybody take it personal!"

"Darned right!" Savitch enthused, Perrault and Aronica clapping him and Chelovek on the back encouragingly.

"Now, we get up there, me and Deke, we get a couple safe, then Joe and Pete whap the hell out of it, and we can *win this goddamned thing!*"

"Yeah!"

"But everybody stays cool, plays within himself, right? Stays in control!"

He stood up and slapped his abdomen. "Now, a couple deep breaths and let's get to it."

Breaking up the huddle and urging Chelovek to the tee with heartfelt good wishes, they didn't even bother to look at Eddie or his partners. This wasn't about mind games anymore; the only truth, the only real victory, would be written on a scorecard and a bank draft, and it wouldn't make a bit of difference who got the upper hand in an insult war. The only thing that counted now was who won at least one of the last two holes. Everything else was utterly and completely irrelevant.

"Do it, Jerrold!" Perrault said, and then they stepped away to allow Chelovek some undisturbed space.

"Tee markers stay where they are," Eddie said. "Your minute's up."

Chelovek gestured for his partners to forget the markers. He could hardly wait, this was going to be so good. He could feel power and authority rippling through his arms and shoulders as he stooped to tee the ball, tree-trunk solidity in his legs, pure focus in a mind that was suddenly able to shut out the whole universe in service of this one mission that would forever change life at Swithen Bairn.

When was the last time anybody here had played two holes of golf for half a million dollars a man?

He could feel all eyes upon him, and he drank it up like mother's milk. He didn't care one whit about where the tee markers were set, that's how confident he was that he was about to *own* these motherfuckers no matter where they hit from.

With theatrical solemnity he slowly brought the clubface to the ball, willing his body to perfect peace and readiness, bidding the world pause for a moment and witness a miracle . . .

It dropped from the sky like a killer asteroid bent on the complete destruction of every life form it encountered.

"You're doubled," Eddie said.

Chapter 42

⊞

THERE ARE TURNING POINTS IN life—like finding out you were adopted, or your father is an escaped war criminal, or the company you devoted your entire adult life to is really owned by the Medellín Cartel and all that talcum powder you've been sending around the world was really heroin and your name was on all the shipping manifests—certain critical moments in which everything you thought you knew and believed is suddenly called into question and after which nothing can ever be quite the same again.

I can't honestly say this was one of those moments for our boys, although the part about nothing ever being the same again would certainly apply. Well, okay, maybe also the part about things not being the way you thought they were, since the thought of being doubled back had never occurred to any of them.

But basically it was really just about money, if you stripped away all the other baggage. And that's what our boys tried to do, remove any other implications that might have been attendant to their new predicament and just treat it as a business problem, a simple proposition to be discussed as would any other commercial matter: calmly, rationally and professionally, as befitted four grown men, none of whom was a neophyte in matters of commerce.

There was no other way to go about it when you got right down to it, but they didn't get right down to it, because to do so required all four of them to be involved, and that was not the situation in the seconds following the thunderbolt that was Eddie's proposal.

"Jerrold?"

Perrault was the first to speak after Eddie, and he called Chelovek's name softly, then again. "Jerrold?"

Chelovek was still on the tee box. He was still holding his club. He was still in his stance, the club held just behind his waiting ball, his shoulders square, his grip relaxed and ready. He'd already taken his last look at the target and was ready to hit.

He'd been like that for nearly a minute now. The same kind of neuronal circuitry that had allowed him to pursue his avocation with a perfectly clear conscience had shifted its programming slightly and was now telling him it was perfectly okay to take his shot, regardless of what his ears, those mischievous and untrustworthy little imps, were trying to tell him they'd just heard.

"Jerry!" Aronica said with more force than Perrault had, but it was too late: Chelovek was taking the club back and twisting his upper body.

Aronica emitted a strangled cry and lurched toward the tee, but there was no way he would get there in time to stop Chelovek from hitting the ball and implicitly accepting Eddie's offer of a double.

Something white and fast appeared in his peripheral vision, and he ducked reflexively to the side just as a pair of golf balls whizzed past his ear and banged into the ground at Chelovek's feet, one hitting him on the ankle, the other knocking his ball off the tee.

Chelovek, already at the top of his turn, staggered backward off balance and looked behind him, startled. "What the hell . . . !"

"Come on down here, buddy," Perrault said gently, his hand still outstretched in the follow-through from his throw.

Chelovek blinked several times, then did as he was told, passing a panting Aronica and wondering why the engineer had the look of a cornered rat on his face.

As he walked, something in his brain decided to replay the last several minutes of his life for him, complete with soundtrack, and his steps slowed as Eddie's words finally seeped in. Then his knees threatened to buckle, so he stopped for a second and used his club as a crutch to balance himself.

He looked around as the world started to come back into focus. "Where's Deke?" he asked.

Aronica, getting up and brushing himself off, pointed off to the side, where Savitch was still actively trying to vomit the abject terror out of his system.

Chelovek grimaced at the sight, which for some strange reason had the effect of finally returning him to reality.

"Yecch," he said, probably the most apt comment he'd made all week.

THE OWNERS HAD COURTEOUSLY REMOVED themselves to a flat grassy area out of earshot of the boys, who were sitting on the ground near the tee box. The sound of an unseen hummingbird in the nearby honey-suckle bushes was accompanied by the raucous screech of a macaw trying to claim the territory. Crickets had already taken up their synchronized, early-evening chirping. Everywhere the unmistakable sounds of nightfall, normally signaling a period of serenity, only grated on the raw nerve endings of our boys, unaware of the beauty of the sinking sun and seeing instead only a cosmic clock counting down the last minutes of their deadline. As Eddie had said when they'd set up the match, it ended at sundown.

Eddie's offer of a double brought the stakes up to a million dollars a man.

"Okay," Chelovek said, fully recovered now, but a part of him wishing he could spend the rest of his life in that blissful state of sweet denial he'd been rudely shaken out of scant moments ago, "here's the bottom line: If we turn it down, three of us are out a quarter million each and Deke's out a million and a quarter." He raised his eyebrows by way of inquiry, inviting confirmation of his analysis.

"Well, I daresay you hit it right on the head there, Jerrold," Perrault said.

"Yep," Aronica agreed. "That really clears things up for me. By God, that was helpful!"

"Okay, okay, fuck the both'a you guys. Jeez, just tryin' to get us to think about this thing rationally . . ."

"There's no way to think about this rationally," Savitch wheezed, still wiping traces of stomach bile from his mouth along with some milky-looking antacid he'd been trying to get down his throat.

"There damned well better be," Chelovek said.

"Do we even have the right to take the double?" Aronica asked rhetorically. "Deke agreed to cover everything above a quarter mil a man, but that was a while ago, and now it could cost him over three million."

"And therefore . . . ?" Perrault stretched his legs out in front of him and leaned back on his hands.

"It's Deke's decision," Aronica answered, folding his arms across his chest as an indication that the ball was now in Savitch's court and the rest need only await his pleasure.

"Horseshit!" Chelovek belched. "You saying we're giving him the right to kiss off a quarter million each of our dough?" He forced a mirthless laugh. "That'll be the day!"

Perrault exchanged glances with Aronica and Savitch, then said to Chelovek, "Are you telling me you want to *accept* the double?"

"Absolutely."

"What the hell do you mean, absolutely!" Savitch cried. "That doesn't cost you a goddamned thing!"

"Doesn't—What are you, nuts or something? Of course it—"

"No!" Savitch shrieked again, getting angry at Chelovek's failure to sympathize with, or even comprehend, the real implications. "If we turn him down right now, you're out a quarter of a million. If we accept and *then* lose, you're still out only a quarter million!" He looked around to make sure everyone was following, then jerked a thumb at his chest. "*I'm* the only one who gets killed if we accept and lose! This is a goddamned *three-million-dollar decision* for me!"

Chelovek stared at him dumbly for a second, then closed his mouth and nodded. "You got a point there."

"Fuckin'-A right I do!"

"So it *is* Deke's decision," Aronica repeated.

"No way," Chelovek said. "I'm not gonna let him make the call to leave my quarter million on the table and walk away."

"Which puts us right back to square one," Perrault concluded correctly.

"OKAY, THERE'S ONLY ONE WAY out."

The others looked hopefully at Aronica.

"We gotta put up the difference ourselves," he said. "Savitch covers the second quarter mil, just like he said he would, and we each come up with the rest on our own."

"That's another half million a man," Perrault calculated. "Forget it."

"Good idea, Joe," Chelovek chimed in. "I'm all for it."

"You're fulla shit," Perrault threw back at him. "You don't have it."

"Oh, yeah? Says who!"

"Come off it, Jerry," Aronica said. "You know he's right."

"Then why'd you even propose it, you stupid sonofabitch!"

It was a good question, and square one was starting to look like home.

.

THEY SAT QUIETLY, CLEVER IDEAS being in painfully short supply. Even the willingness to *voice* an idea was waning rapidly, as each suggestion was greeted by an escalating level of derision, sarcasm and outright belligerence.

"What if we win?" Chelovek asked after a particularly awkward interval.

One or two eyebrows shot up, and Chelovek took it as a sign to explore the matter. "What if we beat these guys and walk home with a million each?"

"Seven-fifty each," Savitch said.

"What?" Chelovek said in astonishment.

"You only risk seven-fifty each, that's all you get to win. I'm the guy putting up the second quarter mil, remember?"

"That's only if we agree to that arrangement," Perrault reminded Savitch. "And I don't recall anybody saying we do."

"And besides," Chelovek added with a malicious grin, "we get ten percent of that second quarter mil, or did you forget that?"

"*You* can forget that, buster," Savitch spat at him. "That was back when—"

"You piece'a-shit welcher!" Chelovek roared. "I don't fucking believe this! We had a deal, and now—"

"Deal, my ass! And besides, I still say you don't have the dough to back—"

"Forget it." Aronica said it quietly, but it managed to stop the fierce ground war in its tracks.

"Forget what?" Perrault asked.

"Winning." Aronica had a twig in his hand and was idly scratching lines in the dirt adjacent to the coral cart path.

"What's with him?" Chelovek said, then fell silent with the others.

Aronica stopped scratching and looked up. "There's something wrong with the stars."

Perrault felt something cold ripple down his spine. "What?"

Aronica pointed up at the sky without looking at it. "The stars. They, uh . . ."

Chelovek looked upward; indeed, faint stars were beginning to appear as the rays of the low-hanging sun cast huge pillars of light outward from the horizon. "They what?"

Aronica sighed, resigned to just say what he had to say and take what came. "They're not in the right place."

Now the ripple threatened to turn into a full-fledged seizure, and an icy fear gripped Perrault's heart. He could see the same kind of nameless dread on Savitch's face. Aronica had his faults, but he was as firmly grounded as anyone Perrault knew, and to hear him suddenly start talking like—

A raucous laugh erupted out of Chelovek, shattering the eerie silence. "The stars!" he managed to choke out, and then started laughing again.

Aronica looked at him, his face completely devoid of expression.

"Jesus, Joe . . ." Chelovek wiped at his eyes. "What the hell are you talking about? You telling me the big-deal scientist believes in *astrology*, f'Chrissakes? Oh, this is really too—"

"Not astrology, you low-life moron," Aronica said. *"Astronomy!"*

He turned around and pointed to a spot low on the horizon, just to the right of the main house and opposite where the sun was getting ready to drown itself in the sea. "Orion," he said. "Right there!"

"What about it?" Savitch asked, trying to make a shape out of the faint stars that were barely visible.

"It came up . . . What I'm saying here . . . It came up early yesterday."

He turned back around to face his partners. "It was in the wrong place, don't you see? I watched it every night we've been here, and I'm telling you: *It's in the wrong place!"*

Jaw agape, Perrault stared at him.

So did Savitch. "You're starting to weird me out a little, Joe." He looked around; the nighttime sounds seemed louder, and as the gap between sun and water narrowed, he got the awful feeling that he was going blind. "I don't like any of this."

Chelovek dropped his head into his hands. "And I don't believe I'm even hearing it."

Savitch, miffed that their fears could be so easily dismissed, said, "But Joe thinks—"

"Joe? Joe thinks?" Chelovek scrambled to his feet and slapped his hands together to shake off the grass. "Well, some goddamned scientist our Mr. Aronica turns out to be. Where do you come up with cockamamy bullshit like this?"

He walked closer to Aronica and squatted down in front of him. "Listen, pal, you don't want the double, just say so, goddamnit, but don't try to freak the rest of us into going along!"

"I didn't say I wasn't going for the double," Aronica protested weakly.

"That's my money we'd be losing!" Savitch wailed.

"Tough," Perrault shot back with real venom, tired of the self-pitying whining. "What exactly are you going to do about it?"

"Where did all that dough come from anyway?" Aronica asks. "When the hell do you even work, playing golf six days a week!"

"He doesn't," Perrault said.

"Whaddaya mean, he doesn't?" Chelovek asked, his curiosity momentarily pushing aside the problem they were facing.

Fact was, Savitch really didn't have to work. The computers quite literally did all the work for him. They were hooked into damned near every market in the world, so when, say, they sensed a high-volatility currency take a minor dip on the Frankfurt exchange, they bought a large block of it and sold it simultaneously in Chicago, before the dip had time to reach the U.S. currency markets. The difference was small, usually on the order of a few pennies, but do it often enough with big enough blocks and it was little different from minting money.

The same technique applied to equities, too. "But stocks are more complicated," Savitch explained. "I'm working on that." Actually, he wasn't working on anything; the work was being done by a programmer he'd hired, a former hacker who'd broken into NORAD's computers and bargained his way out of a federal sentence by agreeing to do something productive with his talent, Savitch having promised the court that he had the perfect outlet for the precocious delinquent's energies.

"So all you do is turn the machines on in the morning and shut them off at night?" Chelovek said in amazement and not a small measure of admiration and envy.

"Doesn't even do that," Perrault said. "They're on all the time. All he does is count his money when he gets home from playing golf, isn't that right, *buddy*?"

"And give you ten percent!" Savitch threw in acidly.

"Aah," Chelovek said as realization dawned. "So there's more to medicine than just running up phony tests!"

"You shut the hell up, Jerry!" Savitch said threateningly. "Some goddamned friend you turned out to be!"

"I told you, Deke, I thought you had a—"

"And that woulda made it okay?"

"Ask your wife the same question, asshole. She *knew* you didn't have a heart condition!"

"Quiet down a second," Perrault warned. Eddie had broken off from his people and was walking in their direction.

Chelovek, still on his feet, semiconsciously drew closer to his partners.

·

"YOU FELLAS HAVIN' ANY LUCK coming to a decision?"

Eddie was answered with much foot-shuffling and noncommittal mumbling. To everyone's surprise, it was Savitch who took him on.

"Seems there may be a little ambiguity in the rules, Eddie."

"Oh? How's that?"

"They don't deal with a situation in which one player covers other players' bets."

Eddie laughed and reached for his cigarettes. "You're a real piece'a work, you are, Deke."

He shook out a cigarette and pulled it from the pack with his teeth. The glow from his lighter lit his face from below, and the sudden apparition of hooded eyes and facial features illuminated by firelight against the darkening sky was eerie, and caused the boys to shrink back and then to feel like idiots for having done so. Savitch even forgot to ask him what he'd meant by that remark, but Eddie was ready to explain anyway.

"You based your whole career on making a casino out of other men's dreams, and now you want special rules to protect you?"

"I just want it to be fair."

"Fair!" Eddie knocked the ash off his cigarette with an impatient flick of his wrist. A glowing ember twirled lazily to the ground. "Who the hell asked you to stake your partners? *You* set up the situation, *you* worry about making it fair! That's no concern of ours, just like we agreed last night."

He stuck the cigarette in his mouth, his eyes going narrow from the acrid smoke, and indicated the sky behind him. "Almost sundown. Another couple minutes, you're going to forfeit."

"Bullshit!" It was Chelovek's turn to show he wasn't afraid. "Says who?"

"The rules we agreed on. We offered a double; you either accept it or you lose. It's that simple."

And it *was* that simple.

THE SUN WAS NEARING HALFWAY gone, and the refractive glimmer of its deep orange light as it passed through many miles of humid and unstable air made it look as if its surface was breaking apart.

"The way I see it," Perrault said, "any one of us can veto accepting the double."

"How do you figure that?" Savitch asked him.

"Because none of us has the right to commit another's money against his will. If I elect to quit, to pay the half million and walk away? There's nothing anybody can do about it. You can't make me risk more."

"We don't have to." Chelovek sat back down, cross-legged on the grass. "Deke, we can keep on going without committing a guy who doesn't want to pony up the extra."

"How?"

"Three of us can agree to accept the double and cover the one guy's losses if we blow it."

Savitch tried to absorb this new option, adding up what it would imply for him personally, when Aronica said, "Two of you, Jerry."

"What the hell's that supposed to mean?"

"It means I'm out. Period." Aronica sighed, and hung his head. "We're not going to win. I don't know why, but we're not going to, and every one of us knows it."

"What is it, the goddamned stars again?"

Before he could answer, Savitch had rolled to his knees and was pointing at Aronica. "You can't do that!" he hissed. "That's a million extra of my dough you're throwing down the john with your crummy two hunnerd 'n' fifty grand!"

"So sue me."

"I've a feeling," Perrault said, "that if we were thinking about this as a team instead of each only for himself, a solution might be at hand."

Aronica was resolute, they could see that. This scientist, who eschewed superstition in any form and prided himself on healthy skepticism and down-right cynicism toward anything that smacked of pseudoscientific malarkey, had been frightened speechless by something he couldn't even name.

Further debate with him was going to be useless, and that left only Savitch and Chelovek. "You and me, Deke! The two of us, let's show these faggots how real men get things done!"

"Don't be an idiot, Jerrold," Perrault warned. "You can't possibly—"

"You stay out'a this, you piece'a chickenshit! Wasn't for you, I'd never have—"

"What, Jerrold . . . diddled Deke's wife? That was my fault?"

"You goddamned right it—"

"Jerry!"

Chelovek turned at the harsh sound of Aronica's voice.

"It's no good, bud. The two of you playin' against the two best balls of those three?"

"But you two can still play with us, even if you're not in the bet!" Chelovek argued, desperation apparent in every syllable.

"Now how do you figure that?" Perrault asked him. " 'I say, Eddie, we're out of the match. Mind if we give our buddies here a hand so they can win four million from you?' "

"We're responsible for the money as a group, remember?" Chelovek said. "That means you're only out as far as the four of us are concerned. How we divvy things among ourselves, that's an internal matter, and it's none of their business."

"In that case," Perrault said, "we get a share if we win."

"And Jerry and I cover the loss?" Savitch sputtered. "You're outta your mind!"

"Fine," Aronica said. "Then I'm throwing *my* badge on the table, and you can play on your own."

The ideas were becoming more absurd, the creativity more exhausted, and only the wretched futility of this match and their lives remained ascendant. Four grown men sat and watched, helpless and miserable, as their fate was determined by a minor star setting at the end of an otherwise ordinary day.

"That's it?" Savitch said, so piteously that the others, despite their own impending doom, actually felt sorry for him.

" 'Not with a bang but a whimper,' " Perrault said, "as Eliot put it."

"Yeah, well *fuck you*," Chelovek said, "as I put it."

Heads turned slowly westward. The last thin crescent of fire narrowed to a point and disappeared, the dying sun finally sinking beneath the waves and dragging the last vestiges of their hopes down with it.

It was night, and it was over.

Chapter 43

HAVING ALREADY GONE THROUGH DENIAL and anger as a group, they quickly graduated to the next stage of dying, a kind of morbid and isolated desolation in which each of them could wallow alone in his own brand of despair.

It didn't last long. They could hear the owners stirring as the reason for their courteous patience winked out in the western sky.

Chelovek drew a loud, shuddering breath that seemed about to break into sobbing, but he held it together and managed to keep his voice relatively steady. "Might's well go face the music."

Perrault, in silent agreement, unfolded his legs and slowly began to rise. He bent over to give the blood a little time to move into his head. "Guess we may as well try to behave like good sports."

"Why?" Savitch asked cynically.

"Because it's all we have left, Deke," Aronica answered.

"All *we* have left?" Savitch asked. "You wanna compare wounds, Joe?"

But nobody was in the mood to fight anymore. Depression was giving way to resignation, and any will they might once have harbored to defend their individual honors had been quite thoroughly demolished, just another bleeding lump in a trail of psychic flotsam.

Aronica drew himself up to his full height, ran a hand through his hair and made sure his shirttail wasn't hanging out. The others followed as he led the way to where the owners were returning clubs to bags, stowing balls, markers and tees, and generally tidying up after nearly twelve hours on the course.

Eddie was stretching his arms above his head and yawning. "How 'bout a cold one, boys?"

"You bet," Chelovek answered heartily, or what he thought might pass for heartily under the circumstances.

Eddie gestured to Jake, who walked to the back of his cart and flipped up the lid of the defibrillator. A layer of partially melted ice came right up to the top.

"That keep the equipment cooled down?" Aronica asked, ever the curious engineer.

"Manner'a speaking," the waiter replied. He suddenly plunged his hand through the ice, fished around for a second and came up with a bottle of Heineken, bits of ice clinging to its surface. He switched it to his other hand and shook off the wet one, then slid open a small panel near one of the control knobs, stuck the top of the bottle inside and tilted it downward sharply. A pop, hiss and clatter later, he handed the bottle to Kirkland, reclad in her workout suit, who'd walked up without the astonished Aronica's having noticed.

Jake put his hand back into the ice and began feeling around again. "Nothin' like a cold one after a round, as Eddie always says."

"You are so right, my man," Eddie affirmed. "Can'a Bud, you got one."

"Somewheres . . . here you go." The waiter had retrieved a red-and-silver can and tossed it to Eddie.

"Gonna suds it all up, schmuck," Eddie said as he popped the top and held it out to the side to let the fizzing subside.

"Got lots more. Doc, whaddaya say? Mr. A.?"

Aronica walked up to the cooler and stuck his hand in, then the other one, and then pushed them both farther in, working his fingers so that he could drill down through all the ice.

"Gonna get frostbit, Mr. A.," Jake said. "Sure I can't—"

Perrault, dazed and confused, moved up beside Aronica and pointed to the machine. "I thought that was a—"

Aronica got his arms all the way down to a smooth slab of plastic, which was the bottom of the bin. There was nothing there but the cooler, and Aronica finally pulled his arms back out.

Eddie was standing behind them, polishing off the last of his beer. "It's a nice surprise when it's all over, we pop the lid and it's just a cooler full'a brews. Gives people a good laugh."

"But you coulda phoned in for beers anytime you wanted," Perrault said, his gentrified aplomb threatening to leave him again. "Whaddaya need to carry around a loud, goddamned industrial-strength goddamned portable goddamned beer wagon—"

"On account'a you never know in match play when the round's gonna end, see? 'Specially with this weird-o-rama doubling thing you guys came up with. Man's gotta be ready for when the time's right. Isn't that right, Joe?"

"How the fuck should I know, Eddie?" Aronica replied, his voice like flint striking steel.

"Well, you were ready when you came up with that Arondium stuff, weren't you? I mean, wasn't like you were studying molecules and atoms for years and tryin' to figure out *how* to make it, was it?"

"What are you talking about?" Perrault said crossly.

Eddie looked at Aronica and frowned. "Doesn't he know how you invented that shit, Joe?"

I do. He'd found it at the bottom of a mixing vessel the morning after he'd abandoned it in disgust on a lab table after failing, for the millionth time, to come up with a metal alloy that could be used to reinforce picnic baskets and be made in quantity on the cheap.

"It was an accident, you said," Eddie continued. "In't that right?"

"Lots of things start as accidents," Aronica said defensively. "Guy who invented those peel-off notes, that was an accident: He'd been looking for a super glue, and all he got was—"

"Yeah, you told us that already."

"But the genius, see, the real genius was, he saw that it was useful anyway!" Aronica had gotten a bit shrill and thought it best to stop.

His handout instructing emcees on how to introduce him when guest-speaking took pains to characterize real genius not so much as the ability to accomplish what you'd set out to accomplish, which was more about persistence and discipline than raw brilliance, but to recognize, even when an experiment had gone astray and might have been discarded, that in fact something extraordinary, albeit unexpected, might have resulted instead.

"So it's kind of like those Pulitzer photographs, that it?" Eddie asked.

"What do you mean?" Aronica asked warily.

"Well—hey, Jake, gimme another one, 'cept this time hand it to me, 'kay?—seems to me, half the time the shutterbug didn't even know he had the shot until he got into the lab. He's sitting in some darkroom dribbling chemicals all over the photo paper, and then he sees some snap he didn't even remember he took, on account'a he was scared shitless at the time and just holding his camera up in the air with the motor drive going, see? But then he spots this shot and he's like, Whoa! Lookit this! and some magazine prints it and he gets a Pulitzer."

Eddie reached behind Perrault to get his beer from Jake. "Something like that, then? A one-shot deal, never even come close to doing it again?"

Aronica didn't need to respond, somehow knowing that if he tried to make it out to be more than that, the matter of what else he'd accomplished in his chosen field would come up, and that something else was in fact precisely nothing.

The miracle metal was the only thing in his life Aronica had been able to point to that justified his existence on this planet, and now Eddie was trying to grind it into dust. *In other words,* his comments seemed to imply, *if you're such a freakin' genius, how come that's the only thing you ever produced?*

"You seem to know an awful lot about materials science," Aronica said, "for a golfer."

"What can I tell you?" Eddie replied. "I read a lot. Now"—he slapped Aronica on the back and nudged Perrault with the bottle—"have a couple beers. You boys look thirsty."

Aronica let himself be led to the cooler, but Perrault demurred. "Gotta do something," he said, turning on his heel and walking away.

"We didn't come up with it," Aronica said.

"With what?" Eddie asked.

"The doubling thing. Wasn't us. It was Sam Coolidge."

"Yeah," Eddie said, wiping a spot of beer from his mouth. "Whatever."

"HEY, ET . . ."

Perrault found Pensecoeur in his cart, drinking from an amber bottle without a label. The Haitian paused in mid-sip at the sound of his nickname, stiffening slightly as the other man approached.

"Uh . . ." Perrault drew up and scratched nervously at the side of his nose. "Mind if I ask you something about your, uh, your grandmother?"

Pensecoeur nodded hesitantly.

"The clinic they sent her to. You know where that was?"

Pensecoeur thought about it for a second. "In the state of New Jersey. A funny name, the city. Like coffee, and a head . . . ?"

It took Perrault a few seconds. "Teaneck?"

Pensecoeur snapped his fingers. "Just so! Why do you ask?"

Perrault closed his eyes and exhaled in blessed relief. "I own a string of clinics, is all. I was rather hoping it wasn't one of mine."

"Ah." He took another sip from the amber bottle. "And it wasn't?"

Perrault shook his head, then patted Pensecoeur's upper arm and squeezed it. "I'm real sorry about your grandmother, Étienne. Truly I am."

"Thank you, Doctor."

"Sometimes, you know, you do things, you've no idea what the, uh . . ." He let go of Pensecoeur and stepped back. "Well, anyway. I'm just sorry."

"Thank you." Pensecoeur held the bottle out. *"S'il vous plaît . . ."*

"What is it?"

"Rum. Very good, from the estate of Barbancourt. Please."

Perrault accepted the bottle and sniffed it first, then took a swallow without bothering to wipe the lip. A heady mix of sweetness, perfume and the ethereal coldness of evaporating alcohol fondled the back of his mouth and throat, and he smiled for the first time in many hours.

"Reminds me of home," Pensecoeur said wistfully. "But this is a nice place, too. I hope I am invited back someday."

Perrault had started to take another swig of the strange and fascinating elixir, but it caught in his throat and he gagged, turning to the side barely in time to avoid spraying a mouthful all over the cart and its occupant.

Pensecoeur had started to get out of the cart to help but laughed instead as he saw that Perrault was all right. "Down an incorrect pipe, *mon ami?*" he said as he took the bottle.

"Invited back?" Perrault was still trying to work the last drops out of his throat but managed to sputter out a few words. "What are you talking about, 'invited back'? Aren't you an owner?"

"An owner!" Pensecoeur looked at him incredulously for a second and then threw back his head and laughed even louder this time. "An owner, *mon dieu!* I am a groundskeeper at a public course in Florida, Lord help me!"

"But . . ." Perrault reached out a hand and steadied himself against one of the struts supporting the golf cart's roof. "But how could you, um, how could you afford—"

"The betting? Oh, *monsieur* . . ." Pensecoeur took a long swig and let the rum take its time going down. "The bets are Monsieur Eddie's . . . I only play."

"ANYBODY UP FOR WALKING BACK?" Kirkland called out. "The bell guys can come and get the carts later."

It was a beautiful, still night, and no one seemed anxious to jump into a bunch of noisy carts and drive them over even noisier paths of crushed coral.

Aronica and Eddie walked together. "You knew you could beat us," the engineer said, "didn't you?"

"We didn't beat you, Joe. You quit." Eddie tossed the empty beer bottle to Jake and caught the full one that came back. "Which was a smart move, because you guys were so primed to self-destruct I coulda beat you with Grandma Moses on my side."

"That's not what I meant. What I meant, you *knew* you were going to win. You knew that we'd either quit or you'd beat us, but there was no way we were gonna come out on top. Not here, not in"—Aronica gulped and kept his eyes on Eddie, not wanting to look up where he knew the brightening stars were twinkling with a malevolence he'd never noticed before—"not in this place."

Eddie turned to him in puzzled surprise, but Aronica was sure he'd detected a moment of hesitation. "Jeez, Joe, you're not gonna come apart on me now, are ya?"

The scientist looked past Eddie and dared a glimpse at the constellation of Orion, only half risen above the horizon. He looked at his watch, pressing a button to illuminate the dial and then felt faint.

"Yeah, some'a the guys, they tell me you been stargazing."

Aronica managed to nod. "Kind of a hobby," he said feebly.

"So you'll be interested in this then: You actually had a few more minutes of decision time than you should have, didja know that?" Eddie pulled a cigarette out of his shirt pocket and lit it, the glow from his lighter creating flickering shadows in the nearby darkness.

"You said sundown," Aronica replied mechanically. "We could all see it setting . . ."

"Right, except that—"

"Be a good fellow and light that thing again." Perrault had slipped up behind them unnoticed.

"Sure." Eddie flicked the lighter on and saw that Perrault had a business card out as well as a scoring pencil from the cart, and he was trying to see enough to be able to write. "What're you doing?"

"Social Security number," Perrault answered.

Eddie laughed and let the lighter go out.

"Hey . . . !"

"Relax, Doc. I was just kiddin' about that. Didn't know you were gonna get so shook up."

Perrault staggered backward, trying to make out Eddie's face in the dark. "The IRS commissioner doesn't really play here?"

"Sure he plays here. All the damned time, but he doesn't report his own bets; you think he's gonna go after you?"

A radio crackled from behind them. "The Piper's on, Eddie," Kirkland said as she emerged from the deepening gloom. "Wants to know what's up."

Eddie nodded at her, then realized she couldn't see him very well and said, "So tell him." He turned back to Perrault. "No, you can lick your wounds in private, Doc. Who knows? Maybe you even learned something here."

Perrault, enormously relieved but still out a quarter of a million dollars, said, "Damned expensive lesson."

"You think so, Pete?"

Perrault mulled it over for a few seconds. "Maybe not."

"Wait," Aronica said. "What was that about sundown? Why'd we get extra minutes? I don't—"

"Hey." It was Chelovek, walking up with Savitch and Pensecoeur. "Carlos said Ted Turner played here once."

"Uh-huh," Eddie affirmed. "Best get cracking now, folks. The Piper's waiting, and that anal bean counter probably hasn't even eaten yet."

"What I was starting to ask," Chelovek said to Pensecoeur, "what was the story with Turner?"

The Haitian pursed his lips and gave a little shrug. "I do not know," he said, motioning for Perrault to follow along back to the main house, "but a week later the gentleman has donated a billion American dollars to the UN."

"YOU KNOW WHAT I'M WONDERING, Eddie?"

"What's that, Deke?"

"What I'm wondering, how does it feel winning two million bucks in a single round of golf?"

Eddie drained the last of his beer, paused for a second, then emitted a most gratifying and prolonged belch. "Ain't about the money."

"Oh, really."

Eddie wiped a hand across his mouth, then tossed the beer into a wire trash can, where it landed with a loud clatter.

"It's *never* about the money, Deke."

Chapter 44

∷

Departure

T O T H E O T H E R G U E S T S M O V I N G about the property, it was just another morning. To our foursome it was the first day of the rest of their . . . ah, you know.

"I don't feel so good," Savitch said.

"No shit." Chelovek winced as he accidentally turned toward a large window through which the sun was dumping its painfully bright rays.

"No, not that; I mean really. My head hurts, my stomach's upset . . ."

"I said, *No shit!*" Chelovek pulled a plastic bottle out of his carry-on, spilled four aspirins into his palm and popped them into his mouth. He bit down on them and began chewing.

"Good God," Perrault said, grimacing, "how can you do that?"

"How can you not?"

"Here comes the plane," Aronica said, pointing out through a different picture window. A light twinkled in the sky, starlike but for some side-to-side movement.

"'Bout damned time," Chelovek grumbled.

"God, get a load'a this here," Savitch said. He was looking behind them rather than through the window.

Perrault followed his gaze. "What the—Is that the Piper?"

"Yep." Chelovek closed his eyes and leaned back on the chair. "The hell could he possibly want now . . . our testicles?"

Aronica shook his head. "I think those were already on the bank drafts."

"Gentlemen," the Piper said breathlessly as he drew within range. "A pleasant sleep, I trust?"

"Yeah, swell," Chelovek said without opening his eyes. "You don't got a pot to piss in, ain't nothin' left to worry about, is there?"

"What I meant, I heard you gentlemen were making rather merry last night. A wonder you got any sleep at all."

That was true. Bankrupt and bereft, what else was there to do but drink as much of Eddie's expensive liquor as they possibly could?

"What is it, Saunders?" Perrault inquired.

"Ah, yes. Well." The accountant fiddled nervously with a sheaf of computer printouts. "There is the matter of the bill . . ."

Chelovek opened one eye. "Whadja say?"

"Ah . . . the bill. Yes, that's it. For your stay, of course."

Aronica turned away from his observation of the incoming plane. "The bill."

"Yes, sir. How do you wish to settle it?"

Perrault tried to suppress a laugh, not wishing to give offense to the prissy little clerk, as Chelovek said, "Well, sir, I don't wish to settle it."

"Don't wish—I'm afraid I don't understand."

"I don't want to pay."

"Oh . . . ?"

"Yeah. Invite said I don't have to."

"Ah, I see! Yes, well, the invitation was quite clear on that, Mr. Chelovek. You see, payment is optional only if this was not the most memorable vacation you've ever had, hmm? And I trust that was not the case." Here the Piper dared a small, conspiratorial snicker. "I say, not the case at all, hmm?"

"What vacation?"

The Piper turned to Savitch. "Pardon?"

"Were we on vacation? Hey, Pete, were you on vacation?"

"I have a vague recollection . . ."

"Now, see here, gentlemen!" the Piper said with righteous indignation. "You can't—"

"You calling my buddy a liar, Saunders?" Chelovek had both eyes open now.

"What! Certainly not! Why, how could you—"

"Man said he can hardly remember it at all," Savitch explained.

"Yes, but we all know perfectly well—"

Chelovek started to get up. "Saunders—"

"Jerry!" Aronica had been watching all of this with growing horror. His eyes darted back and forth frantically, and he gestured insistently for Chelovek to come over to him, but the adman folded his arms across his chest and refused to budge.

So Aronica, eyes bugging wide, gulping down some fear that seemed utterly disproportionate to the current goings-on, sidled over to Chelovek with one eye on Saunders and with a pathetic half smile apparently intended to temporarily quell the little accountant's ire. "Please, Jerry!" he whispered harshly to Chelovek, his back turned to the others. "Don't—"

"Don't what?" Chelovek demanded loudly, causing Aronica to wince and shrink into himself a little.

"Just don't get him riled, okay? Please! I—"

"You what?" Chelovek unfolded his arms and leaned in toward Aronica, staring up at him intently. "Look at me, Joe. What the hell is wrong with you? What the fuck are you so scared of?"

"Jerry, please . . ." Aronica grimaced in real pain and patted Chelovek's shoulder in an attempt to just get him to stop whatever the hell it was he was doing that was liable to anger Saunders. "This guy . . . this place . . . I don't—" He looked ready to break into tears.

"You know what, Joe?" Chelovek said quietly. When he finally managed to get Aronica to look at him, he said, "You are starting to become one serious goddamned pain in my ass, and if you think you're going to get me to fall for any kinda Fantasy Island, mystic mumbo jumbo voodoo Merlin-the-goddamned-wizard horseshit, you'd best—"

"Jerry, listen'a me, I'm telling you: There is something truly freakin' weird going on, and—"

Chelovek stood up suddenly and before Aronica could stop him yelled out, "Hey, Saunders!"

Aronica put a hand over his eyes and turned away. "Yes, Mr. Chelovek?" the Piper answered, his voice all ice and menace.

"Go away or I'll kill you."

Aronica leaned against the wall to keep himself from collapsing.

"What!" Saunders huffed indignantly. "Well, that hardly constitutes civil—"

Chelovek stood up. He towered over the minuscule clerk, even at a distance. His rumpled hair, bloodshot eyes and general air of take-no-shit spoke volumes. The Piper stared at him for one astonished second, blinked and then scurried away.

"You think this guy, this Piper," Savitch wondered, "you think he looks inna mirror, he sees himself?"

Chelovek sat down and closed his eyes again as Perrault and Savitch laughed at the little man's hasty departure and Savitch's only partially humorous query. Aronica was trying not to throw up.

"You imagine that?" Perrault asked. "We leave two million behind, and Nosferatu wants us to pay for the drinks!"

They waited to see if Savitch would point out that it was three-quarters of a million of their money, a million and a quarter of his, but he didn't. It didn't matter anymore.

"Just bid'niz, is all," Chelovek said. "Man's doin' his job."

I bet I know what you're thinking. You're thinking, if the boys had really learned anything on this trip, they wouldn't have reverted to form and stiffed the resort for the cost of their stay, right? You're thinking that this last bit of miserly petulance somehow takes the edge off whatever moral lesson might attach to this tale and which was my motivation in bothering to relate it to you in the first place, am I right?

Well, get real. This isn't some fairy tale where the born-again sinners renounce their worldly goods, dress in sackcloth and join a monastic order of self-flagellating zealots. These are just ordinary guys, probably a good deal more like you or me than either of us would like to admit, and you'd have to have some completely deranged sense of what's right and fair to expect them to pony up for three hots and a cot after dropping two million bucks to a hotel owner with the brass to even present a bill.

"Hi, guys!"

Savitch and Perrault turned toward the sound of the voice. "Carlos!" Perrault said. "How are you?"

"Good. You fellas?"

"Well, we suck, Carlos," Savitch answered pleasantly. "Seriously, we really suck, you know what I'm saying?"

"Ahh, you lost some money, that it?"

"Manner'a speakin'." Chelovek roused himself to semiwakefulness once again. "You takin' us home?"

"Yeah. Well, sort of. What I mean, it's gonna take us a couple hours to turn the plane around. Fuel, cleaning, check a few things . . ."

Aronica groaned, and Savitch's lips began to grow tight.

Carlos held up his hands. "But if you're in a hurry, what we can do, we can hop a supply flight out of here. Not quite the Gulfstream, not by a long damned shot, but it's wheels-up in a half hour. So it's totally up to you guys."

"Uh-huh." Aronica nodded a few times, then sat down and looked up at the steward. "Carlos, I think I speak for my fellow travelers here . . ."

"Sir?"

Aronica lowered his voice. *"Get us the fuck off this island as quick as you can!"*

Carlos nodded vigorously. "I hear you, and I'm on it. Sit tight."

"I say, Carlos!" Perrault yelled loudly. "Hold it a second!"

The others turned to see what was up with Perrault, who was pointing out the window toward where a ground crew was bustling about in preparation for receiving the incoming jet. "Is that . . . ?"

Carlos followed his finger. "Selby Kirkland. You know her?"

"Do I—We played golf with her!"

"That Eddie, what a softie!" Carlos grinned and shook his head. "Gives her time off so she can play."

He turned to go and get things ready, calling back over his shoulder, "That any way to run a business?"

THE LIGHT GLIMMERING IN THE distance resolved itself into two lights, and then three, as the plane closed in on the runway. On the ramp visible through the large window, a tow was pulling an aging 737 into place.

"My fault, fellas," Aronica said out of nowhere. "And I'm sorry."

"What are you talking about?" Perrault asked.

"Why we lost. I'da brought my plain old cubs, this never woulda happened. We coulda beat those guys."

"Not sure that's true, Joe," Savitch said. "But what the heck happened anyway? How come that stick went flat like that?"

Aronica shrugged and didn't offer an answer. Outside the window they could see a fuel truck pull up to the 737. Nearby, Carlos had the beer cooler/phony defibrillator, absent the batteries, on a hand truck and was wheeling it onto the ramp.

"If any of us let the squad down, it was me," Perrault said. "Because I thought Pensecoeur was going to kill me."

"He wasn't all that good, Pete," Aronica said.

"Not in golf, Joe, I meant *literally* kill me. Like do a Nicholson on my head."

"What made you think that?"

Perrault shifted uncomfortably on his chair. "I thought for sure it was one of my clinics that took advantage of his grandmother. And that he knew it. Could hardly hold a club after that."

"Was it?" Chelovek asked.

Perrault shook his head. "Talked to him afterward. Wish I'd done that sooner."

"Think it woulda made a difference?" Savitch asked. "'Cuz you get right down to it, maybe it was me blew the whole thing."

"You? How do you figure?"

"When you guys found out I . . . that I, uh, played a little loose with my handicap 'n' all, I got rattled. It was me shoulda carried the day out there, and I didn't."

"I thought it was on account'a you findin' out about me and Binky," Chelovek said.

"Yeah, that, too."

"I'm sorry, Deke. You know that."

"Yeah. But the only reason I wanted to choke you to death was because Binky was too far away for me to do it to her."

That got some nervous laughter, but it was mostly so they wouldn't have to dwell on the depth of Savitch's pain.

"What the hell is this," Aronica said, "morning confessional? What's got into you guys?"

"You started it, Joe," Perrault argued back. "Don't you even feel bad about being ready to cheat with those clubs?"

"Feel bad? Hah! Compared to the shit you guys been pullin' your whole adult lives, I'm a candidate for sainthood!"

I think Aronica was just whistling past the graveyard. Knowing he'd be leaving the island soon, he was trying to jerk himself back into the real world.

"Well, we can make up all the excuses in the world," Savitch said, "but the bottom line is, we were up against some darned good golfers."

"We were just up against ourselves, Deke," Perrault mused. "I don't know about you boys, but it is not going to be a pretty scene when I get home."

"I'm not even *going* home," Savitch said.

"Come on, Deke," Aronica said with surprisingly gentle sympathy.

"What's there for me?"

"Your wife, for one thing!"

Savitch seemed to shrink on his seat. "My wife, yeah. That's a good one." He sighed and leaned his head back, twisting it to see Chelovek, mouth agape and snoring lightly. "Starting to think that bastard really did do me a favor. I can hardly wait to see her lawyer's face when he starts trying to divide up the assets!" The thought elevated his spirits instantly, and he giggled in delicious anticipation. "Almost worth it just to see that!"

The momentary lightness disappeared quickly. Savitch's lack of residual anger at Chelovek might be simplistically explained just as he'd put it, that Chelovek had actually done him a favor, but he knew that the real favor wasn't helping him to realize that his wife was the type of woman who would cheat on him. Rather, it was the hollowness of his own life that had thrown up light-years of empty space between himself and Binky and robbed her of the warmth and attention she'd rightfully expected from her husband. As his self-absorption increased along with his bank account and waistline, so had her sense of isolation and despair, to the point that her trysts with Chelovek seemed not so much like infidelity as a rightful claim to the comfort and solace she was being denied in her joke of a marriage.

True, she might have had the decency not to seek for it among her husband's friends, but could she really be faulted for wishing some small measure of defiant revenge in the bargain?

None of which excused Chelovek's abhorrent behavior, but Savitch was smart enough to know that it was a completely separate issue, and for the hundredth time that day he tried to shake it off. "So what about you, Pete? You gonna try to make an honest buck healing the sick?"

Perrault took no offense, and actually seemed to consider the question seriously. "Don't know that it can even be done, all this new managed-care folderol. I was thinking, though . . ."

"Thinking what?" Chelovek said to their surprise; they'd thought he'd been asleep.

"Thinking perhaps I'd phone up Sam. See what he's up to, his clinic and whatnot."

Prepared for an onslaught of derision, or at the very least some skeptical sneering, Perrault wasn't at all prepared for nothing.

"If you're not going home," Chelovek said to Savitch, "what about your computers?"

Savitch was rubbing his temples but stopped to reach into his carry-on and fumble around for something. "Heck with 'em. Whole life revolving around a bunch of freakin' machines . . ."

"Bunch'a ATMs, practically. How can you walk away from machines that print money in your basement?"

Perrault opened his own bag and found a bottle of water, which he tossed to Savitch. "Alcohol dries you out, is why you feel so awful."

Savitch screwed off the top and took a long pull. "Way I figure it," he said, wiping his mouth, "sooner or later somebody's gonna catch on to the kind of crap I do. Shut down the whole stupid carnival, once everybody admits it's just high-tech robbery."

"Jeez Louise!" Aronica said, throwing up his hands and letting them fall into his lap. "Drop a few bucks and you guys get religion?" He turned to Chelovek. "What about you, Jerry, hah? What's your story? You gonna quit the ad game, maybe go join a monastery?"

"Actually, I got a pretty nifty idea."

"Really. Another Clio candidate?" Aronica jabbed Savitch in the ribs: *This is gonna be good!*

Chelovek stayed quiet at first, unable or unwilling to come up with a snappy retort. "Got an idea for a car radio that can't be stolen."

"You and a thousand other guys."

"Maybe. But this one's simple and foolproof."

"How's it work, Jerrold?" Perrault asked him.

Chelovek looked over to see if he was asking a serious question, then decided maybe he was and started to explain. 'Steada making the radio hard to steal, you make it hard to *find*."

"Been done," Aronica said. "They always find it."

"Not this one," Chelovek said with a smile. "This one doesn't exist. Well, not exactly." He grew animated as he elaborated. "What you do, you scatter the parts all over the car. Tuner goes in the trunk, power supply under a seat, tape mechanism on the left side'a the dash, disc slot on the right . . . maybe the controls right on the steering wheel. Now . . ."

He sat back and spread his hands. "Guy breaks into your car, goes after your rig—what the hell's he supposed to steal? All there is, there's parts all over the place, and even if he could get all of 'em out, which'd take him two hours, what's he gonna do with 'em?"

Silence followed as he folded his arms and waited for a reaction. The most obvious candidate to speak first was Aronica, the engineer, and the others looked at him expectantly. "Now, why would you go and start up a risky new venture when your business is already bringin' in so much dough?"

"You think it's a good idea?"

"That's not the point, Jerry. The point is—"

"What I'm askin' you, is it a good idea!"

"Hell yes, it's a good idea! It's a *great* idea! The world's full'a great ideas, but it takes dough to get 'em up and running, and why the hell would you want to take that chance!"

"Because it's a good idea," Chelovek said, and leaned his head back again. "You tell people it's something they can use, you can tell 'em with a straight face."

"Wait a minute," Perrault said. "You mean you're going to get out of advertising? But you won a Clio!"

Chelovek stiffened at the mention of his award. "Let me tell you something about my Clio, Pete." He spoke without lifting his head again. "Couple years ago, they had the awards show, the whole thing was falling apart. Outfit that put it on, they were going bankrupt, and it was total chaos."

Chelovek paused for a few seconds before continuing. "So we're sitting there, hundreds of us, black tie, the whole works, and nobody has any idea what the hell is going on, and there isn't anybody from the Clio outfit even showed up.

"One guy, he sees all those hundreds of statues sitting on a table on the stage . . . he gets up, walks to the front and he grabs one!" Chelovek made a swiping motion with his hand. "I mean, he just takes the thing, right off the table, and heads for the door!"

"You're pullin' my leg," Aronica said.

"I shit you not." Chelovek bolted upright and looked at him. "Inside'a thirty seconds, the whole place goes berserk. Everybody's runnin' up to the stage, they're grabbin' these Clios by the handful and running out the back door. Guys're punching each other, tackling each other, statuettes are flyin' all over the place."

Chelovek stopped and looked down at his shoes, then leaned back again. "I saw one on the floor, I tucked it under my jacket, and I split."

There was only silence from his friends, and after a while Chelovek shifted to a more comfortable position and said to Aronica, "Any more questions, Joe?"

"Ah, you gone over the edge, too, Jerry. Christ . . ." Aronica started to shake his head, but it made him dizzy and nauseous, so he stopped.

"Awful lot of sarcasm, Joe," Perrault said, "especially from a guy who thinks somebody reached up and rearranged all the stars."

Aronica hadn't gotten five minutes into his attempt to restore some sanity to his worldview when Perrault's sarcastic jibe brought the stabbing hollowness in his belly back with a vengeance. He looked around, half expecting the

Piper to be hovering—literally—nearby. "All right, all right. You guys're telling me you're not spooked, so how come you're all acting like something important happened when all we did, we lost a bunch'a money!"

"Sometimes," Chelovek said, "something important happens, first thing you gotta do is know it happened."

"And what's that supposed to mean?"

"Kinda like your miracle metal, Joe." Chelovek rolled his head forward and rubbed the back of his neck. "You said it yourself: Trick isn't necessarily to create something. That's not the genius, right? The genius is recognizing it when it drops into your lap."

"So what are you tellin' me here?"

Chelovek stood up to stretch but quickly sat back down. "What I'm tellin' you, if all you come away with from here is a thinner wallet and a Halloween story, then you're a bigger schmuck than you were before."

Aronica stared at him without moving for a few seconds, then screwed up his face and jumped up, flapping a dismissive hand in Chelovek's direction as he walked off. "Leave me alone! You're all fulla shit!"

Aronica went to the picture window and saw the Gulfstream less than a mile away, the outline of its wings and tail quivering as heat waves rippled through the humid air.

On the ramp Selby Kirkland was detaching the fueling hose from the underside of the 737. As soon as she had it stowed and the static protector cable from the nose wheel unclipped, Carlos reappeared. He yanked the top of the hand truck so it leaned backward and resumed wheeling the portable cooler, right to the loading belt extending outward from the plane's belly.

Aronica felt a fresh wave of nausea welling up.

"NOT EXACTLY THE LAP O' LUXURY, this," Chelovek grumbled as they boarded the plane. "Betcha anything the Piper cooked this up special for us."

"We could have waited for the bizjet," Perrault reminded him. "Nobody said we had to take this thing."

"Hell with it," Aronica said as his eyes took in the six rows of tattered passenger seats at the very front of the cargo plane. He also noticed that they all faced forward, despite Carlos's assurances that the owners of Swithen Bairn had faced them backward in the interests of passenger safety. Just proved he was right: The real reason for the absence of windows in the Gulfstream was so resort guests couldn't figure out where the place was. At least in this plane there was a built-in excuse: It was designed as a cargo plane, so there was no need for windows.

"Right," Savitch agreed readily. "Just get this puppy up and get me the heck outta here."

"Say, look at that!" Perrault called from the bottom of the airstairs. He was pointing at the Gulfstream, which was in the act of disgorging its passengers.

"What about it?" Savitch asked just as Aronica stuck his head back out to see what was going on.

"Guess who's coming to golf?" Perrault answered, inclining his chin toward the people just coming down the stairway.

"Hey," Aronica exclaimed, "isn't that—"

"Most certainly is," Perrault confirmed.

The four of them watched as the executive director of the Tobacco Institute led the way, followed by Kenneth Starr and a very fit-looking Charles Keating, whose general air of good health didn't comport well with his early release from prison for medical reasons. Donald Trump and Leona Helmsley came down together but split off immediately when they reached the tarmac, Trump almost bumping into Jerry Falwell and Helmsley nearly knocking over Don King, who'd been engrossed in animated conversation with Dr. Laura Schlessinger as Henry Kravis trailed behind.

Suddenly feeling better for some reason, the foursome trooped into the 737. Two resort workers were already seated in the back row; they were joined by Carlos after he had pulled the forward door closed. Aronica decided not to confront the steward with his bit of dissembling regarding aircraft configuration—what would be the point?

"At least there's some good food on board," Carlos said when he'd noticed their disappointed expressions. "Not as fancy as the Gulfstream, because we have no kitchen facilities, but it'll do."

The engines began their whiny spool-up, and one of the pilots, who had boarded before the passengers to do the preflight, came on the intercom. "Strap in, guys; we're off in a couple minutes."

Even as Aronica and Perrault began fiddling with frayed seat belts that looked like they predated the dawn of aviation, the creaking plane lurched forward and made an immediate sharp left off the ramp and onto the taxiway.

Chelovek, still standing with his hand on the lid of the overhead bin, nearly toppled over onto Perrault. "Jesus H.! We didn't even get the stupid speech yet!"

"This isn't a scheduled carrier, Mr. C.," Carlos called from the back row. "We're kinda hitchhiking."

The plane transitioned from the taxiway to the runway without a pause, moving right into a rolling takeoff. A few seconds later it lifted off and into an alarmingly steep climb.

Savitch gripped the arms of his seat so hard his knuckles literally turned white. Perrault turned around to see the workers in the backseat grinning.

"It's a deadhead flight," Carlos explained loudly over the scream of the engines. "Nothing on board, so we're light." He pointed at the cockpit door. "Boys like to horse around a little, see how fast they can get it to climb."

"Swell," Savitch muttered.

A few minutes later, as the plane began to level out, the three employees unbuckled their seat belts and disappeared through the back door into the cargo area. Carlos returned shortly thereafter with some liquor bottles, glasses and napkins. "Ice coming up soon," he said, and disappeared aft again.

"Prob'ly gonna have to take a cab home from the freakin' airport," Chelovek groused morosely.

The flight droned on for about twenty minutes, our boys lost in their own private thoughts, until Perrault said, "I'm starting to feel a little woozy again."

"Me, too," Aronica said. "Plane's been yawing the past few minutes."

"Yawning?" Savitch said. "What the hell's that mean, the plane's been—"

"*Yawing*," Aronica corrected him. He held out his hand, palm down, pointing his fingers left and then right. "Nose kinda swings back and forth a little."

They stayed quiet for a few minutes, the unusual motion becoming more pronounced. "Why's it doing that?" Chelovek asked.

"Turbulence, more'n likely." Although Aronica wondered why there was none of the up-and-down, bouncing movement that usually accompanied unstable air.

The plane soon began making decidedly wider swings, which also devolved from an even rhythm to something more chaotic. Then it seemed to stop altogether, but just as a few relieved breaths were let out, the plane suddenly jerked violently to the left, sending the liquor bottles and glasses crashing to the floor.

"Joe . . . ?" Savitch bleated beseechingly, panic lacing his voice.

"Everybody fasten your seat belts immediately!" the intercom blared. "We're experiencing turbulence, and—"

The announcement stopped as the plane lurched forcefully once again. Aronica waited for it to subside, then yanked off his lap belt and leaped out of his seat. Holding onto the back of the front-row seats, he made his way forward and threw open the door of the cockpit.

"What the hell's going on?" he demanded.

"Sir, get back to your seat right now!" the first officer shouted. "You shouldn't—"

"I'm an aerospace engineer!" Aronica shouted right back, pulling the door shut behind him. "Now, why's she yawing like that?"

The captain shook his head. "Rudder's gone all mushy!" he said through clenched teeth. "Nose is swingin' around so bad I—"

"You kill the yaw damper yet?" Aronica asked as he strapped himself into the jump seat.

"Don't have one," the first officer said from the right seat. "Just trim, and that's unresponsive, too."

"Reduce your speed!" Aronica said with authority. The captain thought about it for less than a second and then reached for the thrust levers. "Nice and easy now," Aronica cautioned.

As the sound of the engines dropped in pitch, the wild swings seemed to diminish slightly, but then a rolling motion made itself apparent. Aronica and the captain looked out the side window simultaneously, and there was no doubt that the wings were beginning to rock.

"How's the pitch?" Aronica asked.

The first officer checked his instruments. "Steady," he reported, then pointed to the turn and bank indicator. "But the roll's getting worse."

"So's the yaw," the captain added. Indeed, looking through the front windshield, Aronica could see the nose of the plane wallowing against the sky. "Not enough air flowing over the control surfaces. I gotta bring the speed back up, or we're gonna lose it."

Aronica nodded, and the captain shoved the thrust levers forward again. The violence of the unstable changes in the plane's attitude increased, but their extent diminished.

"Too slow and we might stall her right out," the captain said. "Too fast . . ."

And we'll break up. Aronica banged his fist angrily into his knee.

"Getting worse, captain," the copilot reported.

The captain nodded in acknowledgment. He pushed the right rudder pedal and then the left; there was hardly any noticeable difference in the attitude instruments.

"Feels like the rudder's falling apart bit by bit," the captain said. He didn't have to add that there was little or nothing he could do about it. "Can't even make heading corrections. Every time I try to turn, it gets worse."

"I'm going aft," Aronica said suddenly when a few more seconds had passed. He left the cockpit and staggered down the aisle, ignoring the shouts from his friends as he fought to keep himself upright.

He opened the door to the cargo area, but the plane heaved over roughly and it slammed shut. He barely got his hand out of the way in time but opened it again and this time quickly hurled himself through the opening. The door banged shut again, sounding like a rifle shot. In the dim light of the compartment, Aronica reached for what looked like an anchored cable, but it came free as soon as he had his weight on it and he crashed into the floor.

The cargo compartment was empty. Staying down, Aronica crawled across the floor and toward another doorway about thirty feet back. Assorted clips, bolts and ropes flew about his head each time the plane reeled convulsively, but there was nothing heavy to seriously impede his progress.

He made it to the second door and reached for the handle. It was locked. He tried to force it, but with the plane bucking and rearing, he could barely even keep his hand on it, and he finally had to let go and let himself be thrown into a wall covered with movers' padding. Waiting for a roll in the opposite direction, he screamed "Open it!" as loud as he could and then launched a roundhouse kick, catching the door square in the middle, just as he flew past it to land in a heap on the opposite side.

"Open up!" he yelled again, and this time the handle turned. Not waiting for more of an invitation, he hung on through another roll cycle and then jumped for the door, falling through it and taking one of the resort workers down with him.

The terrified man, white clearly visible all around his pupils, was so scared he didn't even seem to feel any pain from the fall. Carlos and the other worker were nowhere in sight, but the man pointed to a canvas-covered entryway on the aft wall. Hanging on to overhead hold points, Aronica stumbled his way back, tore at the canvas and burst into the last compartment.

There he saw the reason they'd been reluctant to let him into the cargo area. Strewn about the floor and banging off the walls as the plane bounced around were at least a dozen empty beer cans. Carlos and the other worker were keeping themselves down by hanging on to some anchor points and, between them, held down by cargo straps looped through four eyebolts mounted on the floor, was the phony defibrillator, its top torn away, what remained of its ice rattling around noisily inside along with several dozen cans of beer. An electrical cord, whipping back and forth crazily, ran from the back of the cooler to an outlet overhead.

The plane shuddered sickeningly, and the worker who'd let Aronica in went flying through the canvas-covered opening. Aronica stopped himself by throwing an arm around a structural support, then yelled at Carlos, "Unplug it!"

But Carlos was too petrified to take his hands off the anchor points that were preventing him from being tossed about with every fresh lurch of the dying plane.

"Pull the goddamned plug!" Aronica screamed, unable to keep the hysteria out of his voice. Carlos continued to stare at him uncomprehendingly. The worker who was hunkered down next to him had his eyes closed and was praying fervently.

The plane seemed to be almost completely out of control now, its chaotic movements amplified in the rearmost compartment because of its distance from the centers of pressure and gravity. The sound of the engines rose and fell horribly, like the screams of a wounded animal, and as the tail viciously whipsawed back and forth, it was all Aronica could do to keep from blacking out and letting go of the support, which would surely prove lethal should he be thrown into one of the many metal structures that seemed to jut from every surface.

But if he didn't let go, he was just as dead. He tried to think clearly, to see if there was any pattern at all to the wild heaving that his mind could latch on to. He gave it only a few seconds, then took a deep breath, and as a particularly strong yaw seemed to run out of steam before swinging back in the other direction, he let go and shoved himself in the direction of the cooler.

Momentarily weightless, he hung in the air, helpless and flailing, until the fuselage changed directions once again and the starboard wall came hurtling toward him. Throwing up one arm to protect himself, he reached as far as he could with the other and grabbed hold of another structural support. Just as he was about to slam into the wall, he twisted hard to one side and stuck out his leg to get it past the electrical cord.

When the impact came, his leg was jerked sideways and into the cord, tearing it out of the outlet even as blinding pain shot through his shoulder, forcing him to let go of the strut and fall to the floor. He had just enough sensibility left to wrap himself around another support member, just before he blacked out.

ARONICA THOUGHT HE WAS DROWNING, but the water smelled like good scotch. He sputtered and opened his eyes, then tried to struggle to a sitting position, but his shoulder hurt too much.

"Hey, take it easy there, guy!"

It was Chelovek's voice. As Aronica focused, he saw that Perrault and Savitch were there, too, hovering above him and looking at him with concern.

He ran a finger across his chin and then licked it. "Hell is this?"

"Chivas," Savitch answered. "Only liquid we had handy."

Aronica winced and reached for his shoulder. "Banged up, but not broken," Perrault assured him, pulling on his other arm to help him up.

"Yeah, right," Aronica said skeptically. "You as good an orthopedist as you are a cardiologist?"

Chelovek and Savitch sat back against a bulkhead, laughing, as Perrault threw them an irritated look. "Yes, by all means have yourselves a hearty chuckle. Quite humorous, almost losing our lives."

Aronica, sitting upright, looked around the cargo compartment. It seemed stable now, and the engines had settled back into their usual throaty rumble. Perrault left him to grab some ice out of the cooler, twist it inside of a shirt and bring it back.

Packing it into Aronica's jacket against his shoulder, he said, "What the deuce happened, Joe?"

Over by the cooler, the two workers were crossing themselves frantically, their eyes still wild with fright. "You guys'll be okay," Aronica assured them. "Plane's all right now."

"That's not what they're worried about."

Aronica turned to see Carlos, who'd gathered up other liquor bottles that hadn't been broken, along with several glasses.

"They afraid we're gonna rat they were drinkin' beer?" Chelovek guessed.

Carlos shook his head and sat down heavily. "It was our fault, wasn't it?" he said to Aronica. "We plugged the cooler in, all hell broke loose. We didn't even know that was it, until you came along and yanked it out and everything went back to normal."

Aronica reached out for one of the bottles. Carlos poured him a glass and handed it over.

"Wasn't your fault," Aronica said, taking a grateful sip. "It was mine."

BACK IN THE MAIN CABIN, Chelovek asked him why it had been his fault. "Whud you do, sabotage the plane?"

"Dumb play," Savitch opined, "since he was gonna be on it."

"How did that cooler figure in?" Perrault asked.

"Magnets," the engineer replied bitterly.

"Magnets what?" Perrault asked him.

"Magnets in the fridge. Compressor motor's got big permanent magnets in it, then you crank it up and you got electromagnetism, too. Couple dozen random frequencies pouring out all over the place."

"So what?"

Aronica closed his eyes and rubbed the bridge of his nose between thumb and forefinger. "Seems my miracle metal doesn't like one or two of 'em."

Now Perrault understood. "The rudder."

Aronica nodded. "With the cooler in the back, it's right underneath the tail assembly. Flip on the fridge . . ."

"Rudder turns to mush. Good Lord!"

Chelovek nodded as he absorbed the painful confession. "So it seems Eddie was right about—Hey, wait a minute!"

"Ah, jeez, your golf clubs!" Savitch exclaimed breathlessly as he slumped back on his seat, an astonished look on his face.

"That's why you wanted Eddie to shut off the cooler," Perrault said.

Aronica exhaled and reached for his glass of scotch, not needing a drink so much as needing Savitch to get off this topic, and do so quickly. His arm was shaking, and he had to use his other hand to steady it. It's not easy to maintain equilibrium when a good number of the things whose solidity you used to take for granted suddenly shifted beneath your feet. He was still trying to stave off a bad case of what scuba divers called the dreads, a kind of numbing terror that sets in when you find yourself too far below the surface in water that is too dark, too cold and too lonely.

Aronica was smart enough to know that if he didn't confront his fears head-on, they'd haunt him for the rest of his life. "Carlos," he said, waving for the steward to take the seat next to him.

"Everything okay, Mr. A.?" Carlos asked as he sat.

Aronica took a sip of his drink. "Listen, this is probably kinda dopey, but I gotta ask you something."

"Sure. What's up?"

"Is there anything, uh . . ." Aronica shifted on his seat to get closer so he could keep his voice as low as possible. "Is there anything *weird* about Swithen Bairn?"

When no answer was immediately forthcoming, Aronica, who had been speaking down into his hand to muffle his voice, looked up at the steward but saw a different man sitting there. Maybe not *different*, in the sense of its being another person entirely, but it was a different Carlos, in the same way that the Piper had looked different days before when Savitch had given the mistaken impression that there might be a problem with his funds transfer. It was the same guy, sure, but it also wasn't.

The old Carlos that Aronica knew from the trip over had been a perfectly ordinary service employee, anxious to please, thoroughly professional and happy in his place, although there had been that odd remark of Chelovek's, about whether Carlos should be sweeping floors or running an airline, and Perrault mentioning that sometimes he sounded like a cabdriver and other times like a member of Parliament, or something like that.

Right now, though, it was neither of those things. Right now Aronica thought Carlos looked like somebody altogether different, like somebody older, wiser . . . somebody who knew one whole hell of a lot more than he'd let on when he was pouring drinks or making sandwiches or hanging on to the floor in the cargo area fearing for his life. I've seen a look something like that when a tour pro gets into a strange zone, almost seems to leave his body and thereafter can't do anything wrong.

"Weird?" Carlos replied in a normal voice. Normal in the sense of volume anyway; in timbre and tone it had much the same quality you'd expect from the Secretary of Defense after you just told him you'd accidentally launched a nuclear missile at China.

"Shh!" Aronica looked around to see if they were being overheard. He wished he'd never brought this up, feeling as though one wrong word and his head would start spinning around on his shoulders, but it was too late to take it back, and the man sitting next to him looked like he might not let him drop it so easily. "Okay, maybe weird's not the right word, but . . ."

As something within Carlos started swarming, like a hive of bees coalescing into a single life in preparation for battling an invader, it occurred to Aronica that he really didn't know exactly what it was he was trying to ask, and therefore he didn't have a good way to phrase it. "You ever look up at the sky, Carlos? What I mean is, you know anything about, like, constellations?"

"Constellations . . . what do you mean?"

Aronica thought the steward's eyes were quaking, but it might just have been the vibration from the engines coming through the airframe and up through the seats. "Um, like—"

"Like the Big Dipper?"

"Yeah, like that."

"Ah, sure." Carlos the happy flight attendant reemerged as something fluttered off and was gone. "Mostly when I was a kid, because they taught us that stuff in school."

"Right. Well, it's kind of an interest of mine, so I was just wondering if you—"

"I get you, Mr. A. Astronomy, right? Except that's pretty tough to do at the resort. You know, on account of the sky being so screwed up. But you'd know a lot more about that than me." He started to get up, thinking the conversation was over now that he'd probably disappointed the guest, but was surprised by a viselike grip on his arm.

Aronica gulped a few times but didn't let go, so Carlos tried to gently peel his fingers off his arm. "Mr. A.?"

"Sorry, sorry." Aronica let go but pumped a hand at Carlos so he wouldn't get up. He took another swallow of scotch and calmed himself. "The sky being screwed up?" he said slowly and with some effort.

"Yeah." Carlos rubbed his wrist and tried to inch away without it seeming obvious. "All of that heat and humidity, it does funny things. I don't know any'a that scientific mumbo jumbo, jeez, but you get stuff like what the locals call false sunsets?"

The color drained from Aronica's face, and his hand began shaking again. "You really okay?" Carlos asked solicitously.

"What—" Aronica cleared his throat. "What's a false sunset?"

Carlos, concerned about his guest's ashen features, decided that in the absence of any other clues to the man's condition, he might as well just play along. "Don't ask me why, but sometimes, when everything's just right, you see the sun going down but it's really been down for a while already. Got something to do with rays getting bent, on account'a, um, I think it's got contraptions—"

"Refraction."

Aronica whirled around, startled by the voice that suddenly sounded from behind.

"It's called refraction," Perrault was saying. Aronica couldn't tell how much of the conversation he'd overheard. "Saw it a couple times in Hawaii. Damnedest thing, really."

"Yeah, refraction, that's it!" Carlos exclaimed, glad to have someone else involved.

"Temperature inversion does it," Perrault explained. "Makes the whole atmosphere like a lens. Bends the light from the sun, bounces it off the upper atmosphere and makes it appear to be where it isn't. I say, Joe . . . are you quite all right?"

Aronica, dizzy, gripped the arms of the seat to steady himself. "What about stars?"

"What about 'em?"

"Can it do that to starlight, too?"

"Oh, sure," Carlos said eagerly. "Stars get screwy all the time. Anything on the horizon does. You see 'em, they go down, and a few minutes later it looks like they come back up again. This one time? Down in Honduras? Me an' a couple buddies, we were—"

He stopped talking when he noticed Perrault gesturing for him to vacate his seat. "Gotta go do some stuff, okay?" he said to Aronica as he rose.

Aronica barely seemed to notice that Perrault had sat down next to him.

"Humidity," Perrault said, shaking his head and patting Aronica's arm gently.

Aronica took a deep breath and let it out slowly. "That's why Eddie said we had ten more minutes than we should have."

"And there you were trying to track a bunch of stars—"

"Right on the damned horizon—"

"And they were bouncing all over the place because of a temperature inversion."

Aronica was stone still for a few seconds, then he smiled, then giggled and before too long was laughing so hard he could barely breathe. His contagious hysterics soon spread to Perrault, and neither of them was able to stop long enough to explain to the others what was so funny.

"Ah, I'll be goddamned," Aronica eventually managed to sputter as he swiped at his eyes, and soon the two of them fell silent.

"So, Joe," Perrault asked him after a few minutes had passed, "does that make it any less magical for you?"

Aronica took a long time to think about it. "No," he finally said as he shook his head. "More."

THE NEXT TWO OR THREE minutes passed in silence. Then Aronica looked around and, spotting Carlos, said, "You got some paper and a pen anywhere on board?"

"I've got a pen," Perrault said, reaching into his jacket pocket.

"Sure," Carlos said. "Gotta fill out manifests when I pick up supplies." He pulled a thin briefcase from under his seat and produced a writing tablet.

Pen and paper in hand, Aronica looked up at the ceiling for a few minutes, then began writing, slowly at first but picking up speed as he went along.

"Letter?" Savitch asked him when he wandered by a little later. "To who?"

"FAA," Aronica replied. "Then Boeing."

He worked for a few more minutes, then tore off the sheet and began a second one. "Seems I'm gonna be outta work pretty soon," he said, without a trace of regret.

"Here, here," Perrault responded, pouring a new round of drinks for everybody.

NOW MAYBE YOU HAVE A better understanding of why my own epiphany, whatever it was, paled in comparison to what happened to these four guys. Now maybe you can understand why I thought Eddie was full of it every time I tried to get him to tell me his side of the story and all he would say was "A bunch of guys came down, we played some golf, a little friendly betting money changed hands . . ."

The one time, admittedly after a few drinks, that I had been pestering him and inadvertently employed some phrase having to do with his using golf to save souls instead of hustling money, he threatened never to allow me another step on Swithen Bairn soil if I didn't "f'Chrissakes get a hold of your goddamned self!"

Sure, the versions I heard from the foursome were probably a little skewed, but after all, isn't that kind of the whole point? As Eddie was fond of saying to tour pros who visited Swithen Bairn, many of whose competitive problems were purely psychological, sometimes the things that are only in your head are the realest things of all.

If you spend any time with Eddie Caminetti, it's easy to get carried away, as even the proudly superrational Joe Aronica had, and imagine all sorts of nonsense, to abandon prosaic explanations for odd coincidences because it's more alluring to believe they weren't really coincidences, but Lord knows there's enough of that pseudomystical crap running around as it is. Fact is, there isn't a single shred of evidence that Colin Powell's decision not to accept a vice-presidential nomination had anything to do with his trip to Swithen Bairn two days before his announcement, or that the race started by Ted Turner to give away tons of money and Bill Gates's acceptance of that challenge was in any way related to their trips to the resort. Personally, though, I can hardly wait to see what happens if invitations that have already been sent are ever accepted by . . . um, sorry; promised Eddie I wouldn't say. Although I don't think he'd mind if I mentioned that it includes several members of the International Olympic Committee, CEOs from the tobacco industry, the entire operations staff of a certain tabloid television network and most of the daytime-television talk-show hosts.

One thing's for sure: Jerry Chelovek had no idea how far off base he was when he'd suggested to Eddie that a little advertising would put some butts in the beds. As for me, I still love going down to Swithen Bairn as often as I can, but even though I'm still ranked among the top ten golfers in the world, I won't play Eddie for more than a quarter a hole—and I do mean twenty-five cents—and I'm perfectly happy to pay my hotel bill when I leave.

I also might as well tell you that Sam Coolidge's not-for-profit Inner Cities Clinics corporation received a $2-million endowment from the resort. And I won't be offended if you don't believe me when I tell you that the postdated check was given to him the night *before* our boys played their last match there.

"If you're trying to find the key to the universe," Eddie said to me once, "I have bad news and I have good news. The bad news is, there *is* no key to the universe. The good news is, it's been left unlocked."

WHILE ARONICA WAS WRITING HIS letters, the simple fact that some purposeful activity was under way was enough to create an atmosphere in which nothing else needed to be done.

Once he'd finished, however, there was nothing for any of them to do, which three of them had been doing anyway, except that now it was singularly awkward and uncomfortable. Conversations begging to be conversed floated about in the air, implike and cajoling, each unspoken beginning an admission of cowardice, each missed opportunity to speak up a humiliating failure.

So instead of talking to each other, the boys nursed their private hurts, each convinced that his was not only unique but more painful than any of the others', and they would have been quite surprised to discover that, in fact, none of them was thinking about his career, or his marriage, or his future, or Eddie Caminetti, or even about the economic catastrophe that had brought him to the brink of ruin.

Instead, all of them had just one question on their minds: *Are we still friends?*

The muffled droning of the engines was comforting at first, not only because it indicated smooth operation of the aircraft but because one could, if so inclined, meditate upon the hypnotic sound and drift off with it, which was probably the easiest thing to do in the present circumstances. Before very long, however, the thrumming became insistent, even taunting, as if daring one of them to admit out loud that even the boring sound of jet engines was preferable to some basic human interaction among the four of them.

It seemed interminable until, of all people, Deke Savitch set his drink down with a resigned sigh. "Hey, fellas," he said, unbuckling his seat belt and perching himself on the armrest so he could face the other three. They turned to him expectantly, their faces betraying vast relief at this interruption, barely caring what he had to say so long as he said *something*.

Savitch rubbed his hands together a few times and dropped them in his lap.

"So where we gonna go next year?" he said.

Epilogue

■

I APOLOGIZE FOR THIS LATE-BREAKING addition. It just happened, and there was no time for me to properly weave it into the rest of the story, but I thought you might like to hear about it.

Remember I told you that I pieced together the story by talking to as many people who were involved as I could (with the exception of Eddie Caminetti, who insisted there was no story to tell)? Well, one of those was Joe Aronica, who turned out to be the most forthcoming and the one most willing to share his thoughts. Almost too willing, sometimes, like a degenerate smoker who finally quits and thinks it's now his mission on earth to convert everybody else by telling them about it . . . at length and ad nauseam.

I admit somewhat shamefacedly that I got a little weary of Aronica's new-found urge to purge, an obsession with absolving himself of his perceived transgressions through a combination of frankly embarrassing confessions and tireless efforts at self-improvement, but the guy was so guileless and sincere I resolved to put up with it.

Turns out I was very glad I did, because recently I decided to resolve something that has been nagging at me for months. It was inconceivable at first that I could bring it up to any members of the foursome—you'll see why in a moment—and I'd made a solemn promise to myself never to do that, but before long it was bothering me so much that I had to get it out in the open or drive myself nuts.

Because of the hours I'd spent listening to the reborn Aronica unburden himself, I felt that he was the best candidate to hear me out.

AS I KNEW HE WOULD, Joe enthused rhapsodically when I suggested that I come and pay him a visit. And, as I knew he would, he essentially ignored my invitation to play some golf—can you beat that, blowing off a three-time Player of the Year?—and insisted I come visit his factory instead.

Jerry Chelovek's idea for a car radio that couldn't be stolen did in fact turn out to be a good one, and when he decided not to sell the concept but actually produce the thing himself, he suggested that Joe take on the manufacturing end, and thus was a match born in heaven—or at least Swithen Bairn—and witnessed by Deke Savitch, who signed on as their chief financial officer.

Joe was deliriously proud of the result, a highly automated factory that practically ran itself. Once he got it going, he took over the research-and-development function, too, and was the primary brainpower behind a host of clever options, like plug-in modules so the kids could watch idioic stuff like Barney in the backseat while Mom and Dad pampered their more sophisticated tastes with Howard Stern up front. I initially resisted what I knew was going to be a detailed, two-hour guided tour but soon found myself fascinated, not just by the amazing production floor innovations Joe had invented but by the immense pride he took in all of it without seeming the slightest bit egotistical or self-absorbed.

I didn't think he even remembered that I was the one who'd invited myself out in the first place, but when we went back to his office later in the afternoon and took up seats opposite each other, he said, "So what is it, Al? Why does number two on the money list—"

"Number three."

"I knew that. What's up?"

Now that he'd asked the question, I was tongue-tied. Seeing him so happy and productive, so comfortable in himself for the first time in his life, I just couldn't bring myself to talk about what was on my mind and risk disturbing the equilibrium he'd found.

He looked at his watch. "Almost end of the day. I been here since five this morning as it is, so what do you say to a little nip?"

I knew he'd been working ridiculous numbers of hours, and I also knew from his wife that he'd never been happier or more enthusiastic. Oh, yeah, that's another thing I should have mentioned: Joe was still married, and although I'd not met his wife before his little golf vacation, they sure seemed a tight couple now. "Good idea. A short one."

He poured us each two fingers of an ordinary but quite acceptable scotch, then waited patiently.

"I gotta ask you something, Joe. Been on my mind."

"That much I figured out already. So shoot."

I took another sip. "That last match at the resort—"

"I remember it," he said with an elfin smile.

"I bet you do." And he'd recounted it to me in excruciating detail. "But there's this one thing, and . . . well, you're the only one I really feel comfortable asking about it. Except maybe you're not gonna like hearing it."

"It's history, Al. What do I give a shit?"

"Right." Another sip, then I set the glass down. *Okay, here it is . . .* "Eddie doubled you guys to a million bucks, and basically he, um, he—"

"He blew us right out of the water," Joe finished for me easily. "Turned things around so it didn't have anything to do anymore with did we think we could beat them. He made it so there was no way we could even try. That what you're trying to tell me?"

When I didn't answer, he said, "You think I don't realize what he did, how he engineered the whole thing so there was no way we could possibly win? Even if Deke Savitch offered to cover all of us to the tune of three million of his own bucks, we had no way to know if he really could, so what choice did we have? We had to give up and let it go, quit while we were still at a level we could afford."

I reached for my drink again, surprised to find that there was hardly any left. Joe pulled the bottle back out and poured me another couple of fingers as he shook his head. "C'mon, Al, don't look so glum. You got nothing to tell me I don't already know."

"That wasn't it, Joe."

"Oh, yeah?" There was a slight hesitation as he tilted the bottle back up, but he covered it quickly. "Okay. What, then? What did you want to ask me?"

I fiddled with the tumbler but didn't take a drink. "How come you didn't accept the double?"

Joe knew I wasn't a dummy, so he thought about it for a second or two before answering, trying to understand why I'd ask a question like that. "I told you: None of us could afford to—"

He stopped when he saw me looking down at the floor. "That's not what I'm getting at."

This time he poured himself some more scotch, then sat back as if waiting for a blow to land.

"If you'd accepted that double," I explained, "and done it when there was only a few minutes of sunset left, there wouldn't have been time to finish the match."

"Okay . . ."

"And you guys were all square at that point, right? The score was tied?"

He nodded slowly, something in his brain warning him that I'd not flown over two thousand miles to ask stupid questions.

"So if you'd accepted the double, ten minutes later the match would have been over, because it was Eddie's own rule that it automatically ended at sundown. Neither side would have been ahead at that point . . ."

And the whole thing would have ended in a draw. No blood. Everybody walks away, and nobody owes anybody any money.

I thought I saw several dozen emotions flit across Joe's face in the space of a few seconds, and I seriously feared that he might have a stroke right then and there or go into cardiac arrest, but just as that thought hit me, his face went serene again. He threw his hands up and let them fall on the arms of his chair. "Well, what the hell."

What the hell? "What do you mean, 'What the hell' . . . you were completely wiped out!"

He shrugged and stuck a little finger in his ear, jiggling it back and forth as if trying to dislodge something that itched. "I mean, what the hell, Al. Look."

He stood and walked over to the wall opposite his desk. It was covered with blinds, and he drew them up, revealing a large window that looked out over the entire factory floor. "C'mere."

I stood and walked over, standing side by side with him as we took in the scene below us. People and machines were scurrying all over the place, everybody appearing purposeful and determined, the whole place buzzing and humming like a mechanized beehive.

"This is me now, Al," he said. "I'm really good at this, and it's where I want to spend the rest of my life."

He pointed to the far end of the production floor. "Metal, wires, silicon—they come in over there." Then he pointed to the opposite end. "Tuners, power supplies, amplifiers—that's what goes out at that end. And you know why that happens?"

He waved his hand, taking in the entirety of the factory. "Because I built everything in the middle. Designed it, supervised the construction, made hundreds of changes until it was right . . ."

He dropped the blinds suddenly, startling me, and giving me no place else to look but right into his eyes.

"You think I mind ponying up a lousy quarter mil to get all that?"

My head started reeling, and I had to sit down, especially considering that I'd agonized over this visit for weeks. "So you're not pissed off at Eddie?"

"Pissed off?" Joe looked at me in amazement, then reared back his head and laughed. "Holy Hannah, Al," he said when he was able to catch his breath. "I've played golf with the sneaky sonofabitch three times since we were at Swithen Bairn!"

I could hardly believe it, and said so, but Joe was quite serious.

"All five of us have!" he added.

FIVE?

Seems I'd forgotten all about Sam Coolidge.

Extra-special thanks to:

David Morgan Brenner
Cherie Gruenfeld
The Honorable Robert Morrill

The full story of Ryder Cup captain Al Bellamy's first encounter with Eddie Caminetti was told in the book *The Green*. For more information, please visit: http://Lee-Gruenfeld.com